THE DEAD SAGA
ODIUM

By

USA Today Bestselling

Claire C. Riley

LOVE FOR ODIUM. THE DEAD SAGA SERIES

DEDICATION

The hugest of thanks go to the bestest (← not a real word!) friend that anyone could ever ask for. My Maverick...Elizabeth. The fates were cruel when they placed us on opposite sides of the world, but maybe one day we'll stumble across a worm hole and we can be sucked through it and end up together.
Couldn't do this without you.

Love you,

Claire

FOREWORD

Without rambling on too much, I thought that it would be good for you to know a few things before you read *Odium*: Firstly, before writing this, I asked for some participants on my Facebook page to fill in a 'survival questionnaire,' a simple 'what would you do?' And as a thanks for filling it in, I promised to cast them each as a character. Some would be tiny parts, some would be huge. The parts all depended upon the answers I received. I also never promised that they would live or die. The characters within *Odium* are very loosely based on these participants. Hey, they have to remain fictional characters, after all!

Many parts of *Odium* are also based on the answers that I was given, from 'would you rescue other survivors?' to 'what would you miss the most?' So before you discount anything that a character says or does, be aware that a lot of these answers are based on real answers. I also filled in one of the questionnaires, and my answers (along with the questionnaire) are on my website if you want to take a look.

A lot of research was done for this book. A lot of knowledgeable people were spoken to. Car mechanics, psychologists and preppers. Some of this stuff seemed obvious to me, other stuff blew my mind.

I hope you enjoy ODIUM and the rest of the books in the series, as much as I enjoyed writing it. This series has been a wild ride so far. It was the second book I'd ever written and though I've learned a lot since the start, this book will always remain a firm favorite for me.

If this is your first delve into this series, you better get ready for a wild ride!

Happy reading,

Claire x

ABOUT THE BOOK

The *infection* came.
Humanity fell.
And the *world* everyone knew ended.

But one woman's unwavering determination to live, against all the odds, might just be the only thing to survive this bleak new existence.
When the fate of a young girl hangs in the balance, Nina sacrifices herself and leaves the barricaded city she's living in. Despite this act of selflessness, Nina isn't the same woman she once was. She's bitter, angry, and she wants nothing more than to disappear.
But now she's reluctantly become both protector and family to the girl she climbed the wall for.

The duo set off across the bleak, post-apocalyptic landscape, toward a safe haven that might not exist. While journeying, they meet Mikey—a man on the run from his past and hiding from bigger demons than the ones that walk the earth.

He introduces them to a life they couldn't imagine. A life above the ground. However, this new world continues to bring more dangers, and darker shadows than they knew possible.
And Nina quickly discovers that beyond the wall…
The deaders aren't the only thing to *fear*.
That *love and survival* just might go hand in hand.
And that fear will not be ignored, or *Forgotten*.

ONE

FEAR

Fear can make people do crazy things. Maybe that's what makes me step forward and say something? Maybe. On the other hand, maybe it's the injustice of it all. She doesn't deserve this treatment. Their treatment. None of us do, but like I said before, fear can make people do crazy things.

A once upstanding member of the community will quite willingly bash your brains in; I know this to be true. I have lived it, have seen it, and have breathed it for the past...two years? Three years? God, can it really have been three years already? No, surely not. The years go by so slowly, yet so quickly all at the same time, and I've lost track now. Constantly feeling the icy grip of death upon her neck will do that to a girl. I have had enough now though. Enough of death, enough of being bullied and ordered around, and enough of the torment. I thought the deaders were what you had to fear the most. I was wrong. My stomach rolls in fear and panic, bringing me back to the present.

She can't be more than thirteen, with a tall, lithe body, short strawberry blonde hair, and cute-as-a-button features.

"Stop."

I look around, unsure of who has just spoken. Upon realizing that it was me, I clamp a hand firmly across my mouth in an attempt to seal in the rest of the sentence. If I could kick my own ass, I would.

Lee turns to look at me, his eyebrows furrowing at my interruption. I look around and realize that the gathering crowd has stopped their gawping at the young girl. Now they all stand and stare at the crazy woman who has opened up her big mouth.

Stupid, stupid me.

His grip tightens on her shoulder, his top lip rising in a crude snarl. He isn't the man he used to be; that much is clear. None of us are the same anymore, though Lee seems like more of a dick than most.

Lee turns back to the young girl, seemingly dismissing my request for him to stop.

"You have been found stealing more than your allocated ration. You are therefore sentenced to life outside of our protective walls. Our community will no longer support your kind."

Your kind? What the hell does that even mean?

Her eyes stray to me, a pleading look set in them.

"You are now banished." His words cut her like an axe through wood, and she collapses to the floor with a howl of fright.

This can't be right. She's just a child.

Two men step forward and grab her by the arms, pulling her up to stand.

"You will leave immediately." His words ring in my ears with finality. "You cannot collect your things. You cannot say your goodbyes. You cannot and will not escape your punishment."

"You can't do that." My voice is quiet, my words almost whispered for the fear of what I know will happen if I speak up, but I have to. I can't let this young girl die. Someone has to stand up for her—someone has to stand up to them. I've seen this ending for others far too many times now, and I don't think I can take any more.

Shit, but why does it have to be me?

Lee looks across at me again. "Pardon?" he asks politely. Too politely for my liking. It makes my hollow stomach do a little back flip.

"You can't do that… She's, she's just a child." I step forward. Hardly even a step—more of a shuffle, really. "This is wrong."

Of all the people that I have witnessed be banished, in all the years that I have been here, why does her fate affect me so? There is nothing particularly outstanding about her; she doesn't remind me of anyone I used to know. A younger, less broken me, perhaps? Nope. Just some skinny kid with pretty eyes. So why her and why now?

"We cannot continue to support her kind any longer." He walks toward me. "For humanity to survive, we must stand as one. By stealing, you are singling yourself out. I am thinking of us all. Her kind will kill us all if the…others don't first."

My heart skips a beat at his last words. The others. Yeah, they'll kill us if they get a chance, but still…

"I don't see you starving to death." My eyes narrow at him. *In fact, even the pigs are better fed than us.* I run a hand across my ribs.

His eyes widen at my obtuseness, and I'm surprised that he doesn't give me a nice backhanded slap to go with his fish-bowl look. The crowd gasps at my boldness, and I glance at them with a roll of my eyes.

"And what do you mean *her kind*? She's one of us, not a deader," I continue bitterly.

"Thieves," he spits back.

3

I look at the stale half loaf of bread, now covered in dust and dirt on the ground. My stomach rumbles all the same. I'm always hungry these days. We all are.

How did we even get to a place where people are hungry and begging for scraps from the rulers of this pitiful town, and yet bread is allowed to go stale? I can't fathom this madness.

Her life for some bread.

"She's not a thief; she's a child." My voice cracks on the last word and I clear my throat and say it again. "A child, Lee."

He lowers his head, appearing to consider my words. The crowd has grown restless. I look at them. Some I consider acquaintances; not friends—no, I can't and won't have friends anymore. It's much too dangerous to have friends in this world. Friends get you killed, or they die. Neither scenario sits well with me. Either way I wouldn't ever want any of these cowards for my friends. They'd sooner sell me for food than stand by my side.

The crowd mumbles and shuffles, whispering to each other. Scared, that's how they all look—scared and pitiful, and here I am hating on them. I don't think these things because I'm being cruel though; these are just the basic facts. All the people watching the scene play out are much too thin, their skin is dirty, and their clothes are threadbare. Each one of us is frightened, but that's life these days. The more fear you hold, the more control people like Lee have over you.

Their eyes won't meet mine, and I can't make out what they say. Do they agree with me? Surely they must know that this is wrong— sending yet another civilian to die. Or are they as bloodthirsty as he is? Because he must be bloodthirsty to do this.

Blood and death.

That's what it means to be sent over the wall and away from our town. *Blood and death.* Our wall is fifty feet high, give or take, and made of steel, stone, and whatever else was available when it was first built. Our wall is the toughest yet and is all but impenetrable—so I'm told, though I have never seen the other towns, or their walls. I was here at the beginning, and haven't left since, the walls strengthening, fortifying, and locking us all inside. All but those in charge.

Keep the dead out and the living in—kind of like prison, but reversed, and with dead people. So maybe not, actually. I almost shrug at my own thoughts. Over the years, the walls have been compacted further still with a cement-like substance to fill any holes, and to thicken their outer shells.

Yet, for walls that are supposedly here to protect us from the outside world, I have seen more horrors within them than I would care to recollect.

"It's Nina, isn't it?" Lee finally looks back up at me and I break my reverie and lock eyes with him. He is a cold-hearted bastard.

"Yes." My hands ball into fists in my pockets to stop myself from shaking, and if I'm totally honest, to stop myself from bitch-slapping him right across his creepy old face.

"I don't like this any more than you do, but you have to understand that without the bread, the pigs do not have enough food to live. Without the pigs, *we* do not have enough food to live. We breed them to feed us, and to use as bait for when we send out our scavengers beyond the walls. Without the pigs we would be in a much worse scenario than what we're in currently, and we would most likely starve. Therefore she is condemning us all to death." He looks to the crowd. "All of us." His arms open wide and gesturing, almost god-like. "As if there isn't enough to fear in this new world."

The crowd nods and agrees. Fear. Fear is the biggest weapon now.

Oh, and the army of dead, of course. Yeah, they're pretty badass too.

"No, no, that's not what I was doing. I was just hungry… I thought it was going to be thrown away. I thought…" The young girl cries louder. "I just didn't think," she wails with wide, frightened eyes. She seems suddenly much younger than her teenage years, like a babe in arms, as she cries and begs for forgiveness.

Lee turns to her with a sympathetic frown. "My dear, that is the problem: you didn't think. If everybody acted that way, we would all perish. You are a thief; you have admitted so yourself, and with that in mind I will not alter our strict laws on this matter." He turns to the crowd. "Let this be a lesson to anyone who thinks that they can steal from me." His eyes shift before he corrects himself. "From us."

Asshole.

The two men holding her begin to drag her away with Lee following behind. I, it seems, am being ignored. I should be glad that I haven't received some sort of punishment for my outburst, really, but instead my palms are sweaty because I know that I can't just leave it.

Damn my morals. Where did they come from? And how can I send them back?

I think I get it now, why I want to save this girl: I want to escape with her. I can't keep praying for someone to help me if I'm not willing to help myself. I hate it here, yet I've done nothing to protect myself since I was shown where I stood on this food chain of life.

I hop from foot to foot, my nerves set on edge. I know what I must do, but I know that upon doing it I will condemn myself too. I look around once more at the so-called life that I have been living—dirty, lonely, and trodden down so that we behave as we're told. This is no more civilized than the outside world. Well, I don't think so anyway. Since no one lives out there anymore.

"You can't do this. She'll die," I shout out. My eyes follow the men that continue to drag her since she will not walk, refusing in any way to help them send her to her doom. I don't blame her; I'd do the same. I run after them, ignoring the voices behind me telling me to stop, to hush, to just walk away. The crowd, it seems, knows that I am right, but is unwilling to stand with me.

Cowards.

I grip Lee's shoulder. "Stop, don't do this. She didn't realize what she was doing; she's just a child, for Christ's sake."

He swings around and slaps me hard across my cheek, catching me off guard. The sound ricochets around the small square, and I stumble back a couple of steps with a sharp yelp. My hand grips my cheek as hot tears burn my eyes, but I refuse to cry. Not for this man, not anymore. He glares at me and continues to walk away. I know I'm pushing his patience—a slap will be the least of my worries if I don't shut the hell up—but I don't care. What kind of world is it where we send our children to die for stealing rotten food?

The guards are shoving her up toward the steps leading to the battlement-style walkway at the top of the wall. The rope ladders are being thrown over the top to the other side, ready for her to climb down.

I grip him hard by the shoulder again.

"Please…"

He spins to look at me. "Do you think that I enjoy doing this? Do you? Because I don't, but people must know not to cross the line." Spittle gathers at the side of his mouth. "They have to know how to behave now, or none of us will survive. They have to know who is in charge…"

"In charge of them? That's what you mean, isn't it? We know that already, Lee; you don't need to kill some innocent girl to prove it to us."

"She is hardly innocent, Nina. She stole, and now she must pay for that selfish act." He glares.

I snort. "Please. Teenagers *are* selfish; it's in their DNA. Just because the world has changed, it doesn't mean that human nature has." I flinch when his hand twitches again, bracing myself for another slap or something harder.

He smiles. "You people are all under my watch, and I have been put in this position to protect you all. And if that means sending one girl over the wall into the hellhole beyond, then so be it. That is what I will do to keep it this way."

Now we're getting to the heart of his annoyance. He wants everyone to know that he's the big boss around here, as if we didn't know it already.

"But she'll die." My voice cracks once again.

"Then she should have thought about that before she stole—"

"From the pigs," I interrupt. "She stole some moldy old bread from the pigs. You make it sound worse than it is. Punish her, but for God's sake don't kill her!"

I look at the young girl. Her eyes are pleading with me to save her, but I don't know what more I can say to help.

"Please, Lee," I whisper. "I'll do anything." If I thought it would make a difference, I'd offer myself—my body—to him to try and change his mind, but I have a feeling that he wouldn't want me anyway. I don't have much to offer him, or anyone. My dark hair is limp and dirty from the lack of shampoo. My clothes haven't fared well either: my jeans are covered in holes and are full of stains. However, I think I'm still pretty, despite my dirty face.

Lee is middle-aged, but his skin is weathered and leathery, making him look a lot older than his years. His eyes are sunken from lack of proper nutrition and his hair is gray and thinning.

The young girls screams, and pulls me from my thoughts. The guards are behind her now, forcing her to climb. She's sobbing and begging again, and tears spring to my eyes. My own fear and anger are bubbling to the surface. Fear for her and for me...

"Fine." I swallow down the mammoth-sized lump in my throat. "I'll go with her then."

Did I really just say that? I can't go with her...

Lee stops and turns to me once more, confusion furrowing between his brows. "Do you know what you are saying?"

I wonder what he used to do, who he used to be in his previous life. Life without the *others*, without the walls, without the fear of... everything. It seems like a lifetime ago now. I bet he was a lawyer; everyone hates lawyers, and he seems the type of person people would hate. I know *I* do.

I look at her again. She's crying for her mom, but her mom can't hear her cries now. Her mom is zombie chow, or a zombie; shit, who knows? My blood thumps in my ears, and I know I am more than likely killing myself by doing this. I have no training and no skills. I'm just a chick with an attitude problem and a penchant for being in the wrong place at the wrong time, as is shown by my current situation. I have nothing to offer her in the way of safety; shit, I'll probably get us killed quicker; but then they say there's safety in numbers, right?

"Yes. I understand." I nod and take a deep breath.

Um, actually no. I'm obviously an idiot who has lost her mind. Please stop me before I kill us both.

Pushing past him, I walk toward the steps. The men stop pushing the girl up, and try to grab me and pull me away, obviously thinking that I'm attempting to thwart their murder of her.

Because that's what it is: murder.

When others were forced to leave, I felt nothing. No remorse, no guilt. I certainly didn't feel like it was up to me to try and save the day, but that was different. *They* were different. They were bad: murderers, rapists, real thieves—not a starving child who was desperate. That's what we were told, anyway.

I look back at everyone standing and watching. Not a single other person willing to help. Mothers with their own children in their arms, and men looking ashamedly to their feet. I look away in disgust. Yes, I've definitely had enough of this place, and these people. I'm willing to take my chances out there. I hold my chin up high.

"Get off me, you idiots. I'm not stopping you…" I shrug them off angrily and look up to her. She's four steps up with tears streaming down her pretty, pale face. I know that I am doing the right thing… probably not the brightest idea I've ever had, but then I've always been told I'm reckless.

Perhaps this has nothing to do with her. Perhaps she's just an excuse to leave. I hate this place; I have hated it since I came here. I'm not some dumb blonde running back into the house of horrors, unaware of the murderer upstairs. No, I know exactly what I'm getting myself into, and I couldn't be happier about it.

"I'm going with her." I push past them and begin to climb.

TWO

We stand at the top of the wall, looking out at the lush wasteland beyond. Surprise covers my face, my mouth hanging agape. This was not what I was expecting at all. It seems the world has thrived under its new management—yet another thing that Lee didn't want us to know about.

Wasteland would be the wrong word to describe this oasis. It's lush and green, and alive with vibrant and healthy vegetation. Trees and flowers cover the landscape, tall and flourishing in their beauty. Yet despite this, in between all their magnificence, the horror and destruction remain.

I look down and around the outside base of the wall, but refuse to look the way we have just come. There's nothing—no *one*—around the base for the moment, and for that I'm thankful. In the distance is a town. I can make out the houses and abandoned cars. The place is a wreck, with garbage and things I'd prefer not to think about strewn all over. And then there are the zombies: small, human-shaped figures, far in the distance and far from human anymore. They kinda ruin the picturesque landscape for me.

"Shit," I mutter.

"I'm sorry."

I look at the girl. Her dirty, tear-streaked face stares back at me with...what? Hope, maybe? I don't know what to say to her. This was my decision, and the outcome of my decision must lie at my own feet.

"Don't worry about it. I hated that place anyway," I reply.

"I am, though. I mean, you could die because of me." Her eyes go wide at the thought.

"Yeah, thanks for that." I look away.

Would I still have left if it had been a more forgiving place to live? Probably. It's all well and good trying to keep your moral compass facing sky-high, but that isn't going to stop me from getting eaten. There are no free passes here. No passing *Go* and no collecting two hundred dollars—not that money is worth anything anymore. No, there is only blood and death, and I can't let her live with my death on her conscience if that happens.

"I was thinking about leaving anyway," I add on with a shrug.

I know we need to start climbing down the other side before Lee starts throwing things at us—or whatever the hell they do when people refuse to climb down—but I need to formulate a plan of some sort. If we climb down without a plan, we're screwed. Hell, I guess we're screwed anyway, since I know nothing about survival other than *don't get killed*.

"What's your name?" Her voice makes her sound younger than I believe her to be. Soft and childlike.

"Nina. Yours?"

"My parents used to call me Emily-Rose." She gives me a slight smile. "But these days it's just Emily. Thanks for…trying to help, for coming with me. You didn't have to and I appreciate it." Her voice is quiet, her words mumbled. "I'm not a thief…not normally." Her cheeks flame.

"Like I said, don't worry about it." I shrug again.

I lift a leg over the top of the wall and shuffle myself so that I'm sitting astride it cowgirl-style. If only this was a horse, then I could ride away into the distance and forget all this stuff. Shit. I wonder if there are even any horses left. Emily does the same, her sad eyes staring into my face for some clue as to what we are going to do.

Now that it's actually come to this—sitting atop the Great freaking Wall of China, watching the desolate city in the distance full of monstrous things—I realize that I'm actually pretty pissed off about it all.

I'm pissed off at Lee, and his so-called rules of the *new society*. I'm pissed off at all the other people for not intervening in some way; hell, I'm pissed at her too: Emily-Rose.

"I used to live over there." She points a hand over to the city with a vague smile.

"Yeah?"

"Yeah. Maybe my house is still there." She looks at me with a spark of optimism. Her limp hair clings to her neck, and despite the warm sun that beats down on us, she looks chilled to the bone.

"It probably is," I say, and she smiles wider. "But it's more than likely going to be over-run with zombies." I stick a giant pin in her cheery red balloon and watch her happiness float away. I feel like a real bitch, but ho-hum, so is life. Especially recently.

"We need to get going." My eyes make out a bunch of cars. Looks like it was a huge twenty-car pileup at one time. There could be zombies amid the wreck, but I haven't seen any movement yet. Perhaps all the zombies have skipped this side of town for lack of food. We all know that zombies are herbivores, right? Ha, yeah exactly. Zombies are distinctly carnivores, and this place is crawling with vegetation, so maybe there is just nothing left for them to eat around here—not that they know of, anyway—hence the safety of the walled city, I guess. That was another reason for the walls being so high in the first place, so I'm told: to hide our human smell, and any sounds that we make.

It just all seems so bizarre. I've had long enough to get used to it, but I can't quite grasp the fact of it—any of it. Deaders, for one, and then this crazy-beautiful overgrown world, for two. I can't disguise the shock from my face, while Emily seems unmoved by it all. This just isn't what I expected my first glimpse of the world to look like.

"Where are we going to go?"

"I'm not totally sure, Emily. Maybe we can head for those cars over there, then make a beeline for those trees." I point further out.

I reach for my matted hair, pulling it up into a high bun with a band from around my wrist. To think, my dark hair used to be one of my favorite features. What I would do to have a long, hot shower. I sigh. I still refuse to look down at Lee and his men, but I can hear them shouting at us to get going. I wonder why they haven't followed us up. Perhaps it's the guilt. They know that this is wrong.

"We need to go. Once we hit the ground, we need to run—fast. Do you understand me?"

She nods a yes, but she's busy picking at a hole in her dirty cargo pants. I'm not sure that it's safe for us to go down the ladder together. It was made by Lee and his men, I think, and I can't imagine that they put a whole heap of effort into making it strong; but I'll be damned if either of us is going to be waiting around once we hit the bottom, so we'll have to risk the climb together. I'm told that there's actually another entrance into this place, but no one seems to know where that is. At least, no one willing to tell the civilians of this little hell-hole, anyway. Lee likes to keep important details like an escape route to himself.

The progress is slow. I guess neither of us are in a hurry to die today. The slight breeze rocks the ladder every now and then, and my knuckles go pink from the exertion of holding on. I look up and beyond Emily-Rose, and think I spy Lee looking over at us, but the face is gone before I can be sure.

My feet find purchase on the ground, and I survey our surroundings. The air smells surprisingly clean—fresh, even. The last time I was out here, it stank with the decay of rotting corpses. Now it smells like… What does it smell like? Nothing. Just air. I can't smell car fumes or pollution. Bonus for Mother Nature, I guess. It feels warmer over on this side of the wall too. On the inside, it is always cold. The shadows that the walls cast seemed to prevent any heat from getting to us.

Emily drops down next to me and I steady myself with a deep breath. My nerves are bubbling away in my empty stomach; I'm half glad that I haven't eaten today. Or yesterday, come to think of it.

"Ready?" I look at her deadpan. She is visibly shaking and I know that, no matter what happens now, I have done the right thing.

She nods and swallows loudly. "Let's go."

We begin to run, with Emily lagging behind a little. Our eyes continuously scan around us for movement, but there's nothing—quite literally nothing—around. No zombies, no animals, no direct vegetation…nothing. I guess that's how they have kept the zombies away from us, from our town. They repeatedly clear the area of anything. There are no hiding places. There is nothing to attract the zombies to us. The walls are high and dull-looking. Nothing about them would be spectacular or interesting for a zombie, or shout *'hey, zombie chow over here.'* I guess they may have come and had a little shamble around once upon a time, but not recently. Our little fortress— quote: prison camp—has been built a couple of miles out from another town, and surrounding that…nothing. If there were zombies around, we would see them. I slow to a walk and Emily catches up quickly.

She looks at me expectantly.

"There's nothing here." I gesture around us. "No point in running; we might as well save our energy." I look behind us and then forward again. It feels weird to be out in the open, a warm breeze on my face, fresh air in my lungs. Almost nice.

Emily looks around us and comes to the same conclusion, stress leaving her face almost instantly.

"We still need to be on guard, Emily, so keep a lookout, okay? Don't go all daydreamy on me."

She looks at me and rolls her eyes. "I'm not a kid, you know. Not anymore."

"Sure thing, whatever." I roll mine back at her. "The first thing we need to do is find some weapons," I whisper.

"What type of weapons? I can't fire a gun." She pales even more. I didn't think that was possible; she's ghostly pale as it is.

"We aren't going to find a gun around here; that stuff had to have been looted years ago. But we need something to defend ourselves with—a tree branch for a club, or a rock or something. Anything, really. So keep your eyes peeled."

She nods and looks like she's pondering something before speaking up. "Old Man Riely, who lived down the road from us, he was as mad as a March Hare. He used to be in the army or something like that. I'm pretty sure he would have a gun. In fact, if I remember correctly, he used to have a bomb shelter at the back of his yard—not that anyone knew about it. He dressed it up to look like just a normal shed. I bet that has everything we need in it." She smiles widely at me.

The plan sounds doable, even if I don't believe that there will be anything left for us. I find it hard to believe that it wouldn't have been raided already, but we have nothing to lose. Well, nothing but our lives.

"Okay, sounds like a plan."

She does a little skip next to me and I raise an eyebrow. She's a perky little thing.

"Nina?"

"What?"

"Do you think that we could check on my house? Maybe my parents…"

"How do I say this without sounding like a prize bitch? There is literally *no* chance that your parents are alive, Emily. None at all. If they were, they would have tried to make it to the wall."

Her skip slows, her head lowering as my words sink in. I can't believe that she would be so naive to think that they would be there. Alive, even.

We are about a hundred yards out from the cars now, and have been walking for a good half hour. The road is starting to clutter with luggage and whatnot strewn around. Bushes are scattered along the edge too. I panic upon the realization that they would be a perfect hiding place for any zombies, but thankfully, I can't hear or smell anything that resembles the dead.

I look at some of the luggage as we move through it. Old clothes, photos—I swear I can see a yellow polka-dot bikini.

Christ, what was that person thinking?

We finally reach the cars; I gesture with a finger to my lips, and Emily nods. Her smile is gone, and to be fair, the girl looks serious and ready to kick some zombie ass. With what, though, I'm honestly not sure. I'm more inclined to hide and then run for it, but you know kids: always think they know best.

We crouch down in front of the first car to listen. I try to turn on my Spidey Sense, but I guess my superpower isn't working today. If only. Peeking around the bottom of the car, I don't see anything. Just more crap all over the road. There are old brown bloodstains all around the place, but no body parts. I guess that's a bonus.

We shuffle between the cars, checking under each one for zombies in wait. It's clear, as far as I can tell. We peek in through the car windows as we creep past. There's nothing that we can use on the roadside for a weapon; I can only hope that there is something inside one of the vehicles. I'm not expecting to find anything really; this must be the first place that everyone comes to when they go over the wall.

I check the first one regardless. Chancing a quick look, I see that all the doors are closed and there are no bloodstains on the inside, which is a good sign. However, when I try to open the door I realize that it's locked. I don't want to smash any windows and draw attention to us. Besides, there doesn't seem to be anything inside worth taking, so we move on to the next one.

This car is painted a dull red color, which does nothing to improve my mood, since red reminds me of blood, and blood reminds me of... Well, it puts me in an even fouler mood. When I look inside, I see that the windows are covered with dried blood smears in the shape of handprints. I shudder when I see a baby car seat in the back, filled with sludge, and I lower myself back to the ground. I can't think about things like that now; I've contained my emotions for months and kept strong.

I take a deep breath and raise myself back up slowly, coming face to face with Emily on the other side of the glass. I start and fall back on my ass. She's climbed inside the car and is looking out at me with another one of her cheery smiles. I feel anything but cheery. I mouth at her to get out and she rolls her eyes and continues rooting around. Typical teenager—they never fucking listen.

Her head pops back into view with a smile, and she holds up a penknife for me to see. I nod my approval. It's small, and rusty as shit, but it's something, I guess. And something is always better than nothing. However, my attention is diverted to something else. A smell.

My stomach clenches in anxiety.

It's the smell of the dead.

THREE

I look around us frantically, my heart beating at an insanely high speed, and I wonder if maybe I'm having a heart attack. I clasp a hand to my chest, feeling my racing heart going wild within it, and take a couple of slow breaths.

Breathe. Just breathe, Nina.

I peek around the corner of the car, expecting to come face to face with a deader, but there is nothing. Yet I know there's something here...somewhere. I plead with my ears to find the noise that shouldn't be there, the one that stands out from the rest. I need to see the abomination before it sees me.

There.

A scrape. A low thump. A moan.

Now that I've heard it, I feel stupid that it took me so long to hear it in the first place. Yep, something's here with us. I grit my teeth, slide to the other side of the car, and peek around it. Still nothing.

The stench is getting worse, and it's all I can do to stop myself from praying out loud that there's only one. We may have a chance with one; any more and we're dead. I hope that Emily's heard the noise and is hiding. The last thing I need is her jumping out and drawing attention to us.

I crouch in front of the car and peek up through the windshield right out through the car and out the back window.

There it is. I look at everything but its face. It's the faces that haunt me the most.

A singular rotting deader is lurching our way. I assume that it has no idea we're here yet, since it seems to be minding its own zombie business.

Emily peeks up. Her face puckers into shock and fear and she ducks back down.

Good girl.

Perhaps we can hide from it. If it doesn't know that we're here, then it might just keep on walking. I fall to my knees, and slide myself under the car as quietly as I can, though every noise my body makes on the ground sounds like a fireworks display being set off. I can almost imagine the giant red arrow pointing at my location: *'She is here; dinner is served.'*

It's reached our car, but its feet continue to make their slow shuffle past us. One foot is broken at its ankle and only hangs on by dried-up brown tendons—hence the thump and slide, I guess. I shudder and look away from the sight; that foot is not going to be on for very much longer. My nose is to the ground, like a hound dog on a hunt, as the shuffling moves past.

Finally, I can take a breath. That's one of the biggest problems for me with deaders: they smell like crap and I don't have the stomach for them. Well, the eating-me-to-death part is a huge problem too, I guess.

I let a few minutes pass before I scoot out from under the car. The knee of my pants snags on the rough road, tearing a hole, and I feel my skin graze against stones and grit. I suck in an *ouch*.

Seriously! After everything that I've survived, and I still moan about a little scrape. I tut at myself.

I keep down low as I move around the car. The deader has moved off to the side of the road now and is going away, and as long as it's far from me, I don't care where. I shudder again and creep over to the door of the car to take a peek inside. Emily is curled up on the floor under a blanket, or coats—I have no idea what it is, actually, but damn she looks cozy, even with all the dried blood. I tap on the glass, trying to avoid looking at the baby car seat again, but she doesn't move. I take a furtive glance around me and tap again a little louder, but still nothing.

With a roll of my eyes I crack the door open. The mound of coats and blankets shuffles and then freezes.

"Em…" I whisper, and give her a poke.

She sits up, pulls the covers off her head, and gives me a half-hearted grin as she produces a half-eaten chocolate bar. My stomach lurches at the thought of food. Chocolate, no less. Man, what I would do for that right now, but it's finders keepers out here, and we need to get going regardless in case more of them come for a friendly neighborhood chow-down.

"Come on." I gesture with my head and we continue winding between the cars, slowing every now and then to check inside them. Unfortunately for us, they all seem to be empty, so as we reach the end of the pileup, we're armed with a tree branch for a bat and the small penknife.

Oh-Deep-Joy!

The woods are about a hundred meters from the roadside, and after a serious look around we make a run for it. Moving from tree to tree, the pace is slow, but hell, I guess there's no rush. It's not like the deaders are going anywhere. It's funny how time doesn't hold much meaning anymore. Not like it used to.

My life used to be ruled by the time: a time to wake me up, a time to be at work, a time for lunch, a deadline to meet, getting stuck in a traffic jam for two damn hours. Dinnertime, bedtime, blah blah. The list goes on. So many things I took for granted back then. Hell, I'd do anything to have a last minute deadline to have to work toward now.

Emily holds onto my arm as we come to the edge of the woods. I'm pretty sure there are some houses I can see through the trees. I don't know whether to be grateful or more frightened. A house can mean a brief respite, but it can also mean more deaders. With the sun beginning to set, we could sure use a place to hole up for the night. And considering our weapons stock consists of what is basically a stick and a blunt butter knife, I'm not sure we'd fare too well in a zombie battle. By the smell of things, I'm damn sure some of the evil-dead are nearby. I wrinkle up my nose and gesture for us to go. Either way, we can't stay here.

We dash the last hundred yards as quietly as possible. Despite the rotting smell in the air, the back yard of the house is actually free of deaders. *Happy dance.*

We skirt around the outside of the house, keeping as quiet and as low as possible. There doesn't seem much point, though, since the yard is so overgrown. We would be hard-pressed to be seen amid this mini-jungle.

With that thought in mind, I make a quick glance at our feet with a pounding heart and a sweaty forehead. Score two for survivors of Earth. I can't see anything reaching up to munch on our ankles, but decide not to stick around as if silver-plattering my feet for someone's lunch.

A low moan draws my attention back to the woods. It sounds like we have been smelled out, as more than one other moan joins in the chorus like some strange a cappella show choir.

"Time to go, Emily," I whisper.

By the look on her face, you would think that someone had just given her a fresh bag of popcorn. Seriously, her chirpiness is making me want to smack some of the silly out of her.

"I know this street." She practically skips around to the front of the house, and if I didn't think it was so foolhardy to do so, I would have shouted at her to get her stupid ass back here. Instead I follow with a grumble, grabbing her shoulder before she slips around to the front of the house.

"What are you doing? You can't just walk out there," I shout-whisper in her face.

She turns and looks at me with a big grin.

"That house." She points down the street. I look to where she's pointing, but I'm unable to figure out which one she's talking about. "That's Old Man Riely's house. The one with the bunker in the yard." Her grin splits even wider.

Well shit, this just seems to be going too easy.

I stare unblinking in the direction that she's pointing, trying to work out which house she's talking about.

"That one right on the end, with the dead tree in the yard," she says, her voice all sing-songy.

I watch as a zombie dressed in a brown-crusted dressing gown crosses the front lawn. Seriously, I wish that guy would have tied

24

the knot a little tighter the day the world ended. A shudder runs through me.

"You mean the one with the dead dude in the yard." I look at her pretty eyes as they go wide in recognition. I can't help but think *halleluiah* as she processes the information, and horror crosses her face.

"Now you get it." I stand with my hands on my hips, feeling a little bit like her mother, and I wonder how I got my self-righteous ass into this situation in the first place. She shakes her head and points over my shoulder with a trembling finger.

I spin on my heel and watch as at least four zombies turn the corner. Each one is dressed in its Sunday best, which is basically a rotting, revolting mess of dried blood and dangling entrails. They are all at various stages of decomposition, with several limbs missing, and guts and viscera hanging to the ground from cavernous holes in their stomachs, which under different circumstances would have made them very fucking dead indeed. Instead, gummy and broken-toothed smiles plaster their faces when they catch sight of us, and with arms reaching for us as if in some kind of crazy zombie flash mob, they groan louder and step up their shuffling from slow to shambling. Well, it certainly seems like they smile, anyway.

I guess the thought of crunching down on someone's brain will give you enough incentive to speed up, right?

Well, only if you're a deader, of course.

FOUR

"**S**hit." **I grip my branch tighter**, splinters of dry wood slicing into my hands. The zombies groan louder in unison as if already sensing the feast upon their rotten lips.

"Nina." Emily's voice trembles behind me, but there's no time to turn and look at her. The approaching group of undead have my attention locked tight on them.

"Nina." Emily's voice rings in my ears again, louder and more persistent, and I unwillingly break my stare with deader number one. I'm almost certain he just licked his lips at me. Creepy fucker.

I look at her terrified face and know that we stand no chance in this battle. Hell, did I ever believe we would? There are too many of them, and we are too few. Quickly surveying the area, I sense our opportunity for escape rapidly closing with each passing second. I grab her hand, holding it tightly, and pull her with me out into the street.

Who am I kidding anyway? I'm no Xena: Warrior Princess.

We run as fast as we can, our hands locked tightly together, and head straight for Old Man Riely's house. My legs pump harder than should be possible, considering how weak I know I am, but I guess my body isn't ready to give up right now. Emily trembles as undead moans and groans break out from every direction around us.

Shit, shit, and thrice shit, just for good measure.

My eyes are glued to our destination—the house, our saving grace… I hope. If I look anywhere else, I know that I will see death coming toward me. Dressing Gown Deader Guy has spotted us too, and is greeting us with a full-on frontal. I should call the cops on this guy for indecent exposure. It would be laughable too—to see his shriveled-up gear staring back at me—apart from the small fact that part of his anatomy is entirely missing, leaving a gaping, rotten hole in its place. Bile builds in my throat, but this is no time to get queasy. I release Emily's hand and ready my branch. I need to hit him as hard as I can and keep on running. I'm only going to get one chance at this.

The mantra *'swing batter, batter, batter, swing'* runs through my mind as I cock my arm back with my stick in hand. We draw closer, and his rotting hands reach for me. I swing. I swing with everything I have, hitting him full force in the face. The bone-crunching impact causes the branch to snap in half and fall from my grip, but I don't stop to retrieve it.

Emily once more grabs my hand, and we keep on running. Legs pumping, feet pounding, she drags me around to the back of the house. A soft cry escapes my lips when we enter the empty backyard. *Maybe we won't die today after all,* is my first thought. *The grass is again ridiculously long* (that's my second thought), *and there's no way to tell if anything is buried deep in the blades, but we have to take the risk—there's no time for another route.*

I can see the bunker she's talking about at the end of the yard;

camouflaged as a little wooden shed, unfortunately it's without a doubt going to be locked up tight. I pull her away from it and toward the back door of the house. She resists against my pull, but I'm stronger than she is.

"Emily, there's no time to try and break in right now, not with the zombies closing in. Those doors are meant to withstand practically anything. Your standard house, however—that's a different matter."

I grin as the thought pops into my head and I slam into the back door with my shoulder. It rattles under the force, but doesn't open. I slam my shoulder into it again, harder this time. Pain shoots up and down my arm, causing me to cry out involuntarily. Still the door doesn't budge. I'd feel silly if it weren't for our impending death.

I look at Emily with a frustrated frown. Something cold unexpectedly grabs my ankle and I scream and stamp out on impulse. I look down to see a leathery hand clamped around my ankle, a zombie attached to the other end of it. It's slowly pulling itself out of the overgrown shrubbery beside the door. I stomp on it repeatedly, with my eyes closed tight against the sight, until I feel the skull cave in and the head turn to mush under my boot. I open my eyes and look down to see what remains of the zombie's head.

My shoe and ankle are covered in gunk, and vomit builds in my stomach, slowly making its way up my throat. I swallow it back down and look away. Fear is growing in me, the panic beginning to set in. The cold mush around my leg isn't helping to calm me down either. My breathing is once again rapid, my eyes quickly scanning the yard for any more of the ground dwellers. I can't breathe.

They're coming.
They're coming.
They're coming.

A sob escapes my lips. I want so much to be tough, but I'm just a girl who likes shoes, goddamn it. What do I know about survival? I look at Emily, whose face seems to mirror my own fear.

There's no hope…no hope at all. I turn back to the door, resting my hand on the knob, praying to every god that might be listening to make my wish come true. Impulse makes me turn the handle, turning it clockwise. It turns—it turns ridiculously easily. I shove the door open wide and drag us both in, slamming it shut behind us. A small laugh escapes my lips. I can feel it bubbling away below the surface. I want to slap myself silly for not trying the handle first. My shoulder hurts, my ankle is covered in goo—Jesus, I'm such an idiot! Another hysterical laugh slips out and I clamp a hand over my mouth. I can't lose control now. I can't.

My eyes slowly adjust to the dark that ensnares us. The house is a mess. Belongings are everywhere, blood is on the walls, cupboard doors are open in the kitchen, with items spilling out of them. I reach behind us and click the lock shut as I hear moans enter the yard. Sure, zombies can't open doors, but I feel more secure with it locked, regardless. I pull us away from the door, drawing a curtain across the inside of it, further darkening our surroundings.

My breath catches in my throat, dry and raspy. God, if I could just breathe. If I wasn't so thirsty. If I wasn't so hungry. If I wasn't so tired. *Shit, if I wasn't so damn scared…*

Emily's cold fingers wrap around my hand; her body moves close to mine. I look at her for a second and wonder what's going on in that head of hers. Probably something similar to my own, no doubt.

We stand frozen to the spot, listening for movements within the house. Waiting, patiently waiting for something. There has to be something here; by the looks of the place, whoever lived here didn't escape unscathed. I just need to know how many and where they are. I just need to know if we need to keep on running.

A *thump* sounds from upstairs and at the back door at the same time, and we both jump. Emily still clutches her silver penknife tightly in her hand, like a miniature warrior. Her knuckles have turned white from the strength of her grip. I want to take it from her and arm myself with something, my own fear taking over, but I can't. I think that she is on the brink of a meltdown; the last thing she needs is for me to take away what she clearly sees as her protector.

Wait, *I'm* her protector. Or I thought I was. Better get on with it then.

I move forward as quietly as possible, careful not to step on anything on the floor. Clothes, bowls, plates, cushions, blood. Something glints up at me, and I move a cushion out of the way with the tip of my soggy, bloody foot. A knife stares back up at me. A knife. A huge freaking butcher's knife. I feel a toothy grin spread across my face, and I reach down and grip it in my hand. It's not as big as I first thought, but compared to Emily's knife, it's like the daddy of our little family. Daddy knife saves the day. Yay, go me!

The thump sounds out from above us again, and we move to the foot of the stairs, checking all the corners of the living room as we go. It's not like we really have a choice in the matter. I mean, if there *are* zombies upstairs, we don't want them catching us unaware; therefore the only logical way to be safe is to clear the entire house of zombies. The stairs creak loudly as we climb them side by side. Maybe they aren't loud. Maybe everything just sounds loud right now. For instance, my heart sounds like an orchestra of drums has broken out.

We climb the last step and look into a relatively cheery-looking hallway. Well, if it weren't for the smears of blood everywhere, it would be cheery. Kind of reminds me of my home, actually—white walls, beige carpets, and art on the walls. Every door is closed. Closed and bloody. Still looks kinda homey though. I roll my eyes. Time does that to you—makes you more comfortable with the site of blood. I wonder when the same can be said for zombies. I don't think I'll ever be comfortable around them.

We stand waiting patiently for the noise again, but nothing. Emily coughs. It's small and inconsequential, and clearly a purposeful attempt at a disturbance. The noise has the desired effect, creating a stir behind one of the closed doors. I look at her and she shrugs at me with a slight rise of her mouth. A vain attempt at a smile, I guess.

We creep down the hallway, our soft steps waking up a loose floorboard and producing a loud creaking sound. We both freeze, and I grit my teeth, pausing for a moment. We hear nothing, so we continue moving forward again until we reach the door that quite clearly contains a guest. I tap gently on it and am met with growling and banging from the other side. We both jump backwards in unison, and I can't help but chuckle lightly. I look at Emily. She's as white as a ghost, but trying to contain a frightened laugh too.

What a great zombie takeout team we make.

FIVE

We settle in for the night. It seems zombies still can't smell through walls and doors, and so have wandered out of the yard in search of a more catchable lunch date.

Barring the dead guy upstairs, the house is clear. There's the odd stray body part to keep us company, but neither of us mentions those. We search the house, starting in the kitchen, and come up with a couple of things we can use; however, the most useful items are sitting in a couple of boxes and backpacks by the front door like fucking birthday presents. It seems the owners were on their way out of this madness and were either taken out or had to make a hasty retreat without taking their gear. Boooo for them, but yay for us.

Gotta look at the glass half full, I guess.

Emily looks around warily while we unpack what we've found so far. She keeps staring at the stray limbs scattered around the place as if she thinks they are going to jump up and demand their things back,

Evil Dead style. I snigger at the thought.

Jesus, when did I get so blasé over rotten limbs?

"Chin up, Emily. It's not so bad." I shrug and continue to rummage through the boxes. There's so much good stuff here, I find it difficult to comprehend our luck.

There's a first aid kit containing mainly Band-Aids and some aspirin, but hey, it's better than nothing. Upon further inspection, I find a couple of bandages and some antiseptic cream too. Great, we're covered for boo-boos.

I turn out the backpack and find a lighter and matches, and a big pack of water purification tablets. *Well gee whiz, aren't we the lucky ones today.*

"Nina."

I look at where Emily stands rummaging through a cardboard box. She holds up some canned food and I nearly fall to my knees, I'm so happy. Canned prunes and baked beans never looked so good.

"Can we eat it?" Emily looks like she might start drooling at any moment.

"Hell yeah." I look around for a can opener, and begin to panic when I can't find one. "Shit."

"What?"

I realize that we're both whispering. I'm not sure whether it's to not draw any attention from outside or from upstairs.

"No can opener. Keep looking." I go and check all the drawers in the kitchen, but still come up short. Seems the owners weren't so savvy when it came to packing their stuff up after all. What good is canned food if you can't get into it?

A sharp bang interrupts my thoughts, and I poke my head back into the living room. Emily is stabbing the top of the can with the penknife she found earlier. I'm about to tell her to stop before she stabs herself when the knife finally pierces the can. Juice splutters out of the top and she lifts it to her mouth and swallows it down.

I'm so jealous, I'm about to see red. Fortunately, Emily stops swallowing and hands me the can with shaky hands that can barely contain her excitement.

"You want some?" She licks her lips greedily.

A little shiver of appreciation works its way up my spine, and I take the can without even acknowledging the question and swallow the rest of the prune juices down. I've never tasted anything so good in all my life, and I don't even like prunes.

"Where's your knife? I need to get these bad boys out."

I take the knife and am about to stab a bigger hole in the can when Emily tells me to stop and hands me a can opener from the bottom of one of the boxes. I smile and quickly attach it and cut the lid off, popping the circular metal ring inwards and then prying it back out. Oh dear god, they look like shriveled up old man parts, but I still shove one in my greedy waiting mouth and groan loudly as the explosion of flavors dances over my taste buds.

I snatch another one out, spit out the pit from the now devoured one, and reluctantly hand the can back to Emily. She fills her mouth with a couple and closes her eyes, moaning and savoring the taste. There's nothing but silence as we both chew and think about the flavors in our mouths. Unfortunately, all good things come to an end, just like our can of prunes. Emily wipes her fingers along the inside of the can to get any remaining juice out, but none remains by the look on her sullen face. She looks into it longingly and then discards it to the floor sadly.

"Hey, chin up, Emily. There's more cans in the box, right?"

"Yeah," she replies with a frown. "I never even liked prunes before, you know? Kinda reminded me of…"

"Yep, totally know what you mean, say no more," I interrupt with a snort of hushed laughter.

She looks at me, her head cocking to one side. "I was going to say giant lumps of dog poop. What were *you* going to say?"

"Uh, yeah, that's what I was going to say too." I shrug and look away. "Come on, let's open up something else."

She hands me the can of baked beans and I shudder—yet another thing I despised pre-apocalypse. I open it quickly and sniff at the insides, my stomach doing a little flip at the lumpy contents. Spoons are at a shortage, so it looks like I'm going to need to drink from the can. The sharp edges don't help with the appeal of the lumpy cold mess that lies within. I chug it back and swallow a couple of mouthfuls of the cold beans. This is worse than I thought. It seems the apocalypse has done nothing to alter my taste buds on baked beans.

I shudder again and hand it to an overeager Emily. I feel strangely full. Or maybe my stomach is closing up shop for the day, in the vain hope that I won't try and force anything else disgusting into it. Emily doesn't seem too bothered by it, though, and is swallowing it down with great eagerness. I burp in my most ladylike fashion into my hand and continue sorting through supplies.

It doesn't seem quite real to catch this sort of a break—especially after such a shitty start to the day. I probably shouldn't question it, and yet I do. We should just hang out here for a couple of days, catch up on some sleep, and fill our stomachs with food. Who knows when we are going to get this opportunity again? The doors are locked, the windows partially boarded up, and barring Mr. Deadman walking upstairs, the place seems relatively safe. I pull the curtains to one side and check outside. Zombies are roaming the streets in their masses. I say masses, but there's probably only a handful of them. Still, a handful is a handful, and we are just one young girl and a woman who doesn't know her north from south. I snort to myself. Yeah, maybe once upon a time we were those people. Not now, however.

I might not be Lara Croft yet, but the desperation to live can fill you with a hell of a lot of enthusiasm for surviving, and if that means fighting hand to hand with a walking corpse when you need to, then so be it.

I pull the curtains back in place and take another look around. Everything is covered in a thick layer of dust, and I can't understand why this place hasn't been picked clean. There doesn't seem to be *that* many deaders outside, and Lee's men were always going out to scavenge and coming back with just the bare minimum of supplies. This town isn't too far from the wall—surely, armed to the teeth they could have had the pickings of the place. I repack some of the stuff into the backpack as I think it through. There's an iPad and iPhone in here. Seriously, what were these people thinking? What were they going to do, play *Angry Birds* to keep the boredom at bay? How long would this thing even hold its charge? And a phone, really? I tut to no one in particular, but attract Emily's attention nonetheless.

"What? What is it?" She throws the can into the same pile as the empty prune can.

"People! People are just idiots." I throw the phone to one side. "The stuff they were packing, some of it is just useless crap."

She comes over and joins me, looking through the growing pile of junk. Her hand stops on a pile of photos, and she lifts them, inspecting each one with a sad smile.

"This isn't crap, Nina. This is their life."

"This *was* their life. They're dead now, and all this," I snatch the photos back from her, "is crap. This doesn't help anyone to survive. Not me, and obviously not them either. This just reminds us all of what we have lost."

"It reminds us of what we can have again," she replies softly.

I shake my head. "No, Emily, things will never be the same again. Who knows how many people actually survived the first attacks, and since then? Pfft, anyone left out here is more than likely a deader, too, now. For all we know, those big-assed walls that we were supposedly being protected by…*that* is life, and the people behind them are all that remain, and we all know how wonderful those fuckers are. Those that aren't control freaks and rapists are cowards." Anger and frustration bubble to the surface, threatening to open the floodgates to my tears. I swallow them down, and control it as best I can. "No, this is how it is now, and this—this hellhole we're in, this is life for us now. So yeah, take a good look at some family photos, keep those memories alive, and see if it inspires you. Me? I'm a realist."

"They're not cowards, they're just scared and trying to protect their loved ones," Emily whispers.

"Well, aren't you the forgiving one? Would you be still singing the same tune if I would have left you to go on your own?"

"Stop it," she sobs.

I clench my teeth and try to stop any more words from spilling out of me. I know she's right. The other people behind the walls, what they had to do to survive was just as bad as what I had to go through, but I hate them just the same. I hate them for never helping me, I hate them for watching me suffer, and I hate them for having someone to protect. A family.

I squeeze my eyes shut, my heart beating against my ribs and threatening to break them. I can't control the ambush of anger and pain any longer. I open my eyes and throw the photos up in the air in disgust. I see Emily's eyes fill with more tears, and I turn and storm up the stairs. Mr. Deadman starts banging on his door again like a noisy neighbor.

"Oh, fuck off to you too." I kick his door as I walk past, and he retaliates with a long throaty groan.

My cheeks feel hot and flushed from my little outburst. Or maybe it's from the memories of my life—my real life, and not this awful existence—that are swelling to the surface and causing me to freak out. I want to cry, I want to shout, I want to kill something. I have a good mind to storm in on our little friend and kill him, but there's no real point in taking that risk other than to sedate my wayward temper.

I sit down on the end of the big double bed and pick up yet another happy photo from the bedside table. The couple in it look happy and in love. They're standing on either side of a man, who I presume must be Old Man Riely. He stands in the middle of the couple, an arm draped over each of their shoulders and a smile on his face. Crazy Old Man Riely, it seems, lived with his daughter and her husband. The pain is suddenly unbearable, and I find myself curling up in a ball on the bed, clutching the photo to my chest as I try to contain the flood of tears that threatens to overflow at any minute.

SIX

When I open my eyes, it's dark outside. Shit, it's dark *inside*. Pitch black. I'm momentarily freaked out until I remember where I am. The house is silent; even the dead dude next door has gone quiet. Maybe he's gone to sleep. Do zombies sleep? I shake my head. I know the answer to that: No, zombies don't sleep. They don't tire and they don't give up. They are the worst type of enemy—and only decapitation or destroying the brain somehow can stop them from coming back again and again.

I go back downstairs to find Emily snoozing on the sofa. She's lit a couple of little candles on the table, and they cast playful shadows across her face. She's curled up with a coat over her, snoring quietly and looking peaceful. Her face seems younger now that she is asleep, now that the worry lines have smoothed out with the onset of sweet dreams. I lean over the back of the sofa, staring down at her pretty face, and sigh, jealous of her contentment. Her eyes flutter and open, and she jumps up from her position in shock at me staring down at her. I fall back on my ass, landing in something soft and sticky that I don't dare look at.

"Jesus, Emily!" I stand back up, touching my backside with a grimace. It's covered in whatever I just fell in. And whatever it is, it's lumpy and gross. Just great. And that's the second time that she's made me fall in less than twenty-four hours.

"Sorry, Nina." She looks sheepish, biting down on her bottom lip.

"It's okay. Kinda my fault anyway, I guess."

"What were you doing?"

Now I'm embarrassed. "Uh, well, nothing. I just came down and was checking on you. Hey, you never mentioned that this dude lived with his daughter and her husband."

She shrugs and sits back down with a yawn. "Hardly ever saw them, they were always away on business or something or other. He was pretty much here on his own all the time, from what I could tell anyway." She pauses and continues. "Probably why he was so cranky all the time."

The thought of him being all alone when the world went to shit is way more upsetting than I would have thought. My thoughts stray to who else might have been alone when the dead rose up. Old people, half senile and not understanding why the only people who come to see them anymore want to eat them; sleeping children confused as to why Mommy isn't smiling down on their little cherub cheeks anymore, and instead is reaching in with dead fingers and ripping their tiny, fragile bodies apart. A shudder runs through me, cold trickling into my spine.

"I found some more food, and a bottle of vodka...some other bits and pieces too. You wanna see?" Emily breaks me from my dark thoughts and I nod with a grimace.

She pulls another backpack over to the side of her and begins to pull things out, placing them on the coffee table before her. There's a lot of what I would call crap, but some really useful stuff too: more matches and candles, a flashlight, a Swiss army knife—one of those really cool ones with all the things sticking out of it, some more painkillers and Band-Aids, even some antibiotic cream, and the bottle of vodka. I'm impressed that she kept it packed with the important stuff. It *is* important; I haven't had a drink in years.

I grab it, unscrew the top, and take a long swallow. It burns on its way down, but damn that's the sweetest thing of all. The burning. It reminds me that I'm still alive.

"Can I have some?"

I look at her with a raised eyebrow, the bottle still poised at my lips. "Nope."

"Why not?"

"You're like twelve."

"So? And I'm like…fifteen, actually. Mom used to let me have a drink on special occasions." She looks at me hopefully.

"Does this look like a special occasion?" I take another swig with a raised eyebrow.

Her shoulders slump, like only a teenager's can, and she continues scrounging through the things she has found. I'm still in a little bit of shock that we have been so fortunate. Maybe *fortunate* is the wrong word. If nobody else has found these things, then it must be for a reason. Maybe this area was completely overrun? Maybe other people never made it to this town because they were eaten first? Maybe…?

"So what's the plan, Nina?"

"Like I said earlier, I have no clue." I peek through the living room curtains out onto the front lawn. It's amazing how dark it gets when there aren't any streetlights or house lights to illuminate things. The moon and stars seem to shine brighter than they ever have before. It would be pretty if it weren't for all the zombies out there. Shit, a lot of things would be prettier if it weren't for their rotting sorry asses.

What *are* we going to do? Maybe we can go up to Ben's parents' cabin after all? That's secluded. Before I can think it through any more, Emily's voice interrupts my inner ramblings once again.

"I was at school, you know, when the people started…when they started hurting…" Her voice trails off and I turn from the curtain to look at her. She's sitting and staring into the air in front of her, her face a tormented picture of pain as the memories invade her.

"What did you do?" I take another swig of the vodka and then hand it to her. Underage drinking laws don't apply anymore, I guess; besides, she sure looks like she could use a drink. I sit down next to her, ready to listen. I don't want to, not really. I've listened to more than enough of these horror stories to last me a lifetime, but the kid needs to spill, and I'm the only one listening.

"I was in Math. I freaking hated Math; my teacher, Mrs. Marrion, she was a real bitch." She smiles. "The school fire alarm went off, and I was happy at first, thinking I was getting out of doing algebra, but as we all started to pile out into the halls in an orderly line like Mrs. Marrion told us to, someone started pushing, then more people joined in, until—until the screaming started." Emily wipes her eyes. "God, there was so much screaming, Nina. Then everyone started pushing and shoving even more, and I didn't know what was going on. I just ran like everyone else and headed for the tennis courts where we were supposed to line up for fire drills, but when we got outside, it was like—everyone was like, you know…now what? What do we do? Where do we go? We didn't know what everyone was even running from, so

42

we all just stood there looking at each other. Then they started coming out the doors."

She takes a swig from the bottle and starts coughing. I pat her on the back, leaving my hand in place long after the coughing subsides.

"I didn't understand—I didn't know what they were, or what they could do." She shakes her head, and the tears that had been pooling in her eyes spill down her face. "It was my gym teacher, Mrs. Turion, she was the first one out. She was hissing and um...she didn't look right. She was just standing there, staring at everyone with blood and..." Emily's face scrunches up at the pain of the memory. "I would have loved to be doing algebra right at that moment," she laughs and sniffs at the same time.

My hand moves in comforting circles over her back. I pull her into my arms and rock her, hushing gently while she sobs.

"Amy, a girl I used to talk to in the lunch line, she went over to Mrs. Turion. Amy was so brave." Emily looks at me with such an endearing smile that even though I know what is coming, I can't help but smile and nod. "Amy was crying, but she still went over to her to see if she was okay. I could never have done something like that. Before Amy could even say anything, though, Mrs. Turion grabs her and bites her." The crying gets louder, and Emily reaches for my face to mimic what happened. I dodge her touch—I do not need to feel that. She withdraws her hands and continues. "She bites down on her face—her face! Amy starts screaming and trying to pull away, and there's so much freaking blood, Nina, and no one—not even the other teachers were trying to help her. They were just standing there like statues. Amy finally pulls herself free of Mrs. Turion, and there's a huge hole in her face and half her nose is just *missing*, and blood is spraying everyone who's too close to her. I think I'm going to be sick, but before I can, Mrs. Turion growls, like a dog or something, and reaches for Amy again. And then everyone else is screaming, but still none of us are moving." Sobs wrack Emily's skinny body, and I think her story is over until she speaks again.

"My friend Adam was standing next to me, and he whispered to me…um, something like, 'we have to go, Emily-Rose,' but I couldn't stop watching Mrs. Turion. Adam pulled me by my elbow, and I stumbled back, and he kept pulling me and pulling me until I looked at him. He had blood on his face, Amy's blood, and then I looked at everyone else, and we were all splattered in it. I freaked out then, wiping at my face and crying, and stumbling backwards as Adam pulled me. It seemed to get everyone moving. Slowly, we all started to move away. Mrs. Turion didn't like that. She let go of Amy and started coming for us, and me and Adam ran and ran until I thought I was going to throw up."

Emily cries even harder and I coo into her ear, rocking her in my lap. I've never been the motherly type, and since the world went to hell, I seem to have lost any part of me that gave a shit for another human being. That was beaten out of me at some point or another, but I feel something for this poor girl. Whether it's pity or actual concern, I'm not sure yet.

"Hey, do you still have that chocolate bar from the car?"

She pulls away from me and takes it out of her pocket with a wide grin. "I forgot all about it."

It's like heaven in a purple wrapper. How either of us could have forgotten about it, I don't know. Especially after we were forced to eat cold baked beans and prunes earlier. I shudder at the thought.

We tear the chocolate bar open and divide it in two and I examine it. It doesn't look so good up close, but I'll be damned if I'm not going

44

to eat it anyway. I'm about to take a bite, and by 'bite' I mean 'shove the whole creamy chocolate half into my mouth at once,' when Emily speaks up again.

"What about you?"

I pause. I knew this question was coming. It's one I've avoided up until now. One I haven't been able to speak about, and one I don't ever intend on discussing with anyone.

"I don't want to talk about it, Emily." I nibble the edges of the chocolate. Strangely, it doesn't taste as good as I thought it would. The vodka was way better, and I reach for that instead.

"Please, Nina."

I gulp down too much and stifle a cough. My head is beginning to feel heavy from the drink. I used to be such a great drinker; now I feel like such a girl. Not even a quarter of a bottle gone and I'm getting woozy.

"Nina." She places a hand on my leg and looks at me. "It helps… to talk about it, to get it off your chest." Her bright blue eyes stare up at me with a profound innocence. She's lived through this horror too, but for some reason I feel that my horror is worse. Shit, don't we all. However, she is still the girl she was; I, on the other hand, am not. I'm harder, colder, and much less trusting.

I shake my head and close my eyes. "It won't help, Emily."

"Why not?" Her voice is barely a whisper.

"It just won't. Nothing helps." My eyes are beginning to fill up. Jesus, what is it with this girl and making me cry? Nothing for an entire year and then boom: twice in one day. She makes me feel almost human again. Almost.

I open my eyes and look at her. I feel a tear sliding down my cheek. I don't want to cry, I don't want to think about it.

"Nothing will ever help."

She frowns at me, her chocolate discarded like mine. Taking the bottle from my hands, she takes another drink. There's no cough this time, as if she's sensing that what I'm going to tell her is bad news, like she's hardening up to the fact that I'm not the goody-goody she thought I was.

I shake my head again. "I can't talk about it, Emily. I just can't think about...about." I snatch the bottle back from her and stand up. "I'm done with the chitchat," I snap.

I storm into the kitchen, but I'm not sure why. There's nothing here—we checked earlier—but I need the space. Space from her, space from the memories.

"You can't just keep bottling it all up you know, Nina. One day the bottle will overflow."

She's followed me to the kitchen and I turn to look at her. Her small frame seems so huge, filling the doorway and stopping me from escaping for a second time.

"Well aren't you the profound one all of a sudden?"

"What happened?" she asks again.

"Fuck you! And quit looking at me with those big, sad eyes! It's like you're doing a Bambi impression."

I take another long drink, the alcohol really flooding my system now. This is a stupid rookie mistake, getting drunk. I slam the bottle on the counter, making us both jump.

She looks hurt but doesn't say anything. Just continues to stare at me, one eyebrow rising in an unspoken question.

Push, push, push. That's all she keeps on doing. That's all she's going to keep on doing. I huff out a heavy breath.

"I killed him," I whisper.

"Who?"

"Ben." I look at the floor, the shame flooding my face as his image appears in my mind's eye. His tortured face begging me to…

"Who's Ben?"

"He was my husband, and I killed him."

SEVEN

I look up at her, my features hardening once more when I see the sadness on her face. I don't want her pity.

"We should try and sleep, get some rest for tomorrow." I screw the cap back on the bottle.

"Nina—"

"Don't. Just don't, Emily. I don't want to talk about it, so just drop it. You have no idea what I have been through. That was just the start of the horror for me." I try to push past her, but she stands frozen to the spot like a statue. "I'll take first shift. Sleep upstairs. The bed's comfy, just don't disturb Dead Guy; he's quiet for a change," I bite out. I hope she drops it. Emotionally, I don't think I can go through this right now—or ever. This is always the worst part of getting to know someone since the apocalypse: sharing each other's sordid pasts, each other's journeys through hell. Like any of it matters or makes a freaking difference. It never does, no matter how many times you tell people what happened. It never helps. The guilt, the pain, the horror, it always sticks around like flies on shit.

She finally relents and lets me past with a roll of her eyes. I wonder if it's the cheap thrill of sleeping in a comfortable bed, or if she's just not sure what's left to say to me. Either way I'm done for the night. I have nothing left to say to her about Ben, about my past. Story hour is finished.

Morning breaks, the light slipping in through the aging curtains, and I rouse myself from my dream and sit up with a yawn. Emily's still upstairs, sleeping I presume. I need the toilet so badly, and dash to the bathroom. I never thought I would take such great satisfaction from sitting on a toilet, but there it is. I don't flush. There won't be any water in the tank and even if there was I wouldn't want to attract any attention. It's kind of gross, but back behind the walls we mainly used buckets, so this is an improvement upon that. I can feel my ladylikeness slipping through my fingers with every passing day. While here, I may as well root through the bathroom cabinets and see if there's anything useful. I don't think either of us checked yesterday.

I pull open the door under the sink and move things around. There are lots of shampoos and body washes. Man, what I would do to be able to take a long, hot shower and wash my hair and body. I stink. Everyone stinks these days, yet this doesn't make me feel any better. Neither does the fact that I know I'm becoming accustomed to it. I don't want *Eau de Stink* to become my natural smell. There are some spare toothbrushes, at which I nearly jump for joy. Tearing open the package, I grab the toothpaste and squeeze out a little of the dried-up substance from within, spit on it to soften it, and scrub my teeth until my gums bleed. Even then I don't think that they are clean enough.

These are definitely coming with me. I slip them into one of my many pockets and continue with my search. I find cotton swabs and clean my ears, and then some god's-honest 'dry shampoo'—the kind that you massage into your scalp, but instead of it shaping your hair into place, it does some magical voodoo shit and makes it look, smell, and feel cleaner. It's not the same as using real shampoo and water, but damn this is a luxury. I'm close to tears at the thought of having clean hair again. Pathetic. *I'm so not Lara Croft.*

I pull my out hair band and squeeze out some of the shampoo, rubbing it into my scalp and through to the tips, pulling my fingers through the knots until clumps of dry, dirty, knotty hair come out in my fingers, but still I don't relent. Who knows when I'm going to get the chance to do this again? There's virtually nothing left in the tube, but there's enough to get a start on my roots.

My fingers are sore and red, as is my scalp, by the time I finish. Looking in the mirror above the sink, though, I know that it was worth it. I use makeup remover to wash my face and even under my arms. Who gives a shit if it's not soap? It's just as good. I look almost human again. Clean teeth, relatively clean hair, and a perfume smell to my skin. Who would have thought this is what I would have missed the most? Being clean.

After primping myself for what seems like forever and filling the pockets in my pants with the extra painkillers, cough medicine, and my toothpaste and toothbrushes, I make my way back downstairs and continue my hunt for useful shit.

Rummaging through the boxes again, I find some more food— dried pasta, dried beans, canned tuna fish. I want some more of the prunes we had last night; I think I have a new favorite, but there's no more to be found. I grab a couple of dried cereal bars from the bottom of the box, examining the *Best Before* dates on them and then sniggering to myself and unwrapping them one after another. I bite into them with more enthusiasm than I showed the prunes the previous night. I'm not sure my stomach can take much more of the delights that this house has to offer.

"Is there any more of those?"

I look up to Emily. She looks well rested, and I'm glad. It's probably the best night's sleep she's had since this all began. I wish I could say the same, but the dreams always ruin my slumber.

We fill up on cereal bars and load everything into the backpacks. I'm pretty impressed by what we have: food, medicines (sort of), survival gear (sort of). If we can find a car, we might actually stand a chance of surviving. For what reason though? I can't help but wonder. The world isn't ever going to be the same again, so what's the point of all this? Three years, and not much has changed. I frown and look through a small gap in the back curtains, which are still drawn shut. Survival instincts are a real bitch.

"So what's the plan?"

Jesus, I wish she would stop asking me that question, or at least find a new approach in asking it. She's like a broken record stuck on repeat. And why does she think I have all the answers? I can feel my temper bubbling below the surface.

"Old Man Riely used to have a real big Hummer parked in the garage. Never drove it anywhere, but he'd be damned if he didn't clean that beast every Sunday morning up on his driveway." Emily peeks out into the back yard with me nonchalantly.

"Really?" I turn to look at her, our proximity close enough for her to smell my fresh breath.

"Did you brush your teeth?" She looks around my face and hair with a frown. "Did you take a shower?" Her eyes skim my clean hair and face, a furrow pinching deeper between her eyebrows.

Guilt floods me: she looks positively green with jealousy. I decide to ignore the interrogation. "Does he really have a big-assed car in his garage?"

She tugs her hair behind her ears. "Yeah. Well he used to anyway." Her perky smile is back in place. How do teenagers do that? Just bounce back every time.

"Why didn't you tell me this last night? If it's still here, then…" I stand up with a huff, and go into the kitchen.

"I dunno. I didn't think that it was important last night, I guess."

I rummage through the drawers; I know I saw some keys round here somewhere. I didn't pay attention to them last night, but maybe they're for the Hummer. I slam through a couple of the drawers, shoving things around, and nearly slice my finger off on a pizza cutter. I pause on the item, deep in thought as to whether it could be useful as a weapon, but decide against it. What am I going to do, slice up a portion of zombie face? Urghh.

I move to the next drawer, and my hand finally lands on the keys I had seen, but they aren't the right ones. These aren't even for a car, for God's sake. I slam the drawer shut in anger and lean back against the kitchen counter.

"He might have kept the keys in the garage. My dad used to keep his spare there." She shrugs and I eye up the door to the garage.

"Seriously?"

"Yeah. Something about always having the keys close at hand if we ever needed to make a quick exit."

I really want to be a bitch and ask how that motto fared up for him, but decide it's best to keep my mouth buttoned on that subject. No point in pulling off the Band-Aid for her.

"Where did he keep them?" That seems like a better question to ask, given the circumstances.

"On the wall, right by the door."

"What was he, stupid? What would he have done if someone had broken in?"

Her mouth opens and closes like a fish for a moment as she flounders on a suitable answer.

I put up a hand in protest. "Don't answer that, I honestly don't want to know. Obviously you were all idiots."

Emily is biting on her lower lip, her nostrils flaring at my last comment. I guess she's trying to contain her temper too. Jesus, we were not going to be a good team if our monthly cycles coordinated.

"Nina, do you think we could go look for my parents at some point? I know what you said about them being…" She looks away from me before continuing. "I'd still like to look for them though. Just in case."

"No." I grab my butcher's knife and stand by the door to the garage. This girl seriously has a death wish if she thinks it's a good idea to wander around a zombie-infested town looking for Mommy and Daddy with nothing to defend ourselves with but a crappy butcher's knife and a blunt penknife.

"But…"

"I said no, Emily. They are dead. I know that sounds harsh to you, but you need to deal with this sooner rather than later. Everyone that got left behind is dead." I turn back to the door with a bitter taste in my mouth. Emily says nothing, but her eyes had told me everything I needed to know. I'm a bitch.

"I don't mean to be horrible, Emily…"

"Then why are you?"

I look at her. The words sting, but I know she's right. I *am* being horrible, but I also know that there will be no point in going to look for her family. If they are alive, then they won't be here. There's no point in trying to sugarcoat it for her. My hand is on the doorknob to the garage while my mind is somewhere else.

"Not everyone died, Nina."

"Yeah, we're left with the real charmers of society eh, aren't we, Emily? The evil, and corrupt, the ones who would sooner leave you to die than help you. Yeah, and that's just another solid reason why we can't go looking for your family." I turn the handle carefully, wondering for a moment if it will be locked.

The door abruptly yanks from under my grip and shoves open wide, slapping me in the face with brutal force. I shout out and drop my knife, my hand flying up to my face where I feel hot blood pouring from my nose. I feel blinded by the lights in front of my eyes, but try to push past them as I hear the groaning of a zombie in the kitchen.

Shit!

Emily screams out my name loudly, and I drop to the floor in search of my knife. The blood pours down my face, a heavy throbbing in my nose. My hand mercifully touches the blade and I grip it and stand back up, simultaneously wiping the blood away with the back of my arm.

Emily's back is pressed hard against the kitchen countertop, the cold enamel digging into her bones the further back she leans. A zombie is clawing for her, drooling and slathering over the floor and itself.

She's kicking out at it repeatedly, but with her back pressed against the counter she can't seem to get the force behind the movement to shove it off her.

I don't hesitate as I slam into the zombie's back, my knife plunging into its skull, which is surprisingly covered in pink fluffy hair. *Looks like we have a little pink punk zombie.* The knife slices in to the hilt before the zombie drops to the floor in a heap of rotting flesh and stinky drain smells. Back splatter from the zombie's head covers my face, and I spit and wipe it off my mouth, shouting angrily and kicking it hard in the ribs. Rotten brain tissue mixes with my own blood, which is dripping off the end of my chin.

"Fucking zombie. I only just got myself clean!" I bend and pull my knife out of its head, black congealed blood flying up over my pants, and abruptly stomp over to the garage doorway and charge in without bothering to check first. Stupid? Yeah, but you should never piss off a woman who's just cleaned her hair. "Any more of you fuckers down here?" I beckon them with open arms, my temper boiling over. "Come on, lunch is served!"

It's dark in here, and my hand roots around the walls until I find a switch and flip it. My eyes go wide as I survey the damage. Pink Z must have been stuck in here for months. I wonder if this is where she actually turned, or whether she was locked down here afterwards.

There's blood everywhere, across the walls and floor, even on the ceiling when I look up. The garage door is painted in the same brown-and-black liquid that seems to fill each zombie. Dirty handprints cover everything I can see. Most things have been tipped from their shelves and now cover the floor: tools, old paint cans, and general junk. However, my eyes fall on the most amazing thing I've seen in a while. Filtering through the horrors, they land on the most beautiful black mid-sized Hummer I've ever seen, which sits in the middle of the room.

I'd love to say it's shiny and perfect, but it isn't. It's covered in blood and gunk, and dented to hell and back, but the windows are intact and it's big and powerful-looking.

"Nina?"

Shit, I'd forgotten about Emily. Her voice calls down cautiously to me.

"Come here, there's no more of them." My temper has passed now, even with the blood and gunk that still clings to my face and hair. I grab the band from around my wrist and tie my hair back up in a bun. It was stupid of me to leave it down, really.

A few seconds pass before I hear her hesitant steps in the doorway.

"Oh my God, look at this place."

I turn to look at her. She too is covered in black sludge and brown blood, her shirt is ripped, and she's as pale as a ghost.

"Yeah, but look, Emily. Look at that beauty." I walk up to her and grab her hand, smiling for the first time in what feels like forever. "If we can get that going, if it has gas in it, if we can get the garage door open—Christ, we might have a chance." The excitement in my voice is palpable, yet she seems unperturbed by it.

"That's a lot of *ifs*, Nina."

"It's a shit-load less than we had before, babe." I give her hand a little squeeze and pull her further into the room. "We have to find those keys. They're here somewhere. They have to be." I point to the little hook that's by the door. It's empty, but the fact that both it *and* the Hummer are there means the keys had been hung there at some point previously.

Excitement bubbles in me, and every time I look up at the Beast—as I've decided to so aptly name it—it tingles a little more. The thing is like a tank, with huge tires, high sides, and a mean-looking grille on the front.

On hands and knees we search, rooting through body pieces and sludge. It seems at one time there were two people in here. Pinky must have turned at some point and eaten her little partner in crime. I shudder at the thought and pray they didn't know each other. Though would that matter? Would it be any less horrifying being eaten alive by someone you didn't know? Maybe, maybe not.

"I think I've got them, Nina."

Emily is pulling out boxes from under the precarious pile in the corner. I'm sure at one point they must have been very neatly stacked and put away, but now they are just a huge mound of cardboard on one side of the car. She shifts a box out of the way and the contents spill out of it.

Pots and pans clatter to the floor. They roll and crash into one another. One particularly pesky metal pan lid rolls under the car and out the other side before clattering loudly into the metal garage door. The entire wall of metal rattles, and the sound echoes around the small confines of the room.

We both freeze, staring at each other in horror as the noise bounces around us. I close my eyes and count to ten. Or I start to, but I only make it to four before something crashes into the other side of the garage door. The sound is quickly followed by a groan and another crash. It seems, much to my dismay, that we have visitors.

And I didn't even have time to make up a guest room. Well damn!

EIGHT

Fist after rotting fist hits the outer garage door, each new set of zombie hands making a resounding crash, and I flinch at every single one. I know we need to move—and now—but I feel frozen in place. Why, I have no idea. I just killed one of them less than an hour ago in the kitchen. I'm still covered by the gore and grime from the kill. Yet trapped in this house with Emily, it had still felt vaguely normal, surrounded by furniture and stupid products and shit that I used to have in my own life. Something as simple as a sofa can be a huge source of mental (as well as physical) comfort. The things you take for granted on a daily basis. Even grumpy dead dude upstairs couldn't ruin it for me. Emily was right, not all of the stuff in the boxes was crap. It all meant something. It was all important to someone at some point.

The sounds echoing in to us from out there, makes me remember where we are, what we have survived, and how fucking lucky we are to have gotten this far. However, break time is over now, back to the real world. *Hip, hip hooray.*

Another smash bounces off the door, and Emily yelps and whimpers. Another loud pound makes her grip my upper arms and scream into my face.

"Nina!"

Her nails dig in to my soft flesh as I stare in horror at the weakening garage door and try to scramble my thoughts together. Jesus, it sounds like there are hundreds of them. A slap ricochets off my face, and I stumble backwards from the force of it.

"Jesus, fuck, Emily!" I swing to slap her back, more of a reaction than in actual anger, but the fear in her eyes stops me. She cowers, waiting for the impending impact; her hands cover her face in protection. I lower my hand, feeling the shame fill me.

"Sorry, I thought you were in shock," she yelps.

I frown at her, still trying to contain my temper and not bitch-slap her back. "The keys. We need the keys, now." I swallow down the beating of my heart and try to focus.

She mirrors my action, her chin trembling. The pounding on the door has increased even more, as has my heart rate.

Her eyes are wide. "I found them. They were under the boxes."

"Well, get to it," I yell.

She clambers over to the boxes and starts to throw things out of the way. I try to help her as much as I can, attempting to pile the stuff out of the way of the front of the car. The noise all the time is ever increasing with the incessant moaning that only the dead can make. Well, only them and my mother-in-law, anyway. Damn, that woman could nag.

It sounds like there's a full-scale thunderstorm outside, as fists pound upon metal. I look to the top of the door, and of course—Of. Fucking.

Course.—the door is beginning to come loose from its rusted hinges.

"Got them, Nina. I've got them, I've got them!" She jumps up, slips, and falls back over with a little yelp. Her hand flies back up, still clutching its prized possession. I almost want to give her a roaring round of applause, but I can't hear myself think anymore. Besides, can it be a roaring applause if there's only one person clapping? Anyway, I digress.

She stands again, done with her little comedy sketch moment, and starts to climb back over everything, unlocking the car with a squeal of some sort of emotion. The garage door seems to mirror her sound as it squeals right back at her, as if in self-righteous indignation at our escape plan, the hinges ever loosening.

"Get in!" I shout the order to Emily and hesitantly run back into the kitchen, tripping over Pinky's body on the floor and falling flat on my face with an "Ooomph." I'm standing back up before I've even caught my breath, and running into the living room with yet more blood pouring down my face.

I grab the two bags that we had so carefully packed earlier, slinging one over my shoulder and carrying the other by its strap. I hear a smash from the living room window as I come back through the kitchen, but I ignore the noise and jump over Pinky's decomposing body like I'm an Olympic hurdler. I grab the bottle of vodka from the kitchen counter without a second thought (*What? This is important stuff, don't judge me!*) and run back through to the garage, slamming the door shut behind me.

Emily is in the passenger side of the car waiting patiently for me. Ha, who am I kidding? She's screaming my name out repeatedly like she's a prized fucking opera singer. The garage door has begun its slow descent to the floor. I throw everything into the back of the car and jump into the driver's side. I put on my seat belt and start the engine.

What? Safety first, even in these times! The engine growls loudly, the sound reverberating around the confines of the garage. The sound seems to incense the zombies outside even further.

Did they know that dinner was getting ready to make a run for it? Drive for it? Whatever…either way it is time to get the hell out of here.

The door finally gives way with a heavy screech and a resounding thud. It lands on the floor, and the zombies outside don't wait for an invitation, but charge forward full tilt. Well, as full tilt as something with rotten and decomposing limbs can manage, anyway.

They attempt to clamber over the many obstacles in their way and I can't help but lift an eyebrow in surprise. I think this is all starting to get a bit dramatic; anyone would think this was some crazy horror story. It seems, however, that garage doors and boxes full of junk are a huge stumbling block for the dead. They moan angrily as they flail around and fail to find purchase on anything solid to pull themselves up and over with.

I rev my engine to add some flair to the moment once more, since they kind of ruined the previous moment with their inability to climb. My foot hits the gas pedal, pressing down as hard as I can until the car shoots forward. I chance a look at the gas gauge, happy to see that there's about a quarter of a tank. *Yay for surviving another day in this hellhole.* We roll over the metal door and several zombies at the same time, making the journey somewhat crunchy and uncomfortable.

Bile rises in my throat at the sight and smell that hit us as the car creeps outside gradually, despite my best efforts to get us going quicker. It looks like every zombie for miles around has come to join in the fight for lunch. They stagger from lawns, from behind trees, from inside their houses as if this is a 'meet and greet your friendly new neighbor' session. I should thank them, really: their bodies are making the drive over the garage door much smoother than it should be. That is until they hit the car angrily, pounding the metalwork with their decrepit scrunched-up fists, creating dent after dent in my beautiful Beast, groaning and grunting and leaving bloody, gory smears along the windows.

Old Man Riely would not be impressed.

NINE

The drive out of the street is slow going, hindered by the bodies pressing against us from every angle. Yet there's something deeply satisfying about the sound of their bones crunching as we drive over the fallen. Emily is hiding behind her hands, like the sight of so many zombies pounding on the windows is too much to take in. Every once in a while she peeks through her fingers, sucks in a breath, and covers her face again as the Beast rocks from the onslaught outside.

I could have really done with a spotter to help get us out of here, but I have a feeling Emily's standing on the top of an abyss waiting to fall in; her fear is almost palpable. I can't say I blame her, or that I'm not worried myself. After all, I'm the one who's trying to avoid seeing the deaders' drooling, rotten faces staring in at me, teeth bared, brown sludge free-falling from open wounds that no man or woman should still be alive and moving around after receiving. Yet here they are, and here I am. I bite my lip and swallow hard, my nostrils flaring as

I try to see over them, past them, fucking through them—anywhere but *at* them. It's bad enough that I get to hear their bones crunching and cracking. I force myself to keep pressing on the accelerator, keep moving forward no matter how slow the progress may be.

Once the street widens up, there's more space for me to maneuver and dodge the vehicle free from some of the deaders. I floor it and we speed away, leaving a trail of broken bones, bloody smears, and shattered dreams of a free lunch across the blacktop.

Silence fills the car, and I focus my attention on the road. Or I try to, repeatedly, but I can't help my eyes from straying to the landscape. Cars are overturned and burned out. Emaciated skeletons litter the road. Some hang from their cars, the odd little twitch giving away that there is some form of life still trapped in there; others seem to have been dragged onto the road and torn limb from limb, leaving nothing and no one behind to reminisce about their existence, barring a few bones. Yet the world—the environment—is blooming. Despite the death and destruction that the naked eye sees, when you look a little deeper, the world is alive and well. Grass, trees, and flowers are overgrown and wild, and sprouting up from every surface and crack available to them. Blues, greens, violets, and oranges. It's a horror story wrapped up in a rainbow.

We finally move free from the city and leave the wasted backdrop behind us. The wall stands tall and mighty in my rearview mirror, yet I don't feel any remorse that I'm out here instead of behind its safety. For the first time in a long time I feel free again, like I'm back in charge of my life—however short-lived that may be.

The hours drift by us, mercifully peaceful with no surprises other than the odd stray zombie, who the Beast and I decide to play tag with. It's probably a stupid idea, but I can't resist it. Every time I see one of their emaciated forms staggering down the highway, anger and hatred burn deeper than I knew possible, and before I know it I'm steering the Beast into their legs and smiling a grim reaper's smile at the sound of their bones snapping.

Emily-Rose sleeps fitfully next to me, occasionally shouting out something unintelligible. Even the bumps of the zombies don't wake her. I wish I could still sleep like that. I don't think I've slept for more than two hours at a time since this whole thing happened, and even then it's never a deep sleep. I smile to myself, wondering if it's because she feels safe with me; that's why she sleeps so well. I hope so. Though she irritates me, she's kinda growing on me. But I wonder how much longer I'll be able to keep up the tough girl charade.

The sun is at its highest point in the sky, and I presume it's around lunchtime now. I need to pee, I need to eat, and I need to stretch. I also need to check the map and make sure that I'm heading in the right direction for Ben's parents' cabin, since that's where I've decided to head to. It's the only place I can think of.

I pull the Beast to the side of the road, checking to make sure there's nothing around us before getting out. Emily stirs when I open my door, looking momentarily bewildered and then apologetic.

She climbs out and follows my lead to the back of the truck.

"Sorry, Nina. I didn't mean to fall asleep." She tucks her little bob away from her face with a sheepish smile.

"It's fine." I root through the backpack to find the map I had packed. My bladder is fit to burst, though, and I'm hopping from foot to foot.

"Gotta pee. Won't be a minute. Find the map, it's in there somewhere." I run to the side of the road and crouch down. I can see as far as the eye can, and it's clear. I'm glad for the break. My pee is a deep yellow and I know that I'm dehydrated. The vodka from last night didn't help, and it would also explain the headache, but I don't regret drinking it. In fact, I'd go so much as to say that I can't wait until I can have another drink and feel numb again. Well, numb apart from the bad head, that is.

Aaah, sweet hangover, how I've missed thee. Let me count the ways. Um, none!

When I return, Emily has unfolded the map and laid it out on the floor of the trunk. She's snacking on some nuts and raisins while crouched over, examining it carefully. She looks up at my approach.

"Better now?" She holds the bag of nuts out to me and I greedily grab a handful and throw them in my mouth.

"Much, thanks. So where are we?" I join her over the map and crunch down hungrily on my nut feast.

Her finger trails over the map. "Right about…" She watches my face as her finger moves. I raise an eyebrow at her. I have the distinct impression she has no clue as to where we are. I decide to wait out her ploy, and she relents quickly. "I have no idea." She steps back from the map with one of her typical nonchalant shrugs. "Sorry," she huffs, "again."

I move closer to the map and find where the wall is, tracing the route I think we had taken to Old Man Riely's house and out of the other side of town. There should be a river over to the left somewhere, and if we follow that, it should lead us right to up Woodland Springs, where the cabin is. I stand back up, looking around us.

"What is it?" Emily asks.

"Well, we're going in the right direction, but there's about two hundred and fifty miles between where we are now and where we

66

want to get to. Give or take." I grab another handful of the nuts and lean against the trunk. No point in letting her know how shockingly bad I am at working out distances. Or how bad I am at directions. Or... *I'm falling into the typical female driving cliché, aren't I?*

My clothes are still covered in brown-and-black sticky gunk. I've tried to ignore it up until now, but it's starting to dry and flake, and it smells like dead puppies left out to rot. I think of my little beauty regime in the bathroom earlier with another wistful sigh.

"What's wrong now?"

"Do you always ask so many damn questions?" I snap and close my eyes, raising my face skyward in an attempt at getting my nose away from my own stench for a few seconds. My brain feels like it's going to pop out of my skull at any point.

"Well, you don't talk much."

I open my eyes and look at her: hands on hips, lips pouting, a real Little Miss Attitude. I think I like her even more.

"And...you don't tell me anything. How else am I supposed to find anything out?"

I raise an eyebrow at her as she continues with her rant.

"If we're in this together, then you need to let me in, tell me where we're going, and what I can do to help. Stop being such a bitch to me all the time." Her pout gets pout-ier. If that's even possible.

I stand up and face her silently. "Emily, you're just a kid. You can't fight, you can't read a map—hell, you can't even stay awake when I'm driving through a massive zombie infestation. How are *you*," I point at her, "going to help us?"

Tears spring to her eyes, and once again I feel like the bad guy in all of this. Err, bad girl. Whatever.

"I'm not a kid anymore. I stopped being a kid when I watched my friends and family get ripped to shreds and eaten."

Touché.

"And you don't know that I can't fight. You just presume you're the only one that can do anything. That you're the only one who can save us." Her chin trembles and makes me feel lousier than I already do. I should hug her and apologize. She's right, I *am* being a bitch, and I'm taking it out on her and presuming that she's useless. Instead what comes out of my mouth is…

"Well, *can* you fight?"

She rolls her eyes at me. "Well no, but that's not the point."

I laugh loudly—a full-on guffaw—and eventually she joins in, rubbing her tears away. Then I do grab her, and hug her fiercely. It seems harder to let go of her once I start though. The feel of human contact, of friendship, is a warm and fuzzy one, and one I haven't felt in a long time.

We eventually separate, both of us looking more at ease with each other than we have since this all began.

I take a deep breath. "I'm going to try and get us to my husband's family cabin. It's up at Woodland Springs, north of here. It's secluded, and they used to spend months up there when they retired so it was always well stocked. It's where Ben and I were going to go when… well, it's where we were heading out to when all this happened." I lean over and point to our position on the map. "I don't know if it's safe there, or if there is food there still, but I don't know what else to do or where to go." I shrug.

"This is where we are." I trace my finger upwards and stop at Woodland Springs. "This is where we need to go. There should be a river over to the left of us somewhere." I point in the direction I think is right. "We could do with filling up some water bottles or something." I look down at my filthy clothes. "I would love to try and wash some of this shit off me too."

"Yeah, you do stink," Emily says seriously.

I laugh again. "You don't smell too pretty yourself."

She laughs in return and blushes.

"Can you drive?"

Emily shakes her head. "My dad always promised to teach me when I was old enough. I've sat in one and I know what all the gears and pedals are. Well, what I remember. It's been a long time, you know?"

"That's okay, that's good. If you know the basics, I can teach you as we go."

She smiles like it's family vacation time. I don't have much choice in teaching her, since I can't cover all that road on my own if we want to make it there sometime soon. Besides, it could end up being a great survival skill for her if anything happens to me. I feel the urge to protect her at all costs, and the feeling takes me by surprise. It shouldn't, really. I risked my life just coming over the wall with her, but in some respects I wonder if I had used her as an excuse. I was tired of being stuck in there and being bossed around all the time. I wanted to see what the world had turned into. Not very much, by the looks of things so far.

"We're going to need fuel soon, too. The Beast was only a quarter full, and I wasted most of that revving the shit out of the engine and running over zombies."

"That seems like a good way to waste fuel." She smiles at me.

"Yeah, I think so too." I smile back, but at the back of my mind, I can't help but worry about having to try and get fuel. We were lucky enough to find a car that started in the first place; I can't see that we would be that lucky again.

We load everything back in the trunk and climb in. It seems Old Man Riely was having a garage sale at some point and had piled clothes and ornaments into the boxes in his garage. Emily had managed to grab some of the clothes and throw them into the back for us. They are...well, old man clothes—checked shirts, brown cargo pants with a surprising amount of pockets, old shoes—but thankfully there are one or two women's items. His daughter's, no doubt. I grab a long-ish black dress and a black jacket—it's really not appropriate for an apocalypse, but it's clean, which is a blessing. Emily tries on some of the cargo pants and slips a belt around her waist. I have to make a new hole in the belt leather with my knife to get the pants to stay up, since she's so skinny. Funny: they were too small for me and they're too big for her. Go figure. I shove my feet into my Doc Martens, and revel once again at my good thought to put them on the day it all went to shit. Doc Martens last through anything.

We follow the road to a small turn-off where I can see the river go under a small bridge. I climb out and scout around for any stray zombies, but there's nothing that I can see. That's the good thing about rural areas, I guess: no houses generally means no hordes of zombies, just the occasional lost one. *Poor little lost zombie.*

I fill some old water bottles, and down one of them without thinking. I bite my lip and worry for a second, then decide there's nothing I can do about it now, anyway, and quickly refill the bottle, this time adding one of the water purification tablets we had found earlier before climbing back into the car, feeling less depressed. I'm not sure if it's the fresh air, clean clothes, and lack of zombies, or the fact that we have cleared some of the stress that has been building between us.

Wait, yeah I do. It's definitely the lack of zombies, though clean clothes and a relatively clean conscience are a bonus too.

About half a mile down the road, there's a garage. It's small, with only one or two pumps and a small shop, but its smallness could work to our advantage. There's an array of trees surrounding it, and hopefully we can fill up my Beast and get on the road again without any problems. Of course things never go according to plan when you need them to.

TEN

We pull up to a pump, take a hasty look around, and I jump out when I see the coast is clear.

"Nina," Emily whispers across to me and I look back in at her without replying.

"Will they be turned on?"

I crinkle my forehead up in confusion.

"Don't they turn them off or something at night?"

"Let's hope that someone did a bad job and left them both on when it went to shit," I reply.

I pick up the hose, which dangles down to the ground instead of sitting in its holder, and squeeze the handle grip, silently praying that the end of the world hit this town during the day. Nothing happens for a second or two, but finally, after a weird gurgling sound, fuel squirts out at me, missing my boots by millimeters. That's the last thing I need. Though I do like the smell of gasoline, I can't see it being advisable to get it all over me. I look at the other pump and see its nozzle hanging limply to the ground too. I unscrew the pump cap and push in the nozzle, letting the fuel fill up the Beast for a few minutes before it comes to a shuddering stop. I guess we aren't the only gas thieves around here. I glance in at Emily as I screw the fuel cap back on. She's smiling like it's Christmas. I have the urge to smile back, but fear is tickling at my neck. It's too quiet out here.

I look back up into the sky, watching a couple of birds circle above us, before sliding back into my driver's seat and starting it up, vaguely happy to see the gas gauge jump back up to a quarter full again. At least it will keep us going for a little longer.

"It was on," I smile. "I didn't manage to get much, but some is better than none, huh?"

Emily nods. "Should we look inside?" Emily looks past me at the small convenience store. I follow her gaze. The place looks trashed, and god knows what or who else is in there.

"No, I think we should just keep going. We have enough stuff to get us by for now at least. No point in risking it." Though I'm tempted by the candy stand I can see through the window.

"This could be the last stop we make for a while though. There could be some really useful things in there," she whines.

I glance at the candy rack longingly again. It's tipped to one side and I can't tell if there's anything on it anymore, but the colorful little sign is beckoning me regardless. I unclip my seat belt with a groan, turn off the engine, and slide back out, reaching in and grabbing my knife as I do.

"Okay, but you wait here." I turn and make my way across to the store with Emily falling into step beside me.

"I thought I told you to wait in the car." I don't look at her, but keep going.

"You did." She smirks.

I frown at her while she continues to smile, and I have to look away before I smile too. Damn infectious smile that she has.

The doors are locked tight, so we scout out another way in, only finding a small serving hatch that's partially open—not enough for a normal-sized person to squeeze through, though.

I look at Emily, and then at the size of the gap. Even she's too small, but she takes the lead and pushes up the small window. It's stuck in place, but after a couple of attempts we manage to get it up further, and I boost her in through it and into the dark building beyond.

My heart races as I follow her on my side of the glass to the doors. She turns a little lock on the door while casting a furtive glance behind her, and I push past her as it clicks open and strain for any noise inside.

"See, aren't you glad I came now?" She smirks.

"No," I grip my knife tighter, and let my eyes get used to the shadowy store, taking in the mess lying around. There's not much left of anything; people have clearly raided before us.

"I told you this was pointless," I say to Emily through pinched lips.

She ignores me and continues to root around on a shelf. There are empty packages of cookies, drinks cans, and bags of chips, but nothing more.

I check out the candy rack and, to my surprise, find a bag of Jolly Ranchers, which have fallen behind the stand. A smile breaks the scowl free from my face.

"Woot! Look, Emily, cherry Jolly Ranchers!" I can't hide the childish excitement from my voice. "I used to love these." I rip the package open and grab one, shoving it in my mouth before holding the bag out for Emily to take one.

I won't lie. I few carnal noises may have escaped my lips, but the embarrassment is worth it for the pleasure that is exploding within my mouth.

"Don't move."

A gruff voice barks out from somewhere inside the store, and for a moment I'm not sure that I really heard it. I'm so lost in the moment of the sweet. It's tingly, and the sugar on my tongue is creating a rush of saliva and making me swallow repeatedly. I lean back further against the wall with a satisfied hum. If I die today, then it will have been worth it for this one moment.

"I said, don't move."

Nope, definitely heard it that time. I open my eyes. *Damn, when did I close them?*

A man comes from around the back of one of the aisles, aiming a shotgun at me. I presume it's a shotgun, it could be a semi-automatic nuclear device for all I know about weapons. What I *do* know is that it's big and scary-looking. Unlike the man holding it. Sure, he's big, but even *I* can see he has a rugged charm about him. I swallow the candy whole, nearly choking on it as it goes down.

"How many more of you are there?" He moves closer to us, checking back over his shoulder nervously. His head is shaved, but dark hair has started to grow back.

"How many more of us? What?" Emily looks from me to Gun Guy warily.

"People? Women? Men? Whoever," he half shouts, keeping the gun's aim steady on us.

"No one," Emily whispers. "It's just us two."

"Shut up." I look at her with narrowed eyes and she shrugs at me like it's no big deal.

"Is that your Hummer?" His eyes widen at it, a grin spreading across his tanned face. I want to stamp my feet in frustration.

"Yes. *Our* Hummer. Get it?" I snap back bitchily.

"Not for long." He looks back at us with a smile, and backs toward the door. "Throw me the keys."

"No." I glare.

"Nina, just give him the keys."

"No."

"Yeah, Nina," he mocks from the glass doors. "Just give me the keys, Nina." He smirks at me, but not for long as a zombie slams into the glass behind him and all three of us scream.

"Shut up. More might come if they hear you," he shouts.

"Hey, you screamed too," I shout back.

The zombie bangs its meaty fists against the glass, smearing its mouth across it as if the glass was ice cream and it was cooling itself down from the hot sun.

"I did not." He hits the glass angrily with his fists, right where the zombie is. The zombie doesn't even flinch, but continues its assault on the glass. It really is quite perverted to watch as its tongue licks back and forth, leaving a strange gloop in its wake.

"Yes you did. It was even louder than Emily's scream, and she's just a kid," I snort.

Emily shoves me in the side. "Hey, I'm not a kid."

I roll my eyes at her. "Sorry," I look at him again, "but he did."

"Does it really matter?" she asks exasperatedly.

"YES!" Me and Gun Guy shout in unison.

The shop falls silent as we stare at each other, playing the 'who can give the other the most evil look' game. Eventually Emily breaks the ice.

"Seriously. You don't seem like you want to hurt us, not really, and we obviously don't want to hurt you…" she begins.

"Speak for yourself," I bite back. He raises an eyebrow at me.

"That zombie out there is stopping any of us from getting out of here right now, so can we all just calm down? We are going to need to help each other, not fight." She looks from me to him and then back again. "Nina? Please?"

Gun Guy lowers his gun slowly, all the time keeping watch on me. Good thing, too, because I want that gun before we part ways.

"Fine." I grab another candy and pop it in my mouth. Now that the imminent danger seems to be over, maybe I can finally enjoy it. I stop and look at the scruffy dead person outside. He used to work here, by the looks of his overalls. He's fat and balding, with no arms. Hence all the licking, I guess. I shudder. I wonder what the hell happened to his arms?

"Hey, I wonder what happened to his arms?" Gun Guy shouts over to us with a laugh, while putting his hand up close to the zombie's face. I cringe at the idea that we've had the same thought.

The zombie is going wild on the other side of the glass and tries to bite through it, breaking a couple more of its teeth in the process, and we get to watch the whole glorious spectacle. Fantastic.

Emily has continued rooting through the shop for anything else we can take, seemingly oblivious to the guy with the gun, who might decide to take us hostage and torture us. Wouldn't be the first time. I shudder, and look at him. He's packing some cans into a backpack, and looks like he wouldn't hurt a fly. Not that he doesn't seem like a badass, but the guards behind the wall all had a certain look about them—a soulless look, I guess. Gun guy doesn't, at least not so far. He seems more of an opportunist than anything. I swallow another luxurious mouthful of sweet-tasting saliva.

"Can I have one of those?" Gun Guy is standing in front of me, staring greedily at my bag of candy. I don't want to share them with anyone—certainly not with a gun-wielding maniac. *Especially if this is the last bag in the world.*

"No, they're mine." I clutch the bag tighter.

"Don't be mean."

"Don't be whiny," I retort.

"I could just take them from you," he says childishly, his brown eyes still staring at my candy.

"You could try." I laugh. "But you won't, will you, Gun Guy? Because if you were going to do that, we wouldn't be talking about it." I put them behind my back and out of his immediate reach, narrowing my eyes spitefully at him.

"It's Mikey." He finally looks up at me, his eyes momentarily pausing on my breasts before finding my face.

"So?"

"It's my name." His eyes soften.

"And again, so?" I snort and push past him. I'm pretty sure he calls me a bitch, too, but I don't care; he's not wrong.

I find Emily in the magazine section, flipping through an old teen magazine. She looks up as I come close.

"So what's the plan?"

That question again, really? And so soon after the last time she asked me the same thing.

"Well, we either keep down low until the zombie forgets we're in here and wanders off, or we find another way out. There's usually a back exit, but since we didn't check around the back, I'm wary of going out that way." I shrug at her.

"We could go out through the roof."

78

We both turn to look at our newest and most unlikely companion, who miraculously seems to have found a can of Spam and is subsequently scooping it out with his hands. It's surprising what food survives the end of the world.

ELEVEN

"The roof?" I ask incredulously. "Well aren't you a real Einstein? Yeah, let's go out through the roof. Get serious." Sarcasm drips from me and I turn to face Emily again.

"It's how I got in," he replies dryly.

"Oh…" Well now I feel stupid. I look back at him. He's still eating the Spam. Damn, it smells good, even for Spam.

"I think the word you're looking for is *sorry*." He stops his scooping and looks at me while licking his fingers. I can't decide whether he's trying to be seductive or not, but the image is far from it. Imagine a dog licking out the inside of a can of food, the meat sliding down the outside of the can and falling to the floor. Yeah, real sexy, right?

"Whatever." I roll my eyes. "So, how do we get up to the roof then?"

A bang interrupts our talking as another zombie hits the glass front. This is way too much like *déjà vu* for my liking.

"Come on, we need to go now before more turn up. There's never just one or two." Mikey drops the empty can, grabs my hand, and pulls me toward the back of the store. I, in turn, grab Emily and drag her with us. His hand is sticky and disgusting if I'm totally honest, and I can't help but flinch at his touch.

At the back of the shop is a small storeroom, and in the middle is a pile of chairs, which Mikey must have used to climb down on. He must have made this trip more than once by the looks of this, and I can't help but wonder where he's staying. The store seems pretty secure if you stay out of sight, and though there isn't much food left, there is some, I realize as I stare around the small room. Cans are loaded on some of the shelves, dried pastas and bags of cereal.

"There's still so much food left," I murmur.

Mikey glances around with a shrug. "I guess so. There just aren't many people left in the world to eat it."

My stomach rolls with nerves. We're so lucky to be alive right now; I guess I keep forgetting that.

He climbs up first, and pulls himself up through the hole in the ceiling. I wonder if he's going to leave us down here, but a few seconds later his head pops back through the hole and he reaches down as far as he can with his hand.

"Come on." He looks at us both and I push Emily forward first since she seems less capable than me.

She climbs up partway and grabs his hand, and Mikey half-pulls her while she climbs out. A few more seconds pass before his face pops back through the hole, his hand reaching for me. I slip my candy in my pocket and climb up, gripping his warm, sticky hand in mine. He pulls me up and I find purchase every now and then with my feet. My fingers reach the lip of the access and I start to pull myself out. The boxes beneath me move and I slip, barely holding on until Mikey reaches for me again. His fingers wrap around my arm, and he pulls me up and out as a loud bang sounds out below me. His muscles strain while he does—since I now have nothing to put my feet on, I'm a dead weight. His other hand reaches for me and grabs my other arm as I finally pull free of the hole and we crash backwards. I land awkwardly on his chest as his back slams into the gravelly roof, and we both groan as the air abruptly leaves our lungs.

My body stills at the close contact of him. The smell of his sweat is pungent in the air, yet strangely intoxicating rather than disgusting. Our eyes meet, and a smile flits across his face as his hands roam to my ass and my eyes widen.

Emily giggles from above us. "Come on, you two."

I look up to her, half-blinded by the sun streaming down, and am about to push off of him when he grabs me around my waist and lifts us both up to standing in one fluid movement, his big hands staying firmly on my hips.

I shrug him off, half embarrassed, and half...well, let's just stick with half embarrassed.

"Keep your hands to yourself." I shove him away, and he laughs as he stumbles back, holding his hands up defensively.

"I didn't do anything." He grins, holding his hands up in defense.

I roll my eyes. "Whatever. So what now, Einstein?" I look around us, but can't see a way down. Looking over the ledge, I can see the two zombies are still there, in all their gory glory, though they look a little confused now that they can't see their meal. Stupid zombies. I have an urge to kick a load of gravel down on them, but resist it for fear of yet more embarrassment because of my childish behavior.

"Nina."

Emily's hand touches my shoulder. She stands next to me and peers over the top too.

"We can easily outrun them to the car."

"Yep," I reply dryly. "What about those ones?" I point to the couple coming out of the woods and shambling over to investigate my beautiful Hummer. A sigh leaves my lips. I was hoping to avoid any more blood splatter, at least for today, but it seems like I'm going to have to do some killing. I am not leaving my Beast.

I turn back to Mikey, who's on the other side of the roof on his hands and knees, crouched down looking over the top.

We tiptoe up to him and crouch down too, and take a peek. There are more shamblers around the back coming from the woods, and it's looking more and more likely that we are going to have to wait them out.

I turn back around to look at Emily. "It seems Einstein here isn't as clever as he thinks." I don't even bother to glance at Mikey, but know already that he is giving me the finger.

It's times like this that I wish I still had my iPhone. You know, when you're bored senseless and just want something mind-numbing to do, like play some crappy game on your iPhone. There are only so many cloud zombies a girl can make before her imagination gets bored and switches itself off. Our backs are pressed into the hard, gravelly roof as we stare up into the sky.

"One-legged zombie," Emily laughs, pointing up into the sky.

"You've already done that one," I grumble.

"There can be more than one one-legged zombie."

"Nope, that's not the game." I gaze up at the cloud, trying to come up with something new. "Scarecrow zombie," I suggest.

"That doesn't even make sense," Mikey replies, and turns his head to look at me.

"It so does, look." I point. "The stick is what Emily thought was the leg." I can't help but chuckle and Emily joins in, followed by Mikey. I feel his arm hot and sweaty against mine, but I don't move. I kind of like him being so close to me, against my better judgment, I'm sure.

"I thought it was a…" he begins with a grin.

"Shut up!" I laugh loudly, and dig him in the ribs with my elbow.

"Ow!" He laughs and digs me back.

I laugh and then feel a flush of embarrassment for some reason. "God, I'm bored." I sit up, reaching around to brush the gravel from my back. At least we can't smell the deaders up here, but I can still damn well hear them, and it seems like there are more of them coming and not the other way around. Mikey sits up and brushes the remaining gravel from my back. I flinch at his touch and pull away, going to look over the ledge again.

"Fuck, I cannot stay up here all day. It's hot, and I need to pee."

"Chill out, princess." Mikey gives me a wonky smile. It widens when I lift an eyebrow at him, my mouth opening in shock at his arrogance.

Princess!

"You two go distract them over on the other side of the roof, and when they go over to have a look, you run back over here, and we can all climb down and get away," he continues.

"Do you think I'm stupid? What you mean is that *you'll* climb down. Then we will be stuck up here as zombie bait while you drive off in my Beast. I don't think so." I stand up and cross my arms and Mikey stands and mirrors my action.

"The Beast?" He smirks.

"Yes, *my* Beast." Now that I've said that out loud, I feel a bit ridiculous, actually. It was meant to be my little private pet name for the car. Damn it.

"Now would I leave two pretty ladies like you stranded?"

"Please," I snort. "I've dealt with men like you before, and there is not a chance in hell that we're being the bait."

"Well, I know for a fact that you would leave me in a heartbeat, so I'm not doing it." He narrows his deep brown eyes at me, his smirk vanishing now that he's realized he's not getting his own way.

"Less than a heartbeat, actually," I bite back. He starts to say something but stops himself short, his face going red as he tries to contain his temper.

"I'll do it then."

We both turn to look at Emily in surprise. It seems my little mouse has a backbone after all. Not that I'm going to let her use it. I haven't come this far to let something happen to her now.

"No." Mikey and I stare at each other as we say the same thing in unison, and I roll my eyes at him.

I rub my arms, feeling a chill despite the hot sun blaring down on me. "No, Emily, I'll do it." I look at Mikey. "But you have to promise me that you won't leave her…"

"I won't." He finally looks serious.

"You can't be serious!" Emily shouts.

"Shut up!" I snap at her. I turn my attention back to Mikey. "Not ever. You have to look after her if I can't get to you."

"I will."

"And you don't come back for me."

He nods his head once in understanding. "There's a group of us hiding out in the woods. It's a really safe place. Trust me on this one." He smiles, but it's a grim smile.

"Nina, I can do this." Emily pushes between us and looks into my face. "I can do this, please."

"No, Emily. You go with him. He has a safe place, and I'll be right behind you."

"Nina…" Emily holds onto my arms as if her life depended on them.

"No. You go with him and you don't look back. I'll find you. I promise."

Her eyes look glassy. I hope she's not about to cry. Jesus, one minute I'm playing *Guess the Zombie Cloud*, and the next I feel like I'm waving goodbye to my very existence. Life keeps getting serious far too quickly.

"Don't start with the waterworks, Emily. I told you, I'll be right behind you. Mikey here is going to look after you or else he'll have me to contend with." I walk away at my last comment for fear that I might start crying myself. I look down at my truck again. There are three deaders surrounding it now, though they don't seem to sense anyone is in it, as they aren't grunting like usual. I can't believe I'm going to have to leave my baby. And Emily. I huff out another sigh.

Mikey comes up next to me. "I'll stay, you two go."

I don't bother to look at him. "No, you need to get her away from here. I have no idea where this little happy place of yours is. I'll just get us lost in the woods. It makes more sense, you taking her. I'll be fine, just leave me a clue of some sort so I can track which way you go." My eyes are still watching my truck.

"Don't go after it, Nina. It's not worth it."

"The hell it's not."

"I'm serious."

"So am I," I retort.

He grabs my arms and turns me to face him. What is it with people grabbing me today? His face is still serious, his jaw working hard. "Like I said, there's a group of us hiding out in the woods. We're staying at an old outdoor activity center. It's pretty secure. We have a little food—not much though, which is why I was out on a scouting mission—but that's where we'll be. It's to the north of here. Just keep going straight if you don't catch up to me, and you'll eventually come to a lake. Just keep following it around, I'll be watching for you."

His look is sincere and yet somewhat grim, and for a moment I feel sorry for being such a bitch to him. He doesn't know me, or Emily. He doesn't have to do this—hell, he might just ditch Emily when he gets off the roof, but as I look at his face I don't believe he will. He seems a man of his word, maybe even a man of honor. There aren't many men like him left in the world.

"You don't have to do this, you know. I don't want you to think I'm a fucking coward and need rescuing. I'll distract them and you two can head into the woods. I'll be able to find you." His eyebrows draw together in concern.

I shake my head, looking anywhere but at him. "Stop saying that—I said no. I told you, she'll be safer with you. I don't even know where I'm heading." I finally let my eyes stray to him. His eyes are looking deep into mine, seeming darker than they had before. "I know you're not a coward; this just makes more sense. Let's say you owe me one, okay?"

He nods, still not looking happy about the decision. "I'll hold you to that."

I roll my eyes. "I'm sure you will."

He smirks again before continuing. "Just head north through those trees." He points to between two particularly large trees, whose branches seem to make an archway. "Follow my path. You'll see it and you can catch up to us."

I nod and take a deep breath. Through the archway, follow his path, meet back up. I can do this. I think. My hand dives into my pocket and I pull out my Jolly Ranchers and hold up the pack to him.

"Just one," I warn.

He smiles and reaches in, retrieving two with a smug grin, and walks off.

Dick.

TWELVE

"Come on, wooooooo! Over here. Hey you, Stinkerbell." I grab a handful of gravel and chuck it down onto the waiting deaders. They shamble forward, bumping into one another without flinching, growling and reaching up for me with dirty rotten arms. It's a good thing that I have their attention… I look over at Mikey as he starts to climb down. He offers me a small smile. Emily follows him, looking less than cheery. She still seems reluctant to leave; I give her an angry glare, gesturing for her to move it.

I pick up another handful of gravel and throw it at them. The ones by my Hummer have begun to stumble over to investigate the noise. That will mean fifteen when they all arrive at my happy little location. I can outrun fifteen of them, can't I?

I look back behind me. Both Emily and Mikey are out of sight now, and I shout louder to keep anything from wandering their way.

"Hey, Ugly Joe! Tra, la, laaa." The zombies—though they clearly don't understand a word I'm saying—are becoming increasingly aggressive. They're growling like crazed dogs and drooling black sludge from their mouths while banging their hands on the glass of the store. They won't be breaking in anytime soon, and even if they did, they can't get to me up here, but it's still making me nervous. They can easily wait me out any day.

One particularly fat zombie, with barely a scrap of material to cover her overly large and rotting bosom, is staring up at me like I'm a prize T-bone. Her jaw is hanging loose from her face, swaying with her every move and leaving nothing to the imagination. Fantastic.

I'm totally running out of insults. My sarcasm and insults bag is nearing empty, and I'm not having too much fun staring at Little Miss No-Jaw either, but I don't dare let their attention drop for any length of time in case they smell out Emily. Even the deaders are beginning to look bored with me and I decide that I've given them enough time to get away. Now it's my turn to make a run for it.

I grab a couple of handfuls of gravel and throw them at the zombies. The little stones bounce off their rancid faces, some even sinking into the putrid and pliable flesh, and I turn and run to the other side of the roof before they start to disperse. I've already decided that I'm going for my truck, there's no point in pretending that I'm not, but as I climb down the side fire escape I see more zombies emerging from the woods closest to my beautiful Hummer, obviously attracted by my shouting.

I land with a soft thud, and run as fast as my little legs will carry me, which actually isn't as quick as I would like them to be, if I'm totally honest. I was never good at running or any sort of cardio, come to think of it

I can't seem to slow my momentum, so I shoulder-slam into the side of my truck, swing the door open, and shut it quickly behind me with a whoop of glee and a painful yelp all at the same time.

It's only momentary, though. When I see the keys are missing from the ignition, I curse Emily. Little clean freak must have taken them. When I get my hands on her, she's going to be getting a mouthful of obscenities and a couple of evil glares to boot. Opening the door back up, I see that the zombies have spotted me and are slowly moving in my direction. I run around to the back of the Hummer, grab my backpack, and shrug it onto my shoulders. I glance back over at the oncoming zombies and duck back into the truck. I grab Emily's backpack too, after a moment of consideration; I'm more than sure I can carry it, for at least a little while. These packs contain everything we need to survive, and I'm not about to let them go without a fight. I glance longingly at the boxes of canned food and other such goods that we had packed. There's no way for me to take these with us, and I kick myself for not eating more and filling up on them, instead of just trying to stockpile it all.

Slamming the door shut, I realize that all of the zombies have noticed me now, and new ones are emerging from the woods closest to the truck with every passing second. Sure, they're slow, but it only takes one stupid mistake to get you killed. If there's anything I've learned about zombies, it's their mob mentality. The more there are, the less likely you are to survive.

The smell is getting worse the closer they get, and I gag, fear and bile running through me. I run back toward the shop—to where I had previously climbed down—and head into the woods, ducking under the little archway branch. I pull out my butcher's knife and keep on running, all the time looking at the ground for some sort of path that Mikey was meant to leave for me. There's movement behind me, the zombies moving en masse to follow me. I don't see anyone up ahead, no zombies, no Mikey. I can only pray that Emily and Mikey made it. He promised to keep her safe, and I believe that he'll keep up his end of the bargain. I don't know what it is about her, but she makes me want to care again, and I feel a ridiculous urge to protect her. Ben would be proud. He always wanted a daughter.

My thoughts are running away with themselves and I trip over a log on the ground, the air leaving my lungs in a *woosh*. My face slams into the dirt, and I get a mouthful of forest earth. I spit out leaves and soil, and scramble to my knees clumsily, chancing a look behind me. I can see them in the distance, but they're far back. Zombies are slow and stupid; that's the human race's only saving grace, I suppose. I climb up to stand and reach down for Emily's backpack, my hand touching something soft and squishy.

I look down as a growl emanates from below and eyes spring open to look at me. The ground moves, the leaves and soil parting to reveal a hideous monstrosity. A yelp leaves my throat and I jump back and trip, falling on my ass again.

Seriously, again…

The zombie on the ground begins to crawl toward me, commando style. It's only now that I see that its body is all but decomposed. There's barely anything left of it, yet it still moves. It still feeds, and it still kills. Black, stringy intestines are spilling out from the huge gaping hole where its middle used to be and dragging behind the thing. If it weren't for my imminent departure from this world if I don't move my ass, I would most likely hurl everywhere.

Scrambling backwards, I somehow stumble and half stand back up. "Shit, aah!"

It reaches for me and I kick the thing—because it is not human anymore; this is a living (quote) dead *thing*—a nightmare, to be more precise. I kick it in the face so hard that its head flies backwards, coming clean off its shoulders in one attempt. Yet its mouth is still working as it flies through the air with a spray of black, rotting slime. Growling and snapping away, regardless that it isn't attached to anything anymore. The fresh smell of decomposition hits me, and my mouth floods with water.

I grab for Emily's backpack once more and begin to jog north (the way Mikey had pointed for me to go, since I have no idea which way that is—why the fuck would I?), only stopping once to retch and empty the meager contents of my stomach. The only other problem now is that I've completely lost my bearings on which direction I should be heading.

The sun is beginning to lower and the air is cooling, now that the day is nearly over. Jesus, another day survived; just about, anyway. Who would have thought? I shouldn't joke about it, but it's my only defense, the only mechanism I have left to cope with. Without it, I would be a sniveling wreck of female clichés. I was once, but I learned to harden up quickly. I guess everyone did. For a girl with a penchant for shopping and no survival skills whatsoever, I haven't done too badly, I guess. Until now.

My feet are sore from all the walking. It seems like it's been hours since I left the garage. Since I left my Beast. I pout again at my loss. I shouldn't feel such loss with an item—it's just a thing—but I do. In this world you get attached to things very quickly, and then this is what happens: you lose them, or they die. I swore I wouldn't let myself get attached to anything or anyone again, yet here I am, traipsing through the woods trying to find Emily-Rose like I'm Bear fucking Grylls and can save us all with my super-unique-yet-gross survival skills.

I stop, leaning my back against a tree to catch my breath. I don't even know if I'm going in the right direction. It's like being stuck in a giant rat maze, but with trees and zombies, and no cheese prize at the end of it. My hands are sore from carrying the bags and the knife, and I lower the bag to the ground and take a look around me to make sure that I am alone.

The knife is still smeared in black-and-red sludge from an earlier attack. It's not like I'm completely alone in these woods. I swap the knife to my other hand—not wanting to put it down for even a minute and leave myself unprotected—and flex my hand out. The palm is red and sore from gripping it so tightly for so long. I'm hot and sweaty, and my old man shirt is sticking to me in all the wrong places. Sweat trickles down my brow and stings my eyes, and I rub it away with the back of my hand. Most importantly, I'm thirsty. I haven't had a drink in hours. My water bottle is empty and even my candies aren't giving me any saliva satisfaction anymore.

Mikey said to go north and that there would be a lake or something, but I haven't found a lake yet. I'm not sure how much further I can go. I'm pretty sure that I was going around in circles for at least the first hour before I finally found Mikey's clue to point me in the right direction. A can of Spam —a full one, funnily enough. It must have killed him to leave it behind. At least I'm guessing and hoping that it was his, anyway, since I picked it up and followed the direction I thought it was sending me. The crushing sense of despair and fear builds in my chest, and I let out an involuntary sob, my shoulders sagging in frustration. If I can just go a little further, they could be just over the next incline. Mikey surely couldn't have traveled that far without Emily getting worn out. Unless I really am going in the wrong direction. Or in circles. Fuck! I sob and stomp my foot. I'm being such a girl and I know it.

Hot tears trail down my face. I hear a growl in the distance and sob loudly again. You would think I could catch a break somewhere, but it seems that no, something, somewhere is determined to make me suffer.

I rub the tears away again, and swallow the rest of my sobs back down. I'm going to get myself killed standing here like a big crybaby. *'Don't be such a girl, Nina.'* I hear his voice and pick up Emily's bag. I've been through it twice now in the hopes that I would find it contained nothing useful and I could leave it behind. But it's not useless. There are really important things in here, things—that if I can get the hell out of these woods—are going to help us survive, and I'm not about to give it all up yet, no matter how exhausted and lightheaded I feel.

I push off from the tree and start walking again. Looking up through the tops of the trees, I pray that I find Emily and Mikey soon, before it gets dark. I don't know what I'm going to do if I don't.

THIRTEEN

My tongue sticks to the roof of my mouth, and I think I can hear water. I want to cry again, but I don't want to waste the energy. Mother Nature is a wild and beautiful thing, and out here that shows more than ever, but right now I hate the bitch and wish someone would take a giant fucking lawnmower to this overgrown forest. My legs feel like lead stumps, my arms and hands burn from the exertion of carrying the stupid bloody backpack. That's not a play on words, either. It's covered in blood from a fight with a zombie. Fucking thing nearly got me, too. The sound of water draws my attention to the left and I follow it until I break through a gap in the trees. A large lake is in front of me, with canoes tied up along the bank. The water is calm, and for a moment all I can do is stand and stare at the glassy liquid. Slowly I edge forward until my feet splash in the shallow water. I drop to my knees automatically and grab handfuls of the water, gulping it down and splashing my face.

I'm dizzy with thirst and exhaustion. I've been walking for hours, and I'm almost certain that I've gone in circles all day. The woods just didn't seem that big on the map. I try to process what Mikey had told me, and where to go. Something about going north and finding the lake, and then following it around until I come to his group.

I look across the lake. It's huge. A sob builds in my throat. It's getting dark now, and that's a dangerous time to be out anywhere, let alone when you're lost in the woods with zombies on your tail and exhausted as fuck.

My hair is slick with hot sweat and my head is pounding from dehydration. I untie my hair and grab handfuls of water, and tip it over my head. It takes a couple of minutes to cool me down, but finally my thirst is quenched, and my breathing and temperature seem to be getting back to normal. I stand back up with shaky legs and start walking along the bank, the straps of the bag still digging into the soft flesh on my palms and rubbing at the blisters that have formed until I know that they have popped. Mikey said he would be watching out for me; I can only hope to God that he is.

Up ahead I can see something in the trees. There's a little light glowing up high, and low murmuring sounds. The woods are dark, the lake is dark, everything is dark now. The blackness surrounds me from every angle, and I can't remember the last time that I felt fear like this. I pause and wait, wondering what the little light could be. Mikey said they had a camp, but this doesn't seem like a camp. Perhaps I'm imagining it. Perhaps I've passed out and am dreaming while zombies slowly shamble in on my position, ready to chow down on my brains.

I traipse deeper into the woods, forcing myself away from the lake edge and shadowing myself against the trees so as not to be seen. As I get closer, the voices get a little louder and my eyes go wide when I realize that I can hear Emily's voice coming from up in the trees.

I half stumble and fall into a clearing.

"Emily?" I look up, my neck straining with the effort, my voice croaky and dry. "Emily!"

"Nina?" There are voices above me, more than just Emily's, and the relief that she is safe and not alone or dead floods me, right before I see a deeper black than just the woods and pass out.

My eyes open and I'm instantly alert but dizzy and nauseous, sitting bolt upright and clutching a hand to my head in pain. Pain shoots through my head. Then pain shoots through my hands. I don't know which part of me to grab.

"Ow, shit! Emily?" I try to stand, but a woman's face comes close to mine. It's too dark to focus on her features properly, and I'm too exhausted to try very hard.

"Stay sitting down." Her hand is firm on my shoulder, yet I resist and try to stand up again. "I said—stay sitting the fuck down. You are in no state to be moving around," the voice snaps at me. I take heed of what it tells me this time, and sit back down.

"Emily?"

Emily comes over to me, but from where I'm not sure. It's so dark out here, I can hardly see a thing, but I can tell I'm outside—that much is clear by the rustle of the trees and the breeze on my face.

"Nina, you're awake." Her arms are around my neck, hugging me to her before I can say anything else. Surprisingly, I find myself hugging her back. Maybe trying to comfort her, or maybe myself, I'm not really sure. I do know that both of us are crying.

Hands finally pry us apart. "How do you feel?" the other voice prompts, though she doesn't sound in the least bit concerned—more like an overly busy doctor being paid to ask the right questions.

"My head hurts, and my hands and feet are sore, but I feel fine apart from that. Where are we?" I croak out, before someone passes me a plastic bottle filled with water. I swallow it down, gulping comically loud.

"We're safe. Where were you?" Emily sobs again, and I vaguely see the other person stand up and leave with a tut. "We were so worried, Nina. You were gone for hours. I thought—I thought that you…"

I place my hand on her arm, or I try to, but it's so dark it could have been a leg, and my hand hurts when I put pressure on it, so I pull it back and clasp it to my chest. "I'm fine, Emily. I just got lost. It takes more than that to kill me. Where's Mikey?" I didn't miss that she said 'we' were so worried. Obviously not so worried that he has bothered to come and see me though.

"He should be back soon." She pauses a fraction before continuing. "He went to find you." I hear something in her voice resembling guilt.

"What did you do, Emily?" I swallow the rest of the bottle of water down, and wipe my mouth with the back of my hand.

"I shouted at him."

"So? *I* shouted at him."

"I told him it was his fault that you had probably been killed. If he wouldn't have shown up, we would have been on the road, and we would have been fine, and…"

"Emily, you don't ever blame someone else," I snap at her, and she stops midsentence. Even in the darkness, I can make out the wetness in her eyes. "If anything ever happens to me…if I die, it's no one's fault but mine. You never blame someone else." I soften my voice. "If I make a mistake out here, it's my fault and mine alone. I'm not your responsibility and I'm no one else's either. Do you understand?" I grab her hand in mine.

"Yes."

I feel guilty for shouting at her. She's right in one sense: it *was* his fault that we got caught in the store; but it was my fault for trying to get my Hummer. I wasted precious time when I should have been trying to catch up to them.

"I'm sorry, Emily. I just don't want anyone being responsible for my life, do you understand that?"

There's no answer and so I prompt her with a nudge.

"I nodded," she replies quietly.

I can tell she's still in a foul mood with me, but I don't know what else to say to make her feel better. Thankfully there's a commotion off to my right that distracts us both. A male voice comes closer as it whispers my name, and I recognize it to be Mikey.

"Nina?" He crouches in front of me, his hands on my shoulders. "Are you okay? Are you bitten? Injured?"

"Hell, no. I'm fine other than my bruised ego," I sulk.

"When did you get back?" In the darkness his face is just a blur, but the concern in his voice is evident. His hands hold my face gently, and I have the urge to shrug him off, but for some reason I don't. His hands feel nice on my face, and the fact that he gives a shit means a lot.

"I have no idea; I kinda collapsed into a clearing when I heard Emily's voice, and then woke up here. Speaking of which, where is here? And where is my stuff?"

"We'll talk more in the morning. Your stuff is safe, but it's hard to explain where we are; you really need to see it to believe it." He stands up and starts to leave just as abruptly as he came. "I'm glad that you're okay," he says while walking away.

I feel kind of weird, like he's just declared something to me, but

I'm stumped as to what. I can't deny that there is an attraction there. I'm not stupid, I can feel it. But whether it is because he's the first male that hasn't tried to demand something off me or because of actual attraction, I don't know. I'm guessing he's feeling something too. I feel uncomfortable with that thought, but since I can't see a damn thing it doesn't seem like we have an awful lot of options right now. The grumpy doctor comes back from wherever she had gone and takes my hands, plastering them in a thick cream and wrapping them in bandages, which hurts so much that it makes me swear until even Emily shouts at me to shut up.

"Can I sleep next to you, Nina?" she asks, after the evil doctor has put away her medical torture bag and we're finally left alone.

"Are we safe? Wherever here is?" I tense up at the thought of sleeping out in the open like this.

"Yes, without doubt." She chuckles. "Just trust me on this one." Emily snuggles in next to me before I can further reply, one arm thrown over my stomach. I don't seem to have much choice, and I'm still beyond exhausted. I feel safe and warm, but something is nagging at me. Something Mikey had said about it being easier for me to see and understand where we are than for him to explain. I can only imagine what I'm going to find when I wake up.

I can hear trees swaying gently, and the deep smell of the forest still surrounds me, but I'll be damned if understand where I am. I try to focus my eyes for a couple of minutes, but the soft breathing and warmth coming from Emily begin to lull my senses and I give in and close my eyes.

Trust her? It seems I have no choice right now.

"Are you serious?" Their faces look shiftily from each other to me and back to each other again. "I am not living up in the trees like a freaking Ewok!"

"Nina, stop overreacting. It's not as bad as you think." Emily rolls her eyes at me and then chances another quick glance at Mikey, who's grinning from ear.

"You can get rid of that stupid smile from your face too," I snap with a growing familiarity. It's a funny world when you can meet someone one day and feel like you have known them your entire life the next.

"Nina…"

"I said no." Though now when I look around, it's actually a pretty clever idea. I'm not telling them that, though. A high ropes activity course is my savior, it seems. Who would have thought? Though I'm not afraid of heights, I never imagined living up in the trees would be a dream come true. It seems like more than just an activity course; there are little huts built into the trees at certain points, and platforms big enough to walk around on and to seat people. In between each platform or hut is a new pathway to get to each stage. Some look easy, with a thin piece of wood to walk across and built-up sides to make it safe. Others look damn-near impossible—to me anyway. I have no idea why anyone would build something so crazy, either.

Mikey is still looking at me, grinning like an idiot.

"What?" I sigh heavily, my eyebrows pinching in as I narrow my gaze on him. My hands are stinging like a bitch, my head has the dull ache of a hangover, but without all the fun of drinking, and now I'm stuck up in the trees with a bunch of people I don't know, don't want to know, and don't trust. I look at Mikey again, whose Little Boy Blue dimples are showing on both cheeks. I roll my eyes. And to make matters worse, I'm stuck with this idiot.

"What? You're still staring!" I huff.

"You've watched *Star Wars*. That's pretty cool, for a girl anyway," he chuckles at me while chewing on a fingernail, and I'm about to come back with a snarky comment that I was forced to watch it by my husband when he interjects.

"Come on, let me introduce you to the others."

I had woken up extremely early, when the sun had risen above the trees and glared down. Emily had rolled over onto her side and away from me, allowing me to sit up and finally look around and examine my surroundings. We were on some sort of wooden platform, with built-up sides to stop us from rolling off the edges. There was no roof, but the trees offered a nice canopy. I rubbed at my eyes, tired and confused, until I stood and realized how high up we actually were. I kicked Emily in the butt to wake her up and she woke with a jump.

Emily and I follow him across one of the narrow beams of wood nestled securely between the branches of a tree. I grip onto the rope dangling down in front of me for security, swapping each one for a new one as we walk and trying not to look down. There's a rope net on either side of the walkway to stop anyone from falling off the narrow beams, and like I said, heights have never been a problem for me, but it still takes a lot of balance and I'm glad when I reach the other side. I have no idea how the hell they got me up here last night. It's like an enigma wrapped in a conundrum wrapped in a big fucking rose-tinted question mark. *Why rose-tinted*, you might ask? Well it sure as hell couldn't have been pretty dragging my passed-out ass up here, now could it?

There are trees to the left of me, but I can see for miles to the right, right over to the other side of the lake that I was edging along the previous night. I shudder at the thought of how close I had come to being zombie chow. If I hadn't heard the voices from the camp, deaders could have found me when I collapsed.

We arrive at a flattened area between the large branches of some trees. They look like they have been woven together like rope, the branches mingling and forming a strong and sophisticated bond. It's covered with a real roof made of wood and what looks like straw. It's kind of like a tree house, but for big kids. Inside there are benches, and there's even a long table. Then there are people—several of them, to be precise—and their eyes are all trained on me and Emily as we enter. I reach for her hand without thinking, like a frightened little kid.

"So, Nina, this is…um. Well, these are…" Mikey scratches his dark shadow of a beard, acting shy and seeming uncomfortable.

"Come on, Mikey, get on with it." A woman with a choppy blonde bob looks up from the table. She looks like she only has one expression—a scowl—and ice-cool blue eyes to match. I recognize her voice from the previous night as the woman that had checked me over. She looks at him, her eyes washing down his body and back up, before those icicle eyes fall on me. I feel uncomfortable under her scrutiny. Shit, I feel uncomfortable under all their *stares*.

Mikey's grin falters before he continues. "Well, these are my friends—I guess, sort of." He scowls back at the woman, though she doesn't seem fazed in the slightest by him. If anything, she seems happier to have had the attention.

"I'm JD," a voice at the back of the little room speaks up. The man stands and comes over to shake my hand. He's tall and well-built, with brown, untidy hair and pale skin. Although he doesn't smile, and there's something about him that seems haunted, his demeanor is relatively friendly. Though I can't see him throwing me a welcome party any time soon, I don't think he'd kick me out, either. I chance a quick but uncomfortable smile as we shake hands.

"I'm Josie." An attractive blonde woman stands up and comes toward me, leaning in for a hug before I can back away from her. It's awkward and clumsy, mainly from my part, but she doesn't seem to notice. Or she doesn't care. She smiles at me warmly and sits back down next to JD, her hand straying to his knee in an overly affectionate way.

"Britta." A hand to the left of me shoots into my line of sight. I turn to look and see a woman with fair skin and pretty, warm blue eyes, her dark blonde hair cut to a manageable, shoulder-length style. I sense an accent of some sort there, too, but I have no idea what. She smiles almost shyly at me, and it lights up her face. Thankfully, she doesn't attempt to hug me like Josie did.

"Crunch." The woman with the choppy blonde hair and a scowl speaks up. She raises an eyebrow at me, and I wonder whether she is daring me to question her ridiculous name, or if she just doesn't like me. Either way her scowl makes up my mind, and I keep my trap shut on the subject of her stupid name.

"I'm Duncan." Another man comes over to me and holds out a hand. He seems pleasant enough, and I can tell he's a real outdoorsy type.

They all continue to stare at me, and I'm guessing this is supposed to be my turn to introduce myself, though the point seems invalid if I'm honest, since Mikey must have told them who I am.

I cross my arms across my chest. "I'm Nina. I guess you know Emily-Rose by now."

There's silence as I wait for a unison chorus of *'Hi Nina,'* like I'm at an AA meeting.

FOURTEEN

"So, you all really live up here in the trees?" I ask between mouthfuls of hot mushroom soup. I'm surprised I can actually get any words out, I'm so ravenous and this is so damn good. It seems Duncan is the group chef around here, and I can see why. If only I had a tasty, crusty roll to dip into it, and a nice glass of red wine too. A girl can dream. A couple of the others—Britta and the loved-up couple—are already done, and have left the rest of us to finish up.

"Yeah. I used to work here…well, I owned it—the activity center—before the, uh… outbreak or whatever. Somehow, I escaped and got myself up here, and slowly the group has grown. Mikey seems to be the one bringing in—"

"The strays," Crunch butts in.

I narrow my eyes at her, but she seems completely unperturbed by everything and everyone.

Duncan tuts. "I was going to say 'brings in the survivors he stumbles across,' since he does most of the scavenging and scouting for us. Well, at least from the local shops and houses," Duncan replies before he drains the last of his soup by picking up his bowl and tipping it into his mouth.

"You say 'local' like they're next door, Duncan." Mikey is leaning back against the wooden wall, once again biting at his nails. Him doing the scavenging would explain why he seems to know his way around, I guess.

"It's a good thing that they aren't *too* local, Mikey. The safety of this place isn't just the height we're at, but the reclusiveness of it, and the fact that the survival equipment is here for us to use. Anywhere else and I don't think we would have been so lucky." Duncan's eyes are warm and caring, but the seriousness of his tone is nothing to miss. "We can survive for—well, for as long as we need up here, as long as we're careful about it and don't attract too much attention to ourselves."

"And you say 'he brings in the survivors' like he does that a lot. When me and Emily met Mikey, he was about to take my Hummer and leave our asses stranded," I snipe, giving a hefty glare in Mikey's direction.

"Maybe he should have," Crunch mumbles under her breath.

"Shoulda, woulda, coulda," I snap back, giving her another glare, to which she rolls her eyes.

"I wouldn't have really left you. You're both far too pretty to be left out here in this big bad scary world without a man to look after you." Mikey smirks, his eyes lingering on me a moment longer than necessary.

"We didn't need your help, we were doing just fine without you. In fact, since meeting you we've actually been worse off." Which is true really, if you leave out the incident at Old Man Riely's house.

"Please," Mikey snorts. "You two girls made a rookie mistake when you didn't bother to arm yourself or search the store for people before food. You're just lucky it was me that found you and no one else. Anyone would think that you were new to all this." He waves his arms around his head and laughs.

I look at Emily, not sure what to say. Everything he said is right, and this world *is* kinda new to us.

"Where are you two ladies from, anyway?" Duncan asks.

I hesitate for a moment before deciding to play the honesty card. "Well, we've been behind the walls since the world went to shit. Well, after the first few initial weeks, anyway." I shrug, and feel a shiver of uncertainty as everyone stares at us open-mouthed. "What? You never met someone from behind the walls before?"

"Not anyone that lived for very long." Crunch looks up at me. "Most either get eaten or killed."

I feel my forehead crease in frustration. "You say that likes it's two different things."

"It is," Crunch replies.

I drag a hand across my face. "You're giving me a headache." I have no idea what they're all talking about. Getting eaten and getting killed are the same thing. Getting eaten and killed or getting bitten and dying, however, are very different.

"What was it like in your cushy little home?" Crunch continues to snipe at me like she has a fucking clue what it's really like behind those damn walls.

"Cushy? It was hardly cushy," Emily shouts.

I turn to look at her with a smile. *That's my girl.*

"How hard could it be, little girl?" Crunch glares up through her lashes. "Did you have the dead beating at your door every morning? No? Well perhaps it was having a nice warm bed, three meals a day, and some friendly neighbors that made it so damn hard for you?"

Crunch slams her spoon down into her bowl and leaves the room before me or Emily can reply.

They really have no idea what it was like if *that's* how they imagined it.

Silence falls across the little lunchroom. I chance a glance at Mikey and Duncan, who are both still staring at me as if wanting to know more about my life behind the walls. Well, tough luck. After the warm welcome we just received from Crunch, I'm not about to come clean with all my nightmares.

"Moving on from this now," I snap, and look down at my hands. This is not what I want to talk about.

"So, you're really from behind the walls?" Mikey asks, leaning forward in his chair like it's fucking story time, like he hasn't heard me tell them to move on from the discussion. "How long have you been out?"

"What was it like in there?" Duncan butts in.

"This isn't moving on," I tut.

"You have to tell us something!" Mikey glowers at me, his hand hitting the table with a thud, making Emily jump.

"I don't have to tell you shit, actually. But if you're really so insistent, it was hell. We were starved, beaten, robbed of everything from our belongings to our pride and dignity, and…" I pinch the bridge of my nose. I don't want to talk about that place anymore. It's over, it's done with. "Let's just say it wasn't all peaches and cream, okay?" I look up at him, my look and mood darkening by the second.

Duncan looks shocked and nods, while Mikey continues to glower but relents. He turns his attention back to Duncan. "Well, we have things pretty good out here, don't we, Duncan?"

"Well, we make do with what we have."

"Things would be a hell of a lot easier if we could get inside the base though." Mikey stares at Duncan as he stands, but Duncan doesn't rise to the bait. "All I'm saying is that we need more weapons—fact." Mikey pushes off from the wall and leaves. It seems like this is a discussion that they have had before.

Emily, Duncan, and I sit in silence for a while before Emily stands with a huff and leaves too.

"Okay, I give up," I say. "What's the base?" I look at my empty bowl and know that I could easily eat ten more. The hollow in my stomach is still there, but for now, it has at least stopped growling so loudly.

"It's the hub of the activity center."

"Aah, okay, what's the activity center? Not being funny here or anything, but I'm not an outdoor type of girl, if you know what I mean." I stand and stretch, feeling the soup sloshing in my belly, making me need to pee.

"It's where you are—here. Ravendale Outdoor Activity Center." Duncan stands too, and collects everyone's bowls and spoons, piling them all into a small basket. We walk out the door together—well, we lower our heads as we duck outside, since there is no actual door, per se. "This was my business. My dream, I guess. I'd only been open a couple of months when the outbreak happened. My third set of team-building exercises were underway and going really well." He stares out through the trees before continuing. "They're still there."

I look out to where he's looking and then back to him. Since all I can see is trees, I'm guessing he's lost in his own reverie for the moment.

"Earth to Duncan. *Who's* still there?" I touch his arm.

"My customers." He turns to look at me. "My staff—everyone. Some of them were out on a canoe trip when it all started. When they got back…it was like hell itself had invaded earth." He stops talking and walking and turns to me with a grimace. "Sorry." He shakes off his darkened mood. "You're more than welcome to stay here for as long as you want. The more people that are helping out, the safer we all are."

"I'm not sure I'll be staying." I like him and I think that he deserves a real answer—no bullshit. "I promised myself that I would get Emily somewhere safe, and well, this place seems as safe as any I've found yet."

"So, why wouldn't you stay?" His mouth puckers into confusion.

"Because I have nothing to offer you all. I can't fight, I have zero survival skills, and I mean, I'm more of a liability than anything." I shrug honestly.

He laughs. "What? And you think leaving us with a temperamental teenager is going to be more helpful to us? Besides, maybe at one time you had nothing to offer, maybe at one time you couldn't even fight, but there is strength in you, Nina. Emily told us how you have been protecting her. You're a strong woman, both mentally and physically, even if you don't want to believe it yourself yet."

I try to defend my words, but I know that he's right, and decide to continue with my whole *'honesty is the best policy'* line. "I don't want to get attached to anyone, and the best way to do that is to be on my own."

"And you think that you're not already attached to Emily-Rose?" He lifts an eyebrow at me and smiles.

A breeze washes through the trees, rustling the leaves. Being this high up, with the sun and the smell of nature, anyone would be forgiven in thinking that we were safe; but there's always more to fear in this world.

I turn and look at Duncan with a more critical eye. "Why weren't you allowed behind the wall?"

He holds his hands up in mock defense. "Why weren't you?"

"I was."

"Yet here you are, both of you." He raises an eyebrow at me again.

"We were kicked out." I pause. "Well, Emily was kicked out. I sorta decided that I wanted to leave. So I'll ask you again: why weren't you allowed behind the walls?" I step back from him.

"Calm yourself. I never tried to get behind the walls; I didn't want to leave here. Besides, I wouldn't have been able to make it that far without being…eaten or whatever." He swallows loudly, and I want to tease him about being a big scaredy-cat to ease the tension, but decide to keep my mouth shut—again. I'm getting good at this whole not putting my foot in it thing.

We start walking until we get to one of the platforms we need to cross using the high ropes. I can see the others on the next platform, and I know that my only way to get to them is by using the damn ropes. *Now* who's the big scaredy-cat? Duncan's hands move around my waist and I jump at his touch. He looks at me and smiles sheepishly.

"There are ropes and harnesses to stop you from falling. I'll show you later on how to tie them so you can do this yourself if you want. Some of the harnesses are still there, but others have broken, and some parts of the course weren't completed, so we didn't have anything to get us from point A to point B." He goes back to fiddling with the rope around my waist, reaching down between my legs and pulling it up on either side of them. "I'm hoping that in time we can finish this place, make it even better and more secure. We could build a perimeter around it and make it a real home. Find more people and…"

"Easy, don't get ahead of yourself." My cheeks feel hot with embarrassment, since he's still crouched down between my legs.

Duncan grins and stands back up, checking his knots. "Sorry, and yeah, I know. I just think we could really make this work."

"I got that." I smile, and I'm sure I feel my face crack at the action. I realize that we seem much higher up than I would have expected us to be. This is meant to be outdoor activities, yet we seem to be at a more extreme height.

"How high are we?" I ask nervously and hold onto the side of the platform.

He finishes tying another knot and makes short work of yet another one, which he attaches to the original one and stands back to assess his work. "Good question. This was the first camping, rope extreme, team-building exercise platform in the country." He smiles from ear to ear at me like a big dumb oaf, yet his cheeriness is lost on me since I have no idea what he's talking about.

"A what?" I ask, dumbfounded.

He grins. "Yeah, I was still working on the name."

He gestures for me to start across to the other walkway, but the path to get to the other side consists of small planks of wood held by rope on either side. The idea being, I'm guessing, to step across each moving step without falling. I try the first one out warily. It sways and I grip my rope tighter and try not to yelp. Sure, there's the protective rope net on either side again, but I still don't want to fall.

"Well, you've heard of the high ropes haven't you?"

I move forward slowly, with Duncan following closely behind. Each step makes me sway from side to side, making my stomach lurch. I always hated fairground rides, and this is like the biggest one ever.

"Yeah, I've heard of those. Is this one of those?" Two more and I'll be across. Duncan is right behind me, waiting patiently. Clearly he's more of an old hand at this than I am.

"Sort of. It's the high ropes, but higher. The highest yet, in fact, and it's built into the trees instead of its own premade base, and the best part is…"

I step onto the other side, my feet feeling finally secure without all the swaying. I can't help but smile that I made it across. Duncan joins me and begins to undo all the knots holding us to the long rope above us.

"The best part is that I had huts built, like tree houses, so that it would be a full-on camping, outdoors experience, but in the trees!" He guides me over to the others with a huge grin. They're all sitting looking out over the lake and talking quietly. They're sitting around a large circular metal fire pit in the floor, which—I'm presuming from the lack of trees above this platform—is where some of the cooking comes from, and perhaps even a fire pit for at night to cook marshmallows on. Yeah, I wish.

"Basically, if you think about it as a small scale bio-dome experience, but without the dome—and in the trees." He shrugs and continues. "You live up here, eat up here, use the bathroom up here, and compete in challenges up here. Or that was the idea before…well, you know." His smile fades away.

Bless him, I think with a roll of my eyes.

"Is he telling you how amazing his tree house is?" Britta looks over and smiles.

"Yep." I smile back and take a seat on a log next to Emily.

"I was just telling Nina about her new home. We'll need to teach both of them how to get around the place and give them jobs to do if they're going to stay." Duncan sits down with the group and gives me a knowing look. "The more people there are, the more work there is, but the safer we all are."

Emily looks at me. "We're staying?" She smiles happily.

"Why wouldn't they be staying?" Mikey looks puzzled.

"For now, at least," I reply grimly.

Emily takes my hand and squeezes it tightly, and I try to give her a reassuring smile.

"Has Duncan told you about his customers yet?" Mikey asks, his expression blank. He's talking to me, but seems to be directing his question at Duncan again.

I raise a questioning eyebrow. "Yeah, sorta." I watch the exchange between the two with narrowed eyes, realizing that I'm missing something. "I thought he had. Why?" I sigh.

"Not this again, Mikey. You're like a dog with a bone. We're not going over there; it's too dangerous," Duncan snaps and stands back up. Mikey matches his stance, and they stand foot to foot, looking ready to start swinging at each other any minute. Well, that was a quick turn of events.

"There are guns, crossbows, more harnesses—food, even! We need those things. If those guys come back and find us, we're all screwed, Duncan. I mean, they have guns…we don't. It's a simple equation, adding up to us being killed unless we go and get the weapons."

I stand up too, pulling my hand from Emily's. "Whoa, what guys?" I look from Duncan to Mikey, but neither of them replies, instead choosing to continue their macho standoff with each other. "Well?" I press with more urgency.

"The Forgotten," Mikey says without looking at me. His jaw grinds slowly, the shadow of his beard emphasizing the movement.

A chill runs up my spine. The mood has gone from lighthearted to scary shit in a nanosecond. I don't like it one bit.

"The who?" I bite my lip to hold in my anger and possibly my fear too. Why hadn't they warned me and Emily that there are people looking for them?

"The Forgotten," Crunch says darkly, sounding way creepier than

Mikey had. "They are society's outcasts, the ones they wouldn't let behind the walls, and trust me when I tell you that you do not want to mess with them."

"Well it's a creepy as shit name, but what's the big deal? Surely you're all the big bad Forgotten, too? And you're not so bad." I frown, trying to act every bit the Bond girl, but instead feeling panicky.

"No, we could have gotten behind the walls if we had gotten there in time. The Forgotten were turned away."

My mouth opens and closes before I can find the right words. "They turned people away? Why?"

Crunch looks away from me, her eyes hitting the floor. "Trust me when I say this—I don't say it because I give a shit about you or your kid, I say it because I intend to live. These guys mean serious business. They are not in any way to be messed with. They are the Forgotten. Not the rebels, or the fucking others, or some other shit name that makes them sound like some sort of fucking comedy sketch, and they are not anything to laugh at. They weren't allowed behind the walls because they were deemed as the big, bad, and fucking ugly of society. Not even their own mothers wanted them."

That darn chill runs down my spine again, and I shiver involuntarily.

FIFTEEN

As if they were one entity, each member in our little Kumbaya circle lowers his or her head, which does nothing to improve the tone of my voice in my next rant.

"The Forgotten? Society's outcasts? That's a little too much creepy for my liking, so we'll be leaving right about now. Thanks for the hospitalities and all that." I stand to leave, but Emily tugs on my leg. I look at her and she's silently shaking her head at me. "You can't still want to stay, Emily." I purse my lips tighter.

She nods at me, and then looks toward the rest of the group. "They're staying."

"They're stupid—clearly."

"Hey!" Josie looks at me, her pretty face showing anger instead of the usual cheery smile.

"Hey what? There are people—sorry, *The Forgotten*—traipsing around the woods looking to do god knows what to you, and you're still here? Tell me why, exactly."

"We have nowhere else to go." Britta's eyes seem as large as saucepans as she says this, and I feel like a piece of shit.

Josie looks at JD, seemingly unsure. Up until now, he hasn't really said very much, seeming to be the quiet one of the group.

JD picks up his bottle of water and takes a long drink before speaking. "Leave if you want; that's your choice. If you think you can fare any better out there alone in the world, then there's not much we can do to convince you to stay, and I wouldn't waste my breath trying to sway your decision. If you want to live, however, then you'll see sense and sit back down. These types of people are everywhere; there is no escaping them. So this place, up here, is as good as any other—probably better, in fact. That's the *why* to your question." He says all this without even bothering to look at me.

I sit back down with a huff and Emily pats my knee condescendingly. I scowl at her and she stops. The tension has risen within the group, and I'm not the only one feeling it by the looks of the sullen faces around the camp.

"Can everyone just calm down?" Duncan pleads.

"We'll calm down, Duncan, when you let us go over to the hub and get some more stuff. We've all fought zombies at some point, we can work as a team. We'll be in and out before you know it." Mikey sits back down, and continues to try to reason with Duncan in a friendlier way. "We need you. You know the way around that place; we'll be safer with you there."

Duncan bites his lip. "The last time I went there I saw my co-workers and customers get ripped apart. It is not somewhere I want to go back to anytime soon." Duncan starts to shout and then stops himself, his nostrils flaring as he tries to contain his anger. Even up here, I'm guessing we have to keep the noise down. Sound travels and so do zombies.

"Things haven't changed since you decided to hide yourself away up here you know. That shit's still happening everywhere, you can't just pretend it isn't." Mikey lowers his voice and Duncan sits back down, the anger suddenly lost.

"Mikey's right, Duncan, as much as I hate to admit it. I think we should go—with or without you. Though it would be helpful if you would come, nobody is forcing you." JD speaks up again, and I'm surprised when everyone stops to listen to him without him even having to raise his voice. "It's about time we all stopped pussy-footing around you. You saved our lives by showing us this place and letting us stay here, and for that we're all grateful, but that only gets you so many free cards, and they've all run out now. We're going over there, and I'm asking you to come with us. To help us."

Duncan seems to be off in his own little world with his thoughts, and just as I'm about to ask if we have any weapons at all, he jumps back in.

"It still haunts me."

"It haunts us all, my friend," Mikey replies.

Duncan drags a hand across his face. "They came back from the canoe trip covered in blood. I'll never forget that image for as long as I live. Out of all the other deaths that I have witnessed, that's what has stayed with me all this time, you know?" He looks up at us and we nod in agreement.

Yeah, we all know exactly what he means. The first time I saw someone die—hell, I should say the first time I witnessed those things killing someone—will be burned into my memory forever. It wasn't real, it couldn't be real. But it was.

"It was so unexpected. There was just no warning, no clue, nothing. I mean, I'm a resourceful guy." He gestures around him as if to prove his point. "I can prepare, plan, evaluate, but this...this was something else. They climbed, fell, Jesus…were dragged from the damn canoe, and the blood was just everywhere. I heard the screaming and came running out of the hub. They had been across the other side of the lake when they were attacked." Duncan looks out into the trees and continues. "When I came out and saw all the blood, I thought that they had been attacked by bears or wolves or something. One woman—Halima, I think her name was—she was unconscious, and we carried her inside to the medic's room. The others were telling me about some man in the woods who had attacked them, but before I could concentrate on what they were saying, I needed to stop the bleeding on Halima. I didn't even know where to start." Duncan's eyes met mine and I swallowed the massive lump in my throat.

I don't want to listen to this. I've heard more than my fair share of survivor horror stories this past year. I don't need any more to add to the collection. But there's always something a little bit fascinating about them. As if maybe by hearing more versions of the same story, it will somehow change the outcome. It doesn't, though. It always ends the same: someone dies. Everyone dies.

Duncan looks heartbroken as he continues. "I started trying to clean her up the best I could while one of my Saturday helpers, Sanil, called for an ambulance, but there was no answer. All the lines were dead, and I began to panic that I couldn't stop the bleeding before we could get an ambulance to her. Her breathing got worse and worse," he looks up at us, his eyes damp, "until it just stopped."

Britta stands up and goes to sit with Duncan, draping her arm across his shoulders.

"It's okay, we all know what you have been through, and we have all been there," she says, her accent making each word sound even more pronounced. He continues as if she hasn't even spoken.

"Sanil started to panic, but me, I didn't move. I just stood there watching her, watching the blood…so much blood, just draining out of her and dripping onto the floor. Of course she couldn't have survived that much blood loss. I knew this, but then just as I was accepting that fact, she moved." He looks up to us, his eyes searching our faces for recognition of a similar horror. Of course we all share it and look away from his stare. Shame floods his face as he continues.

"She moved her hand, slowly at first. I thought it was a goddamn miracle happening. Her eyes opened, but they weren't the pretty brown I was used to seeing; they were colorless, cloudy almost. I was surprised she could see anything, but she clearly could because she reached up and grabbed me. I didn't know what she was doing, but I knew something wasn't right. Sanil tried to help me restrain her, but he was just a kid, and she was so strong—it didn't make sense how strong she was! And then she bit him…his face. She leaned up as he tried to hold her down and tore into it like it was nothing, and he screamed and screamed for me to help him, but man, what could I do? Blood was pumping everywhere, so much goddamned blood." A slow tear works its way down Duncan's cheek, and even though I have my own horror story, I can't help but feel some of his pain. What *could* he do? We have all seen it happen. It happens so quickly you don't have time to react, to think about what to do next.

"I ran! I ran out of the room just as everyone was running into it to try and help." Duncan's face is pale—paler than Emily's, and that's saying something. "Then the screaming really started."

I don't know whether to scream at him myself for not helping, for not trying to do more to save everyone. Why didn't he warn them? Shut the door? Anything? But looking at him now, I know that there's no point in voicing my opinion. He's going to be haunted by those screams for the rest of his life, and I think that's punishment enough.

Stillness surrounds us all. Even the birds have stopped their incessant tweeting for the moment, as if caught up in the horror of his story. I need to cough, but don't want to ruin the moment. I have heard these stories, of varying degrees of horror, and I feel a little numb to them all now. I hear the words, but their meaning is lost on me. Another person torn apart, another person eaten, another person dead. It's horrendous, and it's cruel, but it happened.

Duncan sobs loudly. "That's why I can't go back over there. I can't bear to see their faces—faces of the people that I condemned to death because I was too scared to do anything else."

"Stop being such a fucking pussy, Duncan. Shit happens, and it's happened to us all." JD looks up at Duncan, his nostrils flaring, his eyes wild with quiet fury. "You want to know a sob story? I'll give you a sob story." He grinds his teeth loud enough for me to hear him on the other side of the fire pit. "Try watching your girlfriend and baby boy being eaten alive. See if that's an image that will keep you awake night after night, buddy!"

The silence deepens around us at JD's revelation. Josie is clearly alive and kicking, and I realize that they must have only been a couple since the outbreak. She looks uncomfortable, both her hands falling to her lap so as not to provoke JD any more. Her lower lip trembles, but whether it's because of the colorful image that JD has just given us or because he's talking about his life pre-her, I'm not sure.

I'm stumped and feel uncomfortable listening to everyone's little heart-to-hearts. I have no intention of doing the same, and I can only hope that we are about done for the day. Back behind the wall, I would listen to people's stories day in, day out. It was one of the many reasons I wanted to leave: the horror of listening to everyone's stories is just too much. That sounds heartless, but it's the truth. There are only so many times you can listen to people telling you about their loved ones being killed before you become cold to it.

JD stands abruptly and resolutely storms off, his footsteps loud against the wooden flooring. Clearly he's had enough of our little get-together for the day. Josie stays seated, her head low on her chest. Her shoulders are subtly shaking as she stifles down her tears. Emily nudges me in my side and I look at her. She gestures with her head for me to go over to Josie and I shake my head and mouth 'no' at her. She nudges me again, harder this time, and I nearly fall off my log seat. Why she thinks I would give a shit I have no idea, and I push her back, forcing her to slide off the back of her log. I snort a laugh at her and look up, realizing that everyone has been watching our little pushing session, even Josie. My cheeks flame with embarrassment.

I don't want them to think I'm a heartless bitch, but I'm not about to start trying to disprove their thoughts on me. They seem as doomed as the rest of the world, and if Emily wants to go comfort poor little Josie, then she's a big girl now and she can go do it herself.

Emily sits back down on the log without looking at me, but I can hear her huffing.

"He saved me, you know," Josie speaks between sobs. "I was hiding in the storm drains. I'd been living down there since the outbreak, or whatever you want to call it. I had been visiting my boyfriend in jail when everyone started acting nuts. I got out of there as quick as I could and I hid. Before I knew it, I had been there over two months. Every time I thought about leaving and trying to make my way back home, there seemed to be more and more of them. There were no trucks or cars that I could get to. I had no weapons. I was screwed, so I hid." She wipes her sleeve along her nose in the most ladylike fashion she can muster, and continues. "They got in the prison. How do zombies even get into a prison? I mean, that place, of all places, is supposed to be secure."

I shudder at the word *zombie*. I still have a hard time calling them that, though that *is* what they are.

"They followed me back one day when I was out scavenging. I was backed into a corner, and I was trying to make peace with the fact that I was about to die, and then he showed up—JD." Josie gives a small smile before continuing. "If it wasn't for him, I would be dead. Or one of the dead."

"How did he find you?" I ask before I can stop myself.

What do I care? Yet I obviously do.

"I have no idea, I'm just glad that he did." She shrugs. "One of the guards tried to lock everyone inside. I guess he thought the inmates were trying to escape or something, I don't know, but I only just got out. When JD found me, he had escaped from the prison. He had watched his girlfriend and baby boy," she swallows, and I know what's coming, "…they had both been turned, and he had seen it all. Damn near drove him insane watching them day after day. He was a wreck of a man for months, kept talking about killing every last one of them. In the end I made him realize that the best revenge he could have would be to survive."

Every time I think that I have heard the worst story possible, I hear another one. It never gets easier. I can understand how people go crazy; I mean, how much pain can one mind take? I don't think I can take another story. I don't have the stomach or the heart for it. I'm not a tough *G.I. Joe* girl, I'm just a girl who likes shoes and uses sarcasm to hide her feelings. I decide that I'm about done for the moment and make to leave when Crunch pipes up.

"You wanna hear something funny?"

"Yes!" Everyone says at the same time. Crunch smiles and we all give a small laugh. The horrendous stories we just heard are suddenly put to the back of our minds. For now, at least.

"Well, there's blood and guts in my story, the same as everyone else's, but when the outbreak happened, me and my best friend had just been arrested for stealing fancy panties."

Panties? Now this is going to be an interesting story.

SIXTEEN

C runch folds her long legs underneath herself as she begins to talk. "Me and my good buddy Damien were getting high, you know how it is, right?" She looks at us, her smile faltering for a moment before continuing. "Well...maybe not. Anyway, so we'd had way too much to drink and smoke that day and decided to go and get ourselves a little extra cash, since we were both totally broke and wanted to go on partying. We went into a couple of stores but we got thrown straight out. Obviously we weren't the usual clientele for some of the more upper class shops."

I laugh loudly and she looks at me sharply.

She wasn't trying to be funny there, I guess. Whoops.

"Sorry," I mumble and look away, feeling uncomfortable under her glare.

"Anywho...we were passing a trashy version of Victoria's Secret—you know the ones with the real dirty underwear and sex toys?" She smirks and I look at Emily. She may be young, but by the look on her crimson face, apparently she knows what kind of store Crunch is talking about.

"So me and Damien decided to try it out. We're looking at all these sex toys, and underwear, and joking around. Obviously there wasn't much that we could get from there to sell quickly, so we decide to leave, but man, as we get to the door, we get stopped by security. I'm all like, *'What? We haven't done anything, this is harassment.'* And this big burly security guard just looks at us all serious and stern, and he's like, *'can you come this way please, sir? Miss?'"* She mimics the security guard's voice, and everyone laughs. "Which is funny in itself really, since Damien has never been called 'sir' in his life." Crunch fiddles with the studs on her shirt as she continues. "So we end up in one of the back offices and he asks us to empty out our pockets. I had some fancy underwear stuffed down my shirt, but nothing major— lacy things with frills and shit, but then Damien's searched, and he starts pulling out all sorts of crap from his pockets and down the back of his pants. Lube, play gels, fucking dildos as big as my arm, and I'm like, *'dude! What the fuck?'"*

Laughter breaks out from everyone's lips. I have no idea what Damien looks like, but any guy getting caught with a dildo down his pants deserves a round of applause in my opinion.

"I didn't even see him stealing that stuff, I swear. Even the security guard looked shocked and mildly disgusted by how much stuff he'd shoved down his pants. He must have thought we were planning some mass orgy or something." She wipes at the tears in her eyes and continues, looking younger than I'm guessing she is—the carefree, relaxed attitude of a young woman, not a bitter, angry thirty-year-old. "Anyway, I'm rolling around in fits of laughter, no matter how many dirty looks this security guard gives us, you know? I mean, it's freaking hilarious. I couldn't stop myself even if I wanted to. I think this guy is about to get all serious on us and call the real cops, when we hear shouting from inside the store. Shouting and banging and all sorts of weird and wonderful noises." Crunch raises a sardonic eyebrow at me and continues. "The security guard tells us to stay where we were and he'd be right back, like I was planning on leaving that room at that point anyway, right? He locked the door on his way out, and before I could tell him to call me a lawyer and kiss my ass, he was gone...and the screaming began."

Crunch stops laughing and looks at us with a more serious look in her eye. "The screaming seemed to go on for hours, but it could have been minutes. I lost track after a while. I covered my ears with my hands and hid under the desk like a little fucking kid."

I look away from her sorrowful expression, her mood decidedly darker. I look up to the trees, where a bird flits from one branch to the next. I watch it as it looks down at us with its little brown beady eyes. They have it so easy, birds. It's like none of this crap happened to them. They're still free to fly and roam the world without any harm coming to them. Sure, they don't get the friendly neighbors throwing out bread for their morning breakfast anymore, but I'd give up anything on this shit-hole planet to get things to go back to how they were. For just one more day of normalcy. The bird takes off into the sky without a second glance back at me, and I'm brought back down to earth by Crunch's storytelling.

She looks at her feet sadly, her nose stud glinting at me. "I must have drifted off at some point. I know what you're thinking. You're thinking I'm some heartless bitch who doesn't give a shit. Well, I'm not. I had a mother who was a drunk and a father who brought more trouble to our front door than old ladies to a bake sale, so my safe place was always to sleep. I would sleep to drown out the noise from them both arguing and fighting with each other." She shakes her head and I see a slight blush rise in her cheeks, clearly embarrassed by her small revelation. "So, anyway, that's what I did. I woke up to Damien prodding me in the ribs. He looked really scared. I mean," Crunch whistles through her teeth and wrings out her hands, which seem to be full of nervous energy as she recalls the horror of the moment, "I'd never seen Damien scared before—ever. But he looked petrified. He had obviously listened to every damn sound coming from the other side of the door. There were noises coming from behind it now too—moaning and scraping—and I knew right then, there was not a chance in hell I was even attempting to leave through that door."

I haven't realized that I'm leaning forward on my log seat until my neck and back start to hurt. I lean back and look at everyone else, and realize that Crunch's storytelling seems to be having the same effect on everyone in the group. We all sit transfixed by her words. Maybe it's the vulnerability that we can hear in her voice. She's normally such a badass, so fierce in her demeanor, that to see a softer side of her is just—well, it's just bizarre. Or maybe we just want there to be a happy ending for one of us. Any of us.

"What did you do?" Emily asks quietly from next to me, making me jump a little at the sound of her voice. I look at her and scowl, but she pays me no attention.

"We stacked a couple of chairs on top of the table and went out through the tiles in the ceiling. I didn't even know if it could actually be done, but I've seen it in enough movies, you know?"

We all nod in agreement. *I miss watching movies.* The small memory of being curled up on the sofa with Ben watching a movie brings a deeper sadness to my heart than any story I can be told.

"So anyway, we're following the ceiling tunnels through the mall ceiling, tracing the electricity and water pipes or whatever the fuck they were, stopping every now and then when we get to a store to look in and see if we could climb down." She shakes her head. "The things we saw. Damn, it was like God himself set free all of hell. Damien was like a big crybaby. Every single time we stopped to look into a store, he would sob like my mother high on ketamine. I don't know how long we were in there, but I knew that I didn't want to ever leave. I mean, up there it was like we were separate from it all, like it was a dream or something. But there's always an exit, a dead end, or a loose panel that makes you fall through the roof and into the loving arms of one of the undead, right?" She picks up her half-empty bottle of water and takes a swig before standing up to leave.

I stand up abruptly. "Wait, what the fuck happened?"

Why now, why her, and why I give a shit all of a sudden is beyond me, but I do. I want to know what happened. I need to know. Damien isn't here so it's pretty obvious really, but for just a moment I feel the smallest spark of hope. A glimmer of us beating the undead at their own game. Maybe he escaped. Maybe there's hope for the rest of us. Maybe…

"Damien got eaten—obviously. Ripped limb from limb, fucker was still crying for his momma even as they chomped through his throat." Crunch shrugs her shoulders nonchalantly, but I see the look in her eye and know what she hides way down deep, too deep for just anyone to get to. "I've never seen someone in that much pain, and if I could have ended it for him, I would have." She starts to walk away and begins to tie the ropes around her waist to move across to another platform before looking back at all of us sitting in deathly silence. "But damn, that zombie got a beating before it got its meal. Nearly beaten to re-death by a dildo." She smiles at us, but it's grim and a failed attempt at hiding her sadness. "What a way to go, eh?"

None of us say anything as Crunch moves across to another platform, swinging from the ropes that hang high above the ground, like a monkey in the trees, a determined look set as a stony mask on her face. We all sit in silence as her soft sobs for her friend are heard ringing through the trees. We've all been there, we've all had that loss, that pain, but seeing a woman so strong and so broken has affected all of us. Maybe she isn't that strong after all; maybe it's all a front. We all wear a different mask these days.

Silence encompasses our little group. Each one of us is lost in thought, but whether it is because of the stories that have just been shared or because of our own horror stories, I'm not sure. Me? I just need to get some air. Even though we are as in the open as practically possible, I feel like the oxygen has been stripped from my lungs.

"You ok?" Emily's voice seems distant.

I look at her with far away eyes and nod.

Jesus, I need some space.

I can't seem to think with so many people all around me. My gut twists and churns. Perhaps it's the decent food I've had to eat for the past couple of days. My diet behind the walls consisted of, how shall I say this…whatever we were given, which was never enough, and too far between. It's not the food though. It's me. Something in me is changing.

Emily's hand squeezes my leg, and I feel suddenly like a child needing reassurance from its mother. My chin trembles and I take a deep breath.

"I need…to walk." My voice seems hollow and unfamiliar as I croak out the words. "What's the easiest path around? I mean, without all the knots and stuff?" I ask Emily…the group—hell, anyone who's listening.

"There's no way around without the knots. There's a harness, but we use it over on a different platform. I can show you a quick knot and give you some space to practice if you want." Duncan stands and I follow him.

"I'll help." Mikey follows closely behind.

I smile weakly at Emily as I walk away. She seems at ease here, comfortable even. Britta strikes up a conversation with her, but I'm not sure what about. I'm just grateful that she's giving me some space. Now if I could learn how to tie my own stupid knots, I could get some *real* space.

The funny thing about the end of the world is how quickly you adapt. One day you're incapable of changing a fuse in a plug, and the next you're fighting off deaders, building campfires, and saving teenage girls from impending doom. I have begun to like these people. Much more than the people I used to live with. Maybe it's because they have some fight left in them. Shit, maybe the fight never left them. But they are all strong and capable people in their own way, determined to survive no matter what.

Emily and I are told the rules that they live by, and I hold my breath while they explain them, waiting for the kicker, the one rule that I could argue about. But I can't. They're all perfectly reasonable rules that are intended to make each other's lives easier and safer. We all have jobs; some are awful, some are okay, and some—well, they're just plain dangerous, but someone has to do them. The main one is that no one goes anywhere on their own. Apart from Mikey. He is the camp's scavenger, and no one wants to have his job. To be fair, he always votes to go alone anyway. So apart from bathing, fetching cooking and drinking water, and helping Duncan to pick berries and wild mushrooms and other weird shit that he grows, Emily and I don't leave the trees.

Our existence begins to become comfortable, happy almost—as happy as you can be at the end of the world, anyway. Life would be an awful lot easier I didn't receive dirty looks from Crunch on a daily basis, but life can't always be peaches and cream, can it?

Mmmmm, peaches and cream.

SEVENTEEN

"**Y**ou ready to do this, Nina?" Duncan eyes me warily.

I take a deep breath. "Yep, let's do this thing."

Emily touches my arm. "Be careful, okay?" She smiles.

"Always." I smile back and carefully climb down the steps of the main platform with Duncan.

Scavenging is always a tricky business. Even out here, so far from any major civilization, there are deaders. Somehow they always seem to find our little vegetable patch too, like a lost memory of what they used to eat. Either that or they know that at some point humans will come to pick the damn vegetables, and so they wait for us. I shudder at the thought that maybe they have any sense of who or what they are now. Any brain control at all would be horrifying. Would they remember who they used to be? Are they trapped inside the monster that they now are? God I hope not.

Duncan and Britta have been showing me some of their recipes, and tonight I'm cooking a full meal by myself. It's their funeral: I can't cook for shit. My best meal was *number thirty-nine* and *number twenty-two* on the Chinese takeout menu. Duncan is the camp cook, but Britta—damn, that woman knows how to do some great stuff with herbs. She helps make homemade medicines for headaches and tummy troubles, and even knows a great seasoning for rabbit stew. I'm hoping that at some point she's going to show me some of what she knows.

The vegetable patch is closer to the hub than I would have liked, and as we round the corner, the top of the hub comes into view. I'm still yet to see the actual building, since Duncan refuses to go anywhere near there, but every time we come to collect vegetables he goes all glassy-eyed.

Two deaders are, as we have come to expect, standing right in the middle of our patch. Seriously, it's only a little patch, yet every time they end up standing smack dab in the middle of it, trampling some sort of food that we're growing. I drop my bag to the ground and whistle. They both turn at the same time, give an angry snarl, and come for me.

One of them has a face that's a mixture of my next-door neighbor and my old Aunt Sally. Since my Aunt Sally was a six-foot-two transvestite who used to wear the most hideous orange curly wig, and my neighbor had a bust size that most *Playboy* models would be proud of, the rotting semi-male and busty transformation is not something to smile about.

"Jesus fuck," I whisper and shake my head.

The other deader follows right after, one of its blue dungaree straps dangling down around its ankle. It stands on the rhubarb that I've been trying to grow for the last couple of weeks, trampling the

135

leaves with its dirty boots, and I curse again.

As soon as they step out of the vegetable patch, Duncan comes out from behind a tree and lops off Aunt Sally's head. Dungaree Guy turns to look at Duncan and then looks back at me. He seems to be in a state of confusion as to which meal to go for. Thankfully for me, he chooses Duncan. I can't blame him, really; I'm like a skinny taco at about a hundred and five pounds, whereas Duncan is easily twice my build. Does that make him the gourmet meal?

"Nina?" Duncan whispers my name, and I nod and grip my bat tighter.

I run up behind it and slam the bat as hard as I can into the back of its skull, feeling the softening bone crumble upon impact, and black ooze seeps out of the cracks I just made in its head.

Dungaree Guy pauses for a moment, doing a half-turn to look at what just hit him, before he collapses to the floor and starts twitching. Brown and black gloop continue to escape through the hole in the back of his head, bubbling out and releasing a toxic-as-hell smell.

"Man, he reeks." Duncan wafts a hand in front of his nose.

"They're getting worse," I agree. "Do you think, maybe, we could use it to our advantage?" I grab Dungaree Guy's legs and Duncan reaches for the arms, as we drag him to a hole further into the forest.

"Like how?"

"Well, I was thinking that maybe if they can't smell us—like, if they could only smell themselves, then maybe we wouldn't get as many of them."

We both drop the deader at the same time at the edge of the hole and I kick him in. He lands with a soft thud on top of the others we have killed up here over the past couple of weeks.

"R.I.P.," I say, making the sign of the cross as I continue. "So, I'm thinking maybe we could string up a couple of arms and legs around the patch. They might not sense—smell, or whatever—that we come here, and move along. Does that make sense?"

Duncan looks down at the pile of rotting deaders in the pit. No flies surround them, no maggots—nothing. Even insects know not to go near the flesh of the dead. We turn and head back to the vegetable patch.

"Sounds like it's worth trying. I mean, I'm not sure it'll work, but I'll give it a try." Duncan shrugs and smiles at me. I feel strangely proud that I may have come up with a semi-useful plan.

I begin to hack away at Aunt Sally's arms and legs while Duncan goes into the forest to find something to use as rope, muttering something about finding a dog with a bone. Once I've removed all her limbs, I drag her by her shoulders to the pit and kick her in, saying a quick 'R.I.P.' again. I hunt down her head and give it the same treatment.

When I get back to the vegetable patch, Duncan is coming back out of the forest from the side opposite to me. He's looking pretty pleased with himself, too, and carrying a handful of sticks.

"You find your dog and bone?" I laugh.

He looks puzzled. "What? Never mind." He shakes his head. "Okay, I'm gonna need you to help me. This is Dogbane, I need to you to…" He looks at me and smiles. "Dogbane, not dog and bone." He chuckles and sits down with the twigs.

I flush, embarrassed, and sit down with him.

"So, I need you to break these in half and pull out the middle bits." He hands me a couple of sticks and we set to work on them, each doing our own. I look up through my lashes as he squashes the twigs on the ground until they split down the middle and begins to pull out the inside.

I copy him, finding it easier than I thought I would, and then repeat the process with a couple more branches until we have a small pile of ribbony-type bark.

"Now what?"

"We need to tenderize them all and then do what's called a reverse wrap. I'll show you. Do you have any idea where we are going to hang these things? They are going to ruin the smell of my vegetable patch you know." He raises an eyebrow at me and starts rolling the ribbony bark between his fingers.

I pick up a piece and start doing the same. "I know, sorry about that," I chuckle. "If it works, though, at least everything won't keep getting trampled on."

"I guess so," he grumbles.

Forty-five minutes later, and with several smelly rotten limbs hanging around our little vegetable patch, we finally get to picking some of the crops ready for supper—after washing our hands in a stream. Apparently Dogbane is poisonous; good thing I didn't need to lick my fingers or anything. My rhubarb managed to survive, though it's not quite ready to be picked yet; but we manage to pull some potatoes and carrots and onions.

We're about ready to go when I hear movement from over the hill toward the hub, and curiosity gets the better of me. I creep over to the edge and look down on the hub. It's bigger than I thought it would be, with a curved roof and large windows. It's painted white near the top, with wood paneling along the bottom to help it blend into the surroundings. Outside it are a couple of trucks with several people climbing out. They all have guns, from what I can tell, and I realize that these must be the Forgotten.

Duncan grabs the back of my shirt and drags me backwards, and I only just stop myself from yelping loudly.

"What?" I snap.

"Get away from there. We need to get back to the group, quickly." He picks up his basket and knife, and climbs back down the little incline.

I tut, and turn back to see what the Forgotten are going to do. I creep up as high as I can on the little hill, but keep myself low to the ground as I peek over. My breath catches when I see them dragging a deader off the back of the truck. It's shackled with its arms behind its back, and a long pole to its neck to keep it at a distance. It's more horrifying that, even from this distance, I can see that it's a newish deader. The clothes are filthy, but still intact; its skirt flaps around its ankles, but its feet are empty of shoes.

One of the men uses what looks like a length of rope to whip the deader's back, and they all give loud, guttural roars of laughter as the deader tries to turn around. It's clearly not hurt, but it sure looks pissed off; even from this distance I can hear it growling like a fucking bear. I shudder and start to turn away when another man approaches the deader, a long pole in his hand. While the deader is still looking behind it, the man reaches out with the pole, stabbing it into the deader's abdomen. Smoke rises from the end of the pole buried deep in the deader, and as I strain my ears I can hear a strange buzzing noise. The deader turns back to look at the man. Ignoring the pole inside it, it tries to reach its hands forwards for the man holding what I now comprehend as a zapper of some sort.

All the men are laughing again, and are taking turns at either whipping or zapping the deader. My stomach turns. Why would they do that? It's dead and doesn't feel anything. It doesn't care what they do to it, so what's the point in it all? It seems so unnecessary and sadistic.

They're torturing it for no other reason than to satisfy their own urges.

I turn away from them, feeling sick, and climb down the little incline. I run after and finally fall into step beside Duncan. His pace is quicker than when we were on our way here—almost a jog.

"I don't understand what I just saw, Duncan."

"They're twisted and evil." His pace picks up further.

"But, they're survivors like us, they…"

Duncan swings round to look at me. "Look, you have no idea what they are capable of. There were more of us at one point. There's a reason only Mikey goes on the scavenger hunt to the stores."

I stare at him as I realize what he means. "But why would they do that?"

"We need to get back." Duncan turns and carries on walking. "Not everyone in this world is as good as you, Nina."

"You make it sound like I'm a goody two-shoes or something, Dunc," I snort.

"You are, compared to them. They don't give a shit about the dead or the living. They would especially hate you and Emily because you were behind the walls too. They want the power and the control, and they'll do anything to get it."

I follow after him, dumbfounded. I thought the worst in this world to fear was the dead and the prison camp behind the walls, but apparently there are yet more horrors to experience.

As we climb back up the steps, I'm actually glad for all the branches that we have let overgrow the area, since it makes it harder to spot us up here. I look up and see Mikey looking down at us with a grin on his face. It falls when he sees our serious expressions.

"What's up? Are you okay?" Mikey all but pushes Duncan out of the way to get to me and I can't hold in the laugh.

"I'm fine, thank you, Mr. Bodyguard." I shrug him off.

"Forgotten over at the hub again," Duncan says with a sour look. "At least they didn't spot us, but I'm regretting putting out the deader limbs now."

"The what?"

"Your girlfriend here had a great idea about hanging deader limbs around the patch to see if it covered our scent from them." Duncan smiles. I scowl and Mikey just looks damn uncomfortable.

"I'm not his girlfriend." I stare at Mikey, daring him to disagree with me. "But it was a good plan." I turn back to Duncan. "You're right, though. If they go traipsing through the woods, they're going to know that someone has been there recently. Nothing we can do about it now, though. They would have found the vegetable patch and realized eventually anyway."

I stalk off to find Emily and the others before either of them can say anything else. I don't know what irritates me more: the fact that Mikey keeps acting so protective of me, or the fact that I actually like it. And I hate the thought that people think we're a couple. It's not just Duncan, it's Crunch, too, and I've seen the smiles Britta keeps throwing my way whenever Mikey sits next to me. I feel like I'm back in school.

I stomp into my little hut and find Emily sprawled on her camp bed looking at some old photos. She smiles at me, and then laughs at my sour expression, like I'm something to be messed with.

"What's so funny?" I grumble and sit down near her feet.

"You. You're always so…" She shrugs and smiles again.

"What?"

"I don't know—grumpy. It's funny."

"I am *not* always grumpy."

"Yeah, you are, but I still love you." She hugs me awkwardly from behind, and I pat her arm.

"Whatever, get off me." I shrug out of her embrace. "What's that you're looking at?"

Emily holds out the photos to me and I see they are the ones from Old Man Riely's house. Happy faces smile back at me and a lump instantly forms in my throat. I flip through them all. They're the same old photos that everyone has in their own home—or used to: smiling faces, arms holding each other, a couple kissing on their wedding day, an older man and what must have been his wife standing next to my big Hummer.

I don't even realize that I'm crying until my tears drip onto the photos. I rub them away with my hand, and Emily hugs me again. I don't push her off this time.

EIGHTEEN

"So it's agreed, then? We're going over there?"

"Yeah, but it has to be soon. They seem to do a round trip and swing back to the hub after a day or so, leaving us enough time to get over there and get what we need before they even realize." Mikey's voice sounds strained with worry.

"Maybe we could stay there. If we have the resources, then what's stopping us from defending the place? Or maybe if we keep the noises down they will still think that it's full of deaders. Eventually they are going to get bored of looking for us, right?" Britta asks as she serves up dinner to the group.

"I'm going with you." I stand in the doorway of the dining hut, suddenly unsure of myself. The smell of cooked rabbit is making my mouth water. I don't even know if they will let me come, but I'm willing to put myself forward to help either way. I'm a half-decent fighter these days; well maybe not decent, but I can be vicious when I need to be.

Emily turns to look at me, her eyes wide. "But what about dinner?"

I snort loudly. I'm glad that my safety isn't her primary concern anymore, but really? I'm coming second to her dinner!

"Obviously not before dinner, Emily." The smell of the food cooking makes my stomach groan, and I'm pretty damn sure that it can be heard by everyone, but I don't care. Meat is a very rare commodity these days, and by the looks on everyone's faces, they're all looking forward to it too.

JD sits in the corner, his hand on Josie's knee almost affectionately. Almost. It's more possessive than affectionate. "You're more than welcome to come along, but don't think that we won't leave you behind if you get into trouble. We don't go by the whole 'no man gets left behind' motto. If you fall, you die. If you get lost, you die. If you—"

"I get it," I cut him off midsentence. "There's a whole lot of dying going on for me if I get into trouble. Whatever." I had expected them to say no to me, or at the very least be pleased that I want to risk my life for us all and say yes to me. I hadn't expected them to be so cold about it. Well, not them, but JD.

"I'm just saying that you won't get any special treatment just because…"

"She gets it!" Mikey cuts JD off this time, and I'm glad that someone has. Though the look that passes between them is a confusing one.

It's easier to take a seat and ignore it, though, what with dinner being served up and all. Duncan and Britta are damn fine cooks, and my stomach is always appreciative of their offerings.

A bowl is placed in front of me, and as usual, I can tell that there is not nearly enough to fill my stomach. I look at it for a minute or so. Meat, potatoes, carrots, onions—damn, we're almost civilized. Only the sounds of the group slurping and chewing and the occasional moan of pleasure can be heard. I look around at them all, hunched over their bowls and greedily swallowing, and can't help but smile. I tuck into my share of food, and as the explosion of flavors hit my mouth, I release a groan of pleasure too. I don't even realize that I've done it until it's left my mouth. My cheeks flame, but I keep my head ducked and spoon another mouthful in, chewing every last morsel so I can savor the flavor completely.

It's over too soon. There's a motto there somewhere. I show no shame in scooping my hand around the inside of the bowl to get every drop out. When I finish, I lean back in my chair with my eyes closed in sheer, blissful pleasure. I can feel my body relaxing, and give in to the urge to doze off.

"Nina."

I stir from my sleep begrudgingly, opening one eye and then the other. The room is quite dark, dusk is setting in, and Mikey's face is hovering over mine.

"Hey." He smiles at me, and I stretch and smile back.

"Hey yourself. I can't believe I fell asleep like that." I stretch my back out further and hear a series of small cracks. It's a satisfying sound.

"You must have been really tired." He gives a low laugh and looks away. "I thought it best to wake you though. The others left to go to bed, but I didn't want you to be freaked out when you woke up and it was pitch black or something."

Well, that's kind of cute.

"Mikey, is that your idea of an apology for making me live up in the trees like an Ewok?" I laugh.

He laughs back lightly. "That's very cool you know."

I blush and look away. I again don't bother to correct him that it wasn't by choice that I watched the damn movie, but instead move the subject onwards.

"So why did you *really* wake me?" I probe deeper.

"I was bored. You've been sleeping for ages…"

My blush deepens and I'm glad it's dark. I can't believe he sat with me this whole time. *I hope I didn't snore.*

"…and it was getting dark. I thought it best you get to your hut before it gets too dark." He adds on quickly.

I nod in agreement. "Is Emily okay?"

"Yeah, she went to sleep a while ago. She seems pretty happy here. So, you two, you were behind one of the walls for the past year, right?" He bites his fingernails and I have the urge to smack his hand away. God knows how many germs are on those hands.

"Yeah." Talk of the wall is making me feel uncomfortable, and I stand and stretch my legs out.

"What's it like behind them?" He sits on the table with his feet on one of the wooden chairs while he watches me walk around the little hut.

What's it like? Jesus, what a question.

"It's no safer behind them than it is out here, if I'm honest." I look out the little window and stare into the rustling trees and sigh. "Sure, there are no deaders, but behind the wall there are—how can I put this? —let's call them oppressors…"

He stands up and comes over to me. "Yeah, but oppressors you can beat up." He gives a dry laugh and cracks his knuckles. "Especially you. You're a badass, right?"

"Not these ones. Behind the wall, the oppressors are also your protectors. You stand up to them and they kick you out. Which is why I'm here." I can feel him watching me, his eyes boring into the side of my face. For the first time in a long time, I don't feel nervous that a man is looking at me. I feel safe.

"So, what did you do? I mean, what did *they* do?"

I turn and look at him, my eyes wet with unshed tears. "Whatever they wanted to."

I see the look on his face change into so many emotions, in a matter of seconds, before finally landing back on a blank one. "Why did you stay, then?"

"What choice did I have?" I huff. "If I had left, I would have been killed by the dead right away!"

"So why the fuck did you leave in the end? You don't make any sense." He scratches a hand through his stubble angrily, glaring at me.

"Behind the walls, they control everything: the food you eat, the clothes on your back, the water you drink. They get to decide where you sleep, what your job will be. But more importantly, in the end they decide whether you live or die. If you go up against them, they send you back over the wall. So you see it really isn't about being a badass—which I am, I must add, though I never used to be." I look away from him. The haunted look on his face is too much. I don't want his or anyone's sympathy. "I guess when I saw what they were doing to Emily, I just sort of thought 'fuck it.' I wasn't living, I was existing. They took my body first, and my mind slowly went, too, until I saw her face, until I saw how scared she was, and I knew I couldn't stay any longer. If it meant dying, then so be it. At least I'd die for a reason."

Silence encompasses us and I presume he's mulling over what I just told him. If he reads between the lines, the story is pretty clear. I don't want him to ask me any more questions so I decide to ask him one instead.

"How come you weren't behind the wall?"

I hadn't really thought about it before, or maybe it's just that regardless of who these people are, it really is as simple as I just put it, and I feel safer here than I ever did behind the wall.

Mikey looks uncomfortable and his voice seems to miss a beat before he continues. "I, um, I didn't get there in time. When I tried to get in, it was too overrun with zombies, so I had to find somewhere else to hide. I've never bothered to try since. There didn't seem much point. The walled cities are few and far between, and we have a good thing going on here. Or we did."

I can feel him looking at me again and I return his stare. His eyes are soft and dark, a slight smile turning up at the corner of his mouth. I notice, for what seems like the first time, how attractive he actually is. His arms are toned and ridiculously strong, his shoulders broad. "Until the Forgotten showed up, you mean?" I ask. My voice is quieter than I had meant it to be. In an odd way, the Forgotten don't scare me as much as Lee and his little group of idiots did, but maybe that's because I haven't really met them yet. Or maybe it's because Mikey is here with me, and he makes me feel safe—safe and womanly.

Some hair has come loose from my bun, and he reaches over to brush it away from my shoulder. "Yeah, until they showed up."

His touch sends shivers down my spine, but I don't recoil from it. He slowly rubs the lock of my dark hair distractedly between his finger and thumb.

"Because they're dangerous?" Seems like a stupid question to ask, but it's the only one I can think of right now, since my mind has gone blank and I can't seem to look away from his mouth.

"Yeah. Really dangerous." Mikey lets go of the lock of hair. His hand reaches up until the pad of his thumb is under my chin, his rough fingers touching lightly against my cheek.

Our eyes lock, and I can't seem to break free of the stare. Or maybe I don't want to. His touch is caring and honest, the first genuine show of affection from a man in such a long time.

I'm lost for words, and as Mikey leans in close to my face, my breath catches and my eyes flutter closed to match his. Do I want this? Him? I have no idea, but I know that I like him, even if I'm not ready to admit that to anyone else just yet.

"Ahem!"

I open my eyes and look to the doorway where Crunch stands. Her icy glare could kill small animals, maybe even a zombie or two. I pull away from Mikey, uncomfortable now that the moment has been disturbed.

"What?" Mikey stands close to me, his arm across the tops of my shoulders. I move around to the other side of the table, two sets of eyes following me the whole time.

"Sorry, was I interrupting?" Her ice queen death stare follows through into her words, and I force myself to act unaffected by them.

"No," I answer quickly.

"Yes," Mikey answers and stares at me. His eyebrows furrow in confusion at my coldness.

"I need to go get some sleep." I'm standing in front of Crunch now, but she makes no attempt to get out of my way, which is unfortunate for her since I'm not in any mood to be polite. "Move...Now."

She looks at me for a couple more seconds before giving me a sly grin and stepping out of my way. I squeeze past her and go to find Emily. I shake my head at my own stupidity as I hear them start up a whispered argument behind me. It's pretty obvious that she's into him. The icy looks, the snarky attitude. Wait, that could just be her general attitude, come to think of it. Either way, she hasn't liked me since I arrived, that much is clear. And either way, a relationship is the last thing I need to confuse the situation.

I need to speak to Emily tomorrow about what happened before I arrived here at our little camp in the trees. I haven't spent much time with her since we got here. Eating, sleeping, and adjusting to living like monkeys in the trees seem to have taken up most of my time, but now I need to get my ass into gear and sort myself out. There's a lot I don't know about the group, and I think it's imperative that I find out as much as I can.

NINETEEN

The sun blazes down on me, making my skin feel hot and sticky under its rays. The hut I share with Emily is small, with one window and an open doorway, but the sun, goddamn it, has managed to sneak in through that one small window and blaze down upon my face like it's the fucking Messiah and I'm its trusty disciple. I turn over with a grumble, pulling the blanket up over my face, but after a couple of minutes of getting even hotter under the scratchy blanket, I give up.

I sit up with a huff and automatically do what I try to do every morning: I reach for my clock. Of course, it's not there. It hasn't been there for a long time, but old habits die hard, and I hate not knowing the time. It shouldn't matter, but it's annoying more than anything. I look out the window. The sun has moved from its position now, and isn't glaring down at me anymore, so I have a clear view of the trees outside. I'm too awake now to go back to sleep, though I wish I could. I wonder if anyone else is up yet. Duncan always seems to be an early riser, then again, he always seems to be the first to bed, too, whereas I'm always one of the last.

Emily still snores on her camper bed on the other side of the room. I was lucky to make it back here last night since it was so dark. Any darker and I would have had to sleep out in the open again. Not that I'm averse to doing that, but if I have a choice, I'm going to take the uncomfortable wooden bed in my small, crappy, wooden hut in the trees any day.

I need to pee badly, so I take our pee pot into the empty hut next door and relieve myself and then pour it down the 'pee chute,' as we have so fondly named it. It all lands in a large hole way below us and thankfully underground. Why the hell they didn't make the system simpler by just making it so you could pee right into the chute, I don't know. Typical men, I suppose—always making things more complicated than needed. I rinse the pot with some of the water and throw that down too.

When I arrive back at our hut, Emily is stirring. I'm bored as shit, so I don't try to tiptoe around. She looks up at me from her little wooden bed with a smile. There's color back in her cheeks, and I know if things continue the way that they have been for the past few weeks, she'll start getting some more meat on her bones soon. It pleases me to think of her getting healthy again. I smile back at her and sit on the edge of her bed.

"Hey, you okay?" I ask.

"Uh-huh." She yawns and rubs her eyes.

"I'm going to see if anyone is up. You coming?"

"Yeah, sure." She sits up and stretches, reminding me of when I was woken by Mikey last night.

I've thought about him all night: his hand on my cheek and the look in his eye. Do I even *want* to meet someone else? To begin a new relationship? I don't think so, but I feel drawn to Mikey.

"Can I talk to you before we go?"

Emily nods and I continue.

"When you two left me—you know, back at the garage—what happened?"

Emily sits up and looks confused. "What do you mean, Nina? Nothing. We just ran for what seemed like ages. We came across a couple of deaders, but Mikey took care of them, and then when we arrived here and he introduced me to everyone."

"Was everyone nice to you?" *I sound like an idiot!*

"Um, yeah. Well, JD is—well, JD, and Crunch is obviously Crunch, but yeah, everyone was fine. After a couple of hours Mikey and I got restless because you hadn't turned up, and I said that I wanted to go look for you, but he wouldn't let me. He said that he had promised you he would look after me and keep me safe and he wasn't going to break that promise." She smiles at me, but I can't smile back for some reason. "He tried to get some of the others to go with him to find you, but they wouldn't. They said that you were probably a goner by now anyway. That got him all pissy with everyone, and I freaked out and blamed him for—well, you know, your death, and he stormed off."

Emily looks like she might cry, so I reach out and give her knee a little squeeze. "And?" I probe.

"So he said he would go look for you on his own. The others warned him that it was going to be getting dark soon, and you could both end up getting lost and killed, but he went anyway." She smiles more now. "And then you stumbled out into the clearing like you were Superwoman or something."

I snort. "Hardly. I collapsed into the clearing, more like."

"Yeah, but I prefer my version."

I laugh and she unexpectedly leans over and hugs me. I have the urge to push her off again, for several reasons. One being she smells really bad and could do with a good wash, and secondly because I don't hug. In fact, I hate hugs, and she seems to be hugging me more and more recently. Regardless, I force myself to hug her back, to which she squeezes me tighter.

She pulls away and continues. "He was so relieved when he got back and I told him that you were here." She gives another smile. A mischievous one, grinning from ear to ear. "I think he likes you, Nina."

Yeah, I thought that too.

I roll my eyes. "Well, that's not what we're here for, Emily."

Now it's her turn to roll her eyes at me. "Whatever." She pushes past me as she climbs out of her bed.

"Don't 'whatever' me. I'm serious. I'm not interested in anything like that."

She picks up the pee pot as she looks at me. "Nina, it's obvious that you like him too, but whatever, if that's' not what you're here for.'" She grins as she does little quotation marks with one hand and leaves to go to the bathroom, leaving me to stew with my own thoughts. As if I didn't have enough to think about already.

Breakfast consists of not very much this morning. My stomach was just starting to get used to having proper food in it and is unsurprisingly grumbly about the situation. I feel the same way and express as much to Mikey.

"Is there nothing for breakfast? There has to be something more than this shit." Yeah, I sound pissy, and yeah a little bit childish.

"Don't fucking eat it then, give me your share," Crunch snarks at me.

I toss the handful of berries in my mouth with a grim smile in her direction, and she huffs and stands to leave.

"What happened to you?" I ask Britta. Her wrist and hand are bandaged up, and she's favoring her left hand when I know she's right-handed.

"I slipped using the ropes last night. Crunch thinks it's just a sprain and not broken, but it hurts like hell." Britta looks down at her wrists, her face a mask of worry.

"How in God's name did Crunch become camp doctor?" I frown at Britta, but it's Duncan who replies.

"Apparently before she got mixed up with all her old man's crap, she was studying to become a doctor. Got in with the wrong crowd, fucked up her scholarship, and the rest is history. Kept up some of her abilities, though, by patching up other drug-heads." He shakes his head sadly and takes a sip of his tea.

I sit stunned for a few seconds. That wasn't what I expected to hear at all. I look at Britta, who's tenderly rubbing the joint on her wrist.

"I'm sure it'll be fine." My words were supposed to be full of concern, but I know I sound more irritated than anything else when I speak, knowing that it means more work for the rest of us. I feel instantly guilty, but it's too late to take it back.

I reach over and take the mug of hot water with some green leaves floating around in it that Duncan insists is peppermint tea. I taste it and tell him that he's been miss-sold and that if he keeps spouting bullshit like that, he'll get himself a lawsuit for false advertising. Duncan laughs and adds more leaves to my cup.

I'm feeling especially shitty this morning because of how Mikey made me feel last night. Seriously, I was just starting to like this place, and now he's confused me with his weird manly odor, or some crap.

Mikey looks up from biting his nails and smiles in what I assume is his best heartthrob impression.

I roll my eyes. "Seriously, I'm surprised that you haven't gotten a stomach bug, biting your nails all the time. Do you know how many germs are under those things?" I sit down with a kind of body flop thing going on, and then have the urge to laugh at my own behavior.

Mikey doesn't rise to my bait and keeps on biting his nails.

"Are we doing a water run today?" I ask Duncan, who's looking through some binoculars across the lake.

"Yeah," he replies without looking at me.

I huff out my frustrations.

"What is wrong with you today, Nina?" Britta looks at me with concern, giving me a little tsk noise as she does.

"Sorry." I shrug back. "Just hungry, you know?"

"Yes, we are all hungry, but we have to ration the food. Some days we get to eat more, some days we get less, and some days we get nothing. It's just the way it is." Britta seems more impatient with me today, which is totally unlike her. She normally has much more tolerance of everyone's moods.

"Sorry," I repeat. She makes me feel bad for complaining, like a child complaining to her mother that she didn't get any candy. Little brat me, huh?

"It is okay. We all miss things. It is harder some days than others, no?" She smiles at me and I reciprocate. Her accent also seems stronger today than before, or maybe it's just me becoming more aware of these people as individuals and not just as a group.

"You know what I miss?" We all look at Josie. We all miss things, and I guess I just assumed that they would all be the same things.

"Nights out chilling with my friends." She doesn't smile when she says it, but looks down at her hands. "Relaxing and having fun. I mean, there's just no down time, you know? No break from it all. Sometimes I just want to forget about all this stuff, laugh, and have fun again."

JD puts an arm around her and pulls her close, kissing the top of her head affectionately. I think it's the first time I've seen him being affectionate with her, come to think of it. *Hard ass!*

"I miss Sunday mornings." JD looks around at us all. Some of us nod, some of us (okay, just me) raise an eyebrow in confusion.

"Just Sundays? Or is there another day of the week that you were particularly fond of, pre-apocalypse?" I snort. Since no one laughs with me, I figure they either think I'm an asshole or they know better than to mess with JD.

"I hadn't finished," he replies curtly. "As I was saying, I miss Sunday mornings…" He looks at me to see if I'm going to interrupt again, but I hold my hands up in fake surrender. "Waking up to the warmth of your woman's body next to you, and before you have even opened your eyes, you let her scent wash over you. You pull her close and kiss her good morning, your arms wrapped around each other as you enjoy a moment of pure blissful relaxation with each other's closeness, and the moment isn't ruined by having to get up every two fucking minutes to shoot yet another of those dead fuckers."

We all laugh. Even JD smiles, which is another first. Josie looks up at him fondly through her thick lashes. He looks down at her and kisses her on the forehead again. His hands are on either side of her face, and she melts into his touch. I blush and look away from the romantic gesture, and my eyes fall on Mikey. He's looking at me in a way that makes me uncomfortable. Kind of like a panther stalking its prey. I look down at my shoes, feeling like I'm being undressed by Mr. Seductiveness over there.

"I miss taking a hot bath," Britta is the next to speak and break the moment that JD has created. "I used to love taking a hot bath, and I smell now. I hate it. We all smell!"

We all laugh again. It's true. We really do smell. *Especially Emily right now; I really do have to tell her.*

"I miss baths, and showers. I just miss being clean. I stink!" Emily looks up at me mournfully, like an injured lamb going to slaughter. I should tell her not to be so dumb, that it's not *that* bad of a smell...but it *is* that bad, and she does need to wash. So I nod at her instead and she glares back at me.

"Sorry, but you do," I grin, and she replies by pushing me off my chair.

"I miss being safe," Duncan says darkly. "I miss being able to just walk around without a care in the world. I hate that we're constantly in danger, that we have to watch our backs every second of the day. If it's not zombies, it's the Forgotten. I'm sick of it. I just want to feel safe again, I want us all to." His anger rises as he continues. "We deserve that much, don't we? I mean, this isn't living, it's existing."

His hands ball into fists by his sides. He seems really pissed now, not just angry.

"So are you coming, then? To the hub?" Mikey takes the moment to swoop in and pounce on his prey, looking at him seriously. And here I was thinking *I* was the deer he was stalking. All the lightheartedness from our previous discussion is seemingly forgotten.

Duncan nods. "Yes, I'll come."

Mikey smiles widely—happy, I guess, that he finally got his way. He looks around at the group as if sizing us all up, his eyes resting on me for a moment too long before he speaks.

"Great. Well, let's do this, then. So Duncan, JD, Crunch, and I will go to the hub this morning, clear the place of as many deaders as we can, and scrounge up some new gear." He smiles.

"Wait, why the hell isn't Nina going?" Crunch snaps, coming back into the room. I can't help but agree with her.

"Yeah, why the hell aren't I going?"

Both Crunch and I lock stares for a moment before she realizes that this wasn't my doing, and we decide to turn our angry glares on Mikey.

He holds his hands up defensively. "Whoa, calm down, ladies. Someone needs to stay here and protect the others, in case we don't come back. Nina's good at fighting."

"Just not good enough to come with you?" I retaliate.

"Britta's a good fighter," Crunch bites back.

"Yeah, but I sprained my wrist yesterday. I can hardly grip the ropes to get to my bunk, never mind hold a weapon and fight," Britta interjects. "I would love to come and help in any way, but..." She shrugs, letting her words die off.

"I bet Josie's a good fighter." I look at JD.

"She's not going. End of." With that he looks away from me.

I glance at Josie, who offers me a sympathetic smile.

I start to argue that it isn't fair, but Mikey holds a hand up to silence me.

"I know what you're going to say, so save your breath. JD's not going to change his mind about it, and I'm not going to force the issue with him. Just drop it."

I scowl harder. "I'm going."

"Look I'm not willing to risk everybody's lives." Mikey crosses his arms over his chest.

"But you're quite willing to risk *my* life and not hers?" Crunch interrupts.

Crunch stares at him, her jaw grinding angrily before she grabs her bottle of water and storms off again, giving me the final blast from her blues. JD and Mikey exchange a look, of which I miss the meaning.

I huff. "I'm going with you. I told you the last time this was brought up that I was going, and I have not changed my mind about it. I don't want, or expect, any special treatment from any of you." I look at Mikey, and if looks could kill I think he would have croaked by now. Fortunately for him, they can't. He attempts to argue back, but then stops when he realizes that I mean business.

I don't need anyone helping me; I can look after myself. I certainly don't need some guy with a crush trying to protect me and making others in our group hate me.

"Fine," Mikey replies tensely, clearly not happy about me going at all. *Well he can just suck it.*

TWENTY

I start to load up my backpack with bits and pieces that I think might be useful, but finally decide that the only thing I'm going to need is a weapon. Everything else is pointless. Water, Band-Aids, bandages—what's really the point in any of this shit if I fall or get trapped? I may as well leave them with Emily. She could end up needing them more than I do.

My weapon of choice? My butcher's knife. Yeah, it sucks and it's pretty fucking blunt now, but I don't seem to have an awful lot of choice since there aren't any nice weaponry shops around anymore. Anyway, it's gotten me out of quite a few sticky situations so far, so maybe I should be more content with my weapon.

When I see everyone else's weapons, though, I can't help but feel a pang of jealousy. JD has two scythes. There's a hand-held one that looks small and brutal and a larger one with a long wooden handle. Duncan has a pistol of some sort, and a shotgun strapped to his back. Crunch has a sharp-looking curved knife, and my eyes widen at it. *It.*

Is. Awesome. She smiles at me in answer to my drooling stare.

"It's a Kukri knife. My dad used to collect old weapons and shit; history-type stuff. It's from the Ghurkha's army dudes, or something like that anyway. He had no respect for anything but his damn weapons. Always used to say that they would save our lives one day, but I think he meant from goons who would be knocking on our front door, not deaders."

She actually seems genuinely pleased for the first time since I've met her. If she's pleased to have a deadly kick-ass weapon or pleased that she has something that I want, I'm not sure. I guess this is just another side to her fractured personality.

I look at Mikey and realize that he has the best weapon, and one that I want most of all: a machete.

I want it. I want it. I want it! I almost stamp my feet in frustration.

It's long, sharp, and looks extremely deadly. My salivating goes to a whole new level. And Mikey, well, he just looks like something out of a cool comic book. He's changed into a short-sleeved black T-shirt and is wearing a harness of some sort that comes across his shoulders and across his back. With his biceps bulging and his shaved head, I can't help but feel an attraction to him. *Damn it!*

"Put your tongue away," Crunch bites out at me.

Mikey looks at my knife with a deep frown. "You can't be serious?"

"What?" I ask, pretending that I don't know that I am seriously under-skilled, and lacking in the cool-looking weapon department.

"That's all you have?" He gestures with his bad-ass machete.

I look down at my weapon hand as if I had forgotten that my knife was even there. "This? Yeah. This is deadly as hell, I'll have you know." I almost snort at my own comment. Yeah, really deadly, pfft!

"It doesn't even look sharp, Nina," Mikey purses his lips together in a failed attempt to hold in his words. "Look at it!" He gestures angrily again.

"It's fine," I snap back.

"Nina…"

"Mikey, we need to go. We're losing daylight. If she's prepared to risk her life with that piece of crap, then so be it." With that, JD turns and hugs Josie goodbye, whispering something into her ear and making her smile.

Mikey and I glare at each other for a second or two, neither of us willing to back down, though I know for my own safety, I probably should. I mean, he's right—damn him.

Idiot! Me, not him. Well, maybe him too.

How the hell did they all get such totally badass weapons, anyway? What kind of stuff could be over at the hub that would be cooler than these?

Crunch smirks and follows Duncan and JD, ready to climb down. Mikey sheathes his long machete and walks over to me, his steps cautious. He stands directly in front of me, his eyes boring into mine with a look of resignation. He reaches for my hand, and I think about resisting but don't. Taking my knife from my hand, he unhooks a sling from his side and passes it to me. Inside is a shorter-looking machete. It's not as big and cool as the other one, but I couldn't swing that thing anyway. He walks away without saying another word.

I pull out the knife and stare at it. It's sharp and dangerous-looking, far better than my stupid knife. I turn and watch his retreating back as he climbs down the main pole to the ground, my stomach fluttering as I watch his descent.

Stupid man.

The air is once again humid as we trek through the forest, and it's surprisingly clear, apart from the one deader. It doesn't seem to pose a particular threat to any of us as it slowly drags its decrepit body across the forest floor. It groans as we near it, its eyes turning to look at us, one hand reaching up for us clumsily.

JD walks over to it, staring down at its putrid body with something more than hate written on his face. He puts his boot on the side of its head and slowly presses down, taking his time to feel every bone crunch in its head. The zombie's face pops with finality, leaving black gunk and bone where its head once was. I look away with a grimace, and when I look back up, I see JD smile at it and stalk off without a second glance. I look up and catch Mikey watching me with dark eyes. He reaches down, picks up a rock, and continues walking.

I walk behind him, listening to the scrape of metal upon stone, and realize that he's sharpening my knife. My hand instinctively goes to the knife at my waist—the one he has given me. My fingers grip it around its handle. I'm not giving this back, no matter what he says or how sharp he makes my stupid knife. Ungrateful and selfish? Yeah, probably, but I don't care. Weapons like this don't come easy, not in this world, not anymore, and I would be stupid to just give it up.

The walk is hard on my body. I'm tired, and weaker than I will ever admit to anyone because of the crappy early morning and the lack of food. The nerves are beginning to set in too. Why the hell did I decide to come along? I didn't have to. They were going to be doing this regardless of me. Maybe it's my own desire to try and prove to Crunch and JD that I'm not some stupid, feeble woman, that I'm as strong as they are—more so for what I have been through. Or maybe it's because I wanted to be near Mikey. I hate that he has gotten under my skin; it makes me have an entire new bag of reasons to feel guilty in my life.

I'm lost in my own thoughts and don't notice when Duncan falls into step beside me.

"I hope we're not going to regret this," he says quietly, more to himself than me.

"You and me both," I reply without looking at him.

There's silence the rest of the way there, apart from the odd grunt from people tripping on stuff. Okay, so that would just be me that's tripping on stuff.

The hub comes into view again as we pass our vegetable patch, and I'm pleased that my rhubarb is still growing strong and there are no deaders around, thanks to my little zombie repellent. We crouch down behind some rocks on the ridge, looking across at the place where the Forgotten had stopped yesterday and tortured the deader. There's no sign of them or it today, but there's a large patch of brown-black sludge where they were standing. JD hurries off commando-style to make sure that the coast is clear and none of the Forgotten are still over there. A few minutes later he comes back and gives us the all clear, and we set off again, with Duncan by JD's side.

We aim for the back of the building, which Duncan tells us is an emergency exit and therefore less used. I guess he's hoping to come across as little zombie exposure as possible, but that doesn't seem to be JD's or Mikey's aim. They seem to want to clear the building and take back control of it.

We all stand side by side, our backs against the warm cream walls, as Duncan fumbles around for the key. The bastard locked everyone inside when he left. Any respect I have for him is quashed upon that realization.

Stepping out of the heat and into the murky coolness of the hub, Duncan slips a catch at the top of the door so that it won't lock when it closes behind us, and we all take a second or two to collect our thoughts and wits.

JD points to Mikey, giving him some strange hand signal, which—lo and behold!—Mikey actually seems to get. Or at least he nods, looks back at me, and uses the same hand signal. I shrug and tiptoe up behind him.

"What?" I whisper it as quietly as I can, but in the gloom, the sound of my voice seems to echo around us all, and I flinch.

"Stay behind me, okay? We'll stick to the left, Crunch and Duncan to the right, JD will be in the middle. Keep your eyes peeled and stay in formation." His face is serious, concern crinkling at the corners of his eyes.

JD is huffing for us to go, but Mikey is relaxed and calm. Or at least he seems to be.

We make our way down the hallway, checking out side corridors as we pass them, but silence is what envelops us. Nothing but silence until Duncan whispers that we are nearing the center. The canteen is apparently to the left of the center, and that's where Duncan wants to get to. However, when we reach the main part of the building, JD gestures for us to go right. Duncan does that weird argue whisper thing with JD, who blatantly ignores him and keeps on going right. No one in their right mind wants to disagree with JD, so we all follow like lambs to the slaughter.

As we turn the corner, the moaning can finally be heard. The moaning that only the dead make. I watch a nervous Duncan make a sign of the cross and pull out both his guns, ready to protect himself. I grip my knife tighter, my nails digging into the soft flesh underneath as fear trickles into the pit of my stomach.

The stench of death is upon us and I can't seem to breathe through my nose anymore for fear of throwing up. Even with the fear of being eaten to death—or worse, being eaten and turning into one of the deaders—it's still the smell that manages to get to me the most. I can almost taste last night's rabbit threatening to make a reappearance, but I'll be damned if I'm going to lose another meal to these freaks. I swallow down my bile and grit my teeth.

The corridor is lined with doors, and we gather around the first. JD tugs on the handle until it relents and swings open to reveal an empty office. I release the breath that I've been holding and Mikey looks around at me and gives me a grim smile.

JD closes the door and we move as one to the next door. I instinctively hold my breath again. JD's hand pulls on the handle and he opens the door wide, surprising the zombie inside.

It turns, and I swear I see it smile as it comes toward us, stumbling over the clutter on the floor in its eagerness to get to us. It walks with arms raised, bloodied fingers searching us out. There's a *swoosh* as a blade slices through the air, hitting the zombie in the neck, and then a small thud as its head hits the floor. There's no blood—just black sludge, which oozes out of the hole where the head should be as the body falls to its knees and then lands in a heap.

Somehow we have all crowded into the small space of the doorway, and as we step back and close the door, we are finally greeted with the view that we have all been dreading.

Deaders. Lots of them.

TWENTY ONE

"**F**uck!" Crunch breathes out, beating me to the punch line with startling accuracy.

Yes, *fuck* would be it indeed. Or *fucked* may be better. Maybe even *well and truly fucked*. This isn't how we had talked about it going down. In fact, this would be the entire opposite of how we expected it to go down. We had planned on picking them off one by one, or at least two by two. Like Noah's ark, but without the cute animals.

I turn, startled by the noise behind us, and I know for a fact that my eyes have just widened by at least an inch as more zombies round the corner.

"Double fuck!" I beat Crunch to it this time, and the group turns to look behind us too.

"Ten to the rear," Mikey barks out and readies his machete, solidifying his stance.

"Eight to the front," JD shouts back, his voice nearly drowned out by the groaning horde coming toward us.

We stand back to back, giving each other just enough space to move around as the crowd of overzealous zombies draws close.

I haven't realized that I have placed myself between Duncan and Mikey, with JD and Crunch to my rear. As the first of the rotting zombies gets close, Mikey steps out of formation and slices its head from its shoulders in one move. That's the good thing about the older deaders: the muscle and sinew are much weaker and easier to destroy than the newer deaders. The downside to them? They stink to high heaven. I mean, way more than your average deader. Once again there is no blood splatter—just black gunk, which oozes out of the hole, and a fresh wave of putrid stench. Mikey takes another step forward as an overeager female zombie with one arm and a rotten face (showing more bone than flesh) trips on the body of the first deader, and he swings and removes her head too with a satisfying *thwack* sound. Duncan takes aim with his gun and fires into the crowd, but he seemingly misses their brains, since they continue to twitch and writhe to get to us. Dude needs to practice his shooting skills more, if you ask me.

I take a cursory glance behind me, and see that JD and Crunch have also dropped from their positions and are fast approaching the other deaders while attempting to separate and single them out so they're easier to kill.

I dig deep down in me, summoning up some strength of mind to get my ass into gear. After all, I was the one who asked to come on this joyous trip.

My blade is sharp and deadly and I fumble for a moment before I, too, begin hacking away at the deaders that get too close to us. I slice and dice without prejudice. Mikey is covered in black grime, his face contorted with a deadly rage that I haven't seen on him before. Yet his movements remain precise and controlled; only his eyes give it away. The hate, the contempt.

Duncan steps close to a thrashing zombie and fires his gun into its brain. The bullet comes out the back of the deader's skull and hits the one behind it, spraying it with chunks of rotten brown-and-black brain matter. Unfortunately it doesn't kill the deader, just pisses it off, and it moves forward, stumbling over the now brainless deader on the floor, and grabs at Duncan's shirt. It leans over and tries to bite him, but only comes away with a mouthful of shirt. Duncan pushes his gun between himself and the deader and fires haphazardly into it, but the thing barely notices that its insides are being turned to oozing black mush, which is now trickling out of several holes in its intestines, and continues its onslaught regardless. I swing with my arm—wildly, I'll admit—and hit it in the back of the head. The zombie twitches and releases Duncan, turning to look at me instead, my machete still sunk deep in its skull. That's unusual; a deader is normally so focused on the prey directly in front of it. Regardless, I don't get to ponder this obscurity now that I'm its new source of prey.

I take a step back from it as Duncan fires his gun again, but it clicks on empty. Between him reaching for his shotgun and me getting ready to kick the deader away, Mikey somehow realizes what's happening and turns to pull my machete from the back of the deader's skull. He hacks at its skull again, this time making sure its brain is completely destroyed. The zombie grunts once and falls to the floor as Duncan aims his gun at it.

"Sorry," Duncan pants, wiping away the sweat and black gunk from his face with shaky hands. "And thanks."

I shrug a *no problem*, but really feel like peeing myself. JD calls out that it's clear where he and Crunch are, and I nod and make my way to them without looking at Mikey even though I feel like throwing my arms around his neck right here and now and slobbering him with grateful kisses.

They've managed to make their way further down the hall in their fighting, leaving a trail of rotten bodies either missing their heads or with little left of what were once their skulls.

I'm glad that these monsters are dead, yet I feel no joy at their passing. Only relief that they are out of their misery. For all the death and destruction that they have created, we all know that they didn't ask for this, and if they did have a choice in the matter, this is not the way they would have wanted to go.

We regroup, pausing and catching our breaths as we lean against the walls—all but Mikey and JD, who cover both ends of the hallway.

"How many more, Duncan?" Mikey asks as he wipes his blade along the seam of his pants to clear it free of any gunk.

"I'm not sure, um, I don't know how many made it out before…" He mumbles his words.

"Well, for argument's sake, let's just say that none of them made it out. How many more?" JD snaps.

Duncan seems to be going over the mental calculations in his head before coming to an answer that seems to please him. "I think maybe another twenty or so, maybe less." He smiles, but no one reciprocates it. "I thought that we were just getting some supplies. We don't need to clear the building, we're fine where we are."

"I'm not living in the trees for the next twenty years, Duncan. We're clearing this place, end of discussion," JD barks out.

Duncan nods, but he clearly doesn't agree. I don't know where I stand in it all. It would be great to be living on solid ground again,

CLAIRE C. RILEY

but there's something about living up in the trees that actually makes me feel safer, Ewok or not.

"Twenty more then?" Crunch asks with a grim look.

Duncan shrugs, but doesn't say anything. He doesn't need to. Twenty zombies still lurk in this place. Twenty zombies that we need to find and kill before we can even begin to collect the things we need. Twenty more times that the hungry, gory mouths of the dead can try and eat us.

"Let's go." JD moves off around the corner, and we follow him as one and without argument.

There are stains smeared along the walls, handprints and the words *'help us'* written in dried blood. I shudder and look at Duncan. He lowers his gaze away from me and away from the words, knowing only too well that he caused this. He could have saved some of these people if he wouldn't have been such a coward. Instead he locked them all inside and sentenced them to death.

There are the remains of a body or two on the floor, but not enough of either of them remain to be reanimated, and so JD kicks the bloody bones to the side and out of our way. We can hear more growling coming from behind a closed door; we seemed to have riled them all up, by the sounds of it.

"That's the medic's room," Duncan whispers.

I want to shout out *no shit, Sherlock!* since there's a big red cross on the door, but JD turns the handle before I can get my words out. I swallow them down and ready myself as the door opens inwards and reveals to us the five zombies within.

They head straight for us with long, hungry growls, as if mamma didn't give them their last meal before bedtime. Sludge hangs from their jaws and a cold blankness fills their eyes. Their lips peel back to reveal blackened and broken teeth and they push and shove to get past each other and to their meal: us. I shiver and swallow down the stomach acid that has worked its way up my esophagus and into my mouth.

"I got this." Crunch steps forward, and with her two knives, she decapitates the first two zombies with relative ease (if there can be such a thing when killing the living dead). JD follows her in, and when a zombie lunges for him, he deals with it with a quick swoop of his scythe down its middle. From skull to stomach it splits, and everything left inside tumbles into a pile on the floor along with its body.

Crunch laughs as she circles another, kicking it away with her foot until it falls on its back. She stands above it, placing a foot on its chest, and drives her blade through its face slowly and with a maniacal glee that sends shivers down my spine. There is something like contentment in her expression as she pulls the blade back out, gunk spewing out of the hole left by her knife.

The last deader has reached the doorway, and Duncan takes aim with his gun.

"I'm sorry," he whispers as he pulls the trigger and the zombie hits the floor.

From the looks of the random skeletal body pieces lying around, there were more than just these five in here at one time. I realize that there is no way to know for sure how many had been here. This room is the real hub, the beginning of it all for Duncan, and the end of it all for everyone that had been in here. He hangs his head in shame as he looks at the body of the deader he just shot—what was once a young boy. I'm guessing this was the Sanil from his story. There's a huge chunk of the zombie's face missing—his cheek and part of his right eye. Yes, this was definitely Sanil.

"Do you know how many people followed you in here, Duncan?" Mikey asks, his voice quiet.

Duncan shakes his head in response, but doesn't reply.

I notice that Crunch has taken watch by the door while JD is kicking bodies around, trying to get a rough figure. "I think there were maybe three others at one time, but…" JD kicks another body and shrugs. "It's too hard to tell."

I do the quick math and approximate it at around nine more to go, give or take. Give or take are not good odds in situations like these, and I tell everyone so.

We head back down the hallway, listening intently for any sound. When only our footsteps echo back at us after a couple of pit stops inside various rooms, Mikey stops and turns to look at us.

"Wait. Let's try and think about this. Duncan, where would the highest number of people go?" Mikey waits for Duncan to reply.

"What would that matter? Zombies don't think like humans do. They wander, they moan, they attack and kill. They don't relive their final days," Duncan replies coldly.

"Probably not, but what if everyone went to hide? What if they're still there…waiting?" Mikey lets the news sink in for a second before continuing. "Alive or dead, that's more than likely where they are going to be. Think about it. The first deader was trapped in his office, and I'm willing to bet that he locked himself in there when the shit went down and he couldn't escape. He most likely died from hunger in there and then turned." Mikey looks to everyone in the group and we all nod in agreement; it makes sense when you think about it.

"They're probably in the sleeping quarters then. There's a lock on the inside of the door, but no outside exit from there." Duncan's guilt is palpable as he drags a hand across his face in shame at what he has done.

"Okay, so where are those?" Crunch asks. I can see she feels the same as me, and is trying to contain her anger with Duncan. At least for the moment anyway. It must be harder on them; they have all known him for a long time. They're his friends, but I don't think things will ever be the same between them all again. Or maybe they will. The past is the past, right? And we've all done things we are ashamed of.

"We need to get back to the canteen and turn right. The women's are at the bottom of the corridor to the right. The men's are just past the gym." Duncan lets everyone pass him before following behind. I turn around and look at him, and consider going to walk by his side. Don't get me wrong, I think the guy's a douche and all, but there's enough guilt and pain in this world already, and I have a feeling that there's going to be a lot more to come before our time is up.

His eyes are on his feet, and his hands are deep in his pockets and not on his weapons. He looks pale and haunted as he takes a deep shaky breath and closes his eyes. I flinch as one of the doors to his left swings open and a zombie crashes out into the hallway.

It dives for Duncan, and before he can pull his hands from his pockets and reach for his guns to shoot it, it starts to bite into the side of his face. I stare in horror as its dirty hands clasp his skull tightly. It bites down and pulls back, its teeth clinging onto the flesh from Duncan's cheek in its mouth. Duncan screams and hits out at it, and I stand frozen to the spot, unable to do anything but watch as the situation unfolds.

Mikey pushes past me, sending me crashing into a wall as he raises up his machete and brings it down in one swift movement to decapitate the zombie.

Duncan drops to his knees with one hand clutching his face, and trying to stem the flow of blood that's pumping from the wound. He's sobbing and moaning, tears, snot, and blood streaming down his face.

My only thought? *If I would have walked just a little bit slower, that would have been me.*

TWENTY TWO

Mikey helps Duncan up and simultaneously shouts for Crunch to bring the first aid kit. She obliges, dragging out various bandages and creams from the little bag on her back as we all run. We head down the corridor until we reach the canteen and JD drags a couple of chairs away from a table and helps Mikey get Duncan up on it.

They pull Duncan's hand away from his wound and Crunch squirts some liquid into and over the wound without hesitation, bringing about another long, painful scream from Duncan. He thrashes and fights to put his hands to his face, but Mikey and JD stop him.

Crunch leans over further and inspects the hole in his cheek. Reaching for some tweezers, she digs into it and retrieves a tooth, and then squirts the liquid into the hole again, being careful not to get any of it into his eyes.

"Nina, get over here, I need your help." Crunch doesn't bother to look at me, but continues to dig through her bag.

I make my way from the doorway to the group in small steps. I have no idea how we change into zombies. What if it's through a bite and he's going to change at any moment? I don't want to be near him.

"I mean it; get your ass over here, now!" She finally looks up at me, her nostrils flaring at my slowness. There must be something in my look that makes her calm down though. "It's okay, we just need to stop the bleeding and clean the cut. He'll be fine." She stands and looks at me, and I nod and make my way to her, still wary.

"I need you to squirt some more saline into the cut while I prepare some sterile gauze for it. I can't suture it until it stops bleeding, or at least slows."

I pause with a shaky hand on the bottle. "Will this save him?"

"Maybe," she shrugs. "It'll clear the wound of any surface pathogens and debris, and hopefully…" she pauses and takes a deep breath, "and hopefully save him, but I'm not promising shit. This is basically just a cleaner for the wound; I'd need a lot more equipment to go making promises."

I do as she asks, and when Duncan starts to scream again, JD Looks at Crunch and she nods. Before I can ask what the look was all about, JD punches Duncan hard and knocks him out cold.

Crunch leans over, pressing hard onto his face with some gauze. My jaw hangs low as I look from her to JD.

"The more he panics, the harder it is to stop the bleeding," she replies casually.

I nod and look away, a shiver running down my spine. Mikey runs over to one of the doors and starts barricading it so that nothing can follow us in, and JD moves to the door at the back of the room and does the same thing.

"Nina, I need you to hold this in place."

I reach over with shaky hands, trading places with her and holding the gauze against his sticky skin. "Okay."

"Press harder," she snaps.

I nod. Crunch tips her bag out and rummages through all the bits and pieces for something—a needle and a strange-looking thread, by the looks of it. I look down at Duncan. His eyes are rolled back into his head, and his breathing is shallow. The blood has stopped pumping from between my fingers now, and Mikey uses his sleeve to wipe some of it away from Duncan's eyes and nose.

Crunch stands by my side with the needle and thread in hand. "Okay, lift it up and let me see."

I lift up the gauze, which sticks to him a little as I pull it up. It breaks free, releasing a small spurt of fresh blood, but it stops after a second or two and then just oozes. The bite is deep, but thankfully not as bad as I first thought. It seems to be just surface skin and not the deeper flesh; however, it does look swollen and unhealthy. The sight makes me feel queasy again and I'm glad I don't have to look at it anymore, however mean that may seem. I hold the gauze in place while Crunch tapes it. Crunch puts her fingers to Duncan's wrist and does some weird counting thing with her eyes closed before placing his arm back down next to him.

"Well?" JD asks.

She looks worried, but shrugs in her nonchalant way and lowers the needle and thread. "He should be fine as long as an infection doesn't set in. I've cleaned it the best I could, and I'm going to stick a couple of sutures in it since the deader took a lot of flesh." Crunch readies her needle while she talks, and I turn away. "We need to find a lot more antiseptic cream, gauze, painkillers. We're going to need to go back to the medic's room again."

"Okay, I'll go get the medical supplies. Crunch, see what you can do for Duncan. Mikey, you and Nina stay here. Try and see what's left here—and be on your guard, we haven't cleared this room yet." JD storms off to the door without another word. Crunch quickly zips up her bag and follows after him with her weapons in hand.

I look at Duncan on the table. His breathing is shallow, his skin sweaty. I still don't want to get too near him, so I walk away, heading for the kitchens, carrying my small machete.

Mikey catches up to me. Neither of us talk as we clear the room, and then the kitchen area, checking under tables and behind doors for any lurkers. Zombies aren't known for their sneaking, though, so I think we're good for now. Other than a few bloody bones and old blood patches, there are no live deaders—huh, that sounds weird.

I check the pantry, and even when I see it half full of food, I can't smile. I had come so close to death, or at the very least serious injury, that I feel a bit shocked. And poor Duncan. Shit, what if he dies? I pause in my search, lean against one of the boxes of cans, and take a breath or two to calm myself down. Mikey comes into the pantry and looks at me.

"You okay?"

I nod my head yes, and rub a hand across my sweaty forehead. Why this incident scared me so much, I don't know. It's not like I haven't been nearly killed by these things before; I've been fighting them all day. But I guess the truth of the matter is that I felt safe around this group, and it all came as such a fucking shock to the system. One minute we seemed badass and unstoppable, and the next a deader was taking an afternoon snack from Duncan's face.

"I'm fine." I take a steadying breath.

"Crazy shit, huh?" Mikey turns back around and examines the

food and water on the shelves.

"Crazy is one way to put it." I start checking the boxes by my feet, wanting the distraction. "Do you think he'll be okay?"

"I guess so. I mean, I hope so. He's kept us all alive the past year or so, and he's a nice guy, you know?" Mikey opens up a box of cereal bars, tearing one open and shoving it in his mouth greedily.

"Yeah, I guess." I catch the bar he throws me. "It was kind of a dick move locking everyone in here, though, don't you think?"

Mikey shrugs. "Yeah, but then—we all make mistakes. I mean, no one's perfect."

"But his mistake cost a lot of people their lives." I rip open my wrapper and take a big bite. It tastes like shit, but it's food.

Mikey stares at me for a long minute before replying. "So, even if someone tried to make up for their mistakes, you saying they don't deserve a second chance?" He scrunches up his wrapper and throws it to the floor, looking pissed off.

"That's not what I was saying at all, it's just that..." I huff. "He condemned everyone in here to die. He fucking locked the door on them."

"Who says they weren't condemned anyway? Who says we're all not condemned?"

"Whatever, Mikey, I'm not in the mood to argue with you today." I have no idea what crawled up his ass, but I'm too tired and worried to fight him. There are other things way more important going on.

"I'm just saying that he made a mistake, a mistake that he feels guilty enough for. The last thing that he needs is everyone hating on him. He's spent the last couple of years trying to make up for what he did."

I jump when I feel Mikey close behind me, and when I turn and am met with his angry glare, I'm even more confused.

I scowl at him. "How has he tried to make it up? He spent the last however long trying to keep you all away from this place, away from putting these poor people out of their misery!"

"You don't fucking know him enough to comment on this shit, Nina."

"No, and clearly I don't fucking know you either."

"Clearly!" His jaw grinds.

We stand there staring at each other, both of us waiting for the other to say something else. Anger burns within me. I know—I fucking *know*—he gets where I'm coming from, so why he's acting so self-righteous all of a sudden, I don't know.

"Mikey? Nina?" Crunch's voice sounds out from in the kitchen.

I push away from the shelf behind me and walk past Mikey. His hand brushes my waist, making me turn and stare. I shrug away from him with another angry glare.

"We're here," I say coming out of the pantry and passing Crunch.

She eyes me icily, her eyes straying behind me as Mikey emerges from the pantry too.

"Find anything interesting?" she spits out.

"Crunch," Mikey warns, but I don't stick around to see what else they say.

JD is sorting through some supplies on a table next to where Duncan is. Duncan has finally woken and is now sitting up. He offers me a small grimace as I come over.

"How you doing?" I ask.

"It hurts like a bitch, but I'll live," he smiles. "I *will* live, won't I, JD?" He turns to look at JD, who's shaking out two painkillers into his hand.

"Yes. Crunch seems to think so. We just need to keep it dressed

182

and clean, and hope that it doesn't get infected." He hands Duncan the tablets and a small flask to drink from. "If it gets infected, then…"

Duncan throws the tablets in his mouth and takes a swig from the flask, gasping as he swallows. He looks at the flask and then at JD with a crooked, bloody half-grin.

"Found your stash on the way back, my friend. Thought you could use it right about now."

"Didn't even notice what you gave me." Duncan places his hand on JD's shoulder and attempts to smile again, taking another long swig with the other. "Thank you, that softens the blow, I guess."

JD looks away with a shake of his his head. We have all noticed that his bandages have started to soak through with blood again.

"I'm a goner if this gets infected, right?" Duncan screws the lid back on his flask. "Yeah, that's it." He lies back down and closes his eyes.

JD looks behind me as Crunch storms out of the kitchen area, Mikey close behind.

I turn to look. "We found the walk-in pantry. It's pretty much full. There's more than enough food to keep us going for…well, quite a long time." I shrug.

"What's the plan then?" Mikey asks. He doesn't look at me, and that just opens up a whole new bag of weird emotions.

"How are you feeling, Duncan? Do you feel well enough to continue? Or do you want us to head back to camp? We can come back another day and finish this off." JD seems to have a lot of respect for Duncan. I hadn't noticed that until now.

"We've come this far, we should finish it," Duncan replies coldly. "Just give me half an hour for the painkillers to kick in first."

I look outside and see that the sun is beginning to dip. "We won't make it back before nightfall, even if we set off now. That means spending the night here." Everyone follows my gaze, and I guess we all come to the same conclusion. "We could continue tomorrow," I suggest.

JD nods once in agreement. "Mikey, you and I need to find something better than just a couple of tables to jam the doors. We can all eat and sleep without worrying about any of them coming in and catching us unaware. Tomorrow we finish this." He looks at us all, one by one. "We finish them all."

We all nod and set about our tasks. "I'll go scrounge up something we can have to eat," I say as I make my way to the kitchen.

"I'll help," Crunch replies coldly, and follows close behind.

"I guess I'll just sit here on my own then," Duncan retorts through gritted teeth.

"You do that," both Crunch and I reply at the same time.

TWENTY THREE

I'm on edge as we raid the pantry for any sort of meal, waiting for Crunch to say something shitty to me like normal. Or maybe I'm on edge because we're stuck in a building with a bunch of deaders.

I know the pantries are well stocked with cereal bars and energy drinks, but upon further inspection, there are also dried grains, pastas, and rice, which all seems to have lasted fairly well. There are also cans of beans and cold meats, all of which we can use. Somehow, we have to get this all back to our little tree house; it's going to be a pain in the ass, but it will be worth it. I'm getting used to living in the safety of the trees. With the right tools, more harnesses, and some extra weapons, we could make it even better; and this food will help secure our future for the next couple of months.

Months? Jesus, life is short these days.

We find a couple of boxes of ration packs in the walk-in pantry and take them to the group. Sure, a hot meal would go down nicely, but until the place is completely cleared of deaders, it's best to keep things as simple and as quiet as possible. We eat them cold and straight from the package, squeezing the liquidy mush directly into our mouths—which is disgusting, but it's food, and my stomach is grateful even if my taste buds aren't.

The meat and potato stew I have settles well in my stomach, and combined with the freeze-dried coffee (that JD insists we actually can take the risk to heat up without making too much noise), my body is in sensation overload, being so full of food and caffeine. Bliss. I guess it's the little things these days that really make life worth living.

Duncan's bandages have soaked through quite badly, and he seems unsettled with the pain no matter how tough he's pretending to be. What did we expect, though? A zombie took a chunk out of his face; that's bound to stress anybody out. Crunch works on suturing his face together the best she can, but if I'm honest, the job is ugly and will leave a terrible scar. Still, I guess if he lives, that's better than nothing. I have avoided being in close proximity to him for the last hour or so, so when he takes some more painkillers and goes to lie down in the corner of the room for a nap, I take the opportunity to voice my concerns.

"So is anyone going to talk about the elephant in the room, or are we just going to let him pick us off unexpectedly tonight, chowing down on our brains while we sleep?" I throw my empty ration pack onto the table in front of me and reach for another of the silver-foiled delights from the box by my feet.

"He'll be fine," Crunch replies without fully acknowledging my comment or me.

"How do we know that the virus or mutation or whatever causes people to turn into zombies isn't passed by saliva or bites and things? I mean, that's how it's done in all the movies."

"We don't know for certain, but we think that it is just death itself that causes people to…you know…want to eat brains and shit." Mikey is biting his nails again and I shudder. He has somehow washed his hands free of blood and grime from their earlier battles, but the thought of any of the zombie stuff getting into my mouth makes me nauseous.

"Will you get your hands out of your mouth, Mikey? For God's sake, they have all sorts of…well, you know, zombie germs all over them." I put my second pack of food down, suddenly not feeling hungry.

"I told you, it doesn't seem to be passed that way."

"I don't care. It could mutate, it could be slow-developing. And besides that, it's disgusting, so stop it," I huff.

He finally removes his hands from his mouth and leans back in his chair with a raised eyebrow. "Better?"

"Not really," I reply. "So? What are we going to do?"

"We told you: it will be fine. He will be fine. You just have to trust us on this, Nina."

"But…"

"Oh will you stop your whining?" Crunch snaps. "Seriously, Nina. Go back to camp if you're so worried about him. Because we are not leaving him behind."

"I wasn't suggesting that we leave him behind," I reply darkly.

Wasn't I? What the hell was *I suggesting then?*

"Well we're not killing him either," Crunch hisses at me angrily. "He's our friend, more than can be said for you."

"This isn't about friendships, Crunch, this is about survival. And I wasn't suggesting killing him, either. I don't know *what* I'm saying. I just think that we need to watch him, in case he turns into one of them."

Mikey leans forward in his chair. "Ladies, calm down. You'll wake him, and he needs to rest. Nina, we don't know for certain that he won't turn, but we've all had plenty of dealings with zombies now, and I'm sure that we have had plenty of their gunk all over us. The likelihood is that some of it has gotten in us. Maybe through our mouths, or eyes, or whatever. Either way, we all seem fine..."

I try to interject, but he cuts me off.

"... also, Crunch has been bitten before. In truth it wasn't as bad as Duncan's injury, but she's fine, isn't she? She isn't some crazed zombie woman out for blood, is she?"

I look at Crunch with a smirk, and surprisingly she mirrors it.

"Well, maybe not all the time," she laughs.

JD has been silent the entire conversation. I wonder what his opinion is on the matter, but he doesn't seem like the sort of person I would want to piss off, and if he agreed with me I guess he would have said so by now. I pick my ration pack back up and continue squeezing the mush into my mouth. *Yummy.*

As night draws in, Duncan starts sweating like a fat man chasing the lunch truck, and panting heavily. So much so that JD has decided that we need someone on watch at all times, so we take it in shifts to watch him through the night. JD takes the first shift, with Crunch following him. I'm so happy that I'm not on first watch; after eating and all the exertion, I'm exhausted. I barely have time to nod and smile through a *halle-fuckin'-lujah* before I'm asleep.

By the time Crunch wakes me up I would reckon on it being around one in the morning, but who really knows. Everyone is snoring his or her little head off, and I'm not impressed about being woken up one bit. This is what it takes to be a part of a team though: teamwork. There is no '*I*' in '*team*,' as the old saying goes.

I always hated that saying.

Crunch takes my place on the floor, throwing her jacket over herself, her head resting on a small sack of rice.

I stand and stretch, feeling my joints crack and groan with the movement. I never thought I would say this, but I miss our little tree houses. I sit on one of the tables, my feet resting on a chair, and survey the room. The building has been surprisingly quiet since we killed the first horde of zombies. I can only think that the others who were trapped in here when it all went down have either gotten away or are trapped in their bedrooms as Mikey suggested. I shudder at the thought. What a horrible way to go, to starve to death. Not that there is ever a *nice* way to go, but you know what I mean. If Crunch is right and it's death that brings on animation and not a bite or something else, then once one of the survivors died from starvation, the others were all doomed anyway. Probably even too weak to try to escape or fight the deader off them. There was never any hope.

Tears fill my eyes and I rub them away stubbornly. I look around at my sleeping group. JD has his back to me, but I can see his hand wrapped around the handle of his scythe. Crunch also has her knives next to her, and she's snoring softly already. I look at Mikey and see him watching me. It's dark and I'm not sure how much of me he can actually see, but I can see him clearly. His dark eyes, his shaved head, his large shoulders. He closes his eyes and buries his face further down into his jacket.

Jesus, what's wrong with me?

I swore to myself that I wouldn't ever care about another person. Now here I am with a group of people that I'm growing increasingly fond of, looking after a young girl who I really care about, and quite possibly falling for a man I barely know. This can come to no good. No fucking good at all.

I do a lap of the room, checking through the small squares of glass in the doors to see if the corridors outside are clear, and then go to the windows, peeling back the shutters to check the outside.

All is clear and all is quiet everywhere. Zombies don't sleep, so this area must just be amazingly free of the evil things, which is strange since deaders tend to be attracted to old civilization areas. I squeeze the bridge of my nose and sigh. Though my mind is active with thoughts, my body is tired and achy from the fights won earlier. I wish there was time to train; I have a feeling that the people in this group could teach me a hell of a lot about survival.

I may still be alive years after the dead rose, but that is all down to living behind the walls, not actual skills. Sure, I've killed some deaders, but it's the same again—sheer luck. I need real skills, and I need real strength, not just dumb luck. JD and Mikey said that they see the Forgotten ones quite a bit, but I have managed to avoid contact with them so far. But for how long can that continue? I wouldn't last in a battle with another human. Deaders aren't actually that hard to fight, especially these days. They have no muscle strength, and are decomposing at a steady rate. I wonder at what point they stop, you know, being alive-dead? Their brain surely must switch off at some point.

"Could you pass me some water?" Duncan's voice cuts through my morbid thoughts and the room's silence, making me jump.

"Yes. Sorry, I didn't mean to wake you." I hand him an energy drink, and then hesitate. "Do you want your other drink? The one JD gave you."

"No thanks, this will be fine. Better save that for someone more deserving." He takes the energy drink, leans up on one arm, and takes a swig.

"More deserving?" I prompt, with only a touch of confusion.

"Yeah, someone you don't want dead." He stops what he's doing and looks at me. "I heard you earlier, sentencing me to death, Nina. Don't act so coy about it."

"I'm not being coy." I narrow my eyes at him, not that he can see it. The moonlight has gone now since I've let the blinds close tight again. "I didn't say that I wanted you dead, either. You're just jumping to conclusions."

"So, you don't want me dead then?"

"I never said that either," I whisper.

"What if I turn?"

"Then that's a different story," I reply grimly.

"Well, I'm not going to."

I swallow hard. "Good."

"I don't think." His voice cracks.

"What?"

"I don't feel right." Duncan lies back down, his eyes never leaving mine.

"What do you mean, you don't feel right?" I step back from him.

"I can't explain it. I just don't feel right."

My hand covers the weapon at my hip, but I don't grab it. Not yet. "Could be just an infection setting in," I add.

"Could be." He's still watching me. "But we both know what an infection means for me. Look, if I start to turn, Nina, you have to kill me. Don't let me become one of them, don't let me hurt anyone else." His voice chokes out on the last few words.

I nod and then realize that he can't see me, so I add an "okay" to my nod too. He closes his eyes, and is asleep again within seconds.

I muse for a minute that maybe that hadn't actually just happened, that maybe I've fallen asleep on guard and just dreamt that whole conversation. By asking me to kill him if I think he's going to turn, he's also putting me and Emily at risk. There's no way the group will let me kill him and get away with it, unless he's a full-blown deader.

There's also the other thought in my mind: Could I do it? Kill another human being—even one that is just about to turn into one of the undead and kill everyone?

TWENTY FOUR

I am the worst guard ever!

At some point in the early hours, I must have fallen asleep, because when I wake I'm curled up on top of one of the tables. Mikey is sitting in a chair by my head, his legs stretched across onto another chair, and he's watching me.

I think I surprise him when I open my eyes, because his legs slip off the chair, making it squeak along the floor, and he looks around guiltily to make sure that everyone is still sleeping.

Ha, serves him right for being creepy.

The sun seems to be only just coming up. There's an odd warm feeling to the room, or maybe it's because Mikey's dark brown eyes are still staring intently at me. Either way, the moment seems calm and relaxed for a change. I stretch and sit up.

"Sorry." I rub my shoulder back to life. "I don't even remember falling asleep." I grimace.

"No harm, no foul, right?" He smiles.

"I guess." I swing my legs over the edge of the table. "How's Duncan doing?"

"Hot and sweaty, but sleeping like a baby."

We both go over to where Duncan's sleeping, and sure as shit he's drenched in sweat and pale as a ghost. A little shiver tremors through his sleeping form every now and then.

"This doesn't look good," I say, trying to sound every bit the concerned citizen, but actually thinking about my conversation the previous night, and what the fuck I will do if I have to kill poor Duncan, other than—well, kill poor Duncan, obviously.

"He needs antibiotics, and fucking quickly by the looks of it. We need to get back to camp so I can do a run out to find some."

"I didn't see any in the garage."

"No, but there's a town about ten miles from the garage, and another one Duncan's told us about before. I need to ask him about it when he wakes up, though, since I haven't been to that one. It's somewhere across the lake, that much I do know." Mikey shrugs.

"I would have thought you would have scavenged from all the nearby towns by now," I question.

"I've only been here for six months or so. I was…somewhere else before here. Somewhere—not as welcoming," Mikey replies.

I quirk my eyebrow up at him in further question.

"I'd been alone for a long time, Nina, struggling to survive, and stumbled upon Crunch one day, strangely in that little store I found *you* in." He smiles.

I nod, and want to probe further, but my stomach gives a loud echoing rumble, and I stifle a laugh. "Okay, well, I'm going to find something for breakfast."

We make our way into the kitchen again, and scramble to put

together some sort of meal. We arm ourselves with cans of Spam, energy drinks, some more food pouches and protein bars, and make our way back into the diner just in time for everyone waking up. I can't wait to actually *cook* something with the supplies. There's pasta and rice and canned vegetables... My stomach grumbles at my meager offerings, but cold food pouches will have to suffice for now.

Crunch stands when she sees us coming out of the kitchen together. "Where have you two been?" Her eyes narrow in on me.

"Breakfast," Mikey replies as he strides past me, his arms loaded down with some of our goods.

We eat our food in silence, each of us seemingly weighed down by our own troubles. I look around at each of them between mouthfuls of—what's this that I'm eating again? I check the pack—beef stew, yeah right, and try to guess what they're thinking about. Duncan, well that's obvious: he's thinking about turning into a zombie. He looks worse than he did last night, and he's not eating, which in this world is never a good sign. You never know when you will be getting food, so you always stock yourself up on it when you do get some. JD looks like he's thinking up a plan of some kind—he usually is. Crunch is staring into her beans looking pissed off as usual, probably thinking up new ways to make me suffer. When I look at Mikey, I see him watching me with a grin that I can't help reciprocating.

We pack up our supplies after breakfast, and Crunch examines Duncan.

"What's the verdict, Doc?" Duncan jests, but I can see he's in pain and worried as hell.

"I'll be honest with you, Duncan," she sighs. "It's not good. An infection has set in, and without antibiotics, well..." Her voice trails off.

"I can make a run for some. Nina's Hummer might still be at the garage, and I can take off straight from here. I could be back before nightfall," Mikey suggests.

Crunch swallows and looks anywhere but at Duncan before replying. "I'm not sure he has that much time."

"It takes a lot longer than that for an infection to set in and kill someone, Crunch," Mikey snaps.

She shrugs, but offers no explanation. I guess we just don't know much about whatever it is that brings you back to life after you die. No one knows for sure what causes it—no one that I've ever met, anyway. From what the group said last night, it's not the bite per se that kills you, but death itself. Kind of like a 'you're a deader when you're dead' situation, not because you get infected or bitten by them, but literally because you're dead, you turn into them. Crunch's eyes finally meet Duncan's, and for a moment he seems frozen, unblinking and unmoving, before finally looking across at me with a look just short of desperation. I give the tiniest shake of my head and try to let him know that there is no way I'm killing him while he's still human. *No fucking way.* I'm not a murderer, and while he's still human, that's what it would be: murder. Why he's given me the joyous task in the first place, I have no idea, but if I can palm his plan off on someone else and get them to do the gruesome task, I sure as hell will.

Several long minutes go by before any of us speaks. What is there to say? Nothing can make that news any better, and there are a lot of questions running through everyone's heads, without a doubt. Surprisingly, it's Duncan who breaks the heady silence.

"Better get a move on and clear this place while I'm still me then, eh?" He swallows and picks up his gun.

"We should just head back to camp." JD steps forward, his hand resting on Duncan's shoulder.

Duncan shakes his head. "No way, I can't go back there if I'm—dying." He looks down sadly. "It would put everyone at risk—all of you, and the girls. Emily, Josie…Britta." He shakes his head, and a tremor ripples through his body. "Sorry, I'm just cold. No, better help you all as much as I can, while I still can. You never know, I might be all right yet." He looks at Crunch hopefully.

"Yeah." She shrugs and gives a brief but grim smile. Unfortunately I think we all see through her nonchalance.

We ready ourselves to leave the canteen with the intention of going straight to the male and female sleeping quarters. We exit through the doors at the back, and turn right, heading to the women's dorms first. I can smell the deaders inside as we reach the door, and I chance a glance at the rest of the group. Barring Duncan, they all seem to carry the same grim determination on their faces. Duncan just seems to be trying to keep his pain under control, and I wonder if it was a good idea to bring him along after all. He lifts his guns up ready to shoot and looks me in the eye with a shaky breath and a nod to let me know he's okay, but I don't think he is. He seems to be falling fast.

The door is solid with no windows to look through, and as Duncan predicted, it's locked from the inside. Bloody handprints, however, do cover the outside of the door, with long gouge marks and even a couple of what look like broken fingernails wedged into the wood of the door frame. I check behind us and see that Crunch has us covered.

"Shoot it open, Duncan," JD orders, and we all step to one side.

Duncan fires at the handle and blows it away. The noise is loud and echoes along the corridor, and we all wait to see if anything is going to come and greet us with all the noise we just made. There's no sound coming from anywhere, though, so JD kicks it in and we're confronted with an empty room. We enter and scout it out, knowing that something is in here, somewhere.

"Found it," Mikey shouts out from one of the bathrooms. He comes out and shuts the door behind him. "Found what was left of it anyway."

"Eaten?" Duncan asks, coming forward forlornly.

Mikey shakes his head. "No, she ended it."

Duncan opens the door to the bathroom and goes inside. He's in there for several minutes before he comes back out, looking worse than when he went in.

"I think that's Chrissy. She was a good girl, hard worker. She had kids and a husband."

Even from where I'm standing I can see the tears fill his eyes. He's sweating, and I guess it must be taking all of his control not to break down. After all, this was his fault; he sealed their fate when he locked them all in. Shit, I have to stop doing that. What's done is done, like Mikey said.

The rest of the room is clear, so we move on to the men's dorm. It's near the gym, which we check and clear on the way, finding it both covered in blood and disturbingly empty at the same time.

The men's room is locked also, and Duncan happily shoots out the lock on it, seemingly finding some sort of release in shooting things. Who can blame him? JD kicks in the door, and we follow him in, jumping straight into the action as zombies on all sides move toward us with hungry, frustrated growls. I try to count how many there are, but it all seems to be happening too quickly. I kick out at a particularly nasty-looking deader with eyeballs that seem to swivel in their sockets. Its putrid jaw hangs low to its chest as it approaches, and I can see right into the back of its throat. It's like a black, cavernous hole—leading into a cesspool of rotted flesh, by the funky smell of its breath.

I grimace and slash my—sorry, Mikey's—machete across its neck. Well actually it hits its shoulder, but the second slash *definitely* hits the neck! Its head lolls uselessly to one side at an awkward angle, and the lips of the deader continue to work as it moves forward again to grab me. It lets out a throaty groan, like I've just given it a sensual back massage and not tried to lop its head off like I was She-Ra. I swing and hit it again, this time cutting through the rotten, swollen flesh on its neck, releasing yet more toxic gases and black gunk, which splatters my face. The deader's head falls to the floor like a lead weight, quickly followed by its body, which lands with a loud *splat*. It would actually be kind of comical if it wasn't for the splash-back of gore that I get up my legs.

Fucking deaders. I grimace, wiping my face with my sleeve.

Everyone does their part to dispatch of the ugly deaders in their own way, slashing, shooting, and in JD's case, generally fucking the deaders up a bit with his fists and boots before finally killing them. I sit on the end of a bunk trying to catch my breath once the job is done. Stringy sinew and gore cover the floor, and the smell just about turns my stomach over, but since I'm covered in the crap, there's no way to escape the smell, even if I just up and left. Mikey goes to check the bathroom, but comes back without the morbid news he gave us previously.

We did it: we took back the hub. I want to smile, but the feeling seems hollow somehow as I look at the bodies scattered around my feet. All these people—dead. I look to the man partly responsible for their deaths—certainly for making their deaths all the more horrific—and cringe.

Something about Duncan gives me a fresh sense of foreboding. Is it the glazed-over look in his eyes? The sweat glistening on his forehead and the grayness to his skin? Nope, I think it's the hungry look he has on his face while he looks us all over, like we're prime ribs with extra seasoning.

"Uh, Duncan?" I whisper.

He licks his lips with nervous appreciation, and I stand and back-step away from the bunk.

"Duncan?" My hand reaches for the machete at my waist, the previous night's words echoing in my mind. *'Don't let me turn into one of them, Nina.'*

"Sorry, dude," I whisper.

I look around at everyone else, but only Mikey seems to have caught on to my concern. His eyes are watching Duncan with an unhappy but determined frown set in them, and before I can do or say anything else, Duncan lunges toward Crunch with a growl, grabbing her neck with one clumsy hand and raking his nails around it, breaking the skin. Blood oozes out of the cuts, and the smell of the fresh blood spurs him on more; he opens his mouth wide, ready to take a bite of Crunch á la sandwich.

Mikey steps forward, his large machete raised and still full of black gore from his previous kills, and as Crunch ducks out of Duncan's grasp, Mikey swings hard and slices into his head. His skull cracks between his eyes, much like a coconut being split down the middle, with blood and black fluid oozing from the gap Mikey just made. Duncan's mouth continues to move, his teeth snapping away at the air. His eyes still glare at us, but are completely off balance because of the fissure in the middle of his face. Mikey cries out as tears pour from his eyes, and he swings again, slicing his blade into the opening until he hits rapidly graying brain matter. Mercifully, Duncan stops moving, his body going stiff and then falling to the floor like his batteries have just been taken out. My stomach creases in a bout of overwhelming emotions, and I struggle to stay upright.

Crunch screams—not a long, bloodcurdling one; I guess it's more of a yelp—and I flinch and stumble further away. Blood has sprayed up onto Mikey's face like something out of a horror movie, and my hand covers my mouth as I try to contain my own scream, tears, and god knows what else.

"WHAT THE FUCK JUST HAPPENED?" JD spins around and simultaneously shouts at us all, trying to figure out who did what and to whom.

His eyes finally land on Duncan's body, which lies in a crumpled heap on the floor, his blood spilling out of the deep gouge down the middle of his head in a weird mixture of black and red.

Crunch's hand gingerly touches her neck where Duncan had gripped her. Blood is oozing out of the long finger slices across her neck, but thankfully it doesn't look too serious. Mikey sheaths his machete and holds up his hands in defense.

"He turned." Mikey says, his voice like steel. But his eyes...his eyes say everything about how he feels. He reaches down and picks up Duncan's guns. "He turned."

TWENTY FIVE

JD grimly nods, his face tight with anger and pain, and he takes one of the guns that Mikey hands him, hooking it into the waistband of his jeans. He acts tough and unmoved by the situation, but like Mikey, he too has a tell; his pursed lips reveal to me (and anyone who cares to notice) how hard he's finding it.

Mikey turns to me. "Can you shoot?" His brown eyes burrow into mine, and I can tell that he wants to reach out to me, but doesn't. His nonchalance seems only surface deep.

I nod, still at a loss for words, yet deeply grateful that I didn't have to kill Duncan myself. No one would have believed me when I said he had turned, especially Crunch. My thoughts stray to what Duncan had been like on our way through all the rooms. Why hadn't we noticed him changing? He *died,* for fuck's sake. How do you die while walking? I wouldn't have believed that was even possible if it weren't for what just happened. And how the hell did we not know it was happening—right under our noses, for God's sake! How long had *he*

202

known that he was turning into one of them? Last night he said he felt different, but turning into one of the undead is more than just a little bit 'different.'

"Nina?"

I look at Mikey and he offers me a small smile. It's then that I realize he must have heard my conversation with Duncan last night. It's the only reason for him taking over the situation so quickly. He just killed his friend to help me. Yeah, yeah, it helped all of us in the end, but he did it so I wouldn't have to, so that I wouldn't make any more of an enemy out of Crunch. I smile back, glad that at least he wants me to stick around, but also concerned as to how I get myself into these situations in the first place. I'm like a magnet for bad shit happening.

"I'm no hot-shot with it, but yeah, I know how to point and shoot." I take the gun from him and make myself comfortable with it, testing its weight in my palm and checking how to load and fire it like I have previously been shown, and then tuck it safely in my jeans. Mikey offers the shotgun to Crunch, but she declines with a shake of her head.

"I'm better with my Kukris." Her voice is low, brooding almost, and she doesn't bother to catch his eye. Her clothes, like Mikey's, are covered in blood—Duncan's blood. There are sprays of it across her tight, ripped jeans and black tank top, and a large streak of it covering one side of her face, which she hasn't bothered to wipe off yet, giving her appearance a two-tone look.

"Right, well now what?" My voice comes out harsher than I mean it to, receiving a crappy look from Crunch in return.

"Now what? Is that it? Is that all you have to say? Our friend is dead. Someone that cared about us all. He cooked for us, helped us to survive, and all you can say is 'now what?' What the fuck is wrong with you, Nina?"

She's right, of course. It *is* harsh, it *is* uncaring, but this is our reality. We're not in fucking Disneyland anymore. Someone in our group turned and would have gladly eaten us all if we hadn't taken him out first. That's the reality of it. We can mourn later, but right now we need to go. Of course, by the look on her face I can tell she knows this, but it's a great excuse to have another dig at me.

"Yeah, now what?" I shrug.

Crunch comes forward abruptly, a hand raising up one of her knives. I step forward and match her knife with my own in defense, my stomach twisting into knots.

Mikey dives between us and pushes us apart, one hand on either of us to keep us separated. I glare at her, my mouth twisting into a grimace, and I back away.

"All right, ladies. That's enough." He eyes Crunch more than me, since she started it.

"Nina's right." We all look to JD. He's kneeling by Duncan's head. He places a hand over Duncan's eyes and shuts them before standing back up with a deep sigh. "There's nothing we can do for him now, but survive. He would have wanted that."

I almost want to stick my tongue out at Crunch. Almost, but if looks could kill, I'm pretty sure I would be toast already, so I keep my trap shut for now like a good little girl.

"We need to get what we came for and get back to the others." JD eyes Crunch, his hand touching her shoulder affectionately. "I'm going to miss him too, but we can mourn him once we're all together and safe."

Crunch nods, but I don't miss the evil glare I get from her as she leaves with JD. Mikey grabs my hand, holding me back until we're out of earshot.

"Are you okay?" Mikey's hand touches my shoulder.

I try to shrug him off me, but he grips me harder. "I'm fine, Mikey. I survived without you all these years, you know." I ignore the hurt look on his face. "I'm not some feeble woman that you need to keep protecting."

I pull away from him, but his hands catch me around the waist when I try to leave and he spins me back to him, our chests bumping together.

"Don't do that."

I look up at him, our close proximity making me a little breathless. "Do what?"

"Act like you don't give a shit about what just happened—that you don't give a shit about me."

I don't know what to say to that. I want to tell him I *don't* give a shit, but we both know I would be lying. I bite my bottom lip in thought, wondering what I can say that will explain how I feel about him without being a total jerk. Well, any more of a jerk than I already have been.

His hand comes up and tugs my lip free, and he looks at me before leaning in, slowly at first, and then quicker once he sees my fight-or-flight response kick in. He kisses me abruptly, and I push back at him, my body simultaneously betraying me as I groan into the warmth of his mouth, his hands curling into the back of my hair. My lips press roughly against his, hungry almost, and with that thought I finally pull out of his kiss and stare at him, feeling confused. My eyes stay tightly locked on his bloody face while I try to work through my feelings.

I swallow hard, saying the first thing that comes to mind: "You need to brush your teeth." I pull out of his hold, and whether I catch him off guard or he lets me go of his own choice I don't know, but I'm glad that I don't have to explain myself. At least for now.

We reach camp by late afternoon, after packing some food up for the others into our backpacks. We each grab either a harness or a weapon, making the journey back to camp all the more uncomfortable with all the heavy gear. This is why we went through all this, though, and there will be plenty more trips like this in the next few weeks if we want to salvage anything useful from the hub and make the stay up in the trees more comfortable.

Britta is devastated by the loss of Duncan, though she doesn't actually say very much, preferring to keep herself busy with cooking and feeding everyone, seemingly taking over his role. Several times I catch her staring off in to an empty space, her lower lip trembling as she stirs the food in silence. I had known that there was something between them, but honestly hadn't been sure exactly what. Until now, that is.

JD makes me think of what Lee should have been like as a leader. How he should have ruled, and looked after the people behind the walls. Instead, he chose to look after himself, feeling that it was more important that everyone knew he was the big boss man than to actually be a real leader and protect the needy.

It's a true test of character when you have the opportunity that he did, and it's a test he failed. Once the government collapsed and help wasn't being sent anymore, chaos broke out and Lee found his true feet. He was a disciplinarian through and through, but one that bent the rules to his own advantage. A vicious tyrant of a man, not the sort of person that you would want to protect you. He proved that in the years that followed. However, once he had a couple of people on board with his plan, receiving their share of the bounty, everyone else fell in line. What choice did we all have? It was either do as we were told or be thrown out. No one wanted to die, at least not a death that we would be coming back from. A real death, at times, would have been a blessing.

JD is settled in front of the fire, his arm around Josie. The group is quiet, and deep in thought, but looking forward to going back over to the hub tomorrow and getting yet more supplies. Britta seems as broken as Crunch over what happened to Duncan, but at least she doesn't seem to have taken the fact that he got bitten and turned into one of the undead out on me. Unlike Crunch, who seems to still be brooding about my comment from before, and has taken an even bigger dislike to me; or maybe she's just using it as an excuse to hate me even more. I couldn't really give a shit, but the fact is that living in such close proximity means there's no escaping each other when the shit goes down.

Mikey has been trying to get me alone all night; every time I stand to go to my hut, he stands too. Emily is another one that's hardly left my side since we got back. I can't help but be offended that she thought perhaps I wouldn't come back. I've gotten us this far, surely she should have a little more faith in me. I could really do with some space; time to think about everything that's happened this last week and what it all means.

Britta comes and sits down next to me. *Yay, another leech.*

"Nina, I'm going down to the lake to wash up. Would you come with me and keep watch, please?"

I cringe at my nasty thoughts and force a smile at her.

"Sure." I turn to Emily. "Do you want to come?" Both of us could do with a decent wash, especially me. I'm still covered in the grime from the dead, after only a cursory cleanse. I've changed clothes, but these smell bad too—hell, all my stuff smells bad.

She nods and follows us, climbing down after me.

The lake is bitterly cold, even with the sun warming it, but it's a great thing to be getting clean. It's the simple things in life that I miss: clean water, fresh breath, and a hot cup of coffee. I don't have the coffee, but I have the toothbrush and toothpaste that I stole from Old Man Riely's house and the freezing lake, so two out of three ain't bad.

In the center there's a small man-made island, and we swim over to it and all strip out of our filthy clothes, washing them in the water with a bar of soap and then lying them flat out to dry. I dive under the water, letting the cold bite at every part of me, reminding me that I'm still alive. My hair is filthy and I think it's about time I cut it short and made it more manageable. I untie it from its knotty bun and rinse it in the water, scrubbing at my scalp and pulling my fingers through the black tangles with a satisfying groan. I grab the shampoo that I stole from the women's dorm in the hub and scrub my scalp till I think it might bleed, wanting to wash out every bit of the last couple of years. As if this will make a difference. Of course I know it won't, but by God, it will be damn good to smell like something floral for a change.

Yeah, these are the things that I'm thinking about. Vain? Yes, but even when the world has gone to shit, you can't help but want to look your best—even if your best still looks like crap. I guess it reminds you of your previous life, when you took everything for granted, like having a new toothbrush and some toilet paper. I dunk myself under the water, holding my breath for as long as possible before I come to the surface gasping.

I look around, watching Emily for a couple of minutes, swimming and looking as equally happy as I am about getting clean. When all the crap is washed from her face, she looks even less like her age. A young woman and not a child anymore. She's missed out on so much: a childhood, a family, prom. I snort to myself. Of course these things seem petty in comparison to what other people have lost, but it's kids that I feel the most sorry for. They have lost so much more, and for them it must be even harder to come to grips with. What the fuck do I know? Maybe it's easier for their minds. They never really got to see the world pre-apocalypse. For a lot of them, this is all they know. Now that's a dark fucking thought.

"Emily?" I shout over to her. When she looks at me, I hold up the bottle of shampoo, giving it a little taunting shake, and she smiles even wider. I throw it to her and she catches it with a happy laugh.

My eyes scan the surrounding banks and catch a movement at the shoreline. A lone zombie has spotted us and somehow seems to know that it can't go into the water to get to us. That's something that I never thought about before—zombies, can they swim? Clearly not. You learn something new every day. I grab my machete and swim toward the bank. It's difficult going with the water pushing against the machete, and I have to move quickly to stop myself from being cut by the sharp edge. When I get within a couple of feet of the deader, I let myself sink underneath the water and come up closer to it, stepping out in all my naked-assed glory with my machete in hand. It groans and smacks its chops together, its hands reaching for me before I raise my machete high and drop it down across the top of its skull, surprising myself when it makes a clean shot and the deader's bloated body collapses to the ground.

I stare down, looking into its eyes that look right back up at me.

They're empty and lost of any color, and now match its rotten, graying skin. A scruffy beard hangs from its chin, with patches missing from it, and most of its teeth are broken and smashed away. Unlike many zombies, this one was still has all of its appendages intact, but they aren't in good shape. The bones are visible in the fingers, the flesh obviously becoming too thin and weak to contain the bones underneath them when they grabbed for stuff. The deader is in overalls, which were once probably a rich royal blue, but are now a mixture of dried blood and black sludge. Its nametag says *James*. It hits me hard that I feel nothing for him—nothing at all. No sympathy, no hate, just a blank void where emotions should be. This poor man—whoever he once was—is dead, and I couldn't give a shit about it. How did I get like this, so unmoved by death?

"Hey."

I startle and look up as Mikey comes out from behind some trees, his eyes scanning the lake and shoreline and then returning to wash over me with a greedy appreciation.

Pervert. I can't help but smile.

I blush and step into the water to hide some of my nakedness, the water barely covering my breasts as I stay close enough to the shore to talk to him.

"Hey." I stare back, wondering what he's going to do. My body wants him to get undressed and join me, and not because he could do with a good scrub himself, though he could. His clothes are covered in dried blood and filth, as are his face and hands. However, I couldn't give a damn about any of that; it's him that I want near me. My own feelings for him are confusing. After all this time, why I'm suddenly feeling a connection to another man, I don't know. But I am, and the craving for him—for his touch—keeps growing, despite my best efforts to fight it.

"That was some crazy shit over there, huh?" He scratches the back of his neck and smiles almost shyly at me, trying to keep eye contact and not stare at my nakedness below the water.

"Sure was. I don't think I've made any new friends either." I smile, leaning my head back and letting the water wash over it.

Mikey crosses his arms across his chest, making his muscles flex beneath the thin material, and now it's my turn to swallow. "Don't worry about Crunch, she hates everyone—especially anyone I like." He laughs lightly and then swallows hard, seemingly nervous of little old me all of a sudden.

An alarm is going off in my mind, and I put all thoughts of a naked Mikey to rest and dig deeper.

"Me in particular." I stare him down.

Mikey shrugs, but offers no explanation. Yeah, we both know that to be true.

"Did you two have a thing going at one time? If I'm stepping on someone's toes or something, I think I deserve to know." I've already guessed that they did, but want him to finally tell me. Nothing has happened between us yet, but I can feel it growing between us. Blossoming, as fucking cliché as that sounds.

Mikey looks away from me, checking the trees behind him for movements before replying.

"We did at one time, but not recently."

"Right, and is that by her choice or yours?" I narrow my eyes at him, feeling vulnerable in my naked state and not sexy at all anymore.

He shrugs, but again doesn't answer.

"So it was your choice then?" Okay, this isn't anything that I hadn't already guessed, but it seems like there's more to this.

He looks at me, his brown eyes boring into mine, and then I get it. I finally get it.

"Because of me?" I huff. *Well this makes more sense now.*

Mikey nods and rubs the back of his neck, looking like little boy lost.

"No point in being all coy about it now, Mikey. I would have appreciated the heads up though," I snap, though why I'm angry, I don't really know. She had no claim on him, and neither do I, and if he broke up with her when I came along, then at least he tried to do the right thing. But I am mad at him, and at myself.

"I'm sorry. I didn't know what to say. Me and Crunch, it wasn't like this," he gestures between us. "It was mutually convenient. Or so I thought. I guess I didn't realize that she actually liked me so much until after you came to stay with us and I dumped her..." He trails off at the look on my face.

"No wonder she hates my guts! You used her and then dumped her for me." I hit the water angrily, making it splash around me.

"We used each other," he snaps back.

"Jesus! Were you that certain I was a done deal, Mikey? Do I come across as an easy lay to you?"

Mikey steps forward, the toes of his boots dipping in the water. "No, of course not. I just..."

"What? You thought you'd set things up on the long shot, eh?" The looks that JD and Mikey have been exchanging all make sense now, and my cheeks flush with embarrassment.

"Nina. If I would have known...I..." He rubs his hands down his face. "I like you, Nina. I knew that there was something about you when I met you, so when I got back here I broke it off with her. Shit, it's not like we were even dating, we just messed around from time to time. No big deal."

"You were fuck-buddies in your eyes, but to her it was obviously more than that. And it was a big enough deal that you didn't warn me," I snap.

"What do you want me to say? It's not like anything has happened between me and you either. When would be the right time to bring up some shit which doesn't seem relevant anyway? To me it wasn't anything special—to me it was just sex." He stares at me hard.

"That's the problem with men like you," I complain. "You don't think past your dicks. You used her and I won't let you use me." I turn and swim back to the little island, ignoring him shouting for me to come back.

As if there wasn't enough crap going on in the world to worry about, now I have to stress over crazy ex-girlfriends too.

Suppertime is a quiet affair. Britta's cooked a lovely meal for us, but it's a sad thing when there's an empty chair around the table. Sure, there's one less mouth to feed, but there's also less conversation. We eat, but without much conviction or appreciation for the food. I thank Britta and head off to bed with Emily in tow, my thoughts a tumble of Duncan, Crunch, and Mikey, and all those poor bastards that died over at the hub.

"Are you okay, Nina?" Emily climbs into bed after taking her shoes off—scruffy little ankle boots that are nearly falling apart. I make a mental note to try to find her some new ones when we go over to the hub.

"Yeah, Emily. It's just hard being here sometimes." I unlace my Doc Martens and smile, my thoughts wandering to Ben as they always do when I take off my boots.

"Hard? Why?" She snuggles down under her dirty blanket, and I make another mental note to take it to the lake at some point and wash it for her, or at least see if I can pick her up a new one.

"Being around people…behind the walls, it was horrific." I climb onto my bunk, curling up on my side to watch her. She nods and I continue. "You know what it was like, you were there too. It was supposed to be a sanctuary, a place for people to go and be safe."

"So what happened?" She looks genuinely confused. I guess it sort of happened overnight: one day we were safe, the next we were being raped and beaten.

I swallow the bitter taste in my mouth before I continue. "When the government collapsed, I guess they stopped helping. There was no food, no first aid, no weapons. It must have been happening for weeks; we just didn't realize it. The towns behind the walls had to learn to take care of themselves, and someone had to be in charge and make the rules…"

"Why? Why couldn't everyone just get along?" Tears brim in her eyes.

"Because it's human nature to want to control others, to be in charge—to rule. If people won't fall in line, I guess they're classed as a liability."

"With great power comes great responsibility," Emily whispers.

I snort. "Yeah, that's true. Spiderman had it right all along, Em." We both pause on my nickname for her. She smiles at me, accepting of it, and I continue.

"Being here with other people, people that care and help out, I guess I just sort of panic. It's been a long time since I trusted someone. People turned bad behind the walls, everyone out for themselves. I find it hard here because if I want to keep you safe I have to let my guard down and trust these people. I have to put both of our lives in their hands at times, and I guess I just don't like it."

"Thank you." Emily smiles, wiping away her tears with her blanket, and I nearly choke up too. This kid has gotten under my skin, and I know that I'll do everything in my power to protect her. "I don't have any family anymore. It's nice that you care so much."

"We're each other's family now, Emily. You and me, kiddo."

She smiles again, and I know that she's trying her hardest to not go all gushy on me.

"I know that it wasn't easy for you either, but," I take a breath, "I'm just glad that you weren't a little older. What I went through, no one should have to go through." My voice trembles, and I squeeze my eyes shut.

When I open them I see she's closed her own eyes, and I realize that she's fallen asleep. I watch her sleeping for a while, waiting for my own eyes to grow heavy. In some ways, she's so grown up, and yet in others she's still the child she was when the world was destroyed. I stretch and turn onto my back, staring up at the wooden roof above me, and thank Duncan for building this place, and I pray for his soul.

TWENTY SIX

After a breakfast of berries and canned tuna (yeah, great selection, I know), we begin to pack up some weapons and get ready for the trek over to the hub. JD has gone to scout ahead to make sure that the coast is clear for us. Unfortunately, Britta's wrist is still too sore to hold a weapon, and with Emily coming to help carry stuff too, I'm more than a little worried. Duncan was a link in our armor, and with him gone it's left a gaping hole.

Most of the group is feeling pretty cheery to be getting away from camp and wander around the hub; new surroundings are a real mood booster—especially surroundings that have been cleared of deaders. We're about ready to go when we see JD running back through the trees. The look on his face is not good, and I climb down with Mikey to see what's going on.

"The Forgotten," JD pants. "We have to go." He bends over and clutches his knees as he tries to catch his breath, and I see dried blood on the back of his head and down the back of his neck.

"They don't know about this place," Mikey replies, his eyes quickly scanning the distance.

I can hear movements too—and voices.

"They're following me," JD shouts, rubbing his hand carefully across the back of his head and wincing when he sees the blood. "They caught me, but I got away—but they've been following me ever since. They're going to be here any minute. Get everyone together and let's go." JD climbs the steps and out of my view. I hear him shouting to the others, and everyone moving around above us.

Mikey stares after him for a second before grabbing my arm. "Get Emily, get to the shoreline. Leave your stuff, I'll get it for you."

I shrug him off, ever the stubborn bitch, and climb the steps. "I told you, I don't need your help."

"Stop being so stubborn," he snaps after me.

JD rounds everyone up quickly, and despite what Mikey told me, I grab all I can carry and climb down, never letting Emily out of my sight. We head for the water, and when we reach it, Crunch runs off with JD to a small hut by the shoreline and unlocks the door with a key from a large bunch she's carrying.

"Mikey!" She calls him over, and they all begin dragging out canoes and paddles, and I know that she has to be fucking joking. I've never been in a canoe in my life, let alone paddled one. Is that what you do? Paddle?

Everyone but Emily and I begin pushing out into the water and climbing into the canoes without a second thought. None of these people seem like the great outdoorsman type, but hey, what do I know? Perhaps they were all avid canoers in their previous lives. Stranger things have happened, right? Mikey sees my obvious concern and takes control, and as much as it pisses me off, I'm kinda glad for it too.

"Emily you're with Josie, me and Nina will go together." He grabs my bags from my shoulders before I can argue back, and throws them in the canoe before beginning to wade out into the water. He turns back to look at me. "Move it, now!"

Everyone else has taken his lead and gone along with it—even Emily. *Traitor.*

I don't bother to argue with him anymore, and instead wade out with him, all the while watching where Emily is and listening for any noise around us. Josie is giving her clear directions on where to stand, something about stepping over the keel and keeping low.

How I get myself into these situations is beyond me. The water is cold as it seeps into my boots and makes my pants stick to my legs, but I don't have time to think about that as Mikey gives me the same directions I heard Emily getting. Gunshots and hooting are going off in the trees, but I try to ignore them and focus on what he's saying.

"Nina, you need to step directly over the keel."

"The what?" I ask, panicked, my teeth chattering, but not just from the cold. Voices are getting louder behind us.

"… you can run, but you can't hide…"

I turn around, staring at the tree line, waiting for the Forgotten to burst through them at any minute. What is wrong with these people? Why do they want to hurt us?

"Nina! Focus!" Mikey shouts at me, and I turn and try to pay attention. He points to the end of the canoe. "This is the keel. You can't stand in a canoe, it'll tip over if you do. You have to step directly over this part and sit down, keeping your body low and central. Do you understand?"

I nod, and try to do what he says while he holds the canoe as still as possible for me, which is damn near impossible. Even with his help,

I struggle, and I slip and fall on my ass, the water splashing up around me and making the chill in me run through to my bones. The others are just about on board now and have begun to paddle out across the lake while I'm still floundering around trying to get in like a fucking idiot.

Damn it.

I can the feel panic rising, knowing that there are people in the trees behind us who would be willing to do god knows what to us if they catch us.

"Mikey…" I shout out as I fall into the water for the second time. "I can't do this, I can't do it." I may or may not slap the water in frustration too, but we don't need to talk about that.

Mikey comes up behind me and drags me up and shoves me right into the canoe, where I land unceremoniously into the bottom of it with a thud and nearly knock myself out.

"Keep down," he barks out at me when I try to sit up.

He pushes the canoe further out before gripping hold of the sides of it and climbing in. He grabs a paddle and hands me the other one, and starts to paddle furiously away from the shoreline.

"Copy me," he says, while grabbing my hands and putting them in the correct position. "I'll take most of the weight, but I need your help."

His arms move quickly, pulling the paddle as hard as he can through the water, and I copy as best I can. I'm pretty sure that I make it harder at times, though. He turns around to check behind him, and when he looks back, his face has blanched. I look over my shoulder and can see why: several men have come out of the trees and are taking aim at us. Mikey's momentum increases; the muscles in his arms and shoulders strain against the movement, sweat breaking out on his forehead.

The men fire their guns at us several times, shouting and laughing. Mikey shuffles down low, telling me to do the same, while we continue to paddle, and miraculously they miss us. I peep up from my position again, making the boat rock from side to side, and watch as a couple of them run over to the hut to grab a canoe, dragging it to the shore. They push off into the water, but thankfully for us, they obviously know as much about canoeing as I do and deftly fall in several times before seemingly giving up and beginning to shoot at us again. Mikey glances behind us, making sure to steer us in between the other canoes, and continues to keep as low as he can, but doesn't slow in his momentum to get us to the other side of the lake. We're too far away for them to hit us now, but I still panic with every shot that rings out.

"They're going." Mikey speaks first, and I sit up and look behind us, making the boat rock furiously again. "Jesus, careful, Nina."

"Sorry." I look back at him sheepishly, relieved that we are nearing halfway across now, though my heart is still going a million miles an hour. "How do you know how to canoe?" I ask, looking around for Emily. She's talking with Josie, looking worried and emotional.

"Duncan taught us all. This was our bug out plan."

I nod, and feel shame and sadness sweep through me that Duncan isn't here. He was a good man after all, seemingly thinking of everything he could to protect these people. Maybe he was trying to make up for his past mistakes and cover up his own guilt, but either way he just saved our lives. I chance another glance behind us, but the Forgotten—or whoever they are—have definitely taken off. I breathe a sigh of relief that at least they aren't shooting at us anymore.

"What do you think they are going to do? Can they drive around and get to the other side?" I can't help but feel sad that I've lost not one, but *two* homes in the space of a couple of hours, and Duncan's death seems like it was for nothing now, too.

"No, there's no way around. They'd have to go back to the road and take the long way, but I can't see them bothering. It would take hours. As for what they're going to do, well, I don't know. Maybe they won't notice the huts in the trees, maybe they will, but if they do get up there, they won't be able to get from tree to tree and more than likely won't stick around."

A sweat has broken out on his forehead and I lean across and wipe it away with the sleeve of my hoody before it trickles into his eyes. I'm still mad at him, but he just saved me—*again*—and for that I have to be grateful. His muscles tense with every stroke of the paddle, and I'd love to be able to help out, but since I only know two things about canoes—squat and diddly—I don't bother to offer my help. I notice that we have way surpassed the others. I look back at them; their faces are grim but determined.

We paddle in silence for a couple of minutes before he interrupts my thoughts.

"Idiots."

I turn to look behind us and see thick black smoke rising above the trees line. When I look back, Mikey is looking at me. He shakes his head sadly. "I guess they decided to torch it."

"Why would they do that? I mean, what the fuck do they even want?" I shout, making the others look at me. I point behind us and they stare sadly as their homes for the last couple of years burn away.

"Vengeance."

Mikey's voice is cold as he says it, and for a moment I wonder what our little group did to piss these people off so much; then I realize that he means they want vengeance against the world. They were left to rot outside the walls' protection, hence the name *the Forgotten*, I guess.

"You were all the Forgotten though, right? I mean, none of you lived behind the walls, and you don't go around killing people for no reason."

"The Forgotten aren't just any people, Nina. They are bad people. Rapists, murderers, criminals. *They* call themselves the Forgotten, not us, and they think that the world—other survivors—owe them a debt. They weren't just left behind, they were refused entry. They fought and struggled and lost loved ones just to get to the walls, and when they got there they were point blank turned away. They weren't good enough to be allowed behind the walls."

Mikey sounds more pissed off than I would have thought. I can't blame him—it's horrible to think that these people were just turned away, but that's no excuse to go around terrorizing and hurting other innocent people. In all the books I ever read and all the movies I ever watched, it was always the same: the big and bad of society, so to speak, turn on everyone else, and kill and torture and try to control everyone and everything; but I never got it. And now I'm living it and I still don't get it. I get that there are bad people in the world. I'm not stupid. There were before all this happened, and there still are now. And I understand that people turn on each other and some people— well yeah, they're just fucked in the head, I guess. But at a time like this when what you need to do is stand together to protect each other, why the hell would you decide that killing people is a better option?

I think of JD. "JD doesn't go around killing people. Neither do you or Crunch."

"Maybe he would of if he would have been free when it all happened. It's different for him though—he was in prison when it happened. By the time he escaped, he only had one goal in mind, and that was to kill as many zombies as possible. He never wanted to go behind the walls." His eyes bore holes into my face. "The Forgotten were cast aside as the shit of society, in the hopes that they would die and the government would be rid of them once and for all, while everyone else got to live it up without the fear of being mauled to death by a fucking zombie every time they sat down to rest." Mikey avoids my stare, his voice rising as he talks.

"You sound like you agree with them." My eyes narrow.

"Maybe once I did, but not anymore. I know that it wasn't anyone's fault how it all went down in the end. No one asked for this. We could all survive if we stopped killing each other and killed the dead instead, but some people like to think of the end of the world as an excuse to go fucking mental, I guess."

I snort back a laugh. I can't argue with that. I've seen plenty of crazy shit the past couple of years. The things that people will do to survive never fail to amaze me: mothers protecting their children with their own lives and bodies, husbands committing unimaginable acts against others to protect their own families. I guess now that I have Emily and this little surrogate family, I would do almost anything to protect them too. Anyway, maybe if the Forgotten knew the hell behind the walls, they wouldn't be in such a hurry to get behind them. I shudder as I think how much worse it could possibly be if the Forgotten ever did get control of one of the walled cities and their people.

"What are you thinking about? Did I fuck up again?" Mikey's voice breaks through to me and I glance at him, his look pained.

"No." I shake my head. "I was just thinking about how bad it could get for the survivors behind the walls if the Forgotten ever got in."

"They'd tear the place apart."

I nod, knowing what he's saying is true.

"You'd think this world was bad enough with the deaders to fear. But no, there's worse. There are human beings that will do worse to you," I bite out through gritted teeth. "What people have had to do so far to protect their loved ones and survive is hard enough, but what more are they going to have to do to protect themselves?"

"I'll protect you and Emily now."

I look at him, my forehead crinkling in confusion. "We're not your problem, Mikey. I can manage on my own, and I can protect Emily too. I don't need you."

We have made it to the other side of the lake, thankfully, and the canoe sticks in the mud of the shoreline.

He looks at me hard. "I know you don't. You're as tough as old boots, Nina. But I want to." His jaw grinds hard and he looks away so that I can't reply, and jumps out of the canoe.

What the hell do I say to that?

We drag the boats far up into the trees and into a hut almost identical to the one on the other side. Watching the fire burning the trees and our home away on the other side of the lake, there's a deep sense of loss—all of us feeling heartbroken to have lost so much, but relieved that we made it out together and alive. Pain tugs at me again that Duncan died for nothing. He never wanted to go to the hub, but we all convinced him and it got him killed. Now it was for nothing, and we're homeless once more.

"So, what now?" Emily asks.

Still asking that same question, eh, Emily?

I roll my eyes but agree, since I'd like to know what the rest of the bug out plan is.

"I don't know," JD replies. He looks almost lost, and drapes his arm heavily around Josie's shoulders.

"What do you mean, you don't know?" I question.

"I mean that *this* was our plan. Now I don't have a fucking clue what to do or where to go," JD snaps.

"We must have *some* idea where we can go. You must have talked about it at some point," I snap back.

We all stand and stare at each other with blank expressions until Emily pipes up.

"Nina, we could go to your husband's cabin." She looks cheery that she remembered the original plan.

My cheeks go warm at the mention of Ben. Or maybe it's because everyone turns to look at me, some open-mouthed that I have a husband, some with big fucking smirks on their faces, like the cat that got the cream.

"You said it was safe up there. That's where we were heading before Mikey got us stuck in the store." She rolls her eyes at him, oblivious to my awkwardness, Crunch's gloating, and Mikey's anger.

"Sounds like a great plan, Emily. Whereabouts is this cabin then?" Mikey speaks through gritted teeth.

"Woodland Springs I think you said, right, Nina?"

I nod, and swallow hard. I haven't purposely not told Mikey about Ben, but I also haven't been entirely truthful either. I guess that makes two of us keeping secrets. Now I feel like a big fucking hypocrite.

JD nods and grabs a map from his backpack and spreads it out on the floor. He quickly assesses where we are and which way we need to go.

"Mikey, I think if we cut across the field over here, we can skip all the major roads. It should take us straight into the next town. It's some weird hippie town all about saving the planet or some shit, but," he points to the map and Mikey and I lean over to look, "if I remember correctly, when I came through it last time, there was a car dealership on the outskirts. If we can get there and get a car, we could be heading up into the hills by nightfall." He looks to Mikey for agreement and when Mikey nods, he looks to everyone else.

JD folds his map back up and puts it away. "It's a long trek, through some pretty open ground with nowhere to hide, which is a good and a bad thing," he warns.

Everyone agrees that it's the best plan though—hell, it's the only plan— and we load up our things and head off. I purposely try to stay away from Mikey, but he catches up quickly. He doesn't say anything, but I can feel the tension pouring off him, and it only seems to be getting worse with every smirk and glance from Crunch.

"I'm sorry," I whisper, feeling guiltier than I should.

I look at him, but he won't look at me. His eyes stay trained on the floor. I don't know why I think now is the appropriate time to discuss this, but since we're currently out of immediate danger I go with my gut instinct.

"I didn't purposely not tell you."

"You didn't tell me though, did you?" he replies.

"He's dead. It's not like you have anything to worry about." I choke on the words, realizing how much I actually care for Mikey and how much I don't want to lose him.

"Only ghosts."

I don't have an answer for that. He's right. Ben still haunts me, I just hadn't realized how much or how obvious it was to everyone else.

"You fucking judged me when you were keeping your own secrets, Nina." He looks up at me now and I realize how angry he is. He's not hurt at all.

"You're right, I can't defend that, but when you put it into perspective, I'm not as bad as you. So what that I didn't tell you that my husband was dead, that I killed him, that it was all my fault? So fucking what? You used Crunch and you hurt me!" I spin to face him, my own anger mirroring his as I give him a hard push to his chest, making him stumble back "Don't fucking judge me!"

"I didn't use either of you. I told her straight how it was and stopped fucking around with her as soon as I got back to camp. As soon as I realized that I had feelings for you."

I cringe at the thought of him having feelings for me, but feel a little thrill at it too.

"...Sorry, but it is what it is, Nina. I can't help it that she likes me more than I like her." He shrugs. "It was mutually beneficial to both of us, and she knew from the get-go that that's what it was." He grabs my arm to stop me from walking away.

"But you could have told me, warned me even," I huff and look into the distance, watching the smoke still rising into the sky. "You know what she's like, and you made me into her enemy."

"And I'm sorry for that, but what would it have really changed? She would still have hated you because I didn't want her anymore. I can't help how she feels."

Men are so fucking clueless sometimes!

We stare at each other, and I'm lost as to what else to say, which is good since we get interrupted by Britta.

"Guys, you need to come and see this. We have a problem."

I roll my eyes at Mikey and storm off for dramatic effect, not really knowing why, or who I'm angry with anymore.

Maybe the whole fucking world?

TWENTY SEVEN

As we break through the tree line, we see the open fields in front of us. When JD had said fields, I guess I'd just assumed, well— fields. The journey seems incredibly long with no end to the field in sight, but what frightens me more are the horde of zombies that are just casually strolling around, as if they didn't have a care in the world. One or two wouldn't necessarily be a problem. Don't get me wrong, it's always a problem when there are deaders around, but one or two we could handle. This many? No way.

"Okay, so what's the new plan?" I pull my bag off my shoulders, grab my bottle of water, and take a long swig.

"There is no new plan." JD looks at me seriously.

I look around at everyone else's faces and know that I'm not the only one who thinks this is a death trap, but once again, I'm the only one willing to speak up.

"You can't be serious? Look at them!" I nearly drop my water in anger, and quickly screw the lid back on.

"We have to," Crunch snaps. "What else are we going to do? Take the twelve-mile hike around it? Or perhaps we could head back across the lake and see what those douche bags have left for us!"

She hates my guts, but the tension in her shoulders makes it clear that this isn't personal; she's just as worried as I am.

"Well yeah. Why not?" I splutter. "Seriously, what are we in such a goddamned hurry for? You gotta get up for work in the morning or something? Let's take the route around. It might take longer, but it's safer."

"We're doing this, Nina."

"JD, this is obviously a trap. Look at this place!" I feel Emily's hand slip into mine—whether it's to comfort me or her, I don't know. "Someone has rounded these deaders up and left them here. How else do you explain so many in one place, huh? We *have* to go around."

"You don't know what's over the next hill, Nina." He gestures wearily to the field of zombies. "It could be worse than this. Besides, I have a feeling that that's what they want us to do."

"What? Who would do that? And why?" As soon as I say it, I know: the Forgotten.

Goddamn it, if I ever get my hands on one of them, I'll wring their stupid fucking necks.

"In the meantime, while you go check out the other options available to us and continue to argue with me, we're losing daylight. We need to get across this field and get to the cabin; we need to get to safety," JD says while tightening his backpack straps and tucking in his T-shirt.

Even with all that has happened so far today, now that he has a plan, he seems calm again. Losing our home, being captured and beaten… damn, I don't know whether to be annoyed or just plain jealous that he can keep such a cool head about all these things. I wish I had his self-control, but then maybe that's all it really takes—a plan, a direction, anything to help you focus on your survival.

"JD, don't rest all of our fates on the cabin. It might be destroyed, for all I know!"

"It might not." He pulls out a long knife to go along with the scythe in his other hand, completely ignoring my distress.

"Someone else might be living there for all we know."

He looks at me with a raise of his eyebrow. "They might not."

Frustration and anger overflow from me and I dive forward to whoop him upside the head, but Mikey grabs me around the waist and Emily pulls my arm back.

"You're being an idiot. This could get us all killed," I shout, my anger flaring even more.

"It might—"

"*Not!* Yes, I get it," I snap, and struggle out of Mikey's grasp. "I'm fine, get off me."

"Look, Nina, you don't have to come with us. That's your choice. We're going." JD looks around at the others. "That goes for any of you. None of you have to come. That's your choice. But these deaders have been planted here to *force* us to go around, and I'm not doing it. I see freedom on the other side of this field and I'm taking it. If that isn't worth risking my life for, then I don't know what is."

"Freedom? There's no freedom from this, just more damn zombies!" I spit.

"JD," Britta steps forward, "my wrist is still too bad to hold a weapon." Her face creases with worry. "I-I can't…"

"You'll be fine, Britta." Crunch pulls out both of her knives with a smile, and I can't help but wonder if she's smiling because she knows

230

that Britta would be easy bait if anything should happen.

"You know the rules." Britta grimaces. "What do I do, ask the nice zombies not to eat me because I'm having a bad day?"

"Stop whining, you'll be fine. I've got your back." Crunch smiles again.

A chill runs up and down my spine, like a tiny trail of ants. With that smile, I know that I have to go with them. If anything goes wrong, well, let's just say that Crunch seems more likely to stab Britta in the back than help protect her back. When am I going to learn to mind my own damn business?

We slide down the dusty embankment and wait just behind the wooden fence surrounding the field for everyone to regroup. JD heads up the line with Josie behind him, then Britta, with Crunch snapping at her heels. Emily is between Crunch and me; at least I can trust that she wouldn't necessarily hurt Emily. She may not stick around to protect her if there's immediate danger, but she won't sacrifice her. Either way, I'm right behind Emily, and I'll protect her.

Mikey is taking the back of the line to cover us from behind, or to stare at my behind, I'm not sure which. No, surely it's for protection purposes? I turn around and give him a lift of my eyebrow, and he replies with a smirk.

Damn him. My behind!

"Everybody ready?" JD whispers back.

We all give quiet approval and climb over the fence and into hell, trying to make as little noise as possible. Once on the other side of the fence, though, I know that it will make no difference.

The horde are a way off and luckily shambling in the opposite direction, but it won't take long for them to spot us on the open land, so we set off at a steady speed. JD had said to keep it at a brisk jog, to save our reserves for running for our lives, and that's what we do: a slow yet spritely jog through the wonderful countryside. There are birds in the sky and a breeze in the air, and I'm surrounded by over fifty flesh-eating, stinking, ravenous deaders—simply marvelous, huh?

The entire field is surrounded by a waist-high wooden fence—with the exception of one area to the far left, where the fence has collapsed. This does nothing to help the deaders though; it only seems to confuse the hell out of them as they try to escape en masse through the small opening like they're at a bad rock concert. The ground is littered with rotting body parts and bones, and I wonder whether they are from other deaders or from other people that have attempted to cross here. I shudder and try not to look down at the death around my feet.

None of us speak while we jog at our steady pace through the field, each of us lost in our own thoughts and hopes for survival and possible freedom from this nightmarish day. Emily looks behind once or twice and I try to give her a reassuring smile, but it's lost in my own horror-filled expression as we pass another group of deaders to the right, which are moving in our direction.

JD has spotted them and diverts us to a more central location in the hopes of us getting further across the field before we're spotted by the largest group of deaders near the fallen fence. However, it's the low moan of 'suppertime' from a lone deader that finally gives away our location.

We were so intent on the horde to the left and the zombie pile to the right that we are now stuck in the middle of them all—*hey, I'm sure there's a song here somewhere.* Another couple of stragglers have seen us, and are now heading in our direction. We can outrun them easily, but their groans of starvation are alerting the other deaders to our location, and a loud chorus of hunger is erupting around us like it's Christmas and they're carolers.

We're about halfway across now, give or take, with a trail of zombies hot on our tail. Well, maybe not hot on our tail, since zombies are cold and slow, but I've said it once and I'll say it again: it's zombie hordes that you should fear the most. They are much harder to fight. With zombies behind us, and the ones to the left moving in front of us after finally spotting their takeout lunch making a run for it, I know that we are going to have to stop and fight soon. We just need to get a little further though.

Sweat is pouring down my back in what feels like a hot trail of molten lava, and JD shouts for us to run faster but stay in formation. I push myself harder, my leg muscles pumping faster than they've gone in a long time. Emily is getting tired, but I link my hand into hers and run alongside her, pulling her along with me, my breaths getting shallower the faster I run.

The stench of death is closing in on us from all sides, each deader shambling as quick as their rotten asses can go to catch up to us. Britta is whimpering to herself, knowing that she can't fight them off with her injured wrist if they do catch us. Panic sweeps across her face as she looks around and catches Crunch's hardened glare.

The end of the field is finally in sight, but so is our impending doom, as more of the deaders come out from the trees to our right. I look around, knowing our plan is falling apart, our small chance of escape looking hopeless. We're surrounded by them; though the circle of deaders is large, they are closing it with every passing second.

"RUN!" JD bellows at the top of his lungs as if he just read my thoughts, and we finally break formation, each of us striking out on our own to save ourselves.

Emily is tiring, her breaths coming too rapidly, and she breaks out into a fit of coughs as she tries to catch her breath. She tugs on my hand, her eyes pleading with me—for what, I don't know. We can't slow down; our only chance is to make it to the fence and get over it.

A zombie loses its head as it gets too close to JD. His scythe strikes its neck and sprays the ground with thick black blood. Crunch kicks out at another with a scream, and slams her knee on its chest and her Kukri knife into its forehead as it lands on its back. She jumps straight back up and continues to run, pushing away another that gets too close to her.

Mikey's hand touches the bottom of my back as he pushes me onwards. I hadn't realized that I was slowing down until he touched me. I grip the small machete harder, readying myself to protect Emily to the death as she slows down even more. Zombies are getting nearer still, and the exit, that had seemed to be getting closer, now seems to be moving further away as I tire. Britta must have been a runner in her previous life, because she seems to speed past everything and everyone without looking even a little tired. I guess since she can't fight, the only thing she can do is run. Her life literally depends on it.

A noise from behind has me turning, and Mikey takes out a very ugly rotten deader that was crawling along the ground, its long intestines dragging along the floor behind it like Medusa's serpents. I must have run straight over the top of it without even realizing.

JD has practically stopped to fight now, with Josie by his side. She fights like a demon possessed, swinging her baton around with a loud scream and smashing in the softened skulls of the dead, while JD takes their heads as prizes with a quick swoop of his scythe. They find a gap and begin to run again, just as Emily, Mikey, and I pass them by and take the lead.

A deader reaches me, and I swing my machete and slice off both its hands before kicking it to the ground and slamming my foot into its face. I can feel its mouth moving under the sole of my boot, but thankfully not finding purchase and unable to grab me, since I chopped off both its arms like twigs. I lift my boot up and slam it back down on the deader's face before it can move to get up. I feel bone crunching underneath my boot, but it continues to squirm. With the second rise of my foot, I steal Crunch's wonderful move and slam my machete through the deader's forehead with a guttural cry. Blood and gore squirt up around the hole I just made, and I gag as my machete comes free and the smell wafts up to me.

A scream from behind makes me turn to see Josie landing heavily on the ground, her face slamming into the dirt and gore surrounding her. Before she can try to move to get up, zombies attack her from all sides. They launch themselves at her like vicious dogs, snarling and ripping at her flesh. She screams again, louder this time, as bony fingers pull at her skin and split it open like an overripe peach. Their rotten teeth tear holes in her flesh, and the blood that pumps out only feeds their frenzy. I grab Emily's hand, and without a second thought, we run. I glance back over my shoulder and watch JD fighting to get to Josie, slashing and stabbing at the deaders gorging on her insides. As Crunch passes, she grips him by the shoulders and begins to drag him away. He fights her, attempting to shrug her off, but as more and more deaders surround Josie and her screams are drowned out by their angry snarls, he turns and runs in our direction, his face an image of despair, grief, and anger.

TWENTY EIGHT

You fall, you die.

JD's words ring through my mind, and I feel fear for us and pity for him. They were his rules, his words, and that was his girlfriend; he's going to feel that guilt for a long time. I know how that feels.

We reach the fence, and I see Britta is already on the other side, panting and looking like she wants to keep on running, but she seems unsure of leaving us behind.

"Run!" I scream, and slice a stray deader apart as we get close to it. Britta hesitates before turning tail and running.

Fortunately, most seem to be attracted to the blood drowning the ground—Josie's blood. Mikey grips Emily's exhausted body and practically throws her over the fence as I climb up and jump down the other side. I grip her under the arms, drag her up to standing, and continue running without missing a beat, despite my raging heart. The dead are still following—though not many anymore—but I wonder if those that are would be able to push over the wooden fence, even as sturdy as it seems. They seem enraged to the point of insanity that we're escaping, and I don't want to stick around and find out.

The sun has begun to get lower in the sky, the coolness of night arriving, and my feet continue to pound the ground until I think I'll throw up if I don't stop. I slow to a jog and then a fast walk. Everyone copies me until we are far enough away that the smell of the dead still lingers in the air but doesn't assault our senses anymore. I retch as I try to catch my breath. My legs are throbbing, my arms are burning, and my head is dizzy from lack of oxygen.

I collapse to the ground. Emily falls beside me and curls her body into mine to cry. I lay an arm across her, but there's no strength to give her any comfort right now. All around me the group is panting and dry heaving. I close my eyes to stop the world from going dizzy, and only open them when the panting and wheezing quiets.

I open an eye and look to my left. JD is sitting on his own, his knees pulled in to his chest, tears blurring his vision. His teeth are grinding, and his hands are clenching around his weapon repeatedly. I don't know if it is anger or sadness that has taken hold—maybe both— but when he sees me watching, it's like a veil falls across his features. He sniffs and stands up.

"We need to get going."

"Five more minutes," Crunch gasps and sits up, a hand clutching at her side.

"No, we need to go." His face is hardened steel, but he's not immune to the running; his nostrils still flare as he takes in deep breaths.

"Jesus, JD—"

"Come on," I stand, pulling a crying Emily up with me, and stare at Crunch. She rolls her eyes, but nods and stands up too.

"I'm bleeding."

I turn to look at Britta. A long gouge tears up her inner forearm and blood is oozing from it steadily. Crunch opens up her backpack and pulls out her little medical kit without commenting further.

"Sit down."

I eye JD as they both sit and Crunch examines the wound. He doesn't protest, but he isn't happy about it. Personally I'm glad her arm's been gouged open—well, as long as it isn't life-threatening; it means we get to rest more.

"I need to suture it." Crunch rips open a small package and pulls out some latex gloves before slipping them on. She carefully grabs out some more items from her kit before looking up at me. "Help me."

I nod without question and sit by her side. She hands me some of the items and I try to keep my hands steady as I hold them out for her.

"This is going to sting."

Crunch focuses on the wound and takes her water bottle out from her bag, pouring the water over it to flush out any dirt. She then grabs some spray from her bag, spritzing it over the entire area, and Britta yelps and squeezes her eyes closed as Crunch wipes around with a clean wipe, clearing the blood away.

"Keep still. I have to clean it properly. Using water from my bottle won't do much to keep away infection, but this little concoction will." She spritzes it again and wipes once more, shaking her head and pursing her lips, before opening a small packet with what looks like a fishhook with thread running through the end.

"What was that?" I ask, nodding to the bottle and wipe.

"A little something that I put together when I ran out of my medical-grade gear." She looks from me to Britta. "This is going to hurt again," she says grimly.

Emily sits down next to Britta and takes her other hand in her own, her eyes still red raw from crying. They both smile in an attempt to reassure each other, but it doesn't reach any of their eyes.

Crunch pierces the needle through one side of the wound without another word, before grabbing it with her fingers, pulling it out, and then pushing it through the other side. Then she grips it with a pair of tweezers and pulls it all the way out. She pauses for a second, her hand hanging in midair, holding the thread, before she turns to me with a weird expression on her face. Britta is gasping and sobbing, but Crunch is acting like we have all the time in the world, and she's an uncaring bitch. Wait, she *is* an uncaring bitch.

"Watch carefully, I'm going to show you how to do a surgeon's knot."

Her eyes meet mine, and I swallow the large lump that has rammed its ugly head into my throat, and nod with a grimace. Okay, maybe she's not that much of an uncaring bitch.

"You wrap it twice around the tweezers before pulling it through here." She gestures with her head. "Over, under. You got that?"

I nod again.

"You should use the proper equipment for this, but I lost my suture scissors and the other stuff some time ago. These are coming up to the last of the stitches I have, too." She looks up to JD, but he's looking back the way we came, showing no interest for our mini-operation. She shakes her head and continues.

I watch intently as she ties the stitches off, trying to memorize exactly what she does. I have no idea why she wants me to know this, but I figure that it's information well worth knowing. She continues doing the same thing along the full length of the wound until Britta's skin is sewed up a like a prize pig at a slaughterhouse. It's crude and rough-looking, but it may just save her life.

The wound looks ugly, but at least the bleeding has now stopped. I reach into my backpack, pull out my painkillers, and hand two of them to Britta.

Crunch grabs my hand before Britta can take them from me. "No aspirin, okay? It thins the blood."

I nod. "It's not."

Crunch releases my hand and Britta takes the painkillers, safe in the knowledge that I wasn't trying to make her bleed to death. She swallows them greedily before thanking me profusely. Things like this are in short supply, but she's earned these bad boys.

"Are we done?" JD hovers above, his shadow casting eerie patterns over us in the failing daylight.

"Yeah." Crunch gathers all her things and packs them back into her bag before standing.

I stand, actually feeling a little queasy. It's been an incredibly long day, and watching someone being stitched up like this is not something I get to see every day—nor do I want to. Mikey's hand is on my lower back again, and I'm guessing that I'm forgiven for not telling him about Ben. How could he not forgive me though? He can't be jealous of someone who's dead. I realize that I'm happy he's forgiven me. Not that I had anything to be forgiven for, but I'm glad all the same. Once again I'm startled by how strong my feelings are for him. I don't like it. I don't want to be attached to anyone; today only proved that to me. I shrug away from his touch, feeling dirty somehow.

We begin our hike across the remaining field. This one is how it should be, barren of life—and death—and wild with flowers and nature. In a way, it's as if we are in another world, one that hasn't been touched by the evil that now roams the lands, but I can't take away any happiness from the beauty. We lost Josie today. She was a good woman, kind, strong, and beautiful, and her sudden loss will leave a huge impact on the group, especially with JD. He's trying not to show it, his stride still strong and full of confidence, his head raised to watch in all directions, but it's his slumped shoulders that give him away.

The town finally comes into view as nightfall draws close. We are at the very edge of it, and thankfully, we can see the car showroom that JD had been talking about. A lot of the cars are missing, people obviously having the same idea as us, but there are some left. The weirdest thing of all about the town? The lights: traffic lights, street lights, store lights. I haven't seen a light bulb on for years. The second weirdest, but more scary thing? Fucking deaders—everywhere. My jaw is hanging open in wonderment and confusion, and when I finally peel my eyes away from the town back to the rest of my group, I see that they have the same look on their faces as I do.

"What the fuck?" Mikey whispers next to me.

I don't answer him, I can't answer him. I can't make sense of any of this.

It's as if the town has been frozen in time. Everything has been paused, put on hold—apart from the deaders, obviously. They're still wandering around town like they own the fucking place. I guess they kind of do now, actually. Cars are left abandoned where they parked—or crashed. Store signs still swing in the early evening breeze, though they are weathered and worn. Trees and plants are overgrown like the gardener has been on vacation for too long. I squint into the distance and see bones littering the ground, stripped bare of the flesh that lived once upon a time.

I find it strange that after all this time, there is still so much around in the world. Cars are still where they were left, stores have been ransacked and emptied, yet not like you would think. I guess that just goes to show how little there is left of society. I mean, if there aren't even enough people left in the world to strip a town bare of its cars, then that just proves how many people were actually slaughtered when the dead rose, how little of society actually survived. When I think back to my time since leaving the walls, it occurs to me how damn lucky we have been so far. There has been food available—not much, but some; there's been gas still in the pumps; now there are cars still on the forecourt. It seems too convenient, yet that's the horror of it all, really: how suddenly it all started. No one had a chance to save themselves. Two thirds of the world wiped out in a single week. The zombies outnumbered us in every way, a hundred thousand million to one. It makes me even more sickened and furious with the Forgotten, and with Lee and his so-called guards.

At a time when we should all be working together to try to rebuild the world—to rebuild *life* and somehow survive—we are fighting and killing each other, instead of the dead. We should be fearing the deaders; instead we fear the living just as much. Maybe even more.

When will it stop? How *can* it stop, unless we either wipe out the whole damn planet or someone sees sense? The latter seems unlikely given what I have seen the past couple of years, so then how and what must we do to survive? I can defend myself from the dead, and I can shut myself down from people who think that they are the law and want to control me. However, I can't do anything about people who are willing to set traps to kill innocent people for no damn reason other than jealousy and hatred. It goes against everything, against all logic.

We clamber down the hillside and into a small stream, before climbing up the other side and jogging as silently as possible across the deserted street. The night is coming down quickly around us, and as it does, the lights begin to burn brighter. There's a strong smell of the dead, but the main hordes seem to be heading toward the brighter side of town.

A sign stands tall, proudly emblazoned with the words:

Acer Town.

Population 25,672

The world's first eco-friendly, energy self-sufficient town.

Things make much more sense now, even if my brain hasn't come to grips with the circumstances. The lights, while they give us a great view of the streets and any oncoming deaders, also make us more easily spotted, so we stick to trailing down the side of the old stores. We pass an old coffee shop and a florist's as we head for the car showroom and dodge behind a beat up old Chevy, skirting around its lower edges as a deader comes into sight. It doesn't notice, but pauses, raises its head to the sky, and takes a long hard sniff, its head moving from side to side in a weird, graceful dance. We all crouch lower, holding our breaths, until eventually it carries on its merry little way to wherever the hell it's going, and we quickly set back off in the opposite direction. We reach the showroom, initially trying the front entrance and finding it as bright as the Fourth of July, with a handful of deaders milling around and more on the way, so we head around back.

Two deaders are in the alleyway, staring up into the sky like it's a freaking super moon or something. I even pause in my own sneaking to look up and see if there's anything exciting going on, but nope. It seems these deaders are just the strong-thinking type. Or at least they are until JD lops their heads off and they crumple to the floor.

He tries the back door, which is also locked. The alley is dark, seemingly pitch black after the bright lights of the town, and I wonder how the hell anyone can even see anything. "Mikey, get your ass over here."

Mikey goes to the door and pulls out some little screwdriver-type things, fiddles around for a couple of minutes and manages to get the door unlocked.

Impressive.

I look at Emily, who looks exhausted and about to collapse at any moment, but she still smiles up at me. I loop my arm around her tiny waist as we go inside, and Mikey comes back to my side.

He offers me a small smile while putting away his little breaking-and-entering tools and swapping them for his badass machete.

Once inside, we clear the place of any deaders, only finding two strolling around like they're on their fucking lunch breaks. Hey, maybe they were? One deader is wearing what was once a smart gray suit, with a blue tie to match what I'm sure were once his pretty blue eyes. These days, they're more milky-colored and opaque, every bit the unfocused and confused deader. I realize that even a zombie car salesman has an arrogant air about him, as he dodges us several times before we finally whisk up his brain with a knife to the head.

My limbs feel like jelly, aching and weak from the exertion of the day. All I want to do is curl up and sleep for the next year. Actually, what I'd really like to do is take a long, hot shower, have a nice four-course meal, complete with chocolate fudge cake and ice cream, followed up with a nice cold beer; but I'll take sleep over nothing.

We pass the light switches and Britta reaches for them. She looks to us and we all nod, shrug, and grunt in agreement. She flips the switch and the place is swathed in darkness. I swallow hard, the darkness making the noise seem louder than it actually is.

"Electricity?" Crunch speaks first, and I nod, but then realize that she can't see me. The temporary light and now darkness has made spots flash in front of my eyes.

Britta flips a couple more lights and the forecourt lights thankfully go out.

"Let's deal with this tomorrow. We need to rest." JD leads us into a dark room, with a small window letting in only a glimpse of moonlight from outside. There's an old couch in there, which I think Crunch is going to nab, but she doesn't. She pulls the cushions off it, and hands them round for us all to rest our heads on. When she's nice like this, I feel even shittier that I stole her…what? Fuckbuddy? At least when she's being a bitch, I can hate her for it.

None of us speak as we nestle down into our makeshift beds—we're all either too heartbroken or too exhausted. I guess there are just no words left to describe the horror and loss of the day. Emily lies as physically close to me as she can get before passing out into her own personal oblivion. I, however, struggle to stop thinking about the day's events. It's been non-stop since we woke up, and while my body is aching, sore, and tired from all the exertions, my mind is still active.

I lie there for a while staring up at the ceiling, listening to Emily's soft breathing and feeling her warm breath on my neck. Every time my eyes close, an image of death flashes in front of me. Josie's tortured face as she screamed at us to help her while being torn apart, the echoing of the dead's groans, the gunshots from The Forgotten—it all seems too much to take in. How the fuck is this my life now?

I force my eyes to stay open for as long as I can, the constant images battering my brain every time the weight of my eyelids becomes too much. The last time I close them, I think I hear JD sobbing. I feel guilty that I am awake—this is meant to be a private moment for him—so I keep my eyes squeezed closed. And this time, instead of fighting a futile battle to eradicate the nightmares behind my lids, I surrender myself to them.

TWENTY NINE

It was Emily's breath that I felt when I slipped into sleep, and it's Emily's breathing that wakes me, the warmth of it making my skin clammy and uncomfortable. She's still sleeping tightly against me, her face pressed against my collarbone. My own arms are wrapped around her, clinging to her fragile body.

I release my grip, slowly flexing out my hands to get the blood flowing back into them. I pry her face away from me and roll onto my back, staring once more at the ceiling. Light is filtering in through the small window, but not enough to wake anyone else, by the looks of things.

I blink my eyes, letting them adjust to the light and attempting to clear the sleep away. The ceiling is a light gray and speckled with drops of dried blood. I close my eyes against the sight; that is not the sort of thing a girl wants to see when she first wakes up. Or ever. I roll over onto my other side and see Mikey sleeping. I was in the middle of a Nina sandwich and I didn't even know it. He snores lightly, his face smooth of worry for a change, and I can truly take in how handsome he is.

His lips are shapely and full. His hair is beginning to grow back again; short, dark hairs cover his head, giving him an almost Hispanic look. I realize that he probably is, and wonderment hits me that none of those things seem to matter anymore. Color, race, creed—it's all the same to the dead.

I close my eyes and try to get back to sleep—who knows when we'll get the chance to rest like this again?—but the urge to pee is rapidly growing, and I know that I'm going to have to get up soon. I ignore it for as long as possible, but after a few minutes the urgency is too much to bear, and I get up and creep out into the hallway.

I know that we cleared this place last night, and I know it's safe, but it still gives me the chills walking around somewhere I don't know. It doesn't help that the place is gloomy as hell. I pass the light switches and give them a little flick, freaking myself out when they come on. I quickly turn them off and hunt down the toilets. The smell of the toilets makes me gag when I enter and once again my hand strays to the light switch. I flick it and the lights blink twice before staying on. I stare up at the fluorescent tubing in confusion: this just isn't fucking possible. My bladder nudges me and I only just make it to the toilet in time, breathing a sigh of relief that I chose a toilet only half-filled with…well, you get the idea. I finish my business, and when I come out I automatically turn to wash my hands. The soap dispenser is still there, half-filled with dried-up pink gloop, and the towels are on the wall. I hesitantly turn the tap. There's silence and then a groaning, the tap splutters, and eventually water splashes out of it and into the basin. I stare for a few minutes, amazed by the sight of running water, my eyes transfixed on it. I place my hands under the steady stream, biting down on my lip as the water runs between my fingers, and I smile.

I press the soap dispenser a couple of times, until eventually a hard lump of pink soap drops out of the bottom. This was once in liquid form, no doubt, but over the years it has hardened and solidified. However, after rubbing it between my palms under the water, bubbles finally form and I relish in the feel of having clean, floral-smelling hands. I shrug out of my black hoody and stare at my reflection, my tired eyes looking straight back at me. I look older than I should, worn down and exhausted. The yellow fluorescent tubes do nothing for my complexion either. Most of all, though, I look frightened. Fear settled in me the first day of the outbreak and has been there ever since, but it somehow seems more prominent today. My hair is a mass of dark tangles on my head, my skin pasty white and covered in dried blood and grime. My body is too skinny for my height. The image makes me want to cry, not because I'm vain and give a shit anymore about image and beauty, but because I feel like I've been dying on the inside for the past few years and now it's finally showing up on the outside. A tear slides down my cheek, and I watch it making a little path down my dirty face, my eyes following its journey in the mirror. Down past my nose, around the corner of my mouth, down my chin, and…drip, off the end.

"You're beautiful."

My eyes flick up to Mikey and I stare at his reflection behind my own. His eyes are soft and full of concern.

"You should know me better than that, Mikey. I don't give a shit about my looks." I shrug, the words coming out half-choked.

"I know you don't," he replies, coming forward and placing his hands on my shoulders, his face close to mine, "but I wanted you to know anyway. I think you're beautiful. Since I first met you, I can't seem to get you out of my head."

He buries his face in my neck, and for a minute I think that he's going to kiss it, but he doesn't. Instead, he smells me, taking in a deep lungful of my scent.

"You smell like home to me," he breathes against my neck.

My body quivers against the action, embarrassed—because let's face it, I most likely stink—but surprisingly, my heart contracts at his words. *Home.*

"You know what they say about getting attached to people, Mikey," I sigh under his touch.

"No, what?" He glances up at me.

"Don't—because we all die in the end." I swallow down my bitter pill. We have no home, and we'll never be safe.

His fingers trail up and down my arm, drawing lazy circles across my flesh and giving me goose pimples. "Don't talk like that. We'll be okay, Nina."

I make an agreeing noise, but don't reply. He continues to stare at me in the mirror, and I feel self-conscious and finally shrug away from him.

"I told you I'd look after you both and I meant it. Nina—" Mikey puts his hand on my shoulder and turns me to look at him, his eyes pleading with me to say something, wanting me to say anything other than just 'uh huh,' but I've got nothing. My vocabulary has gone out the window, and the only thing I can think to say is the truth, what I really believe...

"Mikey—we're all going to die, I'm good with that. I accepted it a long time ago."

Mikey pauses for a moment before his hand covers mine. His eyes search my face for something, but he comes away unsatisfied. I pull away from him again. His forehead scrunches up. I know he's not confused; I mean, deep down he believes that we're going to die too. We all know it, we just don't want to admit it. But you can't escape this Armageddon. This is forever. I grab my hoody and slip it back over my head like the cloak of death.

"Come on, let's get back to the others. Crunch will have a fit if she finds us." I smile half-heartedly and hope that he will let it drop.

"Don't do that." Mikey grabs my hand. "Don't try and change the subject. This is important, Nina. I want you to know that we're going to be okay, that we'll be safe."

I roll my eyes.

"Don't do that either," he snaps.

"What do you want me to say, Mikey? Everything's going to be all right? I don't believe that it is, and you shouldn't either. We're all going to die. Maybe not today, maybe not tomorrow, but it will happen, that's a fact, so let's not pretend any differently. The undead always win, and as if that wasn't enough to contend with, now I find out that we have more goddamned humans to fear as well. I thought I escaped all that when I left…but I didn't. We're doomed, so get over it."

"I don't believe that."

"Well you're stupid then. You weren't behind the walls. You don't know the horror I escaped from, and for what? This?!" I gesture around us. "What do you do when hell comes upon the world? Run and hide or stand and fight?"

He looks confused for a moment before answering. "Stand and fight, of course."

"Ha," I scoff. "Why?"

"To survive." He looks even more confused.

"To survive? For what purpose? There's nothing left, Mikey! How do you survive hell? There is no escaping hell. I'll stand and fight by your side every day, but I still don't know what we're doing it for."

He stands and pulls his shirt over his head. "It doesn't have to be all doom and gloom." He comes forward, his hand brushing my arm.

"Doesn't it?" I shrug him off. "Josie died yesterday. That could have been any one of us. You, me, Emily."

"But it wasn't—"

"You go out there and tell that to JD and see if you still feel as high and mighty about it."

"Don't turn this around on me, like I'm the bad guy because I'm glad it was her and not you. Does that make me an asshole? Maybe, but I *am* glad it wasn't you." His lips pinch together as he moves to touch me again. "Look, I care about you, that's all I was trying to say. I don't want to fight with you."

"No, you don't even know me, Mikey. What you want to do is to play happy families, like this shit is just going to go away. Like we're going to wake up tomorrow and have two-point-four children, work for the government, and bring home a nice fat paycheck. Well understand this: that's never going to happen. The government abandoned us. Years later and the dead still rise; they surround us every step of the way. There is no happily ever after—not now, not ever!"

"Nina."

Mikey looks hurt, and I know that I should shut my mouth now, but I don't, I can't. I don't want him to get attached to me. That only leads to more pain.

"What? You think I'm a bitch, right? So what? That's me." My arms cross over my chest so tight I'm struggling to breathe.

Mikey shakes his head at me and throws his hands up in the air. "I give up, Nina. I can't win with you." He stalks away from me.

"That's right, Mikey, you go on back to Crunch, she has less baggage than I do," I spit after him.

He stops in the doorway and looks at me, his jaw grinding at his teeth as he tries to come back with a retort.

"You're such a fucking bitch sometimes, Nina."

"Didn't I just say that?" I shout after him.

The door slams shut behind him, and I'm left feeling empty once more. I can't even cry, I feel *that* sorry for myself. Sad, pathetic little me.

I get back to the room as some of the others are stirring. Emily is still fast asleep, but Britta is awake, though she isn't looking too good—but hey she's not dead, so that's a small victory. Still, after what happened with Duncan I'm keeping her away from Emily and keeping my eye on her. Mikey has gone and sat with Crunch, but I refuse to acknowledge his presence even though I long to go over and apologize. JD has emptied out most of his pack and is sorting through his supplies while munching on another delicious ration pack. My stomach gurgles in response, as if sensing the injustice of another stomach but itself being filled. I root through my bag and pull out some of the cereal bars from Old Man Riely's house. *Damn, that seems like a lifetime ago.*

My head is pounding from dehydration; I don't remember the last time I actually had a drink. Emily is going to be thirsty when she wakes up too, I realize. I should have gone looking for a drink while I was up and about. Yesterday was too much for her—she's still just a child; I think that we all keep forgetting that. I stroke a hand across her brow. How had she survived all this time on her own with no one to look after her? I care for her deeply, I suppose like a mother would feel toward a child—though I'm not her mother and a huge part of me doesn't want to her to think of me as one. I want to be able to leave her here with the others and strike out on my own. I know that they will protect her, that much I do trust of them, but I also know that I am already too attached to her to let her go.

"Nina, come with me and Mikey. We need to find some keys for those cars out there and get the fuck out of this town."

I look up at JD, nod and stand, all without saying a word, following both of them out the door. Crunch moves over to take a look at Britta's arm as I leave, giving me a barely concealed glare as she does. I don't care—she should be glad that I'm out of the picture, not even more resentful. We creep through the darkened corridors of the showroom and toward the front, keeping low and out of sight. Deaders are milling around outside, doing their usual deader thing of moaning and shambling and just being generally stinky. I wonder why no one has mentioned what happened to Josie. Why no one is talking about the elephant in the room, but when I look at JD's face, his grim and determined expression tells me everything I need to know.

A small piece of him died with her yesterday. His guilt for leaving her is eating away at him. I feel his pain, but it's human nature to want to survive at any cost, and deep down he knows that he couldn't have saved her anyway. I've been there. Worse, though, is that no one is talking about her, and I can't help but wonder if this is what it will be like for me. When I die, will no one speak of me? Mourn me?

THIRTY

Lucky for us, we find a small cupboard full of car keys in the dead—um, re-dead—saleszombie's office, and we pick through them all until we get several sets that look like they could be a good shot. Walking to the front of the showroom, though, we realize that that's where our luck ends. The car yard is still full of deaders. Old deaders, new deaders, stripper deaders by the looks of some of them—though most deaders could be strippers by their lack of decent clothing these days. I shudder. They all look hungry and eager for a feast on some flesh, their emaciated frames withering away.

Marvelous. Just fucking marvelous.

We shuffle through the keys, choosing which ones supposedly go with certain cars. The keys all look the same to me, but JD and Mikey have gone all macho-men on me like it's the most ridiculous thing in the world.

"Jesus, woman, how can you not see the difference?" JD snaps exasperatedly at me with a shake of his head, and continues to go through the pile.

I shrug noncommittally. There seems no point in arguing since they *do* all seem the same to me. Well, apart from the symbols on some of the fobs. I'm not completely stupid, I know that they're the car logos, but Ben was the car man in our house; I just drove the damn thing and never really paid attention to this stuff. I always wanted a Ford Mustang for some reason, though, but it doesn't seem like the time or the place to bring that up.

There's nothing amazing in the lot, but thank God there's something at least half-decent there. I don't know what we would have done if all we had to choose from were convertibles. Can you imagine anything more horrendous than driving through a zombie-infested land with a drop top? Jesus, the smell alone would be enough to kill you, never mind the mindless zombies that would rip through your roof in seconds.

We pick two cars that we like from our vantage point and work out a strategy of getting to them.

"Just press the fob and see what happens." Mikey reaches for the fob in JD's hand.

"Don't be an idiot. As soon as anything out there moves or makes a sound, those—what do you call them, Nina?"

"Deaders."

"Those deaders are going to be all over the car."

"Okay, so set off a car alarm to one of the other cars, one on the other side of the lot, and distract them." Mikey roots through the pile, pulls out a key, and examines the cars in the lot.

"Wait." My mind stumbles over a thought. "What if the noise attracts the attention of all the deaders in the area? I mean, what if they *all* freaking come? That sign last night said twenty-something thousand. I bet every one of those people are dead, or—deader. Or maybe we do get out to the cars in time, but think about this: we don't know if they even have gas in them, right?" The two men stare at me in silence. "What? Did I say something stupid again?"

"No, you're actually right."

I can't help be feel a shiny little glow of pride.

"Okay, so…?" I prompt.

"We need to find the workshop. If they have a workshop, then they might have some jiffy cans of gas in there. We get some gas, re-group, distract the deaders, and make a run for it." JD, for the first time since I've known him, seems unsure. "Right?"

I look at Mikey, who painfully ignores my stare, but replies to JD all the same.

"Sounds about right. Let's do this."

We all stand and move to the back of the showroom again. There's a door marked *EMPLOYEE BREAKROOM,* and we push it open. It leads to a long corridor with several doors on either side. JD flips the switch and we all blink as most of the long tubes flare to life above us. The corridor is painted in a light green, which Mikey seems disgusted with.

"What's got your panties in a bunch?" I dare to speak and try to patch up our differences.

Mikey still refuses to look at me, but surprisingly replies. "I hate the color green. It reminds me of my mother's pea soup that she used to force me to eat as a kid."

I snort out a laugh. "Mother issues, figures."

He finally looks at me. "I do not have mother issues. Her pea soup was my fucking issue, if you must know."

I hold my hands up. "Okay, sorry." I'm silent a beat before I continue. "It's been proven that green is a calming color, you know."

He raises an eyebrow at me.

"I'm serious," I laugh.

JD joins in the conversation, much to the exasperation of Mikey, who's still trying to be pissed off. "She's right. There was a study done on how color affects your mood, and they found that green—a particular shade, anyway—had a calming and therapeutic effect on people."

I snigger, but can't hide the surprised expression on my face from the fact that that JD knows this stuff too. I decide to drop the topic, since I'm only poking the flames of Mikey's annoyance with me. There's a framed map on the wall showing the showroom and all the other parts of the car lot. We find our bearings, which really isn't difficult, and head off in the direction of the workshop.

"So what about other colors?" Mikey asks after a couple of minutes, surprising both me and JD. JD turns to glower at us.

"Excuse me?" I smirk, playing dumb.

"You know, like, what do other colors do?"

JD huffs as he walks, clearly unimpressed with our unimportant conversation about paint colors and not 'saving our asses,' but you know, sometimes you have to take a break from the serious things in life. Especially after my morbid conversation with Mikey earlier. I look at Mikey's profile, and he turns to look at me too. His mouth quirks at the side as he tries to stop himself from smiling, and my stomach does a little flip. What the fuck is it with this guy? I can't seem to shake him no matter what I do. We're like magnets that are attracted to each other—we keep springing back, no matter how much I force us apart.

"Um, well, purple colors have been said to help with OCD and other disorders. Orange is supposed to make people feel more self-worth and relieve feelings of self-pity—if I remember correctly anyway." I shrug. "I can't remember the rest."

"No way!" Mikey retorts. "All that from a color, huh?"

"You two done?"

I drag my eyes away from Mikey and look at JD.

"Yeah, sorry. I was rambling, wasn't I?" I shrug again apologetically.

JD frowns at me. "This is it." He gestures toward the door on our left and wiggles the handle. "It's locked. Mikey, you're up."

My heart rate picks up automatically. I don't like locked doors. Locked doors have never boded well for my little group or me. I grip my machete tighter, wishing that Crunch were with us with all her mad fighting skills. Damn her. She's like a super weapon. She can fight like an assassin and she's like Dr. Quinn, Medicine Woman—how can I compete with that?

Mikey retrieves his little set of tools and begins to go to work on the door, actively avoiding touching the bloody handprint swiped down the middle of it. It takes longer than the previous night, but it's still only a matter of minutes before he's done. He stands back as JD steps forward, obviously wanting to take the lead on this, as usual. With a turn of the handle, the door swings open and we step into the gloom beyond.

Actually it's not very gloomy at all, since there are windows all along the top of the wall near the ceiling; but still you get the idea, right?

The smell that hits us makes my stomach churn, and the foreboding feeling within me increases. I hate this part. I'm so used to deaders these days, the smell, the moaning, and yes—the fear. It never goes away, but I'm used to it being there, constantly nibbling away at my insides like some kind of stomach ulcer. However, this part—those few seconds before you see them—that's the part I really hate. It's like watching a horror movie: the music has changed and you know that shit is about to get serious, but it's a matter of waiting for the scary thing to jump out and make you spill your popcorn.

Well, it's like this day in and day out for us, constantly waiting for something to happen, and when the smell of them hits me, it's as if the music on my own little horror movie has taken a turn for the worse.

I grind my jaw together and take a deep breath as we go inside. This is definitely the workshop, and from the looks of things, several cars were under repair at the time of the zombie uprising. Several mechanic zombies have spotted us and are slowly shambling toward us. I count three in total, but then another one peeks from around a doorway. Yes—peeks! That's what it seems like anyway. He pops his head inside and then peeks back out again with a groan. His constant peek-hide-groan repetition is freaking me out. What the hell is wrong with him?

JD has already sliced the head off one of the zombies, and Mikey is making short work with another. A deader in a surprisingly tidy-looking suit is making its way behind him. I jog over and slam my machete into the back of its skull, and it drops down to the floor. Mikey turns at the sound behind him and nearly misses his own deader making a grab for him. They scuffle, with Mikey attempting to pull the deader's hands off his clothes as it tries to pull him toward its attractively decaying mouth.

Mikey reaches back and punches it hard in the jaw. Its jaw slides loose from its joints and hangs from its face. It doesn't stop to assess the damage that has been done, but continues to reach for him. At least with half its face hanging down, it doesn't have the strength in its jaw to take a bite of him. Still, the fat black tongue that dangles from deep in its throat (and is now lapping like a puppy looking for its mama's teat) is disgusting enough to make me want to vomit. Both hands are on Mikey's clothes now, and Mikey drops his weapon and struggles to push the deader off him. I run behind the deader and grab the back of its blue overalls and pull as hard as I can. I hear a rip of clothing and Mikey takes this opportunity to pull out of its grip. He reaches for his other weapon—my now sharp-as-fuck butcher knife—and slams it through the deader's forehead without taking a breath. Splatter and brain matter spray around me, and I gasp and turn away with a grimace.

"You have to see this," JD shouts across to us.

I let the heavy deader drop from my grasp, and we head over to where JD is standing while I wipe my sleeves across my face to clear the filth. The fat deader continues to peek out from the office and growl at us, but doesn't make any attempt to come and get us; as we get closer, I can see why.

Deader-dude number four was a huge, flabby guy, and he's caught between a rock and a hard place. No really, he is. What I thought was an office is actually a tool-station-cum-work-area, and his body is pinned to the work surface by a large clamp holding his stomach in place and a filing cabinet pushed up against his back. He snaps at us, and tears at his own body to get free.

"Jesus, that's messed up."

"How is it even stuck there?" Mikey cranes his neck around the deader, jerking back when it reaches for him. "Shit!" He shudders and comes away.

"His stomach." JD assesses without looking, presumably having checked before.

"What?" I grimace and try to look around the rotting zombie.

The sound of ripping draws my attention. The deader, now more than just a little bit infuriated by his inability to move and eat us, has torn—yes, torn—his stomach out of the vice's mouth. A decidedly disgusting splatter hits the floor, as rotted guts and other mushy black insides pile around its feet, and he makes a move for me. Fortunately, the cabinet holds in place just long enough for me to swipe the deader's head away from his shoulders in one slice—okay, okay, maybe two.

THIRTY ONE

"**N**ina!" Mikey grabs me by the shoulders and shoves me roughly to the side as the zombie's snapping head passes by my face. I slam into the filing cabinet with a grimace.

The head lands on the floor with a sickening thud and JD slams his boot into its face, crushing it below his heel until it collapses under the pressure and stops moving altogether.

"You okay?" Mikey looks me over with concern and I shrug him off, feeling stupid and embarrassed.

"Yes, get off, I'm fine." I slip in the black guts on the floor, and grip his arm to steady myself. The smell wafts up to me and my gag reflex kicks in. "Urgh, who would do that to it? That's seriously messed up."

"You should say thank you. He probably just saved that pretty face of yours," JD snarks as I pass him.

"Whatever." I glare back. "Can we just get on with this?"

Both men come out of the little tool shop and look around. We check under all the cars and around the back of everything to make sure that we are completely alone now. We don't want any more surprises.

As we're searching, I come across rows of car batteries all hooked up to a weird wire system. I can't figure it out, so move on to some cupboards with padlocks on them. I realize that my zombie-killing score is better than the guys', and I can't keep the satisfied grin from my face as I grab a hammer and smash the padlock off a cupboard.

"What's there to smile about?" Mikey calls out to me when I finish in my destruction.

"Nothing." I smirk again, and rummage through the tools inside. There's nothing overly useful that I can see, so I move on to the next cupboard.

"Must be something, from the looks of your grin."

"I was just thinking that I killed more of them than either of you two." I pick my hammer back up and smash it down on the next lock until it comes apart.

"You keeping score?" Mikey laughs with a shake of his head.

"No, it's just that you treat me like a little girl, acting like I can't look after myself, and then I manage to prove you wrong and take two of them out to your one." I turn to look at him, my grin back in place. "You could even say that it was three, since I had to rescue you from yours."

Mikey's grin falters.

"I've got an idea." JD calls out before Mikey can reply to me.

We head over to where JD's standing, by some cars up high on a workstation. An entire engine looks to be beside it, and I have no idea where he could be going with this.

"So I was thinking that these cars will have gas in them, maybe we could siphon it out and we've got what we came for, but then I spotted something else." He smiles tightly. It might be the first smile I've ever seen on his face.

"Well, don't keep us hanging, man," Mikey huffs.

JD doesn't answer us, but points. The aim of his finger rests upon a white van and a tow truck. These weren't in for repairs. They were the company's trucks, and therefore will be filled with lots of lovely gasoline. I almost want to cheer at our good fortune and pray that we're right. We quickly head into the actual office, which is next-door to the little tool-station-cum-zombie-torture-chamber. The keys, the blessed fucking keys, are hanging on the wall. I think of Emily's dad, always hanging his keys on the wall in case of an emergency, and wonder if he wasn't as stupid as I first thought. Maybe he was actually onto something.

Mikey climbs in the tow truck, but after a few moments he calls out to us.

"It's dead," he grumbles.

JD jumps in and tries the van. That one makes a soft whining noise but nothing else, and he eventually climbs out looking more pissed off than I previously thought possible.

"This one's dead too," JD snaps. "New plan, I guess."

I turn and walk away to the batteries I had found in the corner of the garage, their wires winding around them like worms in a can.

"Guys..."

JD and Mikey come over, and I don't even have to say anything else. JD puts his arm around my waist and hugs me close. "Sometimes you're not a total pain in my ass, Nina."

I can't help but blush and smile at his backhanded compliment.

Half an hour later and Mikey and JD have swapped the batteries out of the vehicles for the new ones and they both climb in and try them. Both vehicles whine and then start up with a happy roar, which fills the enclosed space. Fucking energy-saving solar panels!

Both men climb down from the vehicles with huge happy faces and I actually do a little cheer. There's just no way to keep it inside me any longer. Both men laugh, and for once I don't feel embarrassed, just thankful that I have them on my side.

"Let's get the others and get the fuck out of Dodge," JD hollers, sounding almost cheery as he leaves the room.

"Why can't we stay here?" Emily whines at me.

"It's not safe here, Em. No place this big is, you know that; it's Zombie 101."

She twirls around on the chair twice more before I stick my foot out to stop her. The twirling is making me nauseous.

"But we have electricity, lights, a refrigerator! We could do so much here," she whines at me again.

"First off, we shouldn't be using the lights if we can help it—it attracts the deaders—and secondly, I'll refer to point one, where there are a shit ton of deaders everywhere." I get down on my knees so I can catch her eye. "Emily, this place is crawling with them. In fact, this place is actually going to continue to attract deaders from everywhere. The lights and noise are what bring them, and unless we turn everything off, they're just going to keep coming, therefore making your point about staying…pointless. We're going, so let's get our stuff together and get gone." I stand back up.

"What if I don't come with you?" She raises an eyebrow at me, just daring me to take her on.

"Don't pull the rebellious teenager card with me. You *are* coming.

I can't make you, but JD and Mikey will. We're sure as shit not leaving you here to die like the rest of this town." I storm out of the room before she can argue with me any more.

Britta is standing in the hallway, seemingly waiting for me to come out.

"What's up, Britta?" I continue down the hallway, with her falling into step beside me.

"I just wanted to say thank you, really."

I stop and look at her, dragging her into a side room before anyone sees us. Turns out we're in a janitor's closet of some sort. Jackpot. There's toilet paper, disinfectant, car polish, and lots of other things.

"No problem, you don't need to thank me." I begin to root through all the items in a search for anything useful.

"Yes, there is. She would have killed me if it came down to that." Britta touches a hand to my shoulder to get my attention.

"You're right and wrong," I say as I grab a bottle of what should be the pink liquid soap. I give it a shake but it's completely solidified, so I put it back. "She wouldn't have killed you as such, but if it came down to you or her, I'm pretty sure she would have tripped you and left you for dead." I offer her a small shrug. "Sorry, that sounds harsh, but—"

"No, I know that you're right. Crunch will be your best friend until it comes to a choice between you or her, and then you're, how do you say? Um…"

"Toast?" I offer.

"Toast?" She looks confused.

"Yeah, you know, like, you're toast—caput."

"Caput?" She looks even more confused. "I don't understand that, but you would be dead. For that I am sure. I need to get strong and able to fight again, and quickly."

I nod. "Yes. Until then, stay close to me."

Before I can say or do anything else, though, Britta leans over and gives me a big hug. I try to resist, but, as the saying goes, resistance is futile, and I feel myself melt into the gesture. I don't know what, if anything I could do to defend Britta against Crunch. Crunch is badass, and I'm…pfft, heck, I don't know, determined? Yeah, real scary, right?

THIRTY TWO

We pack up our stuff and split into two groups, about which there is a massive discussion. It seems that there is trouble in paradise and the harmony is gone from our group since Josie got killed.

Britta doesn't want to stay with Crunch, but I won't let Emily out of my sight. Similarly, Mikey wants to stay with me. I'd be annoyed that he was treating me like a weak woman, but to be fair to him, he's clearly getting the short straw since my little group *is* weak.

Eventually JD decides he and Crunch will take the tow truck, and the rest of us will go in the van. I know that both JD and Crunch wouldn't give a second thought to leaving us behind, but I'm okay with that—if I was going to be stuck with any of this group, I wouldn't want it to be them, anyway. Mikey and I ride up front and let Britta and Emily rest up in the back. Both of them could do with building up their strength again. Hell, we all could, but they are the weakest of us right now. Britta has two weak arms, one from the deaders yesterday and the other from when we were living up in the tree tops. Both seem to be healing nicely, though, and I think a couple more days and she'll be ready to fight again. We find quite a few useful things in the garage—flashlights, radios, walkie-talkies, that sort of thing—and pack everything we can get our hands on. We even manage to raid the vending machines of the last of their chocolate bars, bags of stale chips, and flat sodas. The amazing thing is that because the electricity still works here, the drinks are still cold. I've never tasted something so good in my whole damn life. It's like the amber nectar of life as it pours down my throat, the elixir of the gods, the—well, you get the idea. It's damn refreshing is what it is, and I can't help but count down the minutes until I can have another one.

I notice the lack of internal handles on the van as the girls climb in. "Um, I guess bang if you need anything." I shrug apologetically.

We check out the windows for any stray deaders before we lift the garage door and drive away into the sunset. There aren't any there, but in the daylight we can see that the entire town is crawling with them. No, really. There's a ton of them that don't have any legs anymore and are just crawling around like fucking snakes in a desert.

It seems that I was completely accurate when I told Emily that the lights and noise attract the dead. By my estimations, every night that the lights come on, more and more deaders head for this town. I simply cannot wait to leave this place.

I hit the garage door button to get it to open up and JD heads out first, leading our convoy. I wait until Mikey pulls all the way out before I press the *close* button behind me and quickly climb into our little white repair van. As we follow JD out of the side alley, we come upon a bunch of deaders. JD heads straight for them, but Mikey goes around the bodies littering the street—well, as much as he can anyway. It's not so easy to do when arms and legs are flying all over the damn place.

A hand flicks from under JD's tire and onto the hood of our van with a thud. I can see Crunch turn around to look and start laughing.

Bitch.

Thankfully, since we were already at the edge of town, we don't have far to go before we are out onto the open road and waving bye-bye to the environmentally friendly Acer Town. Thank the fucking gods for that.

I sit back in my chair and watch the landscape passing us by as we follow JD. I feel a strange sort of longing to get to Ben's parents' cabin, now that we're so close. It's still another couple of days' drive, but we could possibly do this with very limited stopping now, and that thought spurs on my giddiness. JD and Mikey seem to think that the place could be relatively untouched, safe even. Jesus, if it is, that would be…

A bubble of happiness builds in my chest. Maybe we could settle down for a while again. We could build defenses from the deaders. The Forgotten—stupid name—don't know where we are, so we would be off their radar. We could maybe find some peace, some happiness. It feels ironic after my little speech with Mikey this morning.

"I'm sorry, Mikey. I shouldn't have been so cold with you today." I look at him; his eyes never leave the road. "I mean, I still believe those things, but in a way, I guess you're right. Maybe there can be some happiness in this world. Maybe it doesn't have to be all doom and gloom."

I wait for him to say something, give me a smile—shit, anything at this point—but what I get is a sidelong look and a shrug of the shoulders.

"Don't be like that," I plead. "I don't want to fight with you anymore. I was wrong, you were right—well, maybe not *right*, but there may be some truth to what you say." I look at him again, and see his mouth quirk up so I continue. "What can I say?"

"Tell me that you like me," he replies.

"What?"

"Tell me that you like me, Nina. No more bullshit. I tried to tell you how I felt this morning. I mean *Jesus,* woman, I'm not an emotional guy, so that shit is hard. But whatever, it's done now, and now I want to hear you tell me you like me. *I* know that you do, but do *you* know that you do?"

"And what if I don't?"

"Don't feel the same, or don't tell me?"

"Both," I snap.

"I don't know." He pauses. "I didn't think about that."

I smirk, playing him at his own game, and don't say anything.

"Woman!" He grabs my thigh and squeezes it. "Tell me, or so help you I'll…"

I crack up laughing. "Fine, fine: I like you, okay? Does that make you feel better?" I snigger. "Is that a nice ego boost for you?"

"Yes, but now what are you gonna do about it?" he asks.

"What do you mean?" I ask, confused. "Do about what?"

"To make it up to me? You made me feel like a total dick this morning. I think that since you're going to be my girlfriend, that you should be, you know, trying to make me feel better somehow." He looks at me and gives me his award-winning smile.

"I'm not making anything up to you, and who said I was your girlfriend?" I splutter. "Jeez, you tell a guy you like him in these apocalypse times, and he goes all stalker on your ass. Maybe you should be trying to *get* me to be your girlfriend, instead of just presuming.

Like with a foot rub or a trip to the movies or something."

He looks at me and we both crack up laughing at the stupidity of it all. *The movies, ha, now wouldn't that be a nice treat?*

"Let's just get to the making up part." He smiles when our laughing calms down. "That's my favorite part of having a girlfriend."

I roll my eyes at him. "Isn't it for all men?"

We drive in silence for a while before Mikey breaks it.

"Tell me about your husband."

Jesus, mood breaker.

I look at him, trying to keep my annoyance from showing. The last thing I want is another fight.

"I don't want to talk about him."

"Why not? You must have had some great times before, well—just before. You know. What was he like? I need to know what I'm up against."

He tries to lighten the mood with a smile, but my heart breaks every time I think about Ben. I don't know, maybe it's time that I put it all to bed. Maybe if I tell someone what happened, I *can* move on.

"He…" I shake my head, the words forming a hard lump in my throat before they can even get out of my mouth. "He was called Ben."

I let the words settle between us, thinking about all the things that I could tell Mikey about him: how great he was at making me feel special all the time, but especially when I was feeling sick; how awful he was at fixing things; how ambitious he had been, but how he lacked motivation. Every memory makes me think about all of our arguments in the weeks before he died, and the guilt builds in me.

"I killed him," I blurt out.

Silence spans between us for what seems like miles, but can only be a couple of seconds.

"Did you mean to?" he finally asks.

I nod my head *yes* and tears form in my eyes. "Yes and no. I can't talk about this, Mikey. I'm sorry."

I look at him; he gives me a sidelong glance and nods.

"It hurts too much to talk about it. Do you understand?" I ask in a pathetically pleading voice, which I want to slap myself silly for having.

"Yeah. We've all done things that we regret, Nina." He glances at me, and his look tells me that he isn't just saying this to make me feel better.

I let the silence swallow up the moment between us.

"What happened to you, Mikey?"

People always seem to like talking about 'their' stories, and what happened to them when the world went to shit. Here I am joining the popular crowd, trying to revisit a past that doesn't matter anymore; but in truth, it *does* matter. It's been eating away at me since it happened. Maybe I can open up if he does—and maybe we can both unburden ourselves. I normally hate this kind of thing, but with Mikey I feel safe, and like I won't be judged.

"Now that, I don't want to talk about." He forces out a laugh.

I look at him in confusion. "Why?" I regret asking instantly.

I didn't want to talk about Ben, and I should know better and respect his privacy, but it just feels strange. I've never come across anyone who didn't want to talk about their story. That's *my* thing.

"I just don't like talking about it. Tell me what happened to you." He glances at me again.

Shit. "I don't want to talk about that," I half-snort out.

"Okay." He furrows his brow at me but lets it slide, since I did the same for him. "What was it like behind the walls?"

"I don't want to talk about that either," I half-whisper.

"This really isn't going very well is it?" he huffs.

I shake my head, lost in my own memories. I stare out the window, watching a couple of deaders stumbling down the road. They seem to speed up a fraction as we pass them, in the hopes of catching us. But thankfully, deaders can't run.

I think back to Lee and wonder what he is doing now, what all the other people trapped inside are doing. My mind flits from image to image of the horrors I endured while behind their so-called protective walls, and a shudder runs through me.

"They were supposed to protect us," I begin. "They were supposed to protect us from the dead, from the evil on the outside, and they did. They just didn't protect us from the evil within." I swallow down the lump, which has appeared again. "The people in charge, they… changed, once the help stopped. Once the government collapsed, I guess. There were no more food drops, no more first aid drops. About six months in, when it all started to go to shit and we knew no more help was coming, everyone started to rebel, thinking it would be better on the outside, or thinking that they would be better being in charge." I huff out my anxiety and chance a look at him. His face is stony, a mask of indifference, but his grinding jaw gives him away.

"When they started to rebel, some of the weak ones got picked off and—well, you know what happens when you die." I think back to that first person behind the walls coming back to life. The panic from everyone. "One of the men there, Lee—he was a nobody, really—he had a gun. He shot her, the woman that turned, and then he turned and shot the guy that was in charge, and declared himself the new leader."

"Then what?"

The image of Lee standing there with his gun in hand, declaring himself in charge, is vivid in my mind. The bloodshed, the tears, the pain…

"Nina."

I look back at Mikey. I hadn't realized that I had stopped talking. "That wasn't the end of it though." I swallow. "Once we were all dependent on him, he took our weapons, he made us work for food, for water, for anything. We paid with…whatever we had, and if we didn't have anything or didn't want to, they either took what they wanted from you or they killed one of your family. One less mouth to feed, they said."

I hear Mikey suck in a breath through his teeth. This is the part I hate.

"What did they do to you, Nina?" I can practically hear his teeth crunching away.

"I didn't have any family." I look at him. "What do you think happened?" I can't keep the bitter edge from my voice. "That wasn't even the worst of it," I huff. "The worst was watching everyone else. Watching them suffer every day, slowly becoming people that they hated. I hated that place, and for a while I hated everyone in there, but it wasn't their fault that they didn't help each other; they had their own families to protect. You just couldn't risk trying to help anyone else, for fear of what would happen to you. Shit, look what happened to *me* when I tried to protect Emily."

"We never knew," he whispers under his breath.

"What? What didn't you know?" I choke back my tears. I will not cry. I've cried enough for a lifetime because of those assholes.

Mikey shakes his head. "Nothing. It doesn't matter now."

THIRTY THREE

The day draws on and the sun rises higher in the sky. One of the girls bangs from the back of the van and I use the walkie talkie to get JD to pull over, since it seems clear.

Mikey starts to pull to the side of the road, but I place my hand on top of his and give it a little squeeze.

"Stay in the middle. We can see all around us then."

He looks confused, but nods and stops the van smack dab in the middle of the road regardless, yet somehow still managing to stay close enough to the tow truck.

We all climb out and I open the back doors for Emily and Britta. They both jump out, looking hot and sweaty and pissed off.

"It is *not* comfy in there." Emily storms off to the side of the road to pee, and I chase after her.

"Don't go on your own, Em. Never go on your own."

I look down at the side of the road and double-check all the way along to make sure no deaders are playing peek-a-boo with us. Satisfied,

I nod my *okay* to her and turn around to give her some privacy.

"This sucks. It's too hot in there."

I listen to her pee, kind of satisfied that she must be getting enough fluids since it goes on for what seems like forever, and then realize that's kind of gross.

"I know, but what can we do?" I shrug, only half listening. It's true, it sucks, but there really isn't anything I can do about it. I would kill to be able to just sleep for half the day.

"Maybe I can come up front with you and Mikey?" Emily comes up beside me and offers me a smile.

"You can't leave Britta back there on her own," I tut.

"Maybe she could squeeze in to the front too?"

"We won't all fit, don't be stupid."

We make our way over to the rest of the group. I can still hear Emily pleading to come in the front with me, but I'm not really listening to her. I'm getting hungry, and my thoughts stray to the chips and sodas we snagged earlier. I want to ration them and make them last, but I'm a weak, weak woman, and I grab my bag from the front seat and pull out one of the cans. My hand moves over the bottle of vodka and I can't help but smile.

"What's got you so happy?" Crunch snaps, half glancing at Mikey.

I pull out my bottle of Vodka with a grin.

"I think a celebration is in order when we get to the cabin." I pull out one of the cans and everyone smiles. What's not to like about a vodka and Coke? I glance down at the can of pop in my hand, seeing that it's orangeade, and shrug. What's not to like about vodka and orangeade? It reminds me of a time before all this crap—shooting and killing, the dead always on the hunt for fresh brains. Yes, a nice cool drink to take the edge off in the evening is just what the doctor ordered. Aaah, normality. Sweet, blessed normality.

"Getting drunk is not an option," JD snaps.

Crunch digs him in the ribs. "Shut the fuck up, grumpy. That's the first good idea this chick has had since I met her."

See? The doctor has literally just ordered it.

I can't help but laugh, and now I'm really eager to get going and get to the cabin.

"Let's get going then. Mikey, you want me to drive for a little bit?" I ask, as we head back to the van.

"That be okay?" He scratches the back of his neck like he does when he's unsure.

"Yeah, you can take over when night hits." I look at Emily's pouty teenage face. "In fact, why don't you get in the back and have a sleep? The rest will do you good."

"Are you trying to get me in your bed, Nina?" He smirks.

"No, I'm trying to get you in *a* bed. There's a difference," I snigger.

"Fine, sounds good. You sure you'll be okay?"

"Yeah. I can take care of myself, you know." I push him playfully.

Jesus, where did this girliness come from? Good lord, I've found my femininity again.

"Em, you're up front with me."

Emily runs over and hugs me, and I shrug her off with a laugh. Now Britta looks pretty pissed off. Can I not get a break?

"You jumping up front too, Britts?" I cut in before she can moan at me too.

She smiles and grabs her stuff from the back.

We climb in the front, and Mikey climbs in the back. JD beeps at us to hurry up, which I think is not only fucking rude, to be honest, but it's also dangerous. I give him the finger to show him my appreciation, and we set off again.

"So, Britta, where are you originally from?" I ask as we pass a group of three or four deaders chowing down on a horse. Or I *think* it's a horse; there's not much left of it anymore—just stringy, dried-out skin and a near-hollow carcass. One deader is gnawing on what looks like a leg bone, but drops it and stands when it catches sight of our car. I watch it in my rearview mirror; it takes a couple of shaky steps before lifting its head to the sky and taking a deep sniff. It smells the horse and turns back to it, seemingly losing interest in us. I breathe a sigh of relief and turn my attention back to Britta.

"Germany, but I've lived over here for a long time now."

"That explains the accent then."

"Yes, I wonder if I still have it sometimes, you know?" She laughs. I nod. "You do," I smile.

Emily smiles happily at me and then at Britta, her big saucer eyes staring widely at us. "Britta was telling me that she used to study graphic design before—well, before all of this. That's what I wanted to do when I grew up." She turns excitedly in her seat so that she can see us both easier.

I feel like I'm in a freak show, and me and Britta are the main attraction. But then, I guess Emily doesn't really have anyone to look up to anymore. No parents, no family, no damn celebrities gracing the cover of whatever trashy magazine they decided to go topless on. Still, it's unnerving to feel so idolized when I haven't done anything to deserve it.

"That's cool. Were you here on a student visa or something, or did you have family living here?" *Nosy me,* I internally scold myself.

"No, no family. They are all back in Germany. They were, I guess," her voice trails off. "I don't know what happened to them.

279

Communications went down, and the last I heard was that they were locking down the house."

Way to go, Nina!

"No news is good news, right?" I offer a smile, but it fails miserably, since in this world, no news is neither a good thing nor a bad thing. It's just no news. I let the van lapse back into silence. We drive for a couple of miles, either staring at the crazy overgrown landscape or watching JD's car in front of us. He keeps to a steady fifty miles per hour, no more, no less, and keeps his truck in the middle of the road.

There's a shape a mile or so down the road, and I begin to make out that it's a car. There are four or five deaders surrounding it, all groaning loudly and banging on the glass. There are definitely people inside, but how many I just don't know. I slow the van down to get a better look, readying myself to stop, but then I see Emily's terrified face and know that I can't. Shit, I wish Mikey were up here.

JD speeds right on past without a second glance, and I presume without a second thought too. Damn him for not giving a shit. Yet as we get closer, I slow down again. Even from inside the van, I can hear the screaming coming from inside the car. I can't just leave these people to die. I make a split second decision.

"Emily, my machete." I bark out the order and slam on the brakes. When she doesn't pass it to me, I reach between her legs and grab it myself. "Britta, you can drive, right?"

She nods at me sullenly, chewing on her bottom lip. A deader turns from the car and groans wickedly. I swear it fucking smiles at me too, happy to see a new meal on the horizon.

"You get her out of here if anything happens to me." I jump out of the van before I lose my nerve, looking back once at Emily. "I love you, Em." And I do, too.

I run at the deader stumbling toward me, raising my machete high, and slash it across its neck. Well, I aim for the neck, but I'm a terrible fucking shot and instead slice across its face, but it still does the trick in stopping brain activity, and the deader drops where it stands with unhappy disgusting and sloppy *thud*.

Another deader turns from the vehicle, its milky eyes focusing in on me, the new food source, and it moans and groans toward me. One of its feet is dragging along the ground, leaving a black smear behind it. I can hear screaming and banging and an engine trying to turn over, but I don't dare look away from the deaders in front of me for anything.

Another deader has caught my scent, its head in the air as it sniffs me out like a bloodhound, and it turns to come for me too. Only when it does do I see that it has no eyes; black holes fill the space in its filthy sunken in face. Deader number one is close enough now, and I swing for it in a panic. My first one misses and I swing back wildly, cutting it through the stomach. Its insides spill onto the blacktop with a sound somewhat akin to vomit hitting the ground, but it comes for me regardless of its loss of intestines and capacity to hold any of my fine meaty face within it.

I scream and swing back and hit its arm, slicing it off. Its other arm reaches for me and I dodge back and stumble to the ground with another loud scream. I hit out without thinking and slice at its legs. I hit one of them and the deader falls to its knees, and I jump back up and away. The car and people that I had tried to save finally revs its engine and screams away in a ball of smoke.

God-fucking-dammit!

I kick at the deader scrambling at my feet and run back to the van. Britta throws the door open before I get there and I dive in, slam it shut, and rev my own engine before driving away myself.

Half a mile down the road, I finally let out the breath that I've been holding. Emily is sobbing next to me, with Britta's comforting arms around her.

"You better pull over," Britta says, and I look at her.

"Why?" My voice is hoarse from screaming.

"Mikey," she simply says.

It's then that I hear the thudding and shouting coming from the back of the van, and for a minute I wonder if a deader got inside somehow and Mikey was fighting it. I look around us quickly, stop the vehicle, and dive out. Going around to the back of the van, I pull open the doors as Mikey shoulder-barges them at the same time, and he falls to the ground with a loud *thud* before scrambling on his knees for his machete.

He jumps up and looks around us frantically, his eyes wide, almost bulging from their sockets.

"What the fuck's going on?" He grabs me by the arms.

"There was another car in trouble..." I begin before he cuts me up.

"What? Tell me you didn't stop. You never stop for anything, Nina!" he shouts, and then looks around us again before dragging me to the front of the van. "Is everyone okay?"

Both Emily and Britta nod at him. Emily quickly resumes her crying.

"Why's she crying?" he shouts again.

"Stop fucking shouting at me. She's crying because—I don't know." I turn to her. "Why are you crying?"

"Because they nearly got you," she sobs.

"What? No they didn't, I was fine..." My voice drifts off as I remember falling to the ground. "I had it all under control."

"Where's JD?" Mikey asks.

"He took off." I shrug, trying to appear nonchalant, like I'm not bothered, even though I am.

"Motherf—okay, girls, get out. You're in the back again. I'm driving."

Emily stops her crying and climbs out, giving me a filthy look as she goes around to the back of the van. I'm not sure if she's pissed that I just put us all in danger, or that she has to go in the back again. Either way, I'm going to need to do some sucking up later.

"Get in." Mikey gestures to the van and I climb in without questioning it.

He slams the door behind me and climbs in the driver's side, his face stony as he starts the vehicle and we set off again, going faster than before. I say nothing through it all, feeling guilty and a little shocked by how pissed everyone is at me. I can't believe that any of them would have just taken off and left the car and all the people inside to die. Then again, the bastards never even tried to help me or thank me, so maybe I should have left them to it. I haven't lived in this world long enough to judge people, I guess.

"You NEVER stop your vehicle. Do you understand?" Mikey cuts into my thoughts.

I nod my agreement but don't say anything, not wanting to provoke him further. In the distance I can see a vehicle, and I wonder if it's JD. As we get closer I can see that it's the car that I tried to save. They've crashed into a tree. Smoke pours from the front of the car, the alarm blaring. I look at Mikey, ready to ask if we should help them.

"Don't even think about it," he snaps as we pass them by.

I look into the car as we do, glad to see two males and one woman, all unconscious. In the distance I can see the deaders approaching, attracted by the noise from the alarm. I shiver and look away. They left me for dead, and that doesn't make it right leaving them for dead, but either way the choice is out of my hands, since I'm not the one in charge of the wheel. I close my eyes to block it all out, but I can't. These are people—people who need help.

"Mikey?" I plead.

"No," he shouts again.

I huff and fold my arms.

THIRTY FOUR

At some point I must drift off, because when I wake it's much darker. Not quite nighttime, but not quite daytime either. I sit up and stretch, glancing sideways at Mikey.

"Hey," I offer, with a bite of my lip. I'm unsure of how he's going to be after our previous argument.

"Hey, you sleep okay?"

"Yeah, thanks." I breathe out a sigh of relief that he's being okay with me. "Have you seen JD's truck anywhere?" I ask, still feeling annoyed at him for bailing on me.

"Yeah, they're behind us. I caught up to them and took the lead. I think JD knew how pissed off I was at him, plus I know these roads better than he does."

I'm dying to know what was said between them, but since he isn't offering the information, I refuse to ask for it. My mouth feels dry and scratchy, and I'm going to need to pee at some point soon. That's one of the positives of being dehydrated: that I don't need to go as often. My stomach grumbles in protest that I left it out of my equation, but I'm not sure I can get any food into it without peeing first.

"I'm hungry," I say, more to myself than Mikey.

"We're stopping pretty soon for the night. I'm beat." Mikey yawns after his statement as if to prove a point, but he didn't need to. The thick black rings under his eyes give him away.

"Have you heard anything from Britta or Emily?" I ask.

He shakes his head no. "Guess they went back to sleep."

I realize that we're driving uphill and wonder whereabouts we are now. The road is rocky and bumpy, and I'm glad that there is at least a little daylight left so that we can avoid hitting any of the trees that are now towering all around us.

"Where are we going?" I ask as I grip the handle of my door when we hit a particularly bumpy part of the path and we rock side to side. I feel guilty about Emily and Britta being in the back of the van, and simultaneously worry about how much shit Emily is going to give me when she gets out.

"Up into the hills," he replies, turning on his high beams as the trees get even more condensed around us.

"Is that safe?"

He looks at me briefly. "Not scared, are you?"

"Uh, yeah. What are you, stupid?" I laugh in exasperation.

"We'd be hard-pressed to get any zombies up here. It's uphill for starters, which makes us up-current or some shit like that—our smell shouldn't pass down the mountain to them—and this road is really steep, making it incredibly hard for them to get up here. That's not to say they can't or won't, but it's the safest place for now, at least." He shrugs.

I hate to admit it, but in all honesty it sounds like pretty sound logic. It's not long until the road flattens out and we finally pull to a stop. Mikey gets out first, and I wait until he tells me it's clear before getting out myself and letting the girls out of the back of the van.

They groan loudly as they stretch themselves out. Emily still seems pretty pissed off at me, but not as much as before, and I wonder if I have Britta to thank for that or just her nature.

JD pulls up a couple of minutes after us, and he and Crunch jump out, both looking tired. I decide right then that I'm not going to say anything to either of them. I can tell that Crunch is waiting for me to, and I'll be damned if I'm going to let her know that she got the better of me or got under my skin in any way. The air smells clean and fresh, not a hint of deader smell around, and it takes all my concentration to not let my guard down.

"There's a light over there." Emily grips my hand and points further through the trees.

Sure enough, she's right: there *is* a light. My hand grips my machete as I quickly scan the area. Everyone has had the same thought and is brandishing some sort of deadly weapon. Even Britta is trying desperately to get a firm grip on her machete.

We creep toward the light, and as we get closer, we see that it's actually a small, green RV nestled between the trees. It's seen better days, too, if I'm honest. No sound is coming from inside, but a dim light is glowing in each of its little windows. The people inside must either be stupid to have the lights on, or know the area as well as—if not better than—Mikey. We tiptoe toward the door, with Crunch trying to peer in through the windows. Standing outside the door, my heart races and I hold my breath. JD clasps the doorknob, and on a whispered count of three, flings the door wide open. What we see is not, let me repeat that, *not* what we expect to see.

Zombies? Yep, that I would expect. Blood, the stench of death? Yep, that works too. However, what we see is a large man who looks to be completely smashed and is slowly sliding off a little sofa and down to the floor. His eyes are fogged over and rimmed with red, and he flinches when he sees us all standing there gawking in at him. He gives a jump and a little scream and then passes out, all in one swift action. His body finishes its descent to the floor, and sits propped up against the camper's little sofa.

None of us say anything as we stand there, open-mouthed and waiting for him to move, wake, or dive up and attack us where we stand. Instead, his chest rises as he takes in a deep breath and lets out an almighty snore. Emily bursts out laughing, and I snort back a laugh myself. Hell, even JD gives a smirk. Jesus, the Iceman is finally thawing out.

Deciding that the dude is just drunk and not about to turn into one of the undead, we all climb inside the little camper and shut the door firmly behind us. Stepping around the inebriated man, we help ourselves to some of his rations. Totally not proud of that, I'll admit it; stealing someone else's food is a shitty thing to do. But to be fair, it didn't look like the poor guy had eaten anything in weeks, and was just slowly drinking himself to death.

We all rest up, alternating between napping, eating, and talking about the best route to Ben's cabin. After a couple of hours, Drunk Guy is still snoring on the floor and even drooling a little down himself, and JD and Crunch discuss killing him before he wakes back up. Britta takes his side—or what she presumes is his side, since he's passed out. I don't want his blood on my hands either, but before I can argue my point, he starts to stir. His eyes flicker open for the briefest of moments before closing again, and we all stop talking and stare at each other.

A few moments later he shifts positions and opens his eyes once more. "Oh, God, it wasn't a dream," he slurs.

He doesn't seem as drunk as before, but he certainly isn't sober. He closes his eyes again, and resumes snoring.

"We should just kill him," Crunch whispers in between eating some dry cereal.

"I can fucking hear you," the drunk shouts, but keeps his eyes closed. "Pass me my bottle, will ya?"

"I think you've had enough, buddy," Mikey coaxes.

The man opens his eyes back up. "I'll tell you when I've had enough. When I'm dead, that's when."

"Told you we should have killed him," Crunch snaps out, louder this time—I'm pretty sure to make sure that he can hear her.

"Maybe you should have, I don't give a shit anymore anyway." The man opens his eyes and pulls himself back up onto the little sofa, and Emily scrambles to the other side of the small space to get away from him. He turns and frowns at her before running a hand across his face. "So, zombies still walking the earth then?" he asks with a hint of mirth to his voice.

"Yep." I nod. My hand is wrapped tightly around my machete in case he makes any attempt to turn on us. He seems to have sobered up far too quickly, but looks set to start drinking again soon.

He stands up and sways, pushing past Crunch in his tiny kitchen, and opens one of the lower cupboards, pulling out a bottle of dark liquid. He unscrews the lid and takes a long swallow of it before turning to stare at us all and letting out a loud belch. He holds the bottle out to us.

"You want some?"

We all shake our heads, and he shrugs and takes another swallow.

"I think you should probably go sleep off the first round before you drink any more, my friend," Mikey offers.

The big guy laughs, quite loudly in fact, and it makes me feel uncomfortable. "The name's Steve, and I haven't been sober for—I don't know. I can't remember the last time I was sober, to be honest." He runs a hand down his face.

"Okay, Steve. Mind telling us why?" I ask.

"Not really. It's none of your fucking business," he snaps at me.

I flinch at his tone, but try not to show it. I've been spoken to worse than that before.

He shakes his head. "I'm sorry, that was rude of me. I'm a little more rattled today than usual." Steve heads back over to his sofa and takes a seat, slipping the bottle between his knees. "You're right, I probably shouldn't drink anymore, but I've been alone for a long time now. Makes you go a little cuckoo after a while, you know?" He makes a whirly gesture at his head and sniggers, but there's no amusement in his voice or his face. He looks sad. Sad and lonely. And he smells of stale alcohol, sweat, and something else that I'd rather not think about too much.

I nod, but I *don't* know how he feels, actually. I've been constantly surrounded by people for as long as I can remember. Some days, I'd do anything for a little alone time, but that isn't safe.

"So, what's the deal then?" Crunch asks, making it blatantly obvious that she's eating his food, almost egging him on to snap at her. She leans on the counter and crunches the cereal with an open mouth and a smile.

"It's a long story…"

"We've got time," she snarks back.

"It's not a happy story." He clears his throat, the words getting stuck.

"I hate happy stories." She smiles back.

I roll my eyes and glare at her, but she pays me no attention, merely continues to crunch through his stale cereal. I'm surprised it actually still crunches, now that I'm thinking about it.

"My wife and I were headed up here. This was our vacation home of sorts, a long time ago, anyway. When everything went to hell, this was supposed to be our hideout. It's way off the road, hidden up in the trees. There's a spring just behind the RV, and we have our own little allotment to grow food. It was the perfect plan, but the damn woman can't navigate for shit." He rolls his eyes. "We got attacked down by the road before the turnoff. Some crazy guys looking for trouble and wanting to take whatever they wanted. We took off into the woods with them chasing after us, managed to lose them and all, but at some point me and the wife got separated too. I headed up here thinking she'd be doing the same thing, but—she never showed up." Steve shakes his head sadly and takes another long swig from his bottle. "I must have told her a thousand times how to work out north from west, but she never listened to me. Damn woman!"

Sounds like my life story, I can't help but think.

"How long ago was that?" Britta asks.

He shrugs. "Couple of months ago now. I searched for her every day for weeks; and I'm a fucking atheist, but I'll be damned if I didn't pray to every type of god available for them to bring her back home to me." He wipes at his eyes. "Never worked though. My baby's gone, and I don't see much reason for living without her."

"What was her name?" I ask, though I'm not really sure why.

He takes a deep breath before answering. "Jane. My baby's names was Jane."

"She could still be alive somewhere." I shrug.

He looks at me, a darkness settled in his eyes. "I think we all know that she's more than likely one of the undead now, sweetheart."

None of us speaks for a while. We let his sad words settle all around us; the only noise to be heard is Crunch's incessant—well, crunching!

Steve seems like a nice enough guy. He lets us crash, even says we can use his bed to sleep on. Emily and Britta aren't sleepy, though, since they slept pretty much all the way here. I'm okay for sleep for now too, but JD, Crunch, and Mikey all look beat, since they did most of the driving. JD doesn't want to leave his safety up to me though—probably thinking of earlier today when he left me to fend for myself. Asshole, he's probably right; I would quite happily let him be eaten alive. I roll my eyes at my own angry thoughts, knowing that I wouldn't. Damn my moral compass again. I really need to smash up the stupid thing.

Crunch and JD are eventually convinced to sleep in the bed, and Mikey takes the couch. He says he can sleep through anything, but I'm almost certain he just doesn't trust me not to get into trouble again without him nearby. He looks un-comfy sleeping upright, his arms folded across his chest. Every now and then his own snores shake him awake and his eyes flit open, scan the room until they land on me, and close again. Every time his does it, Emily laughs. The night is long, but thankfully uneventful. No groans, no moans, just nature: the wind in the trees, the calls of some birds, and the snores from our sleeping group members. Steve eventually nods off again too, his face on the table in front of him, creating a little pool of dribble underneath.

I can't help but wonder where the heck he got his alcohol from. In the years since the deaders rose up, I've hardly seen a drop of the stuff—hence why I'm dragging the bottle of vodka around with me everywhere—yet Steve seems to have an endless supply. I'm nervous, but excited for the morning. Another new place, another new nightmare, yet this place feels different somehow.

Not just that, but we're within spitting distance of the cabin. A thought has been nagging me for a while, something which I've thought about since I first suggested to Emily that we head to the cabin.

What if Ben's parents are still alive?

THIRTY FIVE

Mikey jumps awake for what seems the hundredth time, his deep brown eyes peering around the camper until they land on me. He gives me a little smile, and then leans his head back and closes his eyes again. Jesus, when did this happen—the protectiveness? Anyone would think that I'm a helpless woman, for goodness' sakes, not someone who survived the apocalypse by herself. Well, maybe not completely by herself, but I only had myself to depend on; I sure as hell couldn't rely on the other survivors.

I stand and stretch, working the creaks out of my bones. Morning broke a few hours ago, but everyone is still sleeping—everyone but me. I wonder why that is, why I'm the only one who can't seem to sleep anymore. Whatever, the reason is irrelevant; I'm hungry and awake and sick of listening to everyone else snore. I creep to the door and sneak out. Once outside I take a moment to sniff the air, much like the deaders yesterday, only I'm not sniffing out prey, I'm sniffing out the dead.

The air smells clean and fresh—beautiful almost, the scent of pine and damp soil clinging to it with a sweet desperation. I can smell something else too, but can't put my finger on it. I only know that it isn't death. I swallow hard; It's been a couple of days of non-stop death on our tail, and this blessed reprieve doesn't go unnoticed.

I stray from the RV and find a secluded corner to do my business, but when I get back to camp, Steve is standing in the doorway looking bleary-eyed and tired.

In the daylight I can see that he isn't as old as I first thought. He's only thirty-something, and though he's looking older than his years, his face still holds a baby-like charm to it. He smiles as I approach, and I return the gesture.

"Morning." He nods his hello. "You want coffee?"

I look toward his little fire pit with a pot swinging over the top.

"Are you serious? Coffee? *Real* coffee?" I jog over to the fire and peer down at the bubbling inky liquid in the pan. "Holy crap!" I realize that my voice has gone up an octave or two. I can't remember the last time I had real coffee. JD had some crappy sachets of the stuff back at the tree houses, but this is the real deal.

I plunk myself down by the fire and let the vapors wash over me. My gut churns in expectancy, and I lick my lips.

Steve smiles and stirs the pot. Satisfied, he pours a cup and hands it to me. For a few moments I merely hold it under my nose—not drinking, not even sniffing it, just letting the scent slowly into my lungs.

"I don't have any milk, but I do still have a little sugar."

He holds out a little brown wooden box to me and I pop the lid and see it a quarter full of sugar that has seen better days. I don't even care, though, as I grab a pinch between my thumb and forefinger and sprinkle it in my coffee. I grab a spoon that's handed to me and stir, and only then do I sniff for all my life is worth.

This has got to be the single greatest day of my life.

The door to the RV opens as I'm about to take my first swallow, and JD steps out, his eyes bulging as he strides toward us.

"Is that coffee?" he barks out, his stride never faltering.

I nod frantically, wondering how the hell he smelled it from inside the camper, and take a tentative sip, all the while with JD watching me. I let the hot liquid settle on my tongue before I swallow, basking in the glory of the bitter and the sweetness of it. My senses come alive and I all but groan out loud with the pleasure of it.

"Is it good?" JD licks his lips, still staring at me.

I nod and grin.

"Can I—" JD begins, before Steve shoves a steaming cup under his nose with a chuckle. JD takes the cup and lifts it to his face, breathing it in before turning around and trapping Steve in a great big man sandwich. "Thank you, brother. I owe you big time."

I would choke on my coffee laughing if it weren't for the fact that at that moment I was in pure, unadulterated, spine-tingling pleasure. I look up as Mikey comes out of the camper, closely followed by the Crunch, Britta, and Emily-Rose.

Mikey's eyes go wide as he gets closer and smells the coffee.

"Is that—" he begins, before Steve hands him a cup.

Life offers such little pleasure these days, and coffee is a long-forgotten luxury of the past. How often did we used to take things like this for granted? How many times did you say to yourself, 'I can't even think straight in the morning before I've had my third cup of coffee?' Christ, if only we knew back then to cherish every little thing.

When I think back now to all the food wasted, drinks not drunk, items bought and shoved into the back of my closet and never worn—

well, it makes you realize what a wasteful life we truly led. I appreciate everything these days: food, drinks, clothes. I look down at my well-worn Doc Marten boots and smile. There is no summer wardrobe and winter wardrobe, there is only a 'whatever you can get your hands on' wardrobe. I appreciate my life and everything in it now—even these people. Apocalypses will do that to a girl.

We sit around jovially chatting for the first time in a long time, feeling somewhat safe, relaxed, and sated from the coffee. It's like a blast from the past was all that we needed to give us the energy to carry on. Britta seems to be getting better; she can hold her weapon now, and the gash on her arm is healing nicely—no leaks or infections, and hardly any pain. Everyone seems to be better for the rest.

Steve stands and stretches. "Anyone want some breakfast?"

The camp, so full of chatter and laughing, falls silent as we look at this god among men. What magic card will he pull out this time? Alcohol, coffee…what next—a pack of bacon, a newspaper, and some slippers?

"Um, yeah," I speak hesitantly. "Need any help?" I stand before he replies and follow him as he heads to the RV. My heart sinks when I think he may go inside and get out the box of stale cereal that Crunch had been munching on the previous night. Instead, he goes around the back of the camper, and I follow like a little lost puppy.

The image behind the camper makes my jaw drop and my stomach growl so loudly that Mikey comes running from the fire to see what's wrong. He slams into my back as he sees what I see.

Fruits and vegetables: strawberries, blackberries, raspberries, tomatoes, peppers, carrots. You name it, it's growing—well, that's what it seems like anyway. A wooden fence with a net sits over the top of it all, protecting it from animals. My mouth is dry and I can't seem to form any words at the moment. Lucky for me, Mikey steps in.

"What—is this—where—" He rubs a hand across the back of his neck and swallows.

My eyes have gone dry from my lack of blinking.

"The wife and I used to grow all sorts up here. We used to keep animals too. Nothing too spectacular, couple of chickens and a pig, mostly. Had to put the pig out of her misery a few months back; zombie got her. Poor girl, she never stood a chance. Came out one morning to find it chewing on her hind legs. Guess everyone loves bacon." He gives a little chuckle and shakes his head sadly. "Still got a couple of chickens though."

He strolls off to the back of the RV and pulls open a little hatch along the bottom. A gangly looking chicken hops out, blinks rapidly, clucks at us, and wanders off.

"Shouldn't you catch her?" Mikey asks, licking his lips.

"Naaa, Livvie there's a quick one and she always comes back. She knows a good thing when she has it." Steve chuckles again and reaches into the little compartment. He struggles for a moment and I'm almost tempted to go help him until he comes back out with another chicken in his hands. "Now, Martha here, she's the shy one. Hates being out here, almost like she knows something ain't quite right." He drops her and shoos her away.

Little Martha gives Steve a dirty look with her little beady eyes—or what I would class as a dirty look, anyway—and pecks at the ground. She looks set to run back inside her hidey-hole at any moment, and I can't help but laugh.

"Go on, girl, get!" Steve shoos her further away before he reaches back in and pulls out a drowsy-looking chicken, the sort of chicken that I would think was terminally ill if I saw it at a farm. The sort of chicken that looks like it needs to be put out of its misery, sooner rather than later.

"Is that one okay?" I ask with a grimace.

Steve laughs. "Yeah, this here is Tami. She's as dumb as a bunch of rocks. Ate some of me and the wife's special plants a couple of years back and never quite recovered." He cuddles Tami to his chest, stroking her like a kitten. She clucks softly and nuzzles into him.

"You're a good girl, aren't you, Tami?" He kisses the top of her feathery head gently. "Yes you are."

I glance at Mikey, whose expression I can only imagine mirrors mine. It's sort of a *What the fuck?* kind of look.

"Can we eat them?" Mikey asks.

"Hell no, you can't eat my girls!" Steve snaps, and pulls little Tami closer to him. "Can I eat your little girlfriend there?"

Mikey and I exchange glances, and I try my best to hide my smirk. I dig him in his side.

"Dude, you should say sorry," I smirk. "You can't go around threatening to eat a man's chickens and expect to get breakfast afterwards. At least not without apologizing first; that's just plain rude." I raise an eyebrow and suppress a chuckle. I look across at Steve, who nods in agreement. Shit, I think even poor old dopey Tami agrees with me.

"Uh, sorry, man." Mikey looks confused.

Steve huffs and starts to show us his vegetable patch. It's not big, certainly not as big as I first thought. I guess my eyes saw it as a Garden of Eden type; instead it's more of a patch overflowing with food.

"You can have what you want. I hardly eat a thing these days, but it was the wife's garden and I feel responsible for keeping it going, you know?"

I nod and smile at all the right times, but really my thoughts are on eating. Eating a lot. I want to indulge, splurge, and gorge myself on everything I can see. I'm pretty sure I'm drooling. Damn ration packs and dry cereal bars are finally taking their toll.

Steve sets Tami down and reaches back inside the chickens' little home. "What do you know, the girls have laid us a couple of eggs. Must have known I had company. How about I cook us up some scrambled eggs, mushrooms, and fried tomatoes?"

I want to cry. Not figuratively, but literally.

Steve strokes his chin, looking thoughtfully at his fruits. "Bet I could throw together a nice fruit salad or something with the rest of this stuff too." He grabs a little basket and hands it to me. "You two pick the fruit and I'll go grab some mushrooms."

He wanders off before either of us can say anything. As he strides away I don't see a man, I see a magical being, a king among kings, a sorcerer— okay, well, I'm pretty damn impressed anyway. Coffee *and* eggs?

If I'm dreaming, you better be damn sure not to wake me up.

If I thought that things were jovial before, it's bordering on hysterics for the rest of the day. It's funny how things can change so suddenly. One minute you think you're going to die, and the next you're playing charades around a campfire while eating a fruit salad and drinking home-brewed wine. I would have loved to have met Steve's wife. He talks about her a lot as we all get to know one another. They had met just out of high school and had been together ever since. I felt sad that they weren't together anymore, and I hoped that whatever had happened to her had been quick.

The day passes in a blur, and as the sun begins to set, most of us make our way back inside the camper. I stay behind to help tidy up and put the chickens to bed. I seem strangely attached to Livvie, Martha, and Tami now. They fed me and gave me some much-needed protein, and as I pick up Tami and she nestles in to the crook of my arm, I feel a weird rush of affection for them all.

"It's hard not to care about something so innocent isn't it?" Steve speaks without looking at me.

"Yeah, especially this little gangly one," I chuckle as I tickle her under the neck, much like you would a puppy.

This has got to be the weirdest thing I have encountered in a long time, I muse.

Steve stumbles and falls onto his ass, and I laugh lightheartedly at him. He grumbles but smiles back.

"You should quit drinking, you know?" I put Tami into her little home, and she toddles over to a little bed of leaves and dried grass. "That stuff will kill you," I say, only half joking.

"I know." Steve wipes at his eyes. "Just doesn't seem much point in surviving without her. She was my everything."

"She would want you to live, she would want you to at least try and find some kind of happiness in this world. It's what you would want for her if the situation was reversed." I pat his arm to offer the big brute some kind of comfort.

I think of Ben and how I had felt when—well, I think of Ben. Sadness creeps in the edges, but I refuse to let my bad memories spoil what is the first truly happy day I've had in years.

"I know. I can see that now. It's been hard being on my own all this time, but you're right, she would want me to survive this." He smiles and finishes covering the vegetable patch, and then closes the hatch on the chickens.

"Night girls," he whispers in to them.

I smirk. "Night, ladies."

As we go back inside the camper, I feel a strange kind of melancholy settle over me. I feel like I'm finally letting go of all the pain, guilt, and loss that I've been carrying around with me for years now. It all seems to be drifting away. And while I'm glad about that, I'm also sad. I didn't know when or *if* I would ever be ready to say goodbye to Ben, to the things that happened to me behind the walls, but I think this is it. I'm ready to forgive all of the others—maybe even Lee. I shake my head. No, I don't think I'll ever forgive him and his fucking goons, but I can forgive the other people. They were scared and trying to protect their families; I get that now.

Life is about moving forward, and whether I want it to or not, that's exactly what is happening right now. And maybe it's time for that—to let go.

THIRTY SIX

Steve has been steadily drinking his homebrew throughout the day, and as nighttime approaches he decides to pull out the big guns, regardless of what we had talked about outside.

"Damn, man, is that what I think it is?" JD holds the bottle of, well, 'JD' up to the light. "Jack Daniels. I've missed this stuff." He unscrews the lid and takes a deep breath of it.

"Yeah, help yourself." Steve reaches over and grabs some glasses from one of the cupboards in the little kitchen. "I've been saving that bad boy for a special occasion." He looks at me and winks. "But if this isn't a special occasion, then I don't know what is."

JD pours the whiskey into everyone's glasses—I even let Emily have a little drop. I know she'll hate the stuff, but this may be her only opportunity to ever try it.

"To lost loves." JD raises his glass.

"To survival." Mikey clinks my glass.

"To friendship." Britta clinks my glass too, and I blush a little.

Damn, these people are making me go soft.

"To better drinks," Emily splutters after taking a sip.

I laugh at her, and hold up my glass. "To, uh…come back to me." I shrug.

"To killing zombies." Crunch stares deep into her glass.

"I'll second that one." JD raises his glass again.

"To Jane," Steve mutters.

He raises his glass high and we all do the same.

"To Jane," we echo.

I never got to meet Jane, but she must have been a damn good woman for him to be so affected by her loss. Or maybe it's the not knowing that's eating him up inside. Who knows? I guess he never will—not unless he's unlucky enough to stumble across her walking corpse.

It's later that night, after everyone has gone to sleep, that I find myself wide awake—again. Mikey is asleep opposite me at the table, facedown. Steve is snoring heavily on one end of the little sofa, his near-empty bottle of Jack Daniels in his hand. JD is on the other end snoring like a baby too. Emily, Crunch, and Britta have taken the bed after much persuasion from me. Britta still doesn't trust Crunch, and I don't blame her, but I know she won't do anything here, certainly not while we have a good thing going. She has too much survival instinct for that. Crunch may trip you to save herself, but she isn't a coldblooded killer. I certainly wouldn't leave Emily alone with her if I thought for even a second that she was.

I want to sleep, but I'm not sleepy yet; the day's events are still weighing on my mind. My head feels a little foggy from the alcohol, but thankfully, I'm not too worse for wear because of all the food I've eaten. For the first time in months, my stomach actually feels full, bloated even. It's a good feeling, one I could get used to. I wonder if we could all stay here. Maybe build a little hut or two of our own. Build some security around the place, perhaps. There really isn't a lot of difference between this place and Ben's parents' cabin, from what I remember—just the home comforts—and we're here already.

I watch Steve snoring soundly. I know he would like the company. I bet Livvie, Tami, and Martha would too. I grin. I decide I'm going to suggest it to everyone tomorrow after speaking to Steve. I'm tired of running, tired of moving from one place to another. I just want to stay somewhere for a while. Since I left the city from behind the walls, I've done nothing but run. Maybe this is where we should stay now, build a life here even.

I feel content in my surroundings as I lean back and stretch out my shoulders, finally feeling sleepy. I decide to go check the perimeter once more before calling it a night, maybe grab my bag from the car before it gets too late—it's only a little way down the hill anyway.

I know what you're thinking, that this is the part where the stupid woman goes out into the night alone and gets caught and eaten by zombies. Well, I'm not stupid.

"Mikey," I whisper, and kick him under the table.

He looks up at me with groggy, alcohol-drenched eyes. "What?"

"I'm doing a perimeter check before I go to sleep. Come with me."

"It'll be fine, we haven't seen a thing all day. Just go to sleep, Nina."

He rests his head back on the table with a thud. I count to three in my head, and when he doesn't look back up at me I kick him again.

"Dude, seriously, come with me. I want to go get my bag from the car," I plead.

Mikey makes a weird groany-growly noise, but still doesn't look up at me. "Go to sleep, woman!"

"Fine," I stand with a huff. "I'll go myself."

I am so not going by myself. Even if there are no deaders out there, it's still freaking dark!

I take a couple of tentative steps toward the door, my hand touching the handle before Mikey does his weird growly thing again and stands up.

"Fine," he picks up his machete from under the table, "but you owe me."

"Fine," I snap back with a smirk.

It's dark outside, the moonlight only just peeping through the treetops, but like earlier, the only things I can smell are pine and damp soil. No deaders, no death, and no rotting corpses. Similarly, there's no moaning and groaning of deaders hungry for brains—well, not including Mikey, obviously.

We skirt around Steve's little fence-and-wire rig, using my solar flashlight as our guide. We go around twice, but find nothing. I can't help but smile, and as we go around the second time I dip my hand under the vegetable patch netting and nab a tomato with a grin.

"You really like it here, huh?"

I look at Mikey as I bite the tomato and it spurts onto my tongue. I give out a little moan of satisfaction and nod at him.

We walk down the hill, shining the flashlight all around us into the trees to make sure there aren't any deaders sneaking up on us for a midnight snack, but as with the area around camp, there's nothing. Well, there are trees, obviously, but no dead people.

Our vehicles are just where we left them, hidden away from the path under the canopy of a particularly large tree. I climb up and sit on the hood of the van and Mikey joins me, his grumpiness finally dispersing as the fresh air sobers him up.

"I do, I like it here. I feel safe, and the food! Oh man, the food is amazing," I laugh.

He laughs. "I hate to say it though, Nina, but the food won't last, and this isn't the safest location. It's good, but not great."

"Don't ruin it," I pout.

"*Me* don't ruin it? Isn't it normally *you* who's the voice of reason?"

"Yeah," I smile as I look at his face, "maybe you've converted me, huh?" I chuckle. "Maybe it isn't all doom and gloom after all," I smirk.

He leans over suddenly, his hand touching the side of my face, and before I can stop him he pulls me into a kiss. I falter for a second or two before I give in to him and kiss him back hard. Our tongues dance over one another's, and his fingers make their way to my hair, grip it, and tug me closer to him. I moan into his mouth, my hands finding his waist, tugging up his shirt and touching the hot skin underneath.

He pulls back slowly and smiles at me. Jesus, I feel almost girly under his stare, and I blush furiously, my mind working to think of something else to say. My feelings for him have been growing, and I'm finally learning to trust again. I don't want to do anything to jeopardize that, but then my new motto seems to be the whole 'moving forward' thing, and this is moving forward, I guess.

I smile and clear my throat. "So, before all this, what did you do? You seem to have a few tricks up your sleeve—they can't all be post-apocalypse, surely?" I lean back to stare up at the stars.

"You'd be surprised what I've learned post-apocalypse," he laughs. "I was, uh…" He looks back at me, seeming unsure of himself. He takes a deep breath and continues. "But yeah, I guess before all this…I, um, I was a thief."

That doesn't really surprise me; the knack for getting into places with locked doors kind of gave that game away. I shrug.

"I was a bit of a bad boy," he laughs, "as you women like to put it."

"Don't tar us all with the same brush, Mikey. We're not all as dumb as a box of rocks, you know." I laugh.

"Sorry," he shrugs. "It was my thing." Mikey drags a hand across his face in embarrassment.

"The bad boy thing?" I laugh loudly.

He leans back next to me, one arm across his face. "Shit, this is embarrassing. Yeah, the bad boy thing."

"What made you so bad then, eh? So you did a bit of breaking and entering, what's the big deal?" I can't believe that I'm not more bothered, actually, and am brushing his criminal past off so easily, but these days it doesn't exactly matter what your past was, and I tell him so.

"What if your past follows you?" he asks quietly, staring up into the trees himself now. "It wasn't just breaking and entering, it was worse than that. I mean, I never killed anyone or anything, but—I don't even know why I'm telling you this."

I turn my head to stare at his profile. I haven't seen this side of him before. I've seen protective Mikey, funny Mikey, dangerous Mikey, but this version baffles me and—strangely—makes me like him all the more.

"It's all good, baby." I watch as he turns to look at me. "I don't need to know about that person if you don't want to tell me. It's who we are now that matters. It was a clean slate when the world went to shit."

"Do you really believe that?"

I shrug. "Yeah, everyone deserves to have a second chance, I guess. I mean, obviously it depends what you did, but a little breaking and entering is okay. Like you said, you never killed anyone." I think about Duncan, and know that everyone really does deserve a second chance—especially if you try to make up for all the bad you did previously. Mikey has helped every one of us more times than I can count, so I guess that gets him a *get out of jail free* card.

Silence echoes around us and I think of Ben. My stomach does a flip, and tugs at my insides. I close my eyes and look back up into the sky, finding it hard to breathe.

"Hey." Mikey's hand touches my chin, and turns me to face him again. "What's up with that?"

"Nothing. Like I said, we've all done bad stuff. Things that we regret, and things we had no choice but to do. It just doesn't make it any easier." I swallow. "That being said, we have to learn to let things go, and move on."

Mikey nods in agreement, and I take a steadying breath.

"It's time to put things like that behind us. We need to forget the bad and work on more of the good, because there just isn't enough of the good to go around these days. So maybe you're right." I look at him and he sits up to get a better look at me. "Maybe it really isn't all doom and gloom after all." I smile at him. "You're a good man, Mikey. Everyone can see that, so whatever you did before the world collapsed, it doesn't matter anymore."

He looks panicked but smiles to cover it, and when he goes to say something I press a finger to his lips.

"Will you just kiss me already?"

He stares at me for a second, looking sweetly unsure of himself before he finally leans down and presses his lips against mine. His strong hands cup my face, and his tongue moves against mine—slowly at first, and then faster when I reciprocate and he realizes that I'm not going to kick his ass anytime soon. His body shifts until he's on top of me, his strong arms pinning me in place as he grinds against me and I moan into his mouth. It feels right—no, *he* feels right: the wanting, the desire, the giving and taking. I want him and me, and all of that other crazy shit.

He pulls away, looking into my face, his thumb stroking my lower lip, seemingly trying to decide on his next move. I smile and reach for his hair, grasping it tightly, and pull his face back down to me. His hand paws at my breast through my shirt, his mouth leaving mine and moving to my throat, trailing soft wet kisses down to my chest until it meets material and he pulls it to one side to access my naked flesh.

He lifts up my shirt, pulling my bra to one side as he takes my breast in his mouth, and I moan even louder at the sweet satisfaction. His other hand moves to his jeans, and he fumbles for a minute with the button before nearly falling off the hood, and I laugh loudly. He looks up at me with a grin, and I shove him off me and to one side. He looks hurt and confused, and I smile again as I slide off the hood of the van with a soft thud. I straighten my shirt as he sits up, his eyes following me as I go around the side of the van. I open up the back doors and climb inside. "Are you coming or what?" I call out to him. "It's now or never, bad boy," I laugh.

I hear his feet hit the ground, and a couple of seconds later his face looks in through the doorway with a big grin before he climbs in and shuts the doors behind him.

In the dark, we are Nina and Mikey. We are the people we were, not the people we've been forced to become, and it's good. It's so good. His body on mine, his hands touching me and wanting me, and hell, I fucking need it. I need to be touched like this, and I need to feel truly wanted again by someone—not just used. With each touch and

310

caress, I feel my walls breaking down. With each thrust, I feel myself melting, and my heart letting go of the pain and guilt that I've carried with me. I cry out, my head tilting back towards the ceiling of the van, and he nibbles on my chin, sliding his tongue down my throat as my body wracks with pleasure. When we have wrung every ounce of pleasure from each other, he rolls off me and holds me in his arms. I flinch, waiting for...fuck, *something*, I don't know what. The pain to start, maybe? The memories of the wall—the pain and abuse that I suffered—don't fade that easily I guess, but as I lay in his arms and he kisses the back of my neck, I know now that they just might, given time. I'm not saying it's love, but it's possibly as close to love as I'm ever gonna get.

It's still dark inside the van, though I know it's morning by the sun gleaming in from under the door. My head is resting in the crook of Mikey's arm, and surprisingly, he isn't snoring for once. The air is stuffy in the van and I begin to dress after untangling myself from Mikey's body.

He stirs and opens his eyes, looking up at me with a smile.

"I could get used to this," he says groggily.

"Me too." I lean over and kiss him with a smile. "Come on, though. I can't wait to see what we're having for breakfast today. Maybe Tami laid another egg," I laugh.

"You wanna?" Mikey grins.

"No, last night was just fine for me. Right now I want to eat." I slip my feet into my boots.

"I feel used." He feigns shock.

"Get used to it," I smirk. "Just not right now."

"Really?" He grabs me, and when I try to pull away he drags me down on top of him.

We kiss and I can tell we're both getting carried away, but my stomach rumbles for food and breaks the spell. I laugh and roll off him, and he dresses by the light of my flashlight.

"You ready?" I ask, opening the van doors and stepping out into the bright day. "Jesus." I pinch my nose to get rid of the smell as my eyes widen to the size of saucers. "Mikey!" I scream.

THIRTY SEVEN

My one moment of happiness is broken, crushed, trampled upon by the undead that surround the van and tree line around us. "Mikey!" I scream again, and reach for my machete.

My hand hits air where my machete normally hangs, and I stumble backwards in search of it and bump into Mikey. He pushes me behind him, and I drop to my knees in search of my machete and holder. The moaning is getting louder, the smell of us reaching the dead and drawing their attention to us.

My hand finally lands on my weapon, and I strap it around myself and pull the machete out. Mikey has already jumped down and is fighting with a deader. My heart skips a beat, and in that moment, I know that if he dies now—if the dead get him and I'm left in this shit-hole without him—that I may as well be dead myself. I run the length of the van and jump out with a guttural scream and my machete raised high. Probably not my wisest decision, since noise attracts the creepy dead dudes, but I'm sure it looks pretty awesome!

I land awkwardly on the ground, but stand up quickly and chop through the center of a deader like he's a prime rib and this is a five star restaurant—now all I need is a tasty side sauce. I kick at him as I pull out my machete. His insides are mush, and my machete slides out of him with relative ease, releasing his intestines to the ground. I slice across his neck and take his head from his shoulders, a splatter of black blood and gore spurting out from the hole in his neck where his head once proudly sat.

"Crunch! JD!" I scream their names as more of the dead surround us, and the air gets harder to breathe with the stench of the cold, rotting bodies.

We move back to back, our weapons slashing wildly around us and cutting down anything that gets too close, as we try to make it around to the front of the van. Jesus, they're everywhere. There must be thirty of them. Where the hell did they all come from? Steve said he hadn't seen any in weeks, and even then only the odd one or two.

I can hear more fighting toward the RV, and I hope to God that it is Crunch and JD, and not Emily. I know that she can handle herself, but the thought of her fighting makes my stomach crawl.

A deader reaches for me and I take off his arm in a swift movement that takes even me by surprise. He looks down at it in confusion before reaching for me with his other hand. I take that too, and nearly laugh as his little forehead furrows in frustration, his brain—or whatever it is that makes them tick—still telling him to grab me, but with what exactly? The deader comes forward, face-first this time, and I kick out at him, my foot hitting his left kneecap with a crunch and making him collapse down to the ground. I kick him in the head, he falls backwards, and Mikey stomps on his face, crushing it under his heavy boot as we continue our backwards scuttle.

I chance a glance around me and catch a glimpse of Crunch doing a flying kick, both Kukri knives held high. I don't see what happens when she lands, but I don't hear her scream in pain, either, so I'm guessing that's a good sign she's okay.

My heart is beating wildly, the sound of blood whooshing in my ears making it hard to think straight, and the smell—goddamn, the smell is palpable in the air. I cough and splutter, biting down on the inside of my cheek to stop the vomit from rising, and slash out at a short, curly-haired deader with half its face missing, leaving me with a prime view of the inside of its mouth and teeth. I scream as I do it, a war cry to get it to back the fuck away from me, but it doesn't back away; they never do. They don't care about limbs and missing faces, they care about brains and new flesh to feast on. I think of Emily and fresh panic surges.

A switch in me clicks, and my fear drops into a bottomless pit. I breathe out, step away from Mikey's back, and fight my way back to the RV. Thoughts run wild in my head, but a single goal is in mind.

I can't lose *her*, I can't lose *him*, I can't lose *them*.

Lose? No, I can't, I won't—no fucking way.

Zombies surround the camper, and I want to cry as they pile in and I hear screaming coming from within. I run up behind them, decapitating several that are jammed in the doorway. Several more are inside, but when I look toward the source of the screaming I see that it's Steve and not Emily. Our eyes meet and he stops screaming—possibly through embarrassment, possibly because he knows that his number is up. He reaches for his bottle of Jack Daniels and chugs it back as zombies surround him and dive in on the feast, Steve a la carte. I step up and into the RV, grab the nearest deader and drag it backwards and off Steve.

Its hands reach back for me, attempting to claw at me, but I swat them away and use the deader as a zombie shield as another one stops its slow execution of Steve, stands up, and makes a grab for me too. Meaty intestines hang from his dried-out lips, the blood trailing down its chin like spittle. My little zombie shield is still reaching backwards for me and I grip it firmly under the jaw, tilting its chin up to expose the soft tissue of its neck while avoiding its blackened teeth, and drag my machete across its throat. Gunk pours down and I push harder until I feel my weapon slice through the bones and tendons holding its head in place. Deader guy comes forward and I duck out of his way as I drop my now re-dead deader and send him flying toward the floor. He sprawls out, and then pushes his arms under him, attempting to push himself upwards. I stomp on him and slam my machete through his back and out through his ribcage. Somehow between kicking, stabbing him, and narrowly avoiding his neck and head, I manage to shuffle him into the doorway of the RV. I reach for the handle and pull the door closed on his face. I don't hear the crack, but I know that the impact of the little door on his softened skull does damage, and I'm about to slam it again when Mikey makes it to me and thrusts his machete through dead guy's eye socket just as he looks up. Bad timing for the deader, I guess. Or not. This sack of rotting meat was going to die again today, one way or another.

I duck out of the way as another deader reaches for me. He grips me by the shoulder and tries to bite me, and I yelp and pull with everything I have to get away from him, but I only seem manage to bring him possibly even closer to me as he trips on the deader on the floor and slams into my back. I scream and slap at him in a frantic attempt to shake him off, feeling every bit like a female cliché.

"Down!" Mikey's voice rings loudly in my left ear, and I drop to my knees and out of his way without a second thought.

I feel something cold splash across my back, and when I look back, Mr. Zombie is no more. Mikey grips the front of my jacket and pulls me out of the camper as another one of the zombies turns to me, smacking its lips together in what appears to be sheer zombie delight.

I struggle to get out of Mikey's grip, and scream at him to let me go. Steve is still in there, we can't just leave him. I look past the deader coming toward me and see Steve. He's drinking from his prize bottle of whiskey. A grimace is on his face as the two deaders bite down on various parts of him, his insides tumbling to the floor in a splash of hot red blood and cold dead hands.

Steve's hand is shaky as he tips his favorite golden drink down his throat. It spills down his chin, splashing across the head of the zombie chewing on his stomach. He coughs and splutters back out the liquid, now mixed with his own blood, before the bottle slips from his hands.

His eyes go wider as the deader growls into the cavernous hole it just made, and his hand unintentionally pats away the face chewing on him. He makes a gurgled scream as he loses the fingers on that hand for his trouble.

"He's gone," Mikey shouts, and drags me backwards again. This time I don't fight him on it. This time I can hear Emily screaming from somewhere outside.

I take one last look at Steve, saying a final goodbye to our brief friendship, and turn away from him, knowing that Mikey is right—Steve's gone. But Emily isn't, and she needs me.

I scan our surroundings. More deaders are coming from the tree line. *How the fuck did they find us?*

Mikey grabs my hand and we run toward the screaming. Emily and Britta are fighting off some deaders. They're surrounded, and damn it,

I'm teaching Emily how to shoot if we make it out of this alive. She's still using her stupid little Swiss army knife, like that's going to help. Britta, on the other hand, has a long knife in her hand and is swiping away at the zombies. She's faring well considering she's still injured, but with more deaders on the way, I know she can't keep it up.

Mikey and I run toward them, en route picking up a bloodied Crunch and JD. Crunch is limping and clearly in pain, but she looks focused on getting to the tow truck. I realize that if she gets there before any of us, she'll most likely leave us behind.

"Shit," I breathe out.

Mikey looks at me, and then at Crunch, possibly coming to the same conclusion. Either that or he's just appeasing me, because he nods and pulls me and we run faster. Either way we are all going to have to fight. The deaders are surrounding the tow truck and JD has the keys. Mikey slips on the uneven forest ground and we slide down the incline and end up in the thick of the fight between my girls and the deaders. I grip a zombie by the scruff of its neck and fling it to the ground. Mikey stabs it through the face as I grab another one and toss it to the other side, stabbing my own machete through the center of its head. Thick black blood bursts up from around the wound. It's still tinged red, and I can only assume it hasn't been dead long.

We stumble and push our way toward the tow truck, only stopping for a breath when my legs collide with its front bumper. I kick out at a fat zombie with deep oozing gashes down its face, my stomach gurgling in protest as my foot sinks into its stomach.

"Aaah," I yelp out as I lose my balance. Thank God I'm by the tow truck or I would be on my ass and the zombie would be chowing down.

I grip the bumper and try to shake the damn thing off, but it's like sinking sand, and the more I struggle the more my foot sinks in. Emily reaches out to grab my leg and pull it out, but the zombie lurches for her, and she screams and steps back.

JD strikes it across the back of the skull, and when it goes limp and begins to fall down, pulling me with it, he wraps his arms around its meaty waist and pulls my foot free. He drops fat guy and almost instantly connects his elbow with a zombie's face and makes a run for the door of the truck. We edge around the side of the vehicle, aiming for the back of the truck. I look in through the window and see Crunch staring out at me. She mouths something to JD beside her and I shiver. I know what she just said. I look at JD, our eyes meeting briefly before he turns the key and starts the truck.

My heart leaps into my throat as he revs the engine harder and a grin spreads across Crunch's face.

THIRTY EIGHT

"**N**o!" I scream out, tears springing to my eyes. I grip Emily's hand in mine, ready to thrust her forward in the hopes that he will at least take mercy on her.

JD looks back at me, his eyes flicking to Emily and then Mikey.

"Hurry the fuck up then," he shouts.

Crunch turns to stare at him. She doesn't say anything, but she's pissed off without a doubt, her lip turned up in an angry snarl. Her arm is pumping with blood, and there's a deep gash across her face. All of us run to the back of the truck before JD can change his mind. I grab Emily, hoist her up, and pretty much throw her in the back, finding the strength from somewhere to climb up and in myself. There's virtually no room as Britta and then Mikey climb in, but at least there's plenty to hold onto with all the equipment that normally hoists the cars up in the center of the truck. I grip the rigging with one hand, and my other chops off the fingers of a deader that's holding onto the side of the truck.

JD shifts the truck into reverse and we begin to back down the hill. Zombies follow us as quickly as their bodies can go, which—to be fair—isn't very quick at all, but there are more coming from all angles. They slip on the decline and fall over, bumping and tripping on one another. More are on their way up the hill, and we all—barring Emily, who I warn with threat of a serious ass-whooping if she goes anywhere near the side of the truck—swing our weapons as the deaders get too close to the truck. The path widens and JD swings the truck around to face the right way before putting his foot down and heading off down the hill even faster. I just manage to keep myself in the truck, hanging on with both hands and still gripping my machete. I keep hold of the rusty metal rigging with a death grip as we go over bumps, deaders, and just general forest stuff.

We squeeze the truck back through the gap in the trees that we had originally come through and the truck crashes back on to the road. JD seems to speed up even more, which I didn't think was actually possible in this old truck.

The road flashes past us in a blur, but I don't watch too much. I look at Mikey and Emily, shocked by the realization of my own feelings for them both, and relieved that they are both alive. I swore I wouldn't feel like this again—reliant on other people and actually giving a shit whether they live or die—yet here I am. When I left the walls with Emily, I did it for selfish reasons; she was just my get out card, my excuse to leave. I feel dirty admitting it, but I guess I used this vulnerable young girl. However, I never in a million years thought I would actually learn to love and care for her. I blink back the tears that are building, but when I look at Emily, her face contorted in misery, I let the sobs escape. I half hug her with one of my arms, trying to offer her some condolence for what she just had to go through. I feel like her mother, her friend, her rescuer, all wrapped up in one. And Mikey, Jesus, what the fuck is that all about? How have my feelings grown so much for him?

I look at him grimly watching the road pass by, his jaw grinding in that way it does when he's deep in thought with worry. A single scratch tears down one cheek, leaving a small trickle of blood in its wake. What would I have done if I had lost him back there? My chest tugs in pain at the thought, and I hug Emily harder to me. I feel his eyes on me, but can't look at him, knowing that it would just set me off even more.

I've spent the past the last couple of years building up my own wall, my own protective barrier to block out the pain, and between these two people they have managed to full-out annihilate it. Damn them.

An hour or so later, JD pulls the truck to the side of the road. I slowly release my death grip and flex my fingers. Sensation runs back through into my arms, and I grab Emily and pull her into a fierce bear hug. She starts up her sobbing again, if only just for a few minutes, before we separate and I kiss her forehead.

"You're fine, Em. I got you, okay?"

She nods and wipes the tears away with the back of her hand.

JD steps out of the truck, looking pissed off and—well, just pissed off, really. Crunch however, looks in pain. It dawns on me then that we don't have any of our things. We lost everything. My stomach twists in on itself under the realization. All that time collecting, saving, rationing—for nothing! I feel like I've been punched in the gut. My eyes stray to Emily and Mikey, my friends—well, Britta, and the other two. I guess we should look on the bright side that we are all just safe. For now at least.

I swallow down my anger, climb down from the truck, and go over to check Crunch's arm and face, since I'm the next nurse-in-training after her, but she shrugs away from me. I hear Mikey, Britta, and Emily climb down too, and make their way over to us.

"Let me look, damn you." I grab her arm and a fresh spurt of blood pumps out of the wound.

"I'm fine, go do your girlfriend routine with loverboy over there. I don't need your help," she snaps.

"Calm down, Crunch," JD barks out. Even he seems to be tiring of her drama queen act.

"What is your problem?" I rip a strip of cloth from my shirt. "I know you would have left us all to die up there if it hadn't been for JD, but I don't know what it is that I've done to piss you off so much in the first place. What makes it okay that you would willingly let me die?" I wrap the material tightly around her bleeding arm to stem the blood.

"Please, go do your saint act somewhere else, Nina." She snatches her arm back from me and tries to stare me down, but for once, with her at least, I stand my ground.

"I'm fucking serious, Crunch! With everything else that is going on around here, the last thing I need is your emotional baggage because you can't handle the fact that Mikey likes me more than you. Get a fucking grip, woman. You're becoming an embarrassment." I turn to walk away when I feel Crunch grab both my arms.

Her grip tightens and she slams me to the ground, her weight collapsing onto the back of me as she holds my face into the dirt.

"Is that really what you think this is about, little girl? Please, you don't even know him." Her mouth is close to my ear, and I swear that if she were a snake, her little v-shaped tongue would be hissing down my ear canal right about now. I struggle to shake her off, and by the sounds of it, so is everyone else. Not that I can see with my face in the dirt.

"Crunch, get the fuck off her." Mikey's voice is above me, and I feel her weight shift as he finally drags her off my body.

I climb up and turn around to meet her venomous stare. "I know what I need to know, Crunch."

"You don't know shit!" she laughs. "What, you think he's some good little boy that's come to save you and your kid? He's just like me." She looks at JD. "Just like you. In fact, he's probably worse than both of us put together."

"Crunch, please," Mikey begs.

The sound of his whiny voice releases a whole new set of anger, and I reach back with all my strength and land a punch square on her jaw. She flies backwards and lands on her ass. "He's nothing like you." I turn and walk away from her.

"You have no idea who or what he is!" she screams after me.

"Crunch, shut the fuck up!" Mikey shouts louder to drown her out.

I hear her voice as she stands back up and comes toward me, but when I turn, JD is holding her back. "He's one of them, Nina."

"Crunch, shut up," Mikey pleads again.

I look at them all. Only Crunch and Mikey seem to know what she's talking about; Britta and JD look just as confused as I am.

"One of who?" I ask warily.

"He's one of them, one of the Forgotten. Your perfect guy used to murder and torture innocent people. So you see, Nina, that's why he's better off with me than he'll ever be with you. We'll always share something you won't."

JD has let go of Crunch, and we all stare at Mikey, who looks devastated. But I can't believe that he was ever with the Forgotten. She has to be lying. I can't believe that he ever did any of those things.

"Mikey?" is the only word I manage to get out, my eyebrows furrowing together in confusion. My hand reaches for him, but he steps back from my touch.

He looks at the ground, at the sky—anywhere but at me. My hand goes to my mouth to hold in the horror.

"But, you said…" I begin, but I can't finish the sentence. The sickening feeling in my gut just keeps on growing.

"It's not like you think," he mumbles. I wait for his apology, his explanation, anything, but he offers me nothing but silence and a look filled with shame.

My head swims. I trusted him. I thought he could protect us, and all along he was the bad guy. "As soon as we can get our own truck, we're leaving." I grab Emily and pull her close to me.

"See why it would never work between you two?"

I look up at Crunch and see her smirk, but I can't even come back with a witty, smart-ass retort. I'm too shell-shocked that the man I have fallen in love with would do such horrible things. He told me what the Forgotten did to people—innocent people—and to find out that he was a part of it all along makes me sick to my stomach.

"Nina?" Emily whispers my name.

I look down at her and see my nails are digging in to her flesh. "Sorry." I let her go, feeling numb and broken. I don't know what to do with myself. Where do we go from here now? I still intend on going up to Ben's parents' cabin, but there's no way I want Mikey there. Or Crunch. But what sway do I hold with these people? There's surely no way that JD is going to listen to anything I have to say.

"There's someone coming." Britta's voice breaks through the uncomfortable silence that surrounds the group.

I look back the way we have just come and see what looks like a small freaking army headed our way, but these guys don't look like they are here to help us. I swallow the hard lump in my throat and reach for my machete, feeling almost dirty and traitorous to all the innocent people that Mikey more than likely killed with this very weapon. A fresh burst of anger surges through me.

"Should we go?" Crunch asks, her voice actually sounding a little worried. *Good,* is all I can think.

"There's nowhere to go. We ran out of gas," JD speaks, coming forward and standing next to me with a grimace.

I could be wrong, but it almost feels like he's shunning Crunch. I turn to look at her, but my eyes stray to behind her. She catches my eye and turns to look. Deaders are on their way now too, just to top off my fabulous day all the more. We're trapped between a rock and a hard place.

"Fuck." Mikey is behind me, and it's the first thing he has said in quite a while. The sound of his voice gives me the urge to turn around and punch him square in the jaw like I did to Crunch, but I somehow resist the temptation, keeping my focus on the enemy coming at us from both directions.

Living army to the front, zombie army to the back. Fucking fantastic.

THIRTY NINE

"What do we do?" I ask, my voice sounding way more confident than I feel.

"Same as we always do." JD glances down at me. "Stand and fight." He looks at all of us, making his intentions clear. "Together."

"What *about* him?" Britta looks at Mikey.

"What about him? He's one of us," Crunch snaps back.

"Is he?" Britta replies.

"Yeah, you got a problem with that?" Crunch steps up to Britta, seemingly forgetting that we're about to be either A: eaten to death, or B: shot to death.

I turn away from the approaching enemy to look at Crunch. "We've all got a problem with that." I narrow my eyes at her. "But we'll deal with that—and you—later. Now can we please focus, or there may not be a later for any of us." I turn away from her, my anger bubbling to the surface.

Crunch groans, but drops back into formation with a few

cursory words.

There's not a chance in hell I'm letting her near Ben's cabin if we make it out of here alive. I grind my teeth together. Fucking bitch burst my happy bubble! The vehicles are getting closer, and so are the dead, the smell of them drifting toward us like rotten meat cooking on a barbeque. Okay, so maybe it wasn't just Crunch that burst my happy bubble. The deaders and the psychotic Forgotten had their share in it too.

The trucks stop about a hundred meters in front of us, and someone stands up on the back of one, raising a megaphone to his mouth before speaking.

"Yo, Mikey. How you doing, bro?"

All our eyes go to Mikey. To be fair to him, though, he looks ready to explode with rage.

The guy on the top of the truck speaks again. "What? No welcome party? We've been chasing your ass down for weeks, the least you could do is give us a wave." He laughs heartily into the microphone and looks around at the other men with him. A lot of them have gotten out of their trucks to watch.

The groaning from behind draws my attention. The deaders are getting closer, spurred on by all the noise the dude with the megaphone is making.

"What are we going to do?" I ask quietly.

"Kill these fuckers," JD growls.

"No. They want me. Let me see if I can sort this out. They might let you go." He looks at JD and then me. He looks sad and angry all at the same time, but I'm just pissed off.

"Go on then," I snap. My gut wrenches, the guilt flaming in me even as I say it.

"You're not going over there on your own, Mikey. I've got your back. We can take them." Crunch shoves me out of the way.

"It's me they want." He looks at us all sadly. "I need to do the right thing for once." He places his hand on Crunch's shoulder in the hopes of calming her down, but she seems even more annoyed by it all.

"No you fucking don't, we need to kill these fuckers!"

"Crunch…" I start to talk, but she spins round on me and grabs me in a headlock, her knife quickly trained at my throat. I stop struggling against her, knowing that she's a ticking time bomb and has been waiting for this moment to kill me.

Shit, she really wants to kill me. The realization makes me struggle again. This isn't just some over-the-top jealousy, this is some fucking mental stalker shit going on. Somebody did not get all the dollies when she was growing up, and is having serious issues now.

Everyone steps away from her in a panic, Emily screams, and I'm sure I can hear the guy on the megaphone laughing, but the panic in Mikey's eyes is all I can see right now, because if he's worried, then I'm worried.

"I'll fucking gut her right now, Mikey. You are not going over there, not without a fight. We can take them." She looks to JD for help. "If we stand together, just us three."

My feet are struggling for purchase on the ground, my hands clawing at her arm. She's cutting off my air supply, and I'm not even sure she realizes it. In fact, I'm pretty certain she would prefer to gut me like a pig instead of just suffocate me, but there it is. The smell of the dead is getting closer. Or maybe that's just my death? Shit, it seems like one way or another, I'm going to die today. If I had a choice, it would definitely be this way and not by being eaten alive. Maybe I should be grateful to her?

Black spots swim in front of my vision, and my face feels full and swollen. The whoosh of the blood in my ears sounds slow and sluggish, and my eyes close against the overriding sensations all around me. I hear a dull *thump* and I drop to the ground, my eyes opening upon the impact of my face slamming into the dust.

I stay down, gasping for air. Dirt is flying up all over me, and Emily is by my side—crying again, for fuck's sake. I'd roll my eyes at her if I wasn't trying to concentrate so hard on breathing. I shift onto my side, pain shooting through my lungs as they expand and fill with air. I know I need to get up, I know that the dead are going to be here any second and that I'm in line for their next meal if I don't move my sorry ass. I squeeze my eyes shut, still feeling the dirt flying up around me and wondering what the hell is going on. And laughing—I can hear the goddamn guy with the megaphone, still laughing.

I groan and finally open my eyes, but can't understand what I see when things come into focus. Britta is on the ground, her back against the side of the tow truck, a small slither of blood trailing down from the corner of her mouth. Her eyes are unfocused, her chest unmoving. My hand goes to my mouth to contain my scream.

"Britta?" I hardly recognize my own voice. It's rough and cracks as I try to form words but end up in a coughing fit.

I look around me, clambering up to my knees quickly, half-leaning on Emily for support as I do. JD, Mikey, and Crunch are still fighting. Crunch is fighting—shit—what seems like both of them until Mikey grabs her and slams her to the ground. She lands on her back in front of Britta with a thud, and cries out at what sounds from my position like something just broke inside of her. And I'm talking about ribs, not her fucking broken heart. She grabs her side and curls up into a ball, shouting randomly, and with enough curse words to make even me blush.

"I was just trying to get you to see sense, Mikey. Fuck all of you," she yells out, rolling onto her side and taking a deep breath.

JD shakes his head at her, still as calm as the day I met him.

"Britta?" I ask.

Mikey drops to his knees in front of her and checks her pulse, though I know it's just a charade. We all know she's dead.

He looks across at me, and then back to her with a shake of his head. "She saved your ass."

"Shit." I knew Crunch was going to be the death of her. I look at Crunch still curled on the ground, shouting and struggling for air. "Did she do it? Did she kill Britta?"

"I don't think she meant to. It's reflexes, you know. Britta snuck up on Crunch and caught her unexpectedly." He shrugs.

"She knew exactly what she was doing, and if it wasn't for Britta, I'd be dead," I snap, my body flushing with hot anger.

"Well, that was all very interesting." More laughing from the guy with the megaphone. "But can we just get on with this now? Or would you prefer to be eaten alive by zombies? I'm not really very picky which way you go, as you well know, Mikey, but I do have my orders."

Mikey looks up at the Forgotten, coming toward us on foot. They're looking pretty damn happy with themselves, and I have no idea what's about to happen, but I grab Emily to my side. I'll die protecting her, of that I'm sure. A scream from behind me makes me look away from the Forgotten. Britta has reanimated and is now chewing on Crunch's arm. They are both thrashing around wildly on the ground, Britta to get a better hold, and Crunch to try to get Britta off her. Crunch screams, and smacks out with her one good arm. Blood sprays the ground as Britta frees a chunk of flesh from Crunch's arm. She swallows the lump of meat and moves in for more. Crunch scoots up to her knees, but is pulled straight back down to the ground as Britta wraps her arms around Crunch's body and falls on her, mouth first. Crunch wails and screams in pain as the deader that was once my friend starts feasting on her shoulder. Her fingernails dig into Crunch's face, and the skin breaks, releasing a fresh torrent of blood.

I feel sick to my stomach at what is happening, but I'm immobile, and unable to do anything to stop it. Emily is curled into my side, her body shaking with tears and cries.

"Shit!" JD steps in to help Crunch, stabbing his knife through the center of Britta's forehead in one quick and merciful movement. She stops moving immediately, her jaw releasing Crunch, who scrambles up and away from her, crying loudly, her hand clutching at her face where blood is gushing out. JD pulls his knife out slowly, the knife sticking slightly on Britta's hard skull.

The other deaders finally arrive, and they come forward reaching for us, but so do the Forgotten, who—for some crazy reason—are finding it all hilarious.

"Better choose, Mikey. What are you gonna do?"

I push Emily behind me and slice my machete through the air as a deader gets too close. I slash at its head, and black gunk squirts out of the large gash in its face. I slash again, taking its head clean off, and it drops to the ground. Old deaders are the easiest to kill, but they stink worse than anything I can think of. I back up as another deader gets too close, my machete slamming through the center of its brain. It jams inside the deader's head, so I keep my grip on the handle of my weapon, put one boot on the deader's stomach, and kick out while I pull my weapon free from its putrid body. It falls backwards with a spray of black and rotted blood and guts, and my foot sinks into its stomach.

This is the second time this shit has happened to me now. I grumble.

Mikey is fighting off a couple of deaders and so is JD, but I don't see Crunch anywhere. Then I hear it: her gargled screams from somewhere behind our truck. A shiver runs down my spine for her. I don't think I would want that to be anybody's ending—even my enemies, which for some reason Crunch decided I was. No one deserves to go that way. Not even her.

More and more deaders are coming out from the long grass on either side of the road. The smell of them is overriding all my other feelings. Fight, stomach lurch, fight, don't vomit. Even the Forgotten are killing them now, but there's much more on their team than on ours.

"Mikey!" I cry out. It's involuntary, but it's the first thing that comes out of my mouth when three deaders approach me and I know that I can't fight them all off at once.

I look at him for a split second. I can see how torn he is, the confusion resting heavily on his shoulders. More deaders are coming from the surrounding fields as if they have been lying in wait for us. There is no escaping them; we simply can't kill them all.

"Take us all, Jon, or I'll go down fighting and you'll never get what you want." Mikey cuts another deader from crotch to throat, tearing it in half. Its insides tumble out and onto the ground in a little pile.

JD comes over and shoulder-barges a deader to the ground. Another one trips over the first one's body and JD puts his foot on its head and stamps down angrily while he puts one of Duncan's guns in the other deader's mouth and blows the back of its head away. Brown brain matter sprays the face of another deader directly behind the first, making the sight even more disgusting.

The sound echoes around us. All the deaders seem attracted by the noise, but JD has more than enough bullets for all of them. *Shame he doesn't have enough for the Forgotten too,* I can't help but think bitterly.

A deader drags its body along the ground, its intestines trailing behind it like a length of red rope. I step away from its hands, which are reaching up for me; its teeth are covered in blood, and it's foaming at the mouth like a rabid dog.

My hand clutches at my mouth when I realize that it's Crunch.

"Oh shit," I sob. I hated the bitch, but I never wanted this for her. The deader's eyes search mine for something. Recognition? Mercy, maybe? I'm not sure, but my arm won't move. It seems frozen to my side, my weapon hanging limply between my fingers. I need to take her out, but she's still so human. So—Crunch!

"Jesus." Mikey steps over and puts his machete in the back of her skull. She doesn't flinch from the impact, or even when it exits through the front and tears her mouth open into a gruesome caricature. "Jon, come on man," Mikey shouts louder.

More deaders are coming with every shot of JD's gun. I chance a glance behind me and see that in fact, most of them are ignoring the Forgotten and heading our way. The guy with the megaphone isn't laughing anymore, but he has a massive grin on his face, probably knowing that we have no choice anymore anyway. He could leave us all here to die if he wanted, but for some reason he wants Mikey. Thankfully Mikey wants me, and I want Emily. I'm not sure where that leaves JD, but I'm not leaving the big guy behind if I can help it.

"Fine, fine, get your asses over here before we're overrun," he speaks into the megaphone, even though there's no need to use it. Maybe it makes him feel more important, or maybe he's just an idiot. Either could be true, I guess.

"JD, get over here." Mikey grabs my hand and we turn and run, dragging Emily with us. I don't know what sort of shit I'm getting involved in by going with Mikey, but I don't have a choice, and if we're going to die I want us to go by the gun and not the dead.

We reach the Forgotten's trucks and are pushed around the back of one, where a guy with a couple of teeth missing steps forward, holding out some rope to us all. I flinch away from him and he laughs in my face and grabs Emily instead, and when I reach for her, arms grab me and pull my hands behind my back. A thick rope wraps around my wrists before I can do anything to stop them.

I look around realizing that JD isn't with us, but I can still hear his gun going off, the constant *boom, boom, boom*, thudding in time with my heart. He's surrounded by deaders; there are too many of them, but still he refuses to let them win. His face is a mask of anger and pain as he shoots with what seems like great precision into the crowd of deaders. He shoots one in the chest and another in the face, and then his gun finally clicks on empty, and he brings out his scythe and begins slashing away at them. In the void left after the noise of the gun, I realize that I am screaming.

I'm screaming for someone to help him. I kick out, struggling against my bonds as JD drops to his knees. Still his arms slash out at anything and everything, and still the deaders come, their hungry mouths biting down on any part of him that they can get their rotten teeth into. Mikey is thrown to the ground in front of me, his face slamming into the dirt as Jon puts his boot against the side of his face, forcing him to watch as JD fights for his life, fights for everything and everyone that he has lost—his girlfriend, his baby, Duncan, Josie, and perhaps even Britta and Crunch, too. We all know there is no point, he can't win, but still he fights.

For the first time since meeting him, Jon isn't laughing or smiling, his lips are pulled up into a crude snarl, his mouth moving, speaking words that I can't hear for my own crying. I pull on my ropes as JD

335

finally falls and the deaders surround him, leaping on him like wolves on a lamb, growling and snapping. The blood seems to be everywhere, the puddle growing bigger as I watch.

I continue to scream until my throat burns and the river of JD's blood gets so close that I can almost smell the iron in it.

FORTY

The floor of the van vibrates against my cheek, hot and cold at the same time. Hot blood flowing from somewhere on the back of my painful skull, and cold metal floor of the van. Silence fills the space between my ears—well, silence and a low rumble. Okay, so I guess it's not exactly silent, but it's really quiet, apart from the low rumble of the van's engine. And the pounding from my head.

Shit. This is bad.

I open my eyes, but the world spins and I shut them again quickly, feeling sick and dizzy, a metallic taste in my mouth. God I hope I'm not a zombie, and that's my blood and not the taste of brain. Wouldn't that just fucking suck?

"Is she okay?"

A voice. Mikey's, maybe? Nice to hear he sounds concerned.

Fucker.

"She's fine. You should try worrying about yourself."

Another voice—not Mikey. That Jon guy maybe? Okay, the sound of their voices isn't making me hungry in the slightest. Human it is, I surmise with relief.

"I don't give a shit about me."

Definitely Mikey.

"I can tell. The Bossman is really pissed off at you. You know that, right?"

Jesus, there is worse than Jon? Another boss?

I groan and move my head, the thumping getting worse when I do. "Emily?" I haven't heard her voice since I woke, and I don't recognize mine either when I speak her name. Maybe I *am* a zombie after all.

"Can I go check on her?"

"You sit your ass down. Lex, you go check on her."

I'm about to open my eyes again and try for another peek around the van, when a hand grabs my eyelid and pushes one and then the other open. The light is glaringly bright and I squeal and pull back from the hand.

"Keep still." The hand grabs for my eyelids again but I roll away.

"Get off me!" I groan and curl up into a ball. "Urghh."

"What are you doing to her?" Mikey's voice again, louder this time.

"She's fine, Lex will take care of her." A laugh, deep and throaty.

I can hear scuffling around and more shouting.

"Jesus, fuck, shut up!" I peel my eyes open and kick out at the infamous Lex as he makes another grab for me. "And back the fuck away."

I look up as Jon laughs again, and I scowl. I scoot myself backwards until my back hits something hard, and I push myself up to a sitting position. My expression must be something hilarious since Jon is still laughing. To be fair, it is pretty damn puzzling seeing Mikey pretty much strapped to the wall of the van by a series of ropes.

My eyes flit from Mikey to Jon back to Mikey again. "What the hell?" I look around the small cavity for Emily and realize that she's not here. "Where's Emily?"

If I were a dog, I swear you would be able to see my fur bristling along the back of my neck. As it is, I'm just one very pissed off woman, tied up, and sitting on the really un-comfy floor in the back of a van, with a numb ass and busted skull. Regardless, the outcome is the same and Jon stops laughing abruptly.

"She's in a different vehicle," he replies, tucking his long brown hair behind his ears.

"If you hurt one hair on her head…"

"She'll be fine. As long as your boyfriend here keeps up his end of the bargain, anyway." He smiles but doesn't laugh this time, and my eyes flit to Mikey.

"He's not my boyfriend," I snark. "And will someone tell me what the hell's going on?" I ask through pursed lips.

"Your boyfriend here skipped out on his end of a very important deal." Jon glances at Mikey, but he refuses to look back. "Now I've spent six months hunting him down and I intend to take you back to the Bossman so that you can fulfill the deal."

"What deal?"

Jon turns back to me. "Don't worry your pretty little head about that. Mikey is going to make things right and then you can all be on your merry little way." He smiles, tucking his lank hair behind his ears again.

"And if he doesn't?" I don't even know why I give a shit what Mikey does. The man seems to have turned into a damn mute since we have been back in contact with these guys.

"I'll cut off your arms, let you bleed out, turn into a zombie and watch you eat your daughter." He stares at me, his expression surprisingly blank considering what he just said.

My heart jumps to my throat. I don't know if it's the abruptness of his words that catch me off guard or the fact that I believe him, but my inner bitch seems to settle back down and I decide to shut the hell up. I don't even bother to tell him that Emily isn't my daughter. It all seems irrelevant when you consider having your arms cut off.

I don't know how long we travel for, but my ass has lost all feeling in it, and I have to continually shift from cheek to cheek to even out the numbness.

"Nearly there, Princess." Jon smirks at me again.

Fucking asshole. He doesn't scare me; I survived behind the walls with worse than him, but I worry for Emily. If anything happens to me, what will she do? How will she cope?

I wish I had never met Mikey. My eyes flit to him. He's still strapped to the wall of the van, all limbs kept separate like he's doing a Jumping Jack, and his head is to one side with his eyes closed. He hasn't moved for so long that I can't decide whether he's sleeping or not. That would be typical of him, to go to sleep at a time like this. Men! He finally moves, probably sensing the evil glares I'm throwing his way. He looks up and catches my eye before quickly looking away. He looks broken, and I feel some of my anger sliding away.

"Please…Is Emily okay?" I ask, my voice barely a whisper.

Jon watches me for a minute before speaking into a walkie-talkie. "Anthony, the kid okay?"

We keep eye contact while waiting for Anthony's reply, Jon still smirking, me giving my best death stare. I don't care about me, or about Mikey. I only care about that little girl who has no one else in the world to take care of her.

"Yeah, she's sleeping. Should be heading in in about twenty minutes." Jon raises an eyebrow at me and I nod. Mikey isn't looking at me. I can't blame him; I'm surprised that he hasn't self-combusted with the amount of hate I've been mentally trying to send him, but I need to pull my shit together. We are not going to get out of this and rescue Emily hating on each other.

"So, how's this going to go down?" Mikey asks without looking up.

Jon leans back, stretching his arms above his head and revealing his taut stomach in a lazy gesture. "Oh, I don't know. If I had my way, I'd fucking kill you. Gut you like the traitor pig that you are." He looks at me. "You *and* your bitch."

"Like to see you try." I narrow my eyes at him.

Shit, I need to shut the hell up.

"She's got fire in her belly, Mikey. Just how you like 'em." He laughs again and swats my leg, making me slump sideways. Yeah, Jon's a real comedian. I scowl.

"Well it's a good thing it's not up to you then." Mikey looks at me on the floor, his face pulling into a grimace. "So again I ask, how's this going to go down?"

"Bossman wants you to stick to your end of the bargain, man. You do your thing, and the women go free." Jon pulls his hair away from his face again. God I want to cut that fucking mop off.

"What about Mikey?" I ask.

"What about him? Dude's a dead man walking as far as I'm concerned, and I'm pretty certain as far as Bossman's concerned." Jon slaps a hand across Mikey's face. "Little bitch shouldn't have run."

"But you can't kill him. He's helping you, isn't he?" I struggle to get myself back into a sitting position, careful to keep my legs far from Jon, lest he push me back over.

"Not my decision," he leans over so that his face is close to mine, "or yours. Now shut your mouth before I put something in it to shut you up." He smiles again, and I close my mouth abruptly.

I've dealt with worse than him before, but that doesn't mean I want a recap on it. Now if I could just work out what the hell they want Mikey to do, work an angle on it, get myself untied, find Emily and a truck, and get the fuck out of here, things would be just dandy. Real fucking dandy. I scowl again.

FORTY ONE

"Jon, cover her up," The walkie-talkie crackles to life and I pause in my random brain ramblings.

Jon stands—well, half-crouches—and pulls out some scraps of material from his back pocket. He reaches over to tie it around my face and I dodge out of his way. He knees me in the stomach and I cough and splutter while he puts the blindfold around my eyes.

"Jon, man, you didn't need to do that," Mikey shouts, and I can hear him struggling against his restraints.

"Be glad that's all I did to her. I didn't have to bring either of them in. My orders were to find you, Mikey. Just you. These are just a bonus for the guys." Jon lightly slaps the side of my face, and I can't help it, I whimper, sounding like a little fucking girl.

"If you touch her…"

"You'll what?" Jon laughs. "You don't hold any cards here, Mikey."

"Yes I do. You hurt her *or* Emily, and I won't help you. You'll have nothing over me, and no way to make me do it. Now get away from her." I can hear Mikey's jaw grinding away angrily. Jon doesn't say anything, but I hear him sit back down.

"When this is over, Mikey…"

"When this is over, you'll be letting these two go. You can do what you want with me, but those two go free."

I wish I could see his face. I'm so confused. I hate him for ever being with these guys, after everything he told me about them, everything they did. I still find it hard to believe that he was ever one of them, but there it is. I want to ask him what they want with him, why he left, and why he lied to me, but Jon doesn't seem the chatty type and I don't want another knee to the ribs.

I feel the truck going over more bumpy ground. My ass is banging against the hard metal floor, and my head whips back and forth, making me dizzy again despite being blindfolded. The vehicle slows, and I can hear talking before it moves off again. A fresh trickle of blood seeps from the wound on my head just as another drop falls between my shoulder blades.

I think about what Mikey said—about the Forgotten letting us go. I have no idea where we are in relation to Ben's cabin. Never mind whether we would be safe there. I think of JD, Britta, Crunch, Josie, and Duncan. So many new people, new names and new faces, and now they are all gone. Maybe they had the better end of the deal, being dead?

The van pulls to a stop with a slight screech of brakes. The doors open, but I can't feel sunlight on my face as I'm dragged out of the van. In fact, it smells like we're inside somewhere. Somewhere familiar, but I can't place the smell. It's a smell from before all this happened. A time from my past, of that I'm sure.

I'm pulled along what I assume is a corridor. The smell follows me, my feet sinking into softer flooring than previously, people's voices echoing off the walls and ceiling. I hear a door open and I'm pulled inside.

"Fallon, I'm sorry man. I'm really sorry."

I hear a hard smacking sound, and Mikey grunts.

"This his woman?"

"Yeah."

I hear a click. I know that sound. I recognize it right down to my toes. That's the sound of a gun cocking.

"Wait, wait, don't," Mikey's voice again, to the left of me.

I try to be strong, refusing to cry, but my chin trembles anyway and a stray tear slides from under my blindfold and down my cheek. I don't want to die. It's as simple as that. Not now, and certainly not without getting Emily somewhere safe.

"Why the fuck shouldn't I? After the shit that you pulled?"

"Loverboy says he won't go through with it if we kill her or the kid."

That was definitely Jon's voice again.

"Well, pretty girl like her doesn't need all her fingers, does she?" The voice next to my ear sends shivers down my spine. He grabs my hand, bending my fingers back, and I scream. Sure, I've lived through this type of shit before, but this is worse: I'm helpless—bound and blindfolded—and about to lose my fingers. I scream again and receive a slap for it.

Be strong, Nina, be strong. I take some deep breaths to calm myself.

"You hurt her in any way, her or Emily, and I won't do a fucking thing to help you." Mikey's voice is sounding gruff and raw, strained even. "I'll help you get behind the walls, but you have to promise me that you'll let them go afterwards. Unharmed, and with all their fucking fingers."

Wait, what? The walls? What have they got to do with it?

"Mikey?" I whisper in confusion.

Silence.

"Mikey, what's going on?" I think of the innocent people trapped behind the walls under the control of Lee and all his men. I know the other walled cities are the same, from what Lee had said. Pieces are starting to fall into place. The Forgotten hated everyone behind the walls. They are deeply jealous of those living inside, but they don't know what it was like in there. Would they even care?

"What are you going to do with everyone?"

"We're going to kill every last one of them, princess." The voice next to my ear wasn't Jon. It was the other man's. Fallon—the Bossman. I can feel him untying my blindfold, but I'm not sure I want to look into the face of this man. This man who would slaughter innocent women and children.

The blindfold falls to the floor and I blink for a second, letting my eyes adjust. When I can focus them, I see Jon to the left of me, grinning as usual. Mikey is on the floor, bleeding from a cut lip, and from behind me steps Fallon. He's not so tough-looking—ordinary face, medium height, well-built—but there's something in his eyes that screams *crazy bastard*. Well, there's that and when he turns away from me I see he has *R.I.P.* tattooed onto the back of his shiny bald head.

I swallow hard. "It's not like you think in there; it's horrible."

"Shut up!" Mikey all but screams at me. I look at him, confused, before looking back to Fallon. He stops mid-step and turns back to me.

"What did you just say?" He smiles. Several of his teeth are missing, making him look like even more of a psycho than I previously thought.

"I said…"

"Shut up!" Mikey shouts at me again.

346

Seriously, what the fuck is his problem?

"It's not like you think behind the walls. It's more of a living hell than out here most of the time." I swallow again, the murderous glare coming from Fallon making my skin crawl.

"Fallon, I think she's like a half-wit or something, man," Mikey pleads from the floor. "She doesn't know what she's talking about."

Fallon looks to Mikey and then back to me and I realize my mistake. Mikey always said that the Forgotten hated anyone who lived behind the walls. I guess that includes me right now.

"That right, pretty thing? You a half-wit?" He smiles again.

I nod. I can't speak, and anything I might say would most likely dig my hole deeper right now. Best to nod and agree to being a half-wit, as embarrassing as that is. Embarrassed is better than dead, right?

"Funny, you don't look like a half-wit." He stands toe to toe with me, watching me intently, and I swallow loudly again.

What did he expect from a half-wit? A wonky eye and a gammy leg? Should I start mumbling my words and screaming out that I can see dead people or something? I chance a glance at Mikey, and the panic on his face—not to mention the swollen and bloody eye—all make my stomach twist and roll, and I'm tempted to pee myself just to prove my half-wittedness. Fallon, however, doesn't give me a chance to. Gripping my arm, he drags me over to his desk and pushes me into a chair. Retrieving a pair of handcuffs from his back pocket, he slips one end around my wrist and attaches the other to a hook on the table.

"What are you doing, Fallon? I told you, I won't do anything unless you promise me the women won't come to any harm." Mikey looks up at me from the floor and attempts to stand, but is pushed back down to the ground. "I mean it. You're fucked without me. I'm the only one that can get you in there."

My mind reels. I don't want the Forgotten to get into the walled city. Any of them. The people there, they might be cowards, and they may have sat back and watched other innocents being tortured and sent to their deaths, but they are innocent too. None of them want this, but you do what you have to do to protect your family. I get that now. I guess after being on my own for so long, I forgot. I look up at Fallon by my side. A long curved knife is in his hand. His intent is clear, and I scream.

"Fallon! Get away from her." Mikey scrambles up from the floor and is punched and kicked back down by two other men.

My eyes flit from him to Fallon and back again as the knife gets closer to my throat.

"So you're one of the lucky ones, eh?"

"Hardly." I choke on my words, my throat too dry and too tight.

"Luckier than my girls. My wife, my children. They were denied. Told the cities were full, told them to get away before they attracted too much attention." His voice is rough like gravel. "Told them they weren't good enough. But you, you were good enough, huh?"

The knife tip dips into my cheek, just below my cheekbone. I feel the sting and burn from it, feel the blood trail down my cheek to my neck. I don't move, don't cry out, though the tears run from my eyes as he drags the blade downwards, carving a path of pain in my face.

"NO! Fallon, no, please!"

My eyes lock on Mikey, and I release the sob which has been building inside me. My body screams in pain, screams in fright from what is happening. After all this time, after everything that I have lived through, this is the way I am going to die? Some crazy nut-bag is going to slice me open like a piñata.

"You figure that you're better than others, huh? That you deserve to be there more than us?" His face comes into view, and I blink back into the hatred in those eyes. "You figure that your life is more important than someone else's?" His lip lifts in a snarl.

"No," I sob again, my face stinging even more from the movement. "I was just there." My tears slide into gash along my face, making it sting even more.

"Right time, right place, huh?" He asks again, his features never softening. "Like all the others in there? All those other people that have lived in safety for so long. Well, time to move on and ship out, people. I'm going in there and I'm going to kill every last one of them, and then me and my boys can live in safety for a change."

"You can't do that—they don't deserve that. The people there, they were just—"

"In the right place at the right time?" he interrupts, finishing my sentence. "You said that already."

I nod. "Yes." My voice comes out a squeak, and he presses the knife into the other side of my face.

"So you figure that you're lucky?"

I nod again, then change my mind and shake my head and try to speak, but the words won't come out. It seems like I'm damned if I do and damned if I don't, regardless of what I say. Besides, my current predicament begs to differ that I'm lucky. In fact, the past couple of years beg to differ on whether I'm lucky or not.

He stands and turns to look at Mikey, whose eyes go wide when he sees my face. The knife didn't slice my other cheek, but it did cut into it. There's blood running down both cheeks now, a free flow of blood trailing down my face.

"What do you think, Mikey? You think she's lucky?" Fallon laughs. Despite the situation being completely unfunny, he laughs a full-on belly laugh, the sound echoing around the walls of the room.

It only adds insult to my injury, and despite the pain, despite the humiliation, I feel anger more than anything else. Angry that this piece of shit man could take his anger and vengeance out on me, and on so many people, for something that was beyond their control. We didn't stop him from getting behind the walls. We didn't turn his family away. Yet we're being punished all the same. And for what? For the deep fucking joy of being allowed to live in the so-called sanctuary of the walled city? In the peace and serenity they provided us with? He has no fucking idea the hell we all lived through on a daily basis. It's bad out here, but at least you know who your enemies are. Inside, everyone turned on you.

Thinking about it now, maybe it would serve them all right, to die. Fucking rot in the hell they helped to make. All it would have taken was for us to stand as one and say *no*. When I think of all those guards, with their greedy hands on my skin, their fingers prying and pawing at my flesh, the beatings, the starvation, the lies and fear, torture and humiliation, I could just as well turn my back on all of them for never helping me. I think of Lee's face, his fake regret as he dished out his punishment to people, to his so-called citizens.

I grit my teeth. "I'll tell you who's lucky," I whisper.

Fallon turns to look at me with a huge grin. "Yeah?"

"You."

"Me? How so?" He stops smiling and seems genuinely confused, like a dog chasing a ball that was never thrown in the first place.

"Yeah, you. All of you. You're all fucking lucky that I'm handcuffed to this chair and don't have my machete, because if I did," I look up at him through my wet lashes, the anger burning a cesspit of hate in my stomach lining, "if I did, I'd cut your ugly fucking head off and feed it to the deaders."

He stops smiling, a rage glowing behind his eyes.

I look down at my legs; the blood from my face is dripping off the end of my chin and onto my skirt. I can feel the burn of the knife wound as I flex my face, testing out my mouth's movements. "Who do you think you are?" I look up at him. "You don't know what it was like behind those walls. Who are you to judge anyone, you piece of shit?"

"Sweet mother of God, you have death wish?" He whistles through his teeth.

I grin, hiding the wince of pain from my cheek. "Nope, I just don't care anymore. I'm sick of men like you trying to rule me, trying to be the boss of me. *I* control me, and my fate. So if you're going to kill me, get on with it. This isn't a James Bond movie, and I don't give a shit about your sick plan to destroy the walled city and the people inside it. Most of those people would be better off dead than trapped behind there anyway. Your family was a hell of a lot better off out here than in there. So you go right ahead and do what you have to."

I keep my eyes fixed on him, my body rigid even as he raises his knife up to me again. I can't wait to be rid of this world. I close my eyes and pray I see Ben again soon.

The pounding of feet in the hallway outside forces me to open my eyes back up, just in time for the door to slam open.

Two men run in, dragging a third behind them.

"We got a breach, boss," says the first guy, a blond-haired, intense-looking man. He helps to lay the injured man carefully on the floor.

"He bitten, Malcolm?" Fallon, moves away from me, only glancing backwards once. He goes to look at the man on the floor.

My eyes connect with Mikey's. He mouths *sorry* to me. He looks broken, like he's half the man he was several hours ago. In my eyes, he is. He was a part of this. His handsome face makes my skin crawl, and the sickening thing is—I know I still love him, regardless.

"Yeah, boss, left shoulder."

"What the fuck are you bringing him in here for, then? Kill this fucker and get on with fixing the breach." Fallon turns back to look at me. The two men that dragged in the injured man look at each other uncertainly.

"Boss, this is Noel. He's a good guy." Malcolm steps forward.

Fallon swings around to look at Malcolm again. "Correction—that *was* Noel. Now he's a dead man," he spits.

"But…"

Fallon kneels down in front of Noel abruptly, takes his knife, and plunges it through Noel's skull before anyone knows what is happening. Noel's hand reaches for the blade a second too late, and then flops back down to his side. Blood pumps out around the hilt of the knife, and Fallon takes it in his grip, one hand on the side of Noel's dead face, the other wrapped around the knife, and pulls it out of his skull.

"I hate having to do the grunt work." He stands, wiping the knife on the side of his pants and walking toward me in one easy fluid motion. "Now, where were we?"

FORTY TWO

"Fallon, man, you know I won't help if you hurt her any more. I'm done." Mikey's voice goes up a notch, which is good, since my voice has deserted me. My badass attitude has up and fled for the day. "I mean it!"

'I mean it?' What is he, like five?

Fallon keeps walking toward me regardless of Mikey's words, and I think my heart might hammer a hole in my chest at any time; at least it'll save Fallon from having to do it.

"Please—please don't, god, I'll do anything, fucking anything, but please don't hurt her," Mikey begs.

Fallon stares at me for a long time. I don't know if he's actually considering what Mikey has said, trying to frighten me some more, or if he has actually zoned out and gone off to la la land. Either way, I'm about ready to pee myself in fear—okay, and I just need to pee, as usual.

"Take her to holding." He continues to stare at me while he talks to someone else in the room. I'm lost in la la land with him now, and can't seem to drag myself away, even as someone is unlocking my cuffs.

Emily is crying continuously when they lock me in an empty, dark room with her. So much so that I ask her if they have done anything to her, but she assures me that no, they haven't laid a finger on her, she was just worried about me and Mikey.

I'm touched by her concern, and worried about how she is going to be when Fallon does decide to kill me. Because without a doubt, he is going to. I'm not stupid. Mouthing off at him just about sealed my fate, and if it wasn't for poor old Noel, I would be dead now. Thanks, Noel. And uh, sorry, I guess.

Emily cleans my cuts as best she can using some material from her shirt. We can't dress it and there are no mirrors to see the damage, so I can only go off her assurances that it isn't as bad as it looks. Strangely, that doesn't fill me with a lot of confidence. Go figure, huh.

We curl up together on the cold, bare floor, our arms wrapped tightly around one another, and for the first time in a long time, I realize that I'm frightened—not just zombie frightened, but the fear-of-the-unknown frightened. These are not good people. They are angry, bitter, and messed up in the head people, and I have no idea what is going to happen to us. I worry for the people in the walled city, I worry for Mikey and what they are going to do to him, and I think of the friends we have lost.

"You can't tell anyone that you're from behind the walls. I mean it, Em, you don't breathe a word of that to anybody ever again. You survived by pure luck, if anyone asks. You recount our journey, only I found you at Old Man Riely's house, in his air-raid shelter. You were safe there and there was no reason to leave. That's what you tell anyone, that's what you tell everyone. You got it?"

Emily nods, and continues to sob. If I manage to live through this, which seems highly unlikely, I'm going to teach this girl to grow some balls. She's too soft, and unfortunately she's reaching an age where she's going to be more than just eye candy for men. She needs to toughen up quick if she is going to survive.

"I'm going to miss Britta," Emily's voice whispers up to me in the darkness.

"Me too," I reply sadly.

"She was so brave, trying to help you and fighting Crunch."

"Yeah, and look where it got her." I regret saying it instantly. Not only do I sound ungrateful that someone lost their life for me, but I've upset Emily now. Britta was her friend, and mine. "I'm sorry, Em."

"It's okay, I know you don't mean it. She really cared about you, she said that you were one of the good ones."

"What does that mean?" I ask, speaking into her hair. I don't want to let her go; I need to keep her close, for her sake and for mine.

"I have no idea, but she said that you would save us all." Emily's arms tighten around me.

"Well, clearly she was wrong," I whisper, more to myself than Emily.

This has turned out to be the worst day ever. From waking up I've nearly died over half a dozen times. I mean, that's *way* more than my usual ranking. We've lost yet another home, yet more friends, god knows what they are doing to Mikey or what's going to happen to us. My face hurts, and Emily's hair is sticking in the dried blood, but I don't move to get it out. Exhaustion finally takes me, and I give in to sleep, though it is by no means a restful one, but one filled with nightmares and sadness.

I dream of blood, and death. Friends, family, loved ones, hated ones. Everyone dies. Sooner or later, everyone dies. The dead will rise and eat you alive.

I wake up shaking and dripping in sweat, still wrapped in Emily's arms. I can hear breathing from behind me and flinch away as a hand touches me. Whimpering, I cower and pull Emily to my chest.

"It's okay, it's me, Nina."

Mikey's voice is soothing, and I release Emily and turn to look at him. It's dark, but I can see well enough to tell he's taken a beating. Instinctively I reach for him, wrapping my arms around him and pulling him to me. We stay holding each other for a long time, until the tears I didn't know I was crying dry up, at the very least.

"I'm so sorry I got you mixed up in this, Nina." He pushes my hair back from my face.

"It's not your fault—well, it is, but…shit, I'm sorry. I don't know what to say, Mikey. How could you ever be with these guys?" I hold his hand, trying to show him that I'm not judging him, not anymore. Too much has happened, and it feels like we're too close to death's door for all that pettiness now.

"I—I met them when I couldn't get behind the walls. There was a bunch of us with families, they said it was full, any more would cause overcrowding." He takes a deep breath. "I had my little girl with me, she was six. They wouldn't even let her stay, no matter how much I begged and pleaded with them. They had a database of names, and my name was on the list—it was a prison list. I'd been to prison for a couple of stints, and because of that, my little girl couldn't be safe. We'd traveled so far to get to one of those fucking cities, and then they just turned us away. The dead were everywhere, and there was nowhere else to go. Then Fallon turned up with his family; he had a big-assed army truck and told me we could go with him." Mikey stops and takes another breath, his hand clutching at his ribcage.

"We traveled for a while, meeting up with other people that had been turned away from the cities, helping them. Our convoy got bigger and bigger until we found—this place." He gestures around us and looks up at me, his eyes glistening. "That's when it all went to shit. This place was infested, but we didn't realize it when we first got here. We staked out the place as best we could when we arrived, it seemed secure, and pretty clear for a small town. We moved everyone in, all of our families. Then one night, we were overrun by deaders. I don't know what attracted them, the noise or what, but one minute it was all fine, and then the next there were hundreds of them."

"Like in the woods?" I ask, thinking of poor Steve and his chickens.

"Yeah." He nods his head. "Just like that. It seems like they're attracted to noise and smell. They must have heard us all pulling up, the smell of us all attracted them and brought them right to us. They killed over half of our group—most of the children and wives." Mikey swallows and clears his throat. Even in the dim light, I can see the tears trail down his cheeks. "I lost my daughter, Rosie. I was out fighting, left her with one of the other mothers and her kids, and when I got back, she was…"

I throw my arms around his shoulders and hug him as tight as I can before he winces and I loosen my hold.

"I'm so sorry, baby. I'm so sorry." I kiss him and hug him hard again, finally letting him go.

"It's okay, I've made some sort of peace with it now." He shrugs, and I know he's lying.

"So what happened next?" I ask.

"Fallon went berserk. He lost his wife and three kids that day, sent him over the edge. He started blaming all the *lucky ones* for being able to get behind the walls. He started wanting revenge, talking about breaking into the walled cities and killing everyone inside. Talked about taking down the government, and being in control ourselves for a change."

"That's where you come in?" I ask, already knowing the answer. I've seen Mikey's skills, I know to some degree what he can do.

"Yeah," he nods. "That's where I come in. I made the mistake of telling him what I used to do for a living."

"You were just a small town thief, though—a bad boy, you said." I half laugh at the comment, and hiss as pain stings my face.

"I was, but I got better at it," he smirks. "I started out small time, breaking and entering, and then moved through the ranks until I got noticed and hit the big time. Seems I had a skill for it."

"You say it like you're proud," I say.

"Well, yeah, I am. I can break into anything, any time, any place— any vault, any door. Didn't matter what the job, it was me they called. When the world went to shit, it was me who got us into safe places, all until this place." He shakes his head sadly before continuing. "I was as angry as them too at first. I wanted to make them all pay, but we couldn't get near the cities. When anyone got too close…"

"They shot them," I finished for him.

"Yeah. So we waited. Watching and waiting for the right time. We watched the drops get less and less frequent behind the walls until they stopped altogether, and then we had to find the other way in. In the meantime, Fallon started going crazy, got more and more twisted, until all he talked about was killing. Whenever we went on scavenger hunts, if we ran into people that had been behind the walls, he'd promise to help them and then kill them…but believe me, death was the final thing for them, and they were all grateful for it by that time. He got sicker and sicker with what he was doing, and I started to realize that it wasn't anyone's fault, and I didn't want to be the one to put all those people to death, so I ran. That's when I met the others—and then you, and you told me what it was really like in there."

"Wait, the other way in?"

I feel Mikey shrug the way he does. "Yeah, there's more than one way in. Always has been, it's like a secret entrance."

"Obviously," I mutter. "But then why seal up the main door if there was another way out after all?"

"No idea. To make you all lose hope? To stop anyone from trying to break in. No one was supposed to know about the other entrance, but they had to have an escape route."

It still doesn't make any sense. We were all starving in there. Lee said that even he was starving, that it was too dangerous to open up the main door again and try and find food because the deaders would get in, but then if that's so, why would there be another entrance?

"So what now? Do you know where the secret entrance is?" This could be a total game changer. If there was a way in and out, we could all have somewhere safe to go after all. Well, once we got rid of Lee.

"Of course I know where it is. I'm the only one who does, which is why they needed me so much." Mikey beams, suddenly happy again.

"Why would Lee let us all starve instead of sending people out to find food?"

"Lee?" Mikey raises an eyebrow at me.

"He was our Bossman," I mock.

"He's obviously just a coward. Too frightened to put himself at risk. Most leaders normally are."

It all makes sense now—how such a simple, bland little man like him was in charge, why he was always so severe with everyone: he needed the fear to control everyone, to stop them from wanting to leave. He told us all that the world was rotted and black, but in reality it is very much alive, though still as dangerous as ever. But there was still food available out there, and with an army like his, it is more than possible to protect the citizens. I think I feel more hate for Lee right now than I have ever felt before. I want vengeance, and I want him to suffer.

"Maybe if we explained to Fallon what it's like in there, maybe I could talk to him, get him to understand?" I plead.

"No, he's too far gone." Mikey takes my chin in his thumb and forefinger, trying not to touch the cut that runs down my face. "He doesn't care who he hurts, or who dies. The only way to stop him is to kill him."

I snort. "Looks like we're shit out of luck, then."

"Not necessarily. I still have friends here."

"Didn't seem like it when they were ready to let us die by the roadside," I bite out.

"No, not them guys, they're just as bad as Fallon. They lost too many people, they've been too brainwashed by him. But there are others. Others that I think we could convince to stand with us. The thing is, this place is pretty damn secure now. A few more tweaks to the security and we could be safe here for good. That's what everyone wants these days. Not vengeance."

Maybe things aren't as bad as I first thought. Maybe there is hope for us, for Emily. I look at her curled up. Her eyes are open and she's watching us with tears in them. I hadn't realized that she had woken up and heard everything.

"You okay, Em?" I ask, my hand stroking her head.

"I will be." She sits up, her arms going around both me and Mikey. "Once we kill Fallon."

I flinch. Those are words a child should never have to speak—

murder, death, killing. But this world has made it all a part of her life. In order for us to survive, for her to survive, she's had to grow up, and quickly. If we don't stop Fallon, and soon, she's going to lose all her innocence. All her purity. And without our children having those things, what type of world will this be? Surely not one worth living in. There has to be certain things in the world—hope, innocence, love. And all those people, behind those walls, what about them? This world isn't safe for them, but surely they deserve better than what they have.

"Mikey, we have to kill him. We have to kill Fallon, and then we have to help them all."

"Help who?" He pulls back to look at me.

"Everyone. We have to help everyone behind the walls."

ABOUT THE AUTHOR

Claire C. Riley is USA Today and International bestselling author. Eclectic writer of all things apocalyptic and romance, she enjoys hiking, movie marathon, & old school board games. Claire lives in Manchester England with her husband, three daughters and naughty rescue beagle.

She writes under C. Riley for her thrillers and suspense.

She can be found on Facebook, Instagram, TikTok and more!

For a full list of her works, head over to her Amazon author page.

CONTACT LINKS

Website: www.clairecriley.com

FB page: https://www.facebook.com/ClaireCRileyAuthor/

Amazon: http://amzn.to/1GDpF3I

Reader Group: Riley's Rebels: https://www.facebook.com/groups/

ClaireCRileyFansGroup/

Newsletter Sign-up: http://bit.ly/2xTY2bx

IG: https://www.instagram.com/redheadapocalypse/

Twitter: @ClaireCRiley

Tik Tok: @redheadapocolypse

Made in the USA
Monee, IL
06 July 2024

61329074R00218